ALSO BY DANIEL PUTKOWSKI

An Island Away

Bonk's Bar

Under a Blue Flag

Universal Coverage

Dark Currents

THE
NEXT
TESTAMENT

A Novel

DANIEL PUTKOWSKI

HAWSER
PRESS

THE NEXT TESTAMENT Copyright © 2019 by Daniel Putkowski
All rights reserved. Printed in the United States of America.

ISBN 978-0-9815959-5-5

FIRST HAWSER PRESS TRADE PAPERBACK EDITION NOVEMBER 2019
10 9 8 7 6 5 4 3 2 1

danielputkowski.com

THE
NEXT
TESTAMENT

PROLOGUE.

To whom it may concern:

I wasn't there when it all began, but I had a lot to do with how it ended. So, let's rewind several decades and work forward, more or less to the point right before I became part of what is now considered history.

There had been violence all along. There was the first strike on the World Trade Center in 1993 and then the atrocity that was 9/11. For different reasons but with plenty of damage done, there was Oklahoma City in 1995. There were more than a few attacks at nightclubs, public events, and corporate facilities. Good citizens then might have been wise to see these occurrences not as isolated incidents or the work of lone wolves and psychopaths but as previews to the big show. Of course, connecting the dots in the past is easier than connecting the ones in the future. Fair enough. Still, when people start killing each other and blowing things up not to steal a fortune but because they hate what the other person believes or who they vote for, it's a good idea to figure out a way to calm things down, to address the real issues.

Maybe there were individuals doing the best they could to defuse political and social tensions. I don't know. That was before I was born. At present, no one's done a thorough analysis. Maybe they never will, because the dust has settled. Thank God it has.

In my opinion—and again, I wasn't there but was told by people who were—what kicked off the United States' Second Civil War was the destruction of St. Patrick's Cathedral. A truck loaded with homemade explosives did the job, this one chock-full and perfectly aimed. It hurtled down Fifth Avenue on Easter morning, mounted the stairs, plowed into the doors, and BOOM! Down came the façade and the roof. More than 2,000 people died that instant. Hundreds succumbed to injuries in the weeks that followed. An American icon was transformed into a smoldering hulk.

The President appealed for calm and reconciliation. There was an arm-in-arm peace walk down the same route the truck took. Congressional hearings were held, more anti-terrorism funds allocated. Talking heads rambled on television, radio, and the internet about how to solve the problem. Too little, too late.

The Hibernians armed up with help from the Sons of Jericho, who had been stashing guns and ammo for years. Together they stormed a mosque, machine-gunning everyone and burning down the block. Days later, Black Scimitar, a string of sleeper cells no one ever heard of, woke up and returned the favor twentyfold, shooting up churches and synagogues in various cities.

The Second Civil War had begun.

There was no clean line between North and South as in the First Civil War—as it's now called—and the issue wasn't slavery or states' rights. It was one god versus another god versus no god at all. Alliances shifted on an almost daily basis.

In a matter of weeks, air travel within the country stopped. Railroads barely functioned. Highways became a series of checkpoints between bandit territories. Shortages of everything were everywhere. Banks ran out of cash. The stock market collapsed. The United States' economy was in free fall and took the world's down the drain with it. But let's not get distracted by Europe or Asia.

For two generations, war had been something that happened on television, somewhere else, and to an extremely limited number of people they knew, if any at all. Suddenly, it was in the street where they lived. They were unprepared. Forget combat training. Think basic survival. How does a person, who never so much as watered a plant, eat when the grocery store is empty? The answer is simple. They don't. Missing a meal here and there used to be called a diet. It wasn't long before one meal a day was a luxury. Hungry people do crazy things. They also fall ill quite easily. Pestilence has always been the big brother of war, and it went on a tear with a wickedly mutated version of influenza and something new referred to as Red Death.

Cities saw the worst of the horror. Skyscrapers became death-trap infernos, the same for mass transit. With no functioning emergency services, entire neighborhoods burned for days on end, which wasn't always a bad thing because the smoke covered the stench of rotting bodies. There were a lot of them, mostly victims of disease and malnutrition, but also a fair number from actual fighting. Collecting corpses was a risky proposition due to snipers honing their craft. Thus, vermin and insect populations exploded; disease spread faster. Repeat, repeat, repeat.

The death toll? Who the hell knows? Suffice it to say, there are still vast areas that were once crowded boroughs and suburbs that have since been bulldozed to make work and stop the incessant fires from getting out of control. Scraping them clean also prevented squatting and removed habitat for anyone looking to start their own miniature theocracy.

Combatants demanded non-combatants take sides, resulting in mass movements of people just trying to survive. Opportunists popped up to settle old scores, carve out niches of power, and make fortunes in black markets. Weapons flowed through porous borders as international agitators reveled in Americans killing each other.

Miraculously, parts of the federal government held together thanks to the Joint Chiefs of Staff. Martial law was declared, and the march back to a unified country was in capable hands. It started slowly, with plenty of setbacks, but the generals maintained the obedience of their respective forces. Loyal troops received better pay, a place to spend it, and familial protection on fortified bases. Plus, they had airpower. The ability to hop over trouble spots, parachute troops anywhere, and assault from above limited the splinter groups' ability to make concerted attacks or hold territory without a daily dose of death raining on them.

The action was financed by the longest-term gamblers known to humankind, the Chinese, who have always seen things in terms of centuries. They lent on relatively generous terms, collateralized by the energy resources of the United States of America. It was a good bet. They also provided technical assistance. They never forgot the lessons of how to put down an insurgency. After all, they outlawed religion a century ago, enforcing the edict by any means necessary.

In five years, the coastal areas and some major interior cities were secured. A guerrilla war festered elsewhere until it became more perilous to be a leader than a follower. Special Forces teams and undercover agents assassinated anyone claiming to be in charge. Only the hard core remained in ever-shrinking pockets scattered far and wide. Bombs and bulldozers kept them on the run.

Then, surprise, surprise! Along came the Common Faith. No one expected a new religion to spawn. But it wasn't really new. It was a mishmash of everything from the past, supposedly the best of each minus the worst of them all. The generals endorsed it as part of the solution. Not right away, but soon enough, people who swore never to make peace were shaking hands and slapping backs. Rumors abounded about under-the-table payoffs. They were true; nobody cared. Peace was at hand. Everyone agreed it was time to get back to business, to the way things were, to obesity and video games and vacations in the sun.

The Common Faith became official thanks to a constitutional convention that updated the First Amendment—among others—with the Twenty-Eighth, thereby creating the fourth branch of government. Technically, Common Faith membership was optional. However, practicing or evangelizing any legacy religion was punishable by a five-year prison sentence or the same term working on a chain gang clearing debris left over from the war. Prison was the safer option. Either way, convicts attended mandatory tolerance classes where they learned to be good Common Faith adherents and forget whatever religion for which they'd fought.

A year of peace gave people confidence the worst was over. The economy restarted. Martial law was lifted. In true American tradition, the generals resisted the temptation to be tyrants and voluntarily retired to an advisory board consulted by Congress and the president. They, along with their families and loyal soldiers, joined the Common Faith, setting an example for the nation. A statue of them was erected near the Lincoln Memorial.

The generals deserve credit for pacifying the country, for believing something new would solve an old problem. No one can blame them for a noble effort that ultimately went horribly wrong. On the other hand, the civilians (Congress and executive-branch bureaucrats—some of them, anyway) saddled a nasty beast and rode it hard. I believe they did it intentionally because many of them worship power, and that's what the Common Faith gave them: absolute control of too much. They slipped into the fabric of the religion, taking positions of unelected authority, creating fiefdoms to exploit an unaccountable system, and thus establishing conditions that led to what happened later, years later, after I was born and during my lifetime, a part of which is the account you're about to read.

And here we are, not in the present, but in the not-so-distant past. Within living memory, specifically my memory, you are in the era following the loss of millions in the war, from Red Death, and from the devastating Flu of 2052. Be glad you missed it, or maybe you didn't and just want to find out what really happened from those who did what they were called to do.

What follows was written by someone else. It's accurate and honest. I know because I was there.

CHAPTER 1.

Common Faith Headquarters stood taller than any other building in Philadelphia. Built in record time as a symbol of national reunification, it occupied a chunk of former green space and what had been the National Constitution Center. As a beacon of confidence in a set of beliefs for everyone, the Common Faith symbol glowed day and night from atop the structure. The circle with a broad, level line in the middle could be seen from every direction thanks to regulations limiting other edifices to much lower heights.

Zoe Whelan, perhaps more than the average citizen, drew strength from the light up there. She wasn't the most devout Common Faith follower, not by a long shot. Nonetheless, she appreciated what it had done for a nation rocked by civil war. It brought people together by giving them a unified set of beliefs, a new reason to coexist as opposed to all the old reasons to fight. It hadn't been easy. Two years of wrangling before the constitutional amendment was ratified, and that after a fierce, protracted civil war left the nation in economic ruin.

Worth it, Zoe thought, as she walked north along Sixth Street toward Headquarters. She remembered enough from the bad old days to be grateful for Common Faith's unified structure. Ancient dogmas and disagreements were gone, fifteen years in the past, and now there were people like her to keep it that way. Hence, her presence this day to deal with one of the holdouts, someone who clung to a legacy religion. A Christian, she'd been told; a potential suicide bomber.

She wasn't addressed as Compliance Specialist Zoe Whelan for nothing. She enforced the law—specifically, the Common Faith Mandate, a set of rules defining acceptable and unacceptable religious practices. Specialist she was, too, having been educated in all things Christian. Her colleagues had their own specialties in Judaism, Hinduism, and so on. She was unrivaled in her ability to hunt, capture, and deliver to justice those who would otherwise destroy the peace finally achieved. Did her status put a swagger in her step? Maybe it did. Not that she cared what other people thought. She earned the badge, maintained exemplary standards of the organization, and would tolerate no one who questioned her ability or authority. She was thirty-five and in the best shape of her life.

Two blocks ahead, Zoe saw a searchlight stab the main entrance of Common Faith Headquarters. No doubt SWAT Commander Derek Bentley was putting on a show. She had admonished him a dozen times not to draw unnecessary attention to religious criminals. They reveled in it, fed on it. She'd seen zealots dragged out of failed sieges, smiles on their faces, praising God, claiming He was going to welcome them in heaven. She wondered if they were mostly attention-seeking lunatics as opposed to genuine believers. Either way, better out of sight and therefore out of the minds of others. Every journalist agreed with her, doing their part by only publishing or broadcasting stories after convictions.

Regular Philly cops formed a line at the next intersection. A few reporters chatted casually with them, including Jesse Young, who spotted Zoe as she flashed her badge to one of the uniformed officers.

"Hey, Zoe!" Young called to her. "Is it true the guy's wearing a suicide vest?"

"Don't be a fashion critic," Zoe joked, as she ducked under

the yellow tape.

Young moved in close, lowering his voice. "Let's work a deal on an exclusive."

"Sorry."

"Come on, Zoe," he pleaded. "I make you look good every time."

"That's easy, Jesse," she said with a wink, then turned for the front door of Common Faith Headquarters. He'd been one of her bedroom conquests, better than most, but not a keeper. Ten years her junior, he lacked the experience to balance his eagerness.

"Look at her go," Young remarked to the nearest cop. "Afraid of nothing."

"Not bad-looking either," the cop added, his eyes lingering on the fit body barely concealed by tailored trousers and a light jacket in the October chill.

Derek Bentley himself stopped Zoe at the entrance.

"Tell me, Bentley," Zoe said.

"Guy says he's with the Surviving Few," Bentley replied.

"I busted several of them in South Philly back in August. At the rentals near the coal terminal."

"Yeah, well, this one asked for you specifically. Won't talk to anyone else. But you're not going in there," Bentley said. "He's covered in C4."

"So?" she returned.

"He could launch you into the great beyond."

"Nah," she said. "Nothing to worry about. And turn off the lights."

"How do you know he won't blow the vest?"

"He's a Christian, right?"

"Like it matters."

"Think about it. Suicide is a sin for which he couldn't repent."

"And dying for the cause makes him a saint," countered Bentley.

"Uh, no. Suicide means eternal damnation to them. Relax,

okay? I got this."

"He's serious, Zoe. Talks like he knows you."

"I'm flattered."

"Don't be. He said he has a message straight from God."

"Sounds serious. I better get in there."

She sidestepped Bentley and strode for the front door, silhouetted by the searchlight.

"Stay to the left!" Bentley shouted. "The snipers have better angles from the right!"

Zoe waved off Bentley's advice. She understood these Christians, their desire to be heard, their longing to be important again. Too bad it wasn't going to happen. She'd listen to this fool's message from God or whatever he had to say. Then she'd remind him it was better to be a living believer than a dead martyr. He would argue the point. She would agree to put his message on all the TV networks, let him read it himself if he wanted. Of course, he'd be bundled into a police van before the cameras rolled. It was a pathetically simple trick but worked because people who pulled stunts like this always missed the big picture. They had tunnel vision. Whatever promise met their expectations was the same one that led them deeper into that tunnel. It wasn't long before they were trapped by their own delusion, not to mention the grip of the law.

Zoe yanked open the door, surprised to see all the lobby furniture in a messy pile near the reception desk. The searchlight beam cast odd shadows against the wall, making it difficult to see anyone.

"Hello in there!" Zoe called, loud enough for her voice to carry all the way to the elevator bank.

"Zoe Whelan or nobody!" a man hollered. "Or swear to God, I'll blow this place to kingdom come! You hear me?"

"Take it easy. She's right here," Zoe replied, adding formally, "With whom am I speaking?" Formality charmed many of her captures. They mistook it for respect.

His volume and intensity dropped as he answered, "My…
my… my name is Andrew."

"Mind if I come around and have a look, Andrew? Make sure
you're okay?"

"Please do."

"Thank you."

Zoe took her time edging around the furniture until she
stood on the back side of the reception desk.

"Down here," Andrew said from the darkness.

Shielding her eyes from the searchlight, Zoe spotted a heavy-
set man seated on the floor, leaning against an overturned chair.
Indeed, he was wearing a suicide vest, neat blocks of explosives
wired together, and sweating profusely under it. He seemed to be
in his late fifties, was clean-shaven, and was nearly bald.

"I'm glad you got here before they killed me," Andrew went
on, a detonator switch clearly visible in his right hand.

"No one's going to kill you," Zoe said.

"Yes, they are. It's been foretold."

"Nothing's been foretold, Andrew."

"But it has, Zoe Whelan. Like Daniel, and Ezekiel before him,
a prophet has come."

"I thought no one was to add to or take away from the Christian Bible."

"Oh, dear, have you forgotten 1 John 4?"

"It's been a while. Refresh my memory," prompted Zoe.

"'*Do not believe every spirit, but test the spirits.*' And Amos 3:
'*Surely the Sovereign Lord does nothing without revealing His plans
to His servants, the prophets.*'"

Zoe pretended to think about what she'd been told, then said,
"Sounds like you're mixed up between the New Testament and
the Old. Maybe you're being led astray."

"Impossible. An angel came to me."

"An angel? I'm jealous," she said with a bit too much sarcasm.

"Oh, don't be. The angel spoke of you."

"Are you sure it was me?"

"Incredible, eh? That's the power of God, making the most of the least of us."

Zoe let the possible insult hang there a moment, then asked, "Why didn't the angel come directly to me?"

"Because your journey begins here," answered Andrew with striking confidence.

"Okay, where am I going?" she queried.

"To get the Next Testament," Andrew informed her.

"Really? What's that?"

"God's plan revealed."

He extended a sheet of paper with his left hand.

For the first time in her professional life, Zoe felt a wisp of fear tickle her spine. She immediately recognized the page from a hymnal she confiscated from another member of the Surviving Few. There was no mistaking it as the same page because it bore her own note in the upper corner. "We still believe," she wrote, which was what the suspect she'd arrested with the song book had told her. She placed it in her personal trophy case, a shoebox of memorabilia from every case she closed.

"How did you get that?" she asked.

"The angel brought it to me from your secret collection," he answered. "We could sing together."

Zoe coughed. "I can't hold a tune."

Keeping trophies broke at least three different regulations and an entire section of tolerance laws. Her practice had started unintentionally after her first arrest. She confiscated a tiny, hand-carved crucifix from the perpetrator. At the end of the day, she found it in her jacket pocket. She almost tossed it in a corner trashcan. Then she got the idea of collecting a tchotchke from each conviction. If ever she wanted to write a book or make a documentary about her efforts, the items would be supporting material of a personal nature. Or, she could donate all of it to the Museum of False Truth when she retired.

"Your mother and I were in the church choir together," Andrew admitted, standing and placing the page on the reception desk.

Anyone his age could make that claim, Zoe thought. Didn't make it true. She was more concerned with how he was able to find her unlisted address, get past the doorman, use the daily elevator passcode, break in, and find the box, which she hid in the drop ceiling. She vowed to take the doorman in for questioning. How else could Andrew or one of his group pull off such a burglary without inside help?

Returning to the current issue, she asked, "Where do I get this thing you mentioned, the Next Testament?"

"Oh, that wasn't for me to know."

"Then how will I find it?"

Andrew grinned. He was prepared for this question. "Remember how Jesus revealed himself to Saul on the road to Damascus?"

"Was long before my time, Andrew," Zoe said.

"Well, He will show you the way to the Time of Gathering."

One of the suspects she arrested in South Philly used the same phrase. He was also a confessed member of the Surviving Few, followers of an aging Episcopalian bishop who called himself Father Rabek. The suspect went raving mad in his cell, screaming about the Time of Gathering. Sadly, he died of exhaustion. Her box contained his necklace with the chi rho symbol.

"Who's gathering, Andrew?"

"Those who already know your name. Those who still believe."

"Any particular reason for this gathering?"

"Isn't it obvious?"

The riddles in which these people spoke annoyed Zoe to no end. Why they reverted to ancient metaphors and archaic vocabulary escaped her. Perhaps it was a case of mimicry in pursuit of credibility. If they sounded like the Bible, then they would be believed in the same way.

"I'm sorry," she said, "I'm missing something."

"They're gathering to hear the Next Testament from you, the

Messenger, who will soon get it from the prophet," Andrew explained.

"How can I be a messenger?"

"Because you've been chosen. It's a great honor, one you don't have to hide."

Zoe noticed Andrew wasn't sweating anymore. He seemed completely relaxed.

"Tell me more about the Gathering," she said. "How many people are coming? Will Father Rabek be there?"

"A glorious event," he answered, "with you at the center."

"If I had more details it would be easier."

"The present, the future, all has been foretold," he said, raising the detonator. "Don't be afraid."

"No!" Zoe shouted.

Her cry echoed through the lobby a split second before the glass behind her shattered and a bullet struck Andrew, snapping his head back. His body hung there, his finger pressing the detonator. Then another bullet tore into his throat.

A puff of smoke rose from the vest. Oddly enough, Zoe followed its rise from Andrew's body into the air. Later, she would distinctly remember the moment because the smoke seemed to morph into the form of a bird that soared across the lobby. She would also recall how she leapt for cover, over the pile of furniture toward the blinding rays from outside.

After that, complete darkness.

CHAPTER 2.
MOUNT CARMEL, PENNSYLVANIA
TWO HOURS LATER

The Mollies, they called themselves—a derivation of the Molly Maguires, that band of coal miners who defied the mining syndicates and Pinkertons in the 1870s. The Mollies' leader, Jagger, had been told by her mother that she was descended from those who escaped the hangings in Carbon and Schuylkill Counties by retreating to the woods of Northumberland County. Almost two hundred years later, there was still a union to join but it had no real power. The United States federal government owned the mines now, having taken possession when it nationalized all of America's energy resources during the Second Civil War. Anyone who drilled for oil and gas or dug coal was technically Uncle Sam's employee.

Unlike their forebears, the Mollies were not miners. They were scroungers and scavengers, sometimes thieves, and randomly vandals. Until recently, they numbered six, but last year one was caught, and presently one was close to death. Without immediate help, the roster would be down to four.

A commando team they might have been, for the way Jagger led her sorry group. Each of them had an assigned task and the equipment to get it done. They knew exactly where to go and multiple routes there and back. Together, they hit targets like a hammer, or independently, as nasty little cuts of a very sharp knife. Membership was limited to those related by blood and/or the bonds of time, which in their short lives meant a minimum of two years without screwing up. No one screwed up, not since the state troopers spotted Zach Zarosky siphoning gas on his own. He was stupid for not taking a lookout. But Zach was a junkie and needed something to trade Doc Erbil for a fix. He got jammed up instead. With everything in short supply, troopers made ugly examples of thieves. Since the end of the war, the Pennsylvania state troopers were tasked by the army to maintain security and enforce the law in rural areas. They were more paramilitary organization than cops.

Jagger's present group tested whistle-clean in terms of drug use. She knew a dope addict, a pot toker, or a pill popper when she saw them. Twitchy hands, glazed eyes, and millisecond-long attention spans were telltale signs. Given the stakes of their missions, she paid attention to everything, especially the condition of her people. She couldn't have a weakling or a sissy or, worst of all, someone hopped-up on chemicals who caused a disaster for the rest of them. Although, truth be told, Runt was too young and therefore too simple-minded to grasp exactly what they were doing. She'd learn, Jagger figured. Trial by fire was often the best teacher.

Besides, these were desperate times. At twenty-nine, Jagger was the only one old enough to remember the Second Civil War, and barely at that. Dad went away to fight. He never came back. A few years later, Mom caught the Flu of '52. She died in a puddle of sweat. Jagger was alone to deal with cousins Whip and Crush, whose parents had passed before Mom and Dad, yet weren't old enough to make it on their own. Then there was Runt, a squirmy tyke found in the woods one afternoon. It happened now and then; parents or caretakers died on the move, unintentionally abandoning children. Not that Jagger wanted another mouth at the table. There'd been a hell of an argument between her and Whip about leaving Runt at the local Common Faith Center. Whip won after threatening to quit the Mollies if they all didn't pitch in to raise Runt. Jagger couldn't afford to lose Whip. She climbed better than a ten-legged spider. On top of that, Crush always took Whip's side.

Jagger's little brother, Dylan, would have been the fifth Molly, and at this point she believed there was a chance he might still be. Hence, the current mission: Operation Breakout. It came together last minute. No matter. They knew the territory, knew the stakes, knew that if they did nothing, Dylan was a goner. Caught Red Death, he did, hacking up globs of bloody puke, the first, last, and undeniable symptom. It had the Mollies on edge that they all might get it, too.

No sense going to the clinic where the quack dispensed narcotics to addicts like Denise Walsh in between signing death certificates for miners killed in Girard Number Six. Otherwise, he was useless. There was no cure for Red Death. Not a medical one, anyway.

There were rumors about a certain someone with the ability to heal. Supposedly this guy had powers from God, the same God no one talked about since He'd been replaced by the Common Faith's Universal Creator. Not that Jagger believed in such bullshit, but as soon as she saw blood splatter the sink, the time had come to try whatever could be tried. Dylan was her younger sibling, the last of her father's clan. The problem: said potential healer was locked up for Common-Faith-related crimes, and all the if's that followed. If Operation Breakout went to plan, Jagger would haul his ass out to their trailer and witness some magic. If that worked for Dylan, Jagger would be the first one to extol the virtues of this guy's miraculous talents. If not, off the Poplar Street Bridge the faith-healer would go, thereby silencing the nonsense that people spread around town.

A full hour of stop-and-go jogging along the train tracks put them at the edge of town. Runt limited their speed. Her short legs were only half the hassle, the other half being her perpetual curiosity. She found every stick, every shiny rock, interesting, not to mention the stars overhead. Jagger guessed she was nine or ten years old, maybe older because kids were smaller now for lack of decent food. Runt insisted on cutting her own hair, which left her with a shock of uneven brown layers.

Whip had made a case for leaving Runt behind.

"She's too young," the Mollies' tallest member said. "I'll go down the chute and bust this guy out. Randy Bartok catches her, there's no telling what he'll do." Where Whip got the long legs, Jagger didn't know. Her mom and dad had been two squat bowling pins. Unlike Runt, Whip had Crush clip her head weekly, leaving no more than a quarter inch of fuzz. She wore a knit skull cap for warmth and protection.

"It's Thursday night, ain't it?" Jagger reminded her cousin.

"Yeah, so?"

"Every Thursday night, starting about now, Bartok spends a couple hours with Joannie T. Forget about him. Selman's the one to worry about. No telling where he's prowling."

"Saw him over by Denise Walsh's place earlier."

"Got nothing to do with where he is now," Jagger said.

"Bet you he's back to the well," muttered Crush. No one referred to the Mollies' strongest member as fat. She wasn't fat. It was impossible to gain weight when home was two miles walking from anything and meals were thin or small. Crush was solid, broad-shouldered, square-hipped, and with hands a little too big. She had a pretty smile, the type fools mistook for vulnerability. Her grin was a form of preemptive disarmament that left suckers with their guard down.

"We should be in the clear," insisted Jagger.

"Runt can wait here. Be a lookout," Whip suggested.

Watching their youngest member twist a twig into a small hoop, Jagger nixed the idea. "We're safer together," she said, handing Whip a flask. "Besides, no doubt our target is not only locked up, but chained fast, which means it's going to take more than your scrawny self to do the job."

After a sip of grog and a quiet cough from the potent liquor,

Whip warned, "Whatever happens to her is on you."

"Ain't it always?"

Whip returned the flask then stepped to the center of the tracks, where she had a look both ways. The loaded coal train left hours ago, bound for the docks in Philadelphia. She dreamed of hopping aboard for a ride to the city or anywhere else. People said it was a big country before it hammered itself to shit. Maybe it still was.

"I'm hungry," Runt said.

"We'll feast when Dylan's back on his feet," Jagger promised.

Runt tilted her head toward the ground. "My belly hurts," she groaned.

"Mine, too. Get over here and pay attention." To Whip and Crush, she added, "Display the hardware."

From a crossbody satchel, Whip removed a length of rope and a burlap sack. In a canvas carryall that had been her father's, Crush carried a pry bar and a bolt cutter. Jagger's own bag of tricks contained a tiny oil can, homemade brass knuckles, and a few tools, among other things not relevant to, but possibly useful during, tonight's mission. Everyone had their own flashlight, which they pointed at the same spot on the ground.

Jagger drew a rectangle in the dirt with her knife, then bisected it, explaining, "We're going in through the coal chute. It's on the north side of Bartok's building."

"Anyone walking down Seventh Street will see us," Crush put in.

"Anybody out right now is downing grog at the Pleasant Corner. In case they're wandering drunk, Whip spies from across the street until we pop the coal chute door."

"How? It'll be latched from the inside."

"If Bartok latched it, he'd have to be there every time he takes an off-the-books delivery. That's too often for his lazy ass to be bothered," Jagger explained, then pointed with the knife. "This side of the basement is the coal bunker, sure to be heaped with Black Diamond Special all the way to the boiler that sits over here against the outside wall. We lower Runt in first. She lights the way for the rest of us to drop down so we don't land crooked and twist ankles or bust knees."

She cut the center line with two dashes.

"This is a door between the bunker and the dungeon. No lock. Nothing but a twist of the wrist and we're through to the other side where there's a couple chains bolted to the wall. The guy we want will be shackled to one of them."

"What if there's someone else with him?" asked Whip.

"I'll knock him out," Jagger answered.

"And if our guy wants to fight?"

"I'll knock him out, too. At the far end of the room is a staircase. Straight run to a landing at the top. Door on the left goes to the first floor. Door to the right goes outside. It has a panic bar. Hit it hard and keep going."

"He ain't gonna run for us," Crush said.

"Then we drag him," Jagger said as all their flashlights switched off. "Dylan's counting on us."

The quartet trotted into the center of Mt. Carmel without a sound. In dark clothing and with starlight overhead, anyone looking out a window couldn't be blamed for missing them. Given it was after midnight, there wouldn't be many so inclined. Besides, most of the houses were abandoned due to a combination of war casualties, '52 Flu, and Red Death. The only vehicle on the roll would be Selman's staff car. No one else had money for gas, if there was any gas to be had.

Minutes later, they arrived at the rear of what had been Our Lady of Mount Carmel Catholic Church. Once the Mandate took effect, the building became a local Common Faith Center because it was the largest of the town's religious buildings and in the best condition. It was promptly stripped of any artifice of Christianity. Gone were the stained-glass windows, the handsomely carved pews, and the statues of saints. The cross atop the steeple was replaced with the Common Faith symbol, the Circle and

Line. All other churches and the one synagogue in town were demolished, the land left to the weeds. Director Martin Selman was the first Common Faith official to be stationed in town and here he remained, holding weekly services as well as lording over various social programs.

"Selman's car ain't here," Crush said.

"Telling you," Whip put in, "he's back at the Walsh's place."

"Then we're good," Jagger confirmed.

They hustled south on Lemon Street, which was more alley than street, to Seventh and made a right. At the corner of Market stood a three-story building that once housed a clothing store on the first level. Presently, Selman's enforcer, Randy Bartok, lived on the top floor and kept the second deliberately empty. It was the unofficial jail in the basement the Mollies wanted to penetrate.

After double-checking the street, they crept along the side of the building. Jagger stooped to examine the metal door sealing off the coal chute. Located just above ground level, it was made of cast iron, about two feet wide by one foot tall. Crush opened her bag, took out the pry bar, and wedged the toe under the lower lip.

"Not yet," Jagger cautioned, taking an oil can from her carrier, applying several drops to each hinge.

Crush couldn't help but smirk. As much of a domineering bitch as Jagger was, she thought of everything, which made her smart enough to be the boss, no matter what Whip said.

Just then, Whip hissed the all-clear sign.

"Do it."

Crush leaned against the bar, but the door didn't move. She repositioned it into another spot a few inches to the left, and put her weight on it again. This time, the door opened enough for her callused fingers to fit in the gap. She squatted down, ready to use her legs for more power, when Whip stopped her.

"Everybody down!"

They dropped to the ground, four pairs of eyes scanning for a threat. Actually, three pairs. Runt squeezed hers shut and pressed her hands over her ears. Zach Zarosky's screams still haunted her. When they took him a snack in jail, Zach wouldn't stop yelling about being innocent. To shut him up, the troopers used a muzzle, tearing the skin on his face as they strapped it tight.

"False alarm," Whip said. "Get going."

"Damn it," Crush moaned. "Almost pissed myself."

Seconds later, they had the door open and latched to the wall the way the truck driver did when he delivered coal.

"You first, Runt," Jagger said.

"Can we eat soon?" the girl asked.

"When Dylan's better."

"What if he doesn't get better?"

"He will. That's why we're here."

A second hiss from Whip urged them to hurry.

"Down you go," Jagger said to Runt.

"It's dark in there."

"Shhh."

Runt wiggled into the chute feet first, her hands held by Jagger and Crush. It was only a yard of smooth metal that fed the coal like a spout into the bunker, which was a wooden pen near the boiler. Slowly they lowered Runt into the darkness, until her feet crunched atop the pile of coal.

"I can stand."

"Good. Give us some light."

Runt pointed her beam at the pile beneath the chute.

Jagger went next, followed by Crush. Whip came last, slipping the latch and easing the door closed so as to leave no trace of their entry.

In the bunker, Jagger pointed her flashlight into the space around them.

"Look at all this coal," Crush whispered.

"Not what we came for."

"Target of opportunity, boss. We should fill our bags."

"Won't do shit for Dylan," insisted Jagger, moving toward the door to the dungeon. She knew the way. She'd been a guest of Randy Bartok a couple of years ago when he pinched her for stealing tools from a railroad crew fixing the tracks, a crime she hadn't committed. Didn't matter. Joannie T was out of town and Bartok wanted a date. He hauled Jagger in, locked her up for a week, three days of which she shoveled coal into the boiler and looked at old magazines. The other four days had been less fun upstairs in his quarters. The consolation prize: half a ton of Black Diamond Special for the stove, and a ride home. Since then, Jagger and her Mollies took deep cover when Joannie T was scarce.

Jagger waited for everyone to get their implements in hand and gather close. Seeing them ready, she eased the door open a crack, through which she peered into the dungeon. Sure enough, on the far side sat the person she'd heard about. He perched on a stool, his arms over a table against the wall. Shadows cast by the single bulb overhead indicated movement from his right hand. He's writing something, Jagger thought. Probably a confession to appease Selman and get out of there. At least he wouldn't see them coming.

She signaled her team that there was one person, far side, chain to the right ankle. Two nods and Runt's shrug indicated they understood. Jagger silently counted to three. The heavy door made not a sound as she opened it wide. Whip darted through, followed by Crush and then Runt. Jagger went last.

In a flash, Whip slammed the burlap sack over his head, yanking him off the stool. He landed hard on his ass. A stack of papers on the table scattered in every direction. Jagger held his arms as Whip tied his wrists with a length of rope. Crush jammed the bolt cutters into the chain attached to his ankle and snapped the link. The three of them hoisted him to his feet, and they were headed for the exit in less than thirty seconds total.

Their captive offered no resistance, which made the climb up the stairs easy. His feet found the treads with amazing accuracy. Jagger guessed he was cooperating with the idea that getting out was better than waiting down there until Selman hauled him off to a worse prison. At the top, they turned right, and outside they went into the cold night. Crush steered him with a firm hand on his back. Across the street, down the block, a left turn at the first alley, and they were safely out of sight.

"Hold up," Whip said, at the next intersection. "Where's Runt?"

Jagger spun around, her eyes straining into the dark for their youngest member.

"I'll find her," she promised. "Take him to the trailer."

CHAPTER 3.

In the corridor of Philadelphia's best hospital, people stood out of the way for Hester Thompson. Her heaving bulk needed no introduction. She was the face of the Common Faith. As one of its founders and now Secretary of the Sacred Council, she influenced all matters religious and social for the entire nation. Healthcare, pensions, and education fell under her purview, not to mention the dozens of smaller programs established after the Second Civil War collapsed America's economy.

"Good evening, Secretary Thompson," a cheerful nurse greeted her at the door to the intensive care unit. "How can I help you?"

"If you have to ask, forget it," Thompson growled, wondering how such a twit could work in a place as important as the ICU. Did she think the Secretary of the Sacred Council, a position one step below the president and equal to Speaker of the House, would come to visit just anyone in the hospital? Thompson barged past the nurse and into the ward, with nothing but another heavy breath and her briefcase in hand. It wasn't hard to spot Zoe Whelan's room, not with two armed guards on duty. Thompson ignored them, too, thankful they recognized her and moved aside.

In the room, Lt. Bentley rose to attention.

"Your inability to command the situation landed her here," Thompson said.

"In the case of a religious incident, SWAT defers to Common Faith officials," countered Bentley, "which means Specialist Whelan gave the orders."

"Hmpf," Thompson grunted. "The Christians have another

martyr and a propaganda victory."

"I talked to Zoe's pal Jesse Young. He reported the cause of the explosion as a gas leak."

"When the erased Christian does not return to his tribe of rebels, they'll think what? He failed?"

"Maybe that he succeeded," Bentley answered.

"Clarify that statement."

"I was the first officer to engage the suspect. He demanded to speak to Zoe Whelan. He sounded like he knew her. He said, 'She's one of us. You'll see.'"

"'*She's one of us*,'" Thompson repeated.

"Never heard any of them talk about a compliance specialist like that."

Doctor Wade entered and was immediately questioned.

"What's the prognosis?" Thompson wanted to know.

"She has some minor cuts and abrasions," answered Wade, "and is in stable condition at the moment."

"I asked for the prognosis."

"Blast injuries manifest themselves in many ways. Some don't show up for days or weeks," he explained.

"In other words, you have no idea."

"She's in a deep coma caused by the concussion of the blast. It's a miracle she's alive."

"Something a Christian would say."

Wade bristled. "I'm a founding member of my Common Faith district."

Ignoring the comment, she said, "Tell me what can be done for her, or I'll find someone who can."

"We've had some luck with cognitive stimulus."

"In English."

"Friends and family speaking to her, reading books aloud. The sounds of her favorite television shows playing in the background. Sometimes it helps the brain return to a conscious state."

"Anything else?"

"We wait," sighed Doctor Wade.

"That's all. You're dismissed."

Thompson settled into a chair opposite Bentley. She took out her phone, scrolled through the menus, and found the police recordings from the incident.

"Listen carefully," she instructed Bentley, then tapped the play button.

CS Whelan: *How do I know you're telling me the truth?*

Perpetrator: *The angel brought it to me from your secret collection.*

Thompson stopped the recording. "Forensics found this," she said, taking a plastic evidence bag from her briefcase. "Can you identify the handwriting?"

Bentley examined the hymnal page. He'd seen that writing on a dozen arrest warrants. "It's Zoe's."

"I had no doubt." She put the evidence back in her case then said, "Take this opportunity to make up for your previous mistakes, Lieutenant. Search her apartment. Find this secret collection of hers and bring it to my office."

"Yes, Madam Secretary."

"I suggest you start now."

Bentley exited after a formal salute.

Alone with her unconscious compliance specialist, Thompson opted to read the transcript rather than listen to the recording. She took it from her briefcase.

CS Whelan: *Who's gathering, Andrew?*

Perpetrator: *Those who already know your name. Those who still believe.*

CS Whelan: *Any particular reason for this gathering?*

Perpetrator: *Isn't it obvious?*

CS Whelan: *I'm sorry. I'm missing something.*

Perpetrator: *They're gathering to hear the Next Testament from you, the Messenger, who will soon get it from the prophet.*

CS Whelan: *How can I be a messenger?*

Perpetrator: *Because you've been chosen. It's a great honor, one you don't have to hide.*

Thompson scanned back to another part of the exchange that intrigued her.

CS Whelan: *Why didn't the angel come directly to me?*

Perpetrator: *Because your journey begins here.*

CS Whelan: *Okay. Where am I going?*

Perpetrator: *To get the message, the Next Testament.*

Thompson pondered the entire exchange.

Your journey begins here.

To get the Next Testament.

The Time of Gathering is soon.

People who already know your name. Those who still believe.

Thompson added what Bentley told her about his initial conversation with the suspect.

She's one of us. You'll see.

Had the Christians compromised her most effective compliance specialist? Or, were they playing for the cameras? Was it a way to inspire others to join their cause? Or, perhaps Zoe Whelan had been one of them from the beginning, a sleeper agent reeling in small fish while protecting the big ones. She might have fed information about the Compliance Division to the Christians, thereby giving them everything they needed to plan future attacks and avoid capture. Had they tried to kill her to cover their tracks but failed?

In any case, Thompson could take no risks. She didn't rise to the highest level of civic administration via luck, coincidence, or because she was born into the right family. It was her ability to exploit opportunities for their maximum potential, regardless of cost—financial or human. With that in mind, she considered how her once-unquestionably loyal Zoe Whelan might serve a greater purpose. Her death would lead to a memorial parade for a fallen public servant, at best a minor propaganda victory with a few minutes on the television news. Thompson contrived a more ambitious plot, one that would cast the Christians as villainous insurgents unwilling to leave the Dark Ages for the modern world.

And she knew the best person to implement her scheme. He was an old friend, but not a close one for some years now. He'd become a liability. Rather than dispose of a tarnished asset, she had wisely relocated him. His rare talents were quite useful in moments of crisis. She would put him to work again. If he succeeded, she might welcome him back into the fold with a promotion closer to the mothership. If not, there would be two caskets in the parade.

● ● ●

Jagger circled Bartok's building in ten seconds flat. Without the pry bar, she struggled to open the chute door. Then she dropped onto the pile of coal, bruising her knee, not that she felt a thing. Finally, she took out her flashlight to point the way. She rushed past the boiler into the dungeon, where to her surprise, Runt crawled around the dirt floor gathering scattered sheets of paper.

Only one thing prevented Jagger from a furious scream: the sight of an apple in Runt's hand. Oblivious to Jagger's presence, the little girl placed the pages in a neat pile, then gnawed at the good part of the fruit. She chewed sloppily, a dribble of juice sliding down her chin.

"Hey Runt," Jagger said.

"Hi, boss. Look what I found."

Jagger's own stomach rumbled at the apple held out by that small hand.

"There's more, too," Runt added, pointing to various apples serving as paperweights.

"Good work. Let's sack them and get out of here."

"I'm not done."

Runt slipped the half-eaten apple into her jacket pocket and went back to picking up loose sheets from the floor.

In the interest of avoiding a pointless argument with a ten-year-old, Jagger joined the effort, albeit with greater urgency. In less than a minute, the floor was bare. Still, Runt wasn't happy.

"Too messy. They have to be in order."

This from a kid with apple bits sticking in her teeth, Jagger thought.

"There's a number on the bottom, silly. One, two, three… you know."

Jagger snatched a nearby apple, saying, "Open your mouth."

"Wha—"

The apple stuffed in Runt's maw, Jagger adopted an assuring tone. "We'll sort them when we get home. Okay?"

An affirmative nod from Runt.

"Now let's load up and get the hell out of here."

The apples went into Runt's jacket pockets; the pages they rolled into a log that Jagger stuffed in her own bag. She didn't need them to go flying and give the kid a fit. Up the stairs to the exit took mere seconds, putting them on the verge of escape.

"When I open the door," Jagger said, "run as fast as you can. Straight to the alley."

"Got it, boss."

Jagger shouldered open the door and bolted for the shadows of the next block. Nearly there, she caught the glare of headlights turning the corner to her right. The lights pointed up the street, just missing Jagger and Runt as they entered the relative safety of the alley. Winded and legs aching from the sprint, Jagger tumbled onto a patch of brown grass beside a dilapidated garage.

Squatting beside her, Runt pointed across the street. Director Martin Selman had exited his sedan and stood at the passenger side with the door open. Suddenly a figure bolted from the car.

"Hey, Ian!" Runt called out.

Jagger clamped her hand over Runt's mouth.

Selman looked around to see who had recognized his special guest.

Ian didn't stop. He was a little older than Runt, with longer legs and the kind of motivation that made Jagger glad she'd suffered under Randy Bartok and not that pig, Selman.

Selman leaned against the car and released a hearty guffaw.

"Why'd he run away?" Runt asked.

"I hope you never find out."

CHAPTER 4.

For the Mollies, home was a house trailer sagging over a cement-block foundation like a melting layer cake. A cast-iron stove heated the kitchen and living room. The two bedrooms and bathroom in back got whatever warmth drifted that way. Their fuel of choice was coal but more often they burned wood, which made no sense for a town that shipped trainloads of anthracite every week. Just because it was mined there didn't mean the people were allowed to buy it. Not that the Mollies paid for anything, unless they absolutely couldn't forage for it. With no electricity to run the well pump, they hauled water from the creek that cut through the hollow on the other side of the hill that shielded them from the worst of the weather. For light, they used candles and, once in a while, kerosene lamps, but only if they nabbed a big enough score to afford the oil.

They might have rented a house in town. With more than three-quarters of the houses empty and unclaimed, there were plenty to choose from. But that required a regular job or service in a government program. Within the borough's limits, squatters were swiftly evicted. Therefore, they stuck to the trailer, which was out of sight, out of mind, in terms of residential enforcement.

Neither forthright employment nor the dole appealed to their idea of making a living. They lived as scroungers. The advantage, as Jagger saw it anyway, was not answering to someone who gave less than a shit about them. For example, those poor bastards going into Girard Number Six every day, risking their lives in a place less safe for humans than the bottom of the ocean. What'd they get for their sweat and death-defying good luck for as long as it lasted? Four tons of freeze prevention, aka coal, and a paycheck that bought from mostly empty shelves at a government-regulated store. Better to stick it out in the woods, which was above ground and off the leash. Or so Jagger thought, and she was the boss.

Not sure what to do with their captive, Crush and Whip ushered him inside the trailer where a single kerosene lamp illuminated the living room. It cast a dim glow on Dylan's face as he lay pale and motionless on the couch. When it came to saving his life, Crush and Whip both had their doubts this new guy could do anything. Thankfully, Jagger and Runt showed up before they reached a verdict.

Jagger assembled the group around Dylan. At some point, he had expelled a gob of blood that dried a crusty, burnt red on his white T-shirt. Whip couldn't look at him, opting to stare at the floor instead. Crush couldn't turn away. Runt had no idea what was going on but sensed something awful.

Jagger pulled the bag off the guy's head, revealing no one the others knew. They'd been too young or not from around here.

"This is John Carroll," Jagger said. "Some call him Father Carroll or Preacher John."

Runt looked up at him, finding his steady eyes comforting amid the tension. He had lots of grey hair, kind of straight like her dad's had been. If she remembered correctly. It was hard to remember Dad.

"People say he can perform miracles," Jagger continued. "Has a direct connection to the Man above."

She gave him a nudge toward the couch.

"Has he been to the clinic?" Father Carroll asked.

"That quack ain't worth spit. Besides, I got you," Jagger said.

Carroll stared down at the young man's impassive face. He clearly wasn't breathing. "There's nothing... " he began.

"Don't start with the negative shit!" Jagger interrupted. "All kind of rumors flying around about you. Power from God, they say.

Reminded me of stories from when I was little sitting in church. Sight for the blind. Healing the lepers, whatever the hell they had wrong. All that."

"Maybe we should go outside," suggested Whip. "Let him alone with Dylan."

"Want to miss a miracle?"

"No."

"Then shut it!" To Crush, Jagger snapped, "Get a couple jugs."

Crush went to the cabinet under the kitchen sink, came back with two plastic milk jugs filled with coins. These she dropped at John Carroll's feet.

"Sorry, Preacher," Jagger went on. "Almost forgot the custom. Have to put something in the plate, right? That enough?"

Carroll estimated the coins represented a fortune to these girls. In the near future, it would be a pittance to them, but they had no way of knowing that.

"Hey! I asked you a question."

"Money has nothing to do with it," he answered.

"Alright," Jagger conceded. "Looking for something less tangible. Makes sense for the, uh, philosophical part of the situation. Tell you what. Get Dylan on his feet and we'll all be thanking Jesus. Do the right thing, too, as much as we can for who we are. We got a deal?"

Carroll returned his attention to the young man on the couch. He'd been wracked by malnutrition his whole life. Then Red Death came as it did in waves of vile anguish, reducing him to a mere happenstance of biology.

"On your knees, damn it," Jagger ordered. "Show him we're serious."

Carroll heard them stoop to the floor as he silently prayed for Dylan's soul.

"Want my little brother like he was, just like I heard about them people in the old days. Now say the mumbo jumbo or whatever. Loud and clear. Make sure the Big Man gets the message."

In words he heard himself say too often before, Carroll informed his captor, "Your brother is dead."

Crush looked at Whip who nodded in agreement about what they'd known all along. No one survives Red Death.

"Better get some rest then, Preacher John," Jagger said. "You have a grave to dig in the morning."

CHAPTER 5.

While his district covered a swath of Cumberland County, it was sparsely populated, which meant local Common Faith Director Martin Selman had plenty of time to indulge his passions without the annoyance of doing his job. A dilettante would have been angry by Ian's dash from the car last night. Not Martin Selman. He was a connoisseur. He appreciated the game with all its nuances and subtleties, conquests and failures. If it was too easy, it was not fun. Nor was he concerned that someone saw him and called out Ian's name. What were they going to do? File a complaint? He was the one who received such complaints. And what was there to complain about? The boy and his mother received extraordinary gifts from him, including a complete remodel of their home, plentiful foodstuffs, and gasoline vouchers.

Therefore, Selman awoke in a particularly jocular mood. Although fifty-seven, he appeared at least ten years younger, thanks to quality hair dye, an exercise regimen, and a careful diet except for a monthly gluttonous feast. He dabbled in narcotics rarely, which made them more effective. Self-control rewarded him with envious results in body and mind, thereby setting an example for others, not that many had the means to emulate his lifestyle.

He'd hardly begun his breakfast when a low-flying helicopter rattled his teacup. His cellphone interrupted the trip to the window for a glimpse of such a rare sight. More rare was a call from Secretary Hester Thompson. He answered on the first ring.

"Good morning, Madam Secretary. It's been too long since we last spoke."

"Transportation is on the way. I expect you in my office at ten. Bring your associate."

"We look forward to seeing you."

She disconnected without giving a reason for requesting his presence. He didn't mind. Knowing less built anticipation. He dialed Randolph Bartok, his most effective Common Faith employee.

"Disentangle from Mrs. Telford," Selman began. "The sound of a higher power is in the air. We've been summoned."

"Tying my boots now," Bartok said. "Meet you at the field."

Selman left the remains of his breakfast on the table, took his coat, and drove to the high school, which was a mere fifteen blocks away. There, a state trooper helicopter sat in the middle of the disused football field. Although the game wasn't played anymore for lack of enough students, it was mowed to provide a safe landing spot, as every inhabited town was required to have.

He took a seat in back with Bartok. They donned headsets to shield their ears from the noise and to communicate with the crew.

The co-pilot gave a thumbs-up, informing them, "About ninety nautical miles from here to there. Forty-five minutes of flight time. Buckle up."

Don't rush it! Selman wanted to say. He hadn't flown since the early days of the Common Faith, when he jetted in military transports from city to city, giving lectures about its inevitability.

They rose above Mount Carmel's grid of streets, then swung east by south. Off the left side he saw the breaker, processing plant, and office that was Girard Number Six, the newest coal mine in Pennsylvania. It was opened to help fund the war debt, selling coal to China. A black streak of tailings stretched from the breaker for more than a mile. The refurbished railroad line wound south toward Pottsville along the Shamokin Creek.

From there it was mostly forest and small towns, some abandoned, some not. They flew over Reading, where the damage from heavy fighting left the city in ruins. The Army Corps of Engineers and their bulldozers had cleared it down to the streets.

A terrible shame, thought Selman, a city erased. Then again, plenty of room for proper planning and redevelopment.

More greenspace followed, which left him thinking about how part of the country might have looked when it was only the Native Americans who lived here: forests and wild fields, clean rivers and fresh air. It must have been stunningly beautiful.

Next came the Philadelphia suburbs. Like Reading, they were pocked with empty spaces. Major roads led from formerly somewhere to presently nowhere. The one exception was the new military base in King of Prussia. The former site of the nation's second-largest shopping mall now housed thousands of soldiers, their families, and all manner of fighting equipment.

"Hopefully won't need that anymore," Selman said.

Bartok rocked his head in a noncommittal response. He preferred to conserve his commentary until absolutely necessary and then unload by the paragraph. It fit his brooding nature and hardened face that had taken as many punches as his fists had given to others. The past couple of years he'd kept his hands to himself, opting to brandish a modified ten-gauge shotgun. The weapon's report focused attention far and wide.

Only a few minutes remained in their flight, during which Selman noted how the northern and western parts of Philadelphia contained block after block of tent villages. They ended abruptly where new housing was under construction—uniform buildings of eight stories each.

Then came Center City. Several skyscrapers remained intact, albeit with less occupancy. Of course, Common Faith Headquarters was taller than all of them. The Circle and Line beckoned them to the central helipad, where they landed.

The decision to locate Headquarters in Philadelphia had been hotly debated. The old-guard politicians wanted it in Washington, D.C., but a younger group believed it best to be in Philadelphia. Where the nation began, so shall the new faith. A nostalgic public agreed. Thus, the building was constructed across the park from

Independence Hall, although in much grander fashion than the quaint brick edifice where the founders argued in 1776.

Selman glanced at his watch. The journey lasted forty-five minutes almost to the second. He and Bartok were greeted by a chubby male in the white smock of Common Faith interns. They earned special benefits for their families by serving five years in various menial capacities.

"An honor to meet you, Director Selman," the intern said with a slight bow in the Asian style.

"Please, I'm a humble man," Selman replied. "I'm here to help in any way I can."

"Yes, sir, of course. Please follow me."

They entered the building and took a short elevator ride to the level with offices and meeting spaces for Sacred Council members.

"This is as far as I'm permitted," the intern said. "Secretary Thompson will meet you in the Sanctus Chamber, which is straight ahead. Permission to enter has already been granted."

"Thank you," Selman said, bowing only his head.

They walked through a corridor that grew progressively darker, the one Selman had heard about but had never seen. He'd been sent to Mount Carmel before the building was finished. The hall ended at a set of double doors with a wide gap between them. Almost-blinding light shined through.

"Ready?" Selman asked.

A sharp "Pffft" indicated that Hollywood trickery didn't impress Bartok.

Entering the Sanctus Chamber was like stepping into a cloud. The domed ceiling and circular wall gleamed brilliant white, illuminated by hidden lights. A matching circle in the middle of the space, this one of polished black granite, served as a single, continuous desk for nine council members. The line in the center was made of marble, the ends of which did not touch the circle. At it were three chairs, one slightly elevated for the Secretary and one on each side for her deputies. Currently only the center was occupied by the woman herself, resplendent in the neutral grey robe of her office.

For Selman, it was like entering the Holy of Holies in Solomon's Temple. No, it was better. What a thrill to be in the most sacred place in the nation!

"Secretary Thompson," Selman greeted her as his eyes adjusted, "how wonderful to see you."

"I hope so," she replied, shifting her bulk deeper into the chair and looking at Bartok. "Still fit after all these years, Randy?"

"None the worse for the wear," he said, taking position next to Selman at the edge of the granite circle. He wondered how Thompson or anyone else got to the marble line inside. Up through a hole in the floor? He'd ask Selman later because the Big Lady was going on about a tragedy.

"Last night," she said, "a Christian suicide bomber nearly killed the most effective compliance specialist in the division."

"We thank our Universal Creator they did not succeed," commented Selman.

"He might yet. She's in a coma."

"Oh, my. What can we do?"

"She's from your district. Actually, she was born there before the district existed. We'll get to that later."

Unbeknownst to her visitors, Thompson pressed a floor switch that summoned another intern. She entered from a side door wearing the blue smock of a director trainee and carrying a shoebox, which she placed on the shiny granite in front of them. She bowed and backed away, remaining in the room.

Selman deliberately ignored the box, keeping his eyes focused on the Secretary, who held up her cellphone.

"Listen carefully," she said. "The first voice belongs to Compliance Specialist Zoe Whelan. The second, the man, is the Christian perpetrator."

The conversation between Andrew and Zoe played from the phone.

"Why didn't the angel come directly to me?"
"Because your journey begins here."
"Okay, where am I going?"
"To get the Next Testament."

Selman held up his hand for Thompson to stop the recording. "Excuse the interruption. He said, 'the Next Testament,' correct?"

"You've heard of it?" Thompson asked.

"I might have," Selman replied. "The leftover Christians borrow plenty of terms from the Dark Ages."

In fact, months ago, an informant in Selman's district reported about a former priest, Father John Carroll, who was the spiritual leader of the small group of Christians in Mount Carmel. A modern-day hermit, Carroll claimed to be having visions that he was translating into testimony and prophecy.

"He's calling it the Next Testament," the informant had said. "Radical stuff, from what I gather."

In normal circumstances, Selman would have ignored the tip as someone looking for a reward, and left well enough alone. However, this person was a reliable source, and the nature of Carroll's claims went beyond talk of the Second Coming. He was predicting cataclysmic events of the near future. If, by accident or coincidence, an incident actually correlated to his prophecy, then his status would rise. True or not, people fell for that kind of thing, spreading the message faster than when social media was unregulated. Selman wasn't going to allow a prophet to pop up in his district. A couple dozen people holding prayer sessions in private was one thing. Preaching about God making a radical change-of-course to current events was something else. Selman set a simple trap triggered by the informant, and Carroll was captured. As an ironic joke, Selman gave him sturdy paper to finish writing his prophecies. Father Carroll was still in custody, scribbling away in solitary confinement. Mount Carmel's knot of underground Christians had cause for lamentation, and life went on.

Of course, Selman wasn't going to reveal any of this to Secretary Thompson. Depending on how matters progressed, he could use the priest to advance his own career and possibly end up sitting in this magnificent room where, considering his history, he belonged.

Pretending to scour his memory and with a pleading look at Bartok, Selman said, "No, the Next Testament doesn't sound right. But maybe. I'm not sure. Randy, do you recall something relevant?"

"Have to check my notes," Bartok said.

Thompson was direct. "Other Christian specialists have mentioned rumors but with no substantiation. You know how they talk. 'A prophet has come.' 'The Time of Gathering is now.' 'Prepare to be delivered.' But without evidence, I was inclined to think it was the work of a huckster looking to fleece the flock. Someone selling the sizzle without the steak. We have a wing at Graterford Prison full of them. The fact that one was willing to bomb this building has changed my opinion."

"Indeed. Did Ms. Whelan make any recent reports about this testament or whatever it's called?"

"No."

"Hmmm. Please, continue."

The playback started again.

"How do I know you're telling me the truth?"
"The angel brought me this from your secret collection."
"How did you get that?"

Thompson stopped the recording. She waved at the intern to give Selman a plastic sleeve containing the hymnal page.

"That is what he gave her."

Selman scanned the page. He recognized the song immediately. "A Mighty Fortress is Our God." Written by Martin Luther. A staple of Christian worship for centuries. He placed it on the table beside the shoe box.

"And that," Thompson said, "is the secret collection referred to in the conversation."

Selman resisted the temptation to see the contents. "With your permission, Madam Secretary, I'd like to hear the rest of the exchange without any more visual aids."

"Very well."

The recording played through until its abrupt end.

Selman contemplated what he heard in the context of the hymnal page and what he guessed was in the box. The intern ruined the moment by dumping the contents onto the table after an impatient hand gesture from the Secretary. There was a small pile of items, including a miniature version of the New Testament, various types of crosses, rosary beads, pages of the Old Testament, a piece of stained glass, and more. He would have preferred to pick through them one at a time.

"Leave us," Thompson told the intern, who bowed twice then exited. "Do you understand the problem?" the Common Faith's highest officeholder asked.

"Your best agent might have been compromised by the Christians," ventured Selman.

"Oh, it's worse than that. Friend or foe, she survived an explosion. A miracle, the Christians will say. A validation of their God's power. 'Love your enemy' writ large for the nation to see."

"More like simple good luck," Selman put in, "but I see your point."

"Perhaps she always was a Christian, one planted among us years ago. If not, they might have converted her. Even if she's not and she's fortunate enough to survive, she'll be a living saint to them."

Selman thought for a few seconds while making eye contact with Bartok. Having previously dealt together with random miscreants and vicious troublemakers, they didn't have to speak to acknowledge the path to a solution.

"Trust me, Madam Secretary, there will be no martyrs nor

saints on our watch," Selman said.

"My dear Zoe Whelan is not to be one of them?"

"Not for their side. Let's remember, every good crisis needs a victim."

Thompson grinned. "What does that sound like?"

"Social worker on the mend murdered by religious radicals."

From grin to a hearty chuckle, Thompson did not hide her satisfaction. "I forgot how good you are at this, Martin."

"The opportunity to maintain my reputation is very much appreciated."

"As I said before, Ms. Whelan is from your district. Her family still lives there."

"That's correct," Selman said. "Her mother receives a small pension and her brother is a coal miner."

"Compliance Specialist Whelan will be transferred to the clinic in Mount Carmel today, her family notified after arrival to prevent any drama between here and there."

"Naturally."

"I expect a powerful narrative, Martin, one that discredits their entire existence and establishes the Common Faith as the only alternative. Put the pieces in place as soon as you can and resolve the matter before more bombs go off. Keep me apprised of your progress."

"I shall, Madam Secretary, knowing the Bounty of Faith will be my reward."

"As it always has, Martin."

• • •

"What's that you're humming?" Runt asked. She stood near the growing pile of dirt Father Carroll shoveled out of the hole in which Dylan was to be buried. Jagger had tied a length of rope between his ankles, using her impossible knots. The span was long enough to allow him to walk but not run. Runt had instructions to yell for help if he tried anything stupid. Jagger and the rest were only fifty feet away, inside the trailer getting Dylan ready for his final resting place.

"A hymn," Carroll replied. "A song we used to sing in church."

"We listened to music, but then the power went off. That was a while ago. We could use batteries in the player, but the boss says we have to save them for the flashlights."

"Make your own music," he suggested.

"I do sometimes, especially when I'm out getting wood for the fire."

He went back to digging. Runt stopped him with another question.

"Do you have kids?"

"No, I don't have children."

"Then why do people call you father?"

"It was the title given to me by the church when I became a priest."

Runt mulled that a while. "I try to remember my dad, but it's really hard."

"I'm sure he was a good man."

"Did you know him?"

"I'm sorry. I didn't."

"Do you think he died of Red Death like Dylan?"

Father Carroll replied, "He might have."

"How come we didn't catch the Death but Dylan did?"

"I don't know."

"You don't have a lot of answers," complained Runt.

She walked a few dozen yards away to the start of the trail to the stream. She turned back to Preacher John as she now thought of him. Calling him father didn't make sense if he had no kids. She wondered why he wasn't scared when Jagger told him he was going off the bridge at dusk. Seeing that he stopped digging again, Runt returned to the hole.

"Tell them it's finished," Preacher John said.

Runt did as she was asked, returning with the other three, who carried Dylan's body. He was wrapped in a sheet, secured with loops of rope in a neat pattern. Again, Jagger's impossible knots ensured her little brother would not be disturbed.

Whip and Crush helped Father Carroll out of the hole and were then surprised that Jagger jumped in.

"Bring him to me," she said. "I'll lay my brother to rest the proper way."

It was a tight fit. Jagger squeezed against the end of the grave as Whip and Crush eased Dylan over the edge. She let his feet slide to the bottom, then moved to the side, bending over to lower him by the shoulders until he was in place. From her back pocket she took out Dylan's jackknife. Into the wooden handle, he'd inscribed DYLAN on one side; the other read ANNA. She used to tease him about Anna, a girl from Second Street he saw regularly until she disappeared with her parents. Jagger had hoped Dylan and Anna would someday have children to continue the family line. As it stood, that responsibility fell to her. It was more likely she'd be in the ground next to Dylan than complete the task. She tucked the knife into the loop of rope around his chest, then reached for Crush and Whip to haul her out.

"I'd like to pray for your brother," Father Carroll said.

"Say whatever you want," Jagger told him, taking the shovel in hand. "Not like he's going to complain."

"Blessed are the poor in spirit," Carroll began, "for theirs is the kingdom of heaven."

She ignored the words and put her back into shoveling at a steady pace. The work stemmed her tears.

"Blessed are they who mourn, for they will be comforted. Blessed are the meek, for they will inherit the land. Blessed are they who hunger and thirst for righteousness, for they will be satisfied. Blessed are the merciful, for they will be shown mercy. Blessed are the clean of heart, for they will see God."

Not wanting to be outdone or show weakness, Crush took

the shovel from Jagger for the next layer. Whip stood back with Runt, who was the only one listening to Father Carroll.

"Blessed are the peacemakers, for they will be called the children of God. Blessed are they who are persecuted for the sake of righteousness, for theirs is the kingdom of heaven. Blessed are you when they insult you and persecute you and utter every kind of evil against you because of Me. Rejoice and be glad, for your reward will be great in heaven."

"We'll see about that," Jagger muttered, then finished the job without stopping until there was a mound atop the grave. Sweaty and tired, she propped the shovel on her shoulder and announced the day's orders.

"Everyone wash up, including you," she said, pointing at Father Carroll. "We're going to have a funeral feast."

"With what?" asked Whip.

"If it has to be tree bark, I'll conjure something."

"Is he going to eat with us?"

"Yes."

"Why feed him if he's going off the bridge tonight?"whined Crush.

"The condemned get a last meal."

CHAPTER 6.

Body, Mind, and Soul (BMS for short) it was called, the Common Faith's comprehensive health services program, which was free to all practicing members. Like education, subsidized housing, and retirement pensions, healthcare management had been shifted from various predecessor agencies to the Common Faith. It was a matter of efficiency, replacing all the individual structures with a single one. A nation deeply in debt had to save wherever it could.

Since the transition, all medical facilities bore the Circle and Line emblem, which is why Selman and Bartok sat under the awning at the rear of Philadelphia Central East Hospital in the shadow of the symbol overhead. Inside, Compliance Specialist Whelan was being prepared for transport.

"Tell me your fears," Selman began, noticing his colleague was visibly anxious.

"If our Mount Carmel zealots got word out to their friends here in Philly, then Thompson knows we have John Carroll in the dungeon," Bartok said. "He hasn't seen the light of day in a couple weeks."

"Relax. If the munificent Secretary knew Carroll was in our custody, she would have transferred us to the blistering desert of southern New Mexico," Selman said, to allay Bartok's concern.

"I wouldn't bet on that with your money or mine," Bartok countered. "She's a long-term thinker."

"As am I. Besides, I doubt there's a connection between him and the suicide bomber. Don't assign causation to coincidence.

There's probably a hundred kooks claiming to have written divine revelations, calling them the Next Testament or some such thing."

"Sure about that?"

"Absolutely. It's what I would have done had I not answered the call of the one, true Universal Creator of the Common Faith and written the Original Doctrine that defines our marvelous national religion."

Bartok would have wagered his whole stash on that statement. He never met a guy who played the angles better than Selman, and he'd met some diabolical sons of bitches during the war, when the only rule was there were no rules.

He said, "Carroll doesn't seem crazy. More like a guy with a mild case of Jesus fever, holding hands and telling stories to make people feel good."

"He'll be a raving psycho by the time we're finished telling this particular chapter in the long history of violent insurgents. We'll establish him as the culprit with regards to Whelan's demise. Naturally, he'll perish with her. And then—"

An EMT with the help of two orderlies interrupted Selman when they wheeled Zoe Whelan through the doors toward the waiting ambulance.

"And then I'll be measured for the grey robe of a Sacred Council member with you as my Chief of Personal Security."

"Think it'll buy you that far up the ladder?"

"Why not? Where I almost was is where I most definitely belong."

Enjoy the view, Bartok wanted to tell him. All this goes right, Mount Carmel will be deader than a nuclear test range in terms of his side deals. No more extorting hush money from Christians. No more stealing Bounty of Faith deliveries. Forget unofficial tolls on trucks taking the shortcut on Route 54. Say goodbye to miners' widows, not that he dallied with anyone other than Joannie Telford. It was the availability of others, should she turn sour, that he would miss. He'd lose his percentage of all that and the fun of being top dog. Yeah, no thanks. I'll skip the pension-earning potential for the bundle saved along the way. Next stop, Florida for some gator hunting until a heart attack, cancer, or a self-inflicted gunshot wound did the job.

"One of you in back with me and the patient," the EMT said. "The other can sit up front with the driver."

Selman volunteered to assist with Whelan. Her impassive face bore several scratches and a few small bruises. She breathed normally yet was undisturbed by the bumps in the road. Thus, he relaxed in his comfortable seat by the rear windows to watch the scenery go by.

He remembered the horrific traffic of the East Coast before the war, especially on the Washington Beltway. Presently, it was a steady, unhindered ride at ground level for a closer view of what he'd seen from the helicopter. The vehicles they passed were mostly convoys of construction supplies. Private cars were heavily taxed in favor of more efficient and practically free public transit, which was blossoming now that direct corridors could be built between population centers. Even with the money for a car, gasoline was still rationed through a voucher system. Millions of unwanted vehicles were being recycled to make steel for a nation rebuilding itself.

On the west side of Reading they stopped at a Pennsylvania state trooper checkpoint. When martial law was rescinded, the troopers resumed internal security duties, including enforcement of travel restrictions. The metropolitan areas were mostly free of the inconvenience. However, the hinterlands required monitoring to prevent insurgents from gathering and to clamp down on the black market.

Selman saw a column of men and women in bright red coveralls. Unlike at the end of the First Civil War, there was no going home to the farm. These former rebel fighters were serving their twenty-year sentences in work crews demolishing buildings, rebuilding damaged infrastructure, and attending mandatory tolerance classes provided by the Common Faith.

The next and last checkpoint was at Pottsville, but that was a cursory inspection of documents and they were clear to Mount Carmel.

The ambulance stopped at Bartok's building, where Selman and the enforcer got out.

Selman told the EMT, "Doctor Erbil will take good care of her at the clinic. Thank you for the ride."

Bartok held the door for Selman to enter the former storefront on the ground floor of his premises.

"You really should do something with this space."

"Like what?" asked Bartok.

"A coffee shop."

"I'll think about it." Not that Bartok would give it a moment's consideration. There wasn't a single restaurant in Mount Carmel anymore. Why would anyone buy a cup of coffee?

"Mr. Carroll," Selman called down the stairs. "We've come to have a chat."

He didn't expect a response. Nor did he expect to be staring at a broken chain on the floor of the vacant basement.

"Find him."

• • •

Doctor Erbil had never spoken to Secretary Hester Thompson before. Why would he? Although technically his boss, she was at the top of the pyramid, with at least a dozen people between himself and her. In any case, she had called him personally, giving instructions on exactly what he was to do for patient Zoe Whelan, who would be arriving at his clinic via ambulance. As the only physician for Pennsylvania District 17, he didn't need the Secretary to tell him he was responsible for patient outcomes, but she did, in so many words.

"Her treatment record will be sent to your digital assistant soon. You do have data services out there, correct?"

"Some of the time," Erbil croaked.

"She's in a coma," Thompson continued, without missing a beat.

"Madam Secretary, this is a day clinic," interrupted Erbil. "We don't have the people or equipment to care for a coma patient." The last time he saw someone in a coma had been at least ten years ago, during a rough stretch in med school when he had almost flunked out.

"The Bounty of Faith has no limits, Doctor. You'll get everything you need from Pottsville."

"Thank you."

"Ms. Whelan will be placed in a private room. Only next of kin and official visitors will be allowed to see her. Notify her family after you have her settled in. Use your training to do the best you can. Report to me daily via the secure system, the code for which will be sent in the next five minutes. I want an honest appraisal of her condition."

"I can do that."

"And you shall."

The ambulance arrived before he had time to panic. As he'd been ordered, he placed Whelan in a room on the second floor at the rear of the clinic. He performed a cursory exam, finding her stable, breathing on her own, but unresponsive in any way. He assigned the only other staff member in the building, Nurse Porter, to remain in the room.

"What if someone else comes in for treatment?" Porter asked.

"I'll deal with them."

"I'm still going to need help."

"On the way from Pottsville."

Was it half an hour before a team pulled up to the front door? Doctor Erbil thought it was less, which meant the Secretary must have notified them before speaking with him. They brought everything from extra catheters and feeding tubes, to a heart monitor and spare oxygen cylinders. They knew what they were doing, too. Erbil stayed out of the way while they transformed the room into a temporary ICU.

When they finished, the team leader, a short guy with a ponytail, said, "A neurological team and support staff will be here tomorrow afternoon. Can you handle it until then?"

"We have it covered," Erbil assured him.

"Enjoy."

The support team was gone as quickly as they arrived.

"Keep an eye on her," Erbil told Nurse Porter. "I'll notify her mother."

The Bounty of Faith, he thought, taking a last look at how the room had changed. The Secretary wasn't kidding.

• • •

To stock the shelves, the Mollies rambled through Mount Carmel and surrounding small towns. The government paid no attention to the area except with regard to the flow of coal, which meant no military patrols, no bulldozers knocking things over, and no visitors without travel passes through the checkpoints. The situation was to the Mollies' advantage because abandoned homes and businesses were their prime hunting grounds. They pried up floorboards, tore open walls, and crawled through attics. It wasn't only copper wire and pipe they found. Hidden money, squirreled-away jewelry, lost tools, and yes, cans, jars, and hermetically sealed plastic bags of food were discovered. Jagger was frequently amazed what people forgot or left behind, or what remained when they died before they could use, spend, or eat it. The non-edibles the Mollies sold to Jerry Boyle, who was merchant, warehouse operator, and dealer in all things to all people. His trading post, for lack of a better term, was in the woods off Route 901 behind what had been the little borough of Locust Gap. Anything safe to eat, the Mollies kept for themselves.

After several missions to far-flung Kulpmont, Lavelle, and Ashland yielded nothing, they were down to Jagger's hidden reserves. In fact, she'd been supplementing the table from her stash for the past couple of weeks. Three cans of stew, a bag of red beans, and a box of outdated crackers remained. Nothing else. If Dylan hadn't died, she would have stretched it for a few more days. But he did die, and she needed to honor the dead as well as bolster her gang with a treat for hard work in trying to save him. As for what they would eat tomorrow, they'd find it, steal it, or go hungry.

"I want it thick. No extra water," Jagger told Whip, who did most of the cooking. She dumped the cans of stew into a pot for heating on the stove. Another pot full of beans simmered nearby.

"Got any more where this came from?" Whip asked.

"Don't worry about it."

At the table, Jagger ladled out portions to each of them, including Father Carroll, who folded his hands to pray. She let him go on, then changed the subject to Dylan's antics.

"Remember the time Dylan beat that trooper at darts at the Pleasant Corner?" she began.

"Yeah," Crush said. "Bastard wouldn't pay up until Steve Regan shamed him into it."

"And then he was two dollars short," put in Whip.

Steve Regan owned the Pleasant Corner, Mount Carmel's one and only drinking establishment that sometimes served food. Regan offered Jagger a job there, replacing the bartender-turned-thief who he recently fired and clubbed senseless. Jagger suspected his offer had more to do with how she might look in the cropped shirt and shorts he had in mind than her ability to pour grog and make conversation. She had no good reason not to do a job like that, other than her own desire never to take orders from anyone.

Listening to Whip and Crush go on about Dylan, she resolved to find a score to keep the Mollies together, living as they had been, or to come up with a plan to relocate. Sooner or later they would have to move out of Mount Carmel. Her suspicion was that it would be sooner. There was only so much stuff left behind, and it was becoming harder to find.

Runt stopped the reverie cold when she asked Father Carroll, "Do you have a brother?"

"I did. He died in the war."

"Any other family?"

"The church is my family."

"Good for you," Jagger said, putting her bowl down in front of Runt. "Finish that."

While the kid gobbled several more spoonsful of stew, Jagger went to the kitchen where she stared at the sunset. As soon as the dishes were washed, they would march Preacher John down to the Poplar Street Bridge and off he'd go. Truth be told, he would be her first kill. Not that she hadn't scared the living shit out of several victims by dangling them precariously close to taking a fall to their death. She'd done that and worse, all of which furthered a reputation of murderous capability. But she never had to finish the job. In every case, the victim gave in. Hence, she let them live. It was only fair.

Tonight was different. Preacher John had proven to be a fraud. As a result, Dylan was dead. No, Preacher John hadn't killed him. He failed to save him, which was the same thing. Almost. Contrary to all claims of supernatural powers, he did nothing more than the clinic quack could have done. Less, in fact, if Jagger was honest with herself. The quack might have turned his back and she could have stolen some pills or equipment or whatever. She'd have had a consolation prize. But this great promise of beating Red Death was nonsense. Who told her that, anyway? Joe Grant? Yeah, it was him. Grant was one of the few Mount Carmel residents who still talked about Jesus, albeit on the quiet. So enraged was she, mostly at herself for believing stupid lies, that her memory shut down. She thought of nothing but Carroll's body found on the tracks when the next train passed through, thereby doing a public service of eliminating one six-foot-tall heap of false hope.

"Supper's over," Jagger said. "Wash the dishes and let's get this done before shift change at the mine."

. . .

In terms of mines, Girard Number Six went deeper than most, especially when it came to digging coal. That's where the high-quality anthracite was. Men worked five hundred feet below the surface. They took two packed meals because their shift lasted twelve hours, six days a week. There was a quota, one the federal government established to satisfy America's war debt to China.

By the ton, none of the other gangs came close to the output of Mike Whelan and his team. Part of the success came from the dangerous nature of working in their particular part of the mine. As the most experienced miners, it was their task to remove the columns of coal that supported the ceiling from the areas where the rest of it had already been removed. Of course, taking away this support meant certain collapse of the rock overhead. The trick was to drop the roof along the way, staying ahead of the un-supported area. Not that planet earth always cooperated, because sometimes an entire section came down, whether the pillars were there or not. Other times, it held up longer than expected, lead-ing fools to think it was safe to pass through. Several dozen men had died this way, their bodies entombed forever.

When their shift ended at six, Mike and his crew arrived on the surface to fresh air and a welcome shower in the locker room. Although the water wasn't exactly hot, it was warm. To be clean was to be human again. They all agreed on that, as well as the distinct comfort of sleeping somewhere without fear of being crushed by a million tons of rock.

After he pulled on clean pants, Rat Durkin sidled up to Mike. "I talk to you a minute?" he asked.

"Hearing things again?" Mike guessed.

"Telling you, Mike. I heard it on the way out. Hissing, popping.

Rock's on the move. Running that seam it is."

Sheldon Hunter gave the reason in the form of a question. "What do you expect after taking out the columns?"

"Spent more nights down the hole than you slept under the moon," Rat groused. "Shut up and learn something."

"Go on," Mike said.

"Ain't never been wrong and you all know it," Rat continued. "Called the drop on the east side last year, didn't I? Saved us all and ain't looking for nothing more than a thank you very much. Maybe a glass of grog at the Pleasant Corner if you're feeling generous."

"Are you calling this one?" Mike asked, frustrated by Rat's propensity to ramble.

Rat got to the point. "I'm calling it. We don't move west on Monday, we're dead on Tuesday."

"We're more than three thousand tons short of the quota," Hunter reminded them. "Without pulling the columns we'll never catch up."

"If we have to, we'll blast a section of roof," Mike said. "See how things look after that."

"The whole thing's coming down," Rat told them, slamming his heavy boots into his locker. "Anyone still believes, say your prayers." On that disturbing note, Rat stormed out of the room in his stocking feet.

"He might be right," Hunter suggested.

"He's never been wrong," Mike finished. "Doesn't mean we have a choice."

Just then Superintendent Alvin Filner entered the room. "Mike Whelan still here?" he called out.

"Yeah," Mike replied.

Filner pushed through the other men until he was face to face with Mike. "Get to the clinic soon as you can."

"What happened?"

"A crazy Christian tried to blow up your little sister."

Mike stuffed his feet back into his work boots.

"The boots stay here!" Filner demanded.

Into the bottom locker went his boots, and out came his sneakers, held together with duct tape. A key landed on the bench.

"Take my truck," Filner offered. "The clinic and back. Not enough gas to go anywhere else."

"Got it," Mike acknowledged, then grabbed his coat and bounded for the exit.

• • •

Jagger sent Runt to the far end of the bridge where the road curved away from town. The kid didn't need to see this bit of horror, but with her good eyes she might spot Randy Bartok or one of Mount Carmel's good citizens headed toward them. Whip and Crush helped her manage Preacher John, who offered no resistance whatsoever, which perplexed Jagger. They tied his hands behind his back in the trailer, walked with him in silence for an hour, and were about to give him the heave-ho. He hadn't made a peep, nor tried to run away. She would have died fighting rather than go like a limp dishrag.

"Should I cut his hands loose?" Whip asked.

Crush answered, "Yeah, let's see if this angel can flap his wings and fly."

"Not yet," Jagger told her, then launched into a spittle-laced tirade.

"Healing the sick, feeding the poor—it's all bogus!" she began. "Not a damn true bone in your whole body."

"Then throw me off the bridge," Carroll said.

"Oh, I'm going to see you die just as soon as I'm done. And you're going to listen!" Jagger nudged him toward the gap in the guardrail. A one-inch slip of shoe leather and he'd be gone. But she had more to say.

"You're as bad as Selman and that asshole Bartok. I bet the

three of you sit around the table, carving up two-pound steaks, having a laugh at how people fall for your shit."

"Come on," Whip grumbled. "Give him a shove, and let's get out of here."

"Back off!" Jagger shouted. "I'm in the middle of something."

"No," Carroll interrupted. "You're afraid."

"Anybody scared around here, it ought to be you, Preacher!"

"You're terrified of the consequences."

"Ain't me taking the plunge."

"This is neither the time nor the place for my end. You'll see."

"How do you know?" Jagger asked, pressing her hand into the small of his back.

"My faith tells me I have more work here on earth," Carroll offered.

"Faith in fairy tales? Because from what I seen today, you got nothing the rest of us don't got."

"Push him off already," Crush said.

"Yeah," Whip added. "If he flies away, we'll know his shit's real."

"Help me," Jagger told Crush. "Grab his belt."

Crush moved close and hooked her fingers into the back of his pants, widening her stance for leverage.

"Final words?"

"We'll meet again," Carroll said. "Very soon."

"Car!"

Runt's tinny voice carried down the hill, across the length of the bridge, distracting everyone from the depths below.

"Aww, damn it," Whip moaned.

"Coming fast!" Runt shouted. "A pickup!"

"Come on!" Crush urged. "I ain't waiting for Bartok to kick my ass."

"Not before I give the word," Jagged told her.

"Do it!" Whip hollered as she ran for cover.

Jagger shouted, "Drag him in the road!"

Crush hesitated a split second until she realized that Preacher

John would be hit by whoever was coming in the pickup, a twist she hadn't expected. She yanked hard on Carroll's belt, spinning him away from the edge, toward the driving lane, where he landed hard on his left side.

Father Carroll looked up to see headlights bearing down. Next came the screech of tires. The rear of the pickup kicked out, sending the vehicle skidding sideways down the middle of the bridge. Somehow it righted itself, which only put the blinding headlights back on him. He waited for the inevitable strike of the steel bumper. A long second went by with no impact, no final image, nothing but the reeking scent of tire smoke. Then there was a voice, one he recognized.

"Father Carroll?" Mike Whelan said. "Is that you?"

"Yes, alive and well. Help me up."

Mike took the former priest's arm and pulled him to his feet. "I'm on the way to the clinic. Zoe's been hurt."

"I know. It's been foretold."

"What?"

"I'll explain later. Cut me loose and we'll go together."

Using his pocketknife, Mike sliced the ropes from Carroll's wrists. The two of them got into the pickup and headed for the clinic.

From a spot in the trees at the end of the bridge, Jagger and her crew watched them drive away.

"Thought for sure that truck would have hit him," Crush said.

Whip piled on with, "Should have shoved him off right away."

Runt dared an attempt at making sense of the situation by wondering aloud, "Maybe he is an angel."

At that simple logic, Jagger seethed. "Keep it up," she said, "and we'll all be in the dirt next to Dylan."

CHAPTER 7.

Sitting with a coma patient gave Nurse Porter an odd sensation. She was used to dealing with drug seekers, miners with broken bones, and the lonely geriatric looking for someone to talk to in a depopulated town. Zoe Whelan, on the other hand, was dead, but not quite. The machines said she was alive. She had a regular heartbeat and breathed normally. Yet, there was no waking her, leaving Porter with nothing to do. She couldn't have been more relieved when her patient's mother, Claire Whelan, appeared. Porter guessed her to be mid-sixties, with mostly grey hair and a lean, compact frame that suggested lots of walking.

"My God, Zoe," Claire sighed, touching her daughter's forehead, then snapped at Porter, "What happened to her? Doctor Erbil wouldn't give me any details."

"The transport told me it was a Christian suicide bomber," Porter replied.

"I don't believe that," said Claire.

"It's all I know. I'll give you a moment to be alone."

"My son, Mike, is on his way."

"I'll send him up."

Phew, thought Porter, a good reason to step outside for some fresh air. She sat on the bench that flanked the front door, smoking one of her last five cigarettes. It was a pre-war Marlboro, dry and harsh, that went a long way to tamp down the sudden stress of an exotic case. She swung her feet up on the bench, closed her eyes, and recalled a ski trip with her family from her early teens. They'd gone to a resort in upstate New York. The snow was deep and lush. Late in the day, they came across a group surrounding one of their friends, who'd fallen and broken a leg. The ski patrol splinted it, loaded him aboard a sled, and towed him off. Inspired, she decided to become a nurse.

A fateful decision it turned out to be. Halfway through nursing school she was drafted into the army as a "sixty-eight whiskey," also known as a combat medic. Plenty of horror ensued. At the first opportunity, she left the military, opting for the most mundane assignment she could find. After a string of rural stops, she landed in Mount Carmel last year. While she appreciated the boredom, the desperation depressed her. Anything worse than a severe cold was as likely to kill the person than not. The big production for Zoe Whelan aside, they had nothing stronger than aspirin and basic antibiotics. Doctor Erbil peddled painkillers for cash—that is, the ones he didn't take himself.

She needed a change. A stint in a city would be best. Not at another Common Faith hospital with its scale wages and flaky philosophy on the walls. Private specialty shops were quietly taking root. She'd dig into that during her next weekend off, if she could get Selman to sign a travel pass.

"My sister in there?"

Startled out of her daydream, Porter dropped her cigarette.

"I'm Mike Whelan," he said, retrieving her smoke and giving it back.

Tall and clean he was, unlike so many in this town. Too bad he was a miner. She could tell by the black lines around the edges of his fingernails. Had he another profession, she might have flirted a little on the off chance that her wagon hitched to his might lead to a better place, but miners never left except in boxes.

"I'll take you," Porter offered.

"Just tell me. I'm used to finding my way in the dark."

A sense of humor, Porter thought. That was refreshing.

"Second floor, all the way in the back," she said with a smile. "Your mother's already there."

"Thanks."

Porter didn't watch him go. She might have lowered her guard and followed him with the idea of having some fun, even if it led to nothing else. Instead, she went for a walk around the parking lot.

In Zoe's room, Mike greeted his mother with a warm hug.

"A suicide bomber tried to kill her," Claire said. "They told me he was a Christian, but I don't believe it."

"There's some crazy people out there," Mike warned, then pointed at the doorway where Father Carroll stood. "Look who I found in the middle of the road."

Stunned, Claire gushed, "But Randy Bartok had you!"

"I escaped… with help," explained Carroll. "How's Zoe?"

"They sent her here to die," Claire said.

"There was another reason," he told her, moving close to the bed where Zoe rested.

"Don't forget my daughter is a compliance specialist. The kind that hunts people like you."

"People like us. All that's about to change. I'll explain everything, but first take my hands," Carroll said, extending his arms to either side.

Mike and Claire joined hands with the man who had been the last priest in Mount Carmel.

"Let us pray."

• • •

Nurse Porter saw the second man enter the building. She was pacing the parking lot, smoking the last of that priceless cigarette, contemplating how to find a private clinic, when he quick-stepped to the back entrance where Mike Whelan held the door from inside. A brief glimpse of him in the light revealed his identity. It was Father Carroll, the most wanted man in Mount Carmel. Word on the street was that Selman had ten thousand dollars in reward money for information leading to his capture.

Ten grand would take her a long way from Mount Carmel. It would also make her a rat for denouncing a guy who probably did more for sick people here than Doctor Erbil ever did. During her service in the army, she treated the wounded from both sides. The differences between them were in their minds, not their bodies. If that was a crime, it was for other people to prosecute, people like Compliance Specialist Zoe Whelan. If she lived. Which was unlikely.

She respected his willingness to go in there, pray for his enemy, and support her family. Like her, he tended to both sides, which was more courageous than some of the killers on the battlefield. They might pull the triggers, but they didn't deal with the mess left behind.

Not wanting to encounter him and possibly have to explain why she hadn't reported it, she paced the lot a few more times. At last, she saw him exit the building. He crossed the street and faded into the shadows on Hickory Street.

"God bless," Porter said, stubbed out her cigarette, and walked inside.

CHAPTER 8.

"*E pluribus unum,*" Martin Selman began. "Does anyone know what that means?"

It was nine thirty Saturday morning and nearly every plastic chair in his local Common Faith Center was occupied. Of course, the attendees didn't know the answer to his question. No matter. Selman relished the sound of his own voice, especially when it boomed over the heads of a full house.

"*E pluribus unum,*" he repeated. "From many… one."

He watched the interested cock their heads. Perhaps he underestimated his flock. Inspired by their curiosity, he lowered his volume a notch for a sense of enhanced drama.

"When our nation was tearing itself to pieces, when zealots of various religions and diabolical opportunists attacked and counter-attacked each other during the horrible days of our Second Civil War… we… that is you, and me, and many, many others… we made a giant leap, something no one imagined possible in the modern world."

There hadn't been any fighting in this backwater, but hundreds of residents had traveled to join one particular cause or another. Few returned.

"Tell me about it!" shouted one of the rare survivors. "I was there fighting for peace with the generals."

"Thank you for your service." Selman tolerated the interruption with a condescending nod.

A murmur rippled through the people who remembered their own relatives lost in the conflict. It lasted long enough for

Lenny Donovan to shout, "Keep it down! The man's trying to make a point."

"Right, well, *e pluribus unum*. From many, one. From many religions—Christians, Jews, Muslims, Hindus, Krishnas, and all the others—we forged one: the Common Faith."

A loud cough from the back of the room did nothing to slow Selman's momentum.

"We searched the very depth of our souls and discovered we actually believe most of the same things. Ninety percent of the underlying principles of our religions were the same! Why couldn't we see that? Why couldn't we get along? Why were we killing each other?"

Only the creaking of nervous bodies shifting on plastic chairs replied.

"The answer, my friends, is simple. We drifted so far apart because we allowed ourselves to be blinded by dangerous people. They manipulated us, used us for their benefit while we suffered."

"Not anymore!" Lenny Donovan chimed in.

"No, not anymore," affirmed Selman. "Thanks to good people we share the Bounty of Faith. The Bounty of the Common Faith." He paused for effect and to give his voice a rest.

In the last row, septuagenarian Milton Kessler whispered to his wife, Betty, "That mean he's handing out free stuff today?"

"Nah. BoF rations again," she said. "Soy powder, crackers, canned cheese, and darn awful cookies."

"Was hoping for a gas voucher, get my truck on the road."

"You shouldn't be driving and we both need shoes."

"Shhh," hissed someone sitting to their left.

"Thankfully, our Universal Creator has shown us the way to peace," Selman continued. He wanted to add that Father John Carroll, wherever he was, would not be interrupting the peace.

There were about four hundred people seated before Selman, less than a tenth of the regular crowd at the megachurch where he'd been one of five assistants to the senior pastor. A few seated out there were holdout Christians and would report through their grapevine any mention of their guru.

"Peace is hard work," he said. "Harder work than war."

Unlike his ecclesiastical superior and co-workers at the mega-church, Selman saw the opportunity to be part of something bigger than anything since Constantine converted to Christianity and effectively started what would go on to become the most powerful belief system in the world. At least for a time it was. Then came the rivals, which, depending upon one's perspective, were generally equal in membership and geographical control. While some were state religions, none achieved the kind of depth and scope of the Common Faith.

A constitutional amendment enshrined the Common Faith in a whole new branch of government, which was a good thing because the First Amendment did need updating, all of it. If a citizen wanted to express religious beliefs, the law required they fall within the proscriptions people like him developed. Otherwise, a compliance specialist would be sent to investigate, and if necessary, prosecute violations. An appeal could be made to the Sacred Council. Their rulings were final. The Supreme Court had been relieved of jurisdiction over religious matters.

Selman understood the trajectory of the Common Faith when it was nothing but the idea of a few congressmembers looking to restore order in a country fighting itself. One of them, didn't matter who specifically, had asked the question, "Why are there umpteen religions when they all have so much in common?" Indeed, why? The answer was as practical as the question. "Because no one dared to point out the obvious and bring them all together." Of course, the goal was easier said than done. What made it possible was the Second Civil War, which began as a series of terrorist attacks and reprisals prompted by religious disagreements and socio-economic feuds that evolved into violence on a colossal scale.

The weak-minded followed the dedicated radicals until a

more potent alternative got their attention. The Common Faith was that alternative. It swelled in popularity because it exercised Earthly authority in the form of immediately accessible benefits from food handouts to affordable housing, day care to job training, as well as the ability to level fines and prosecute crimes deemed of a religious nature.

Hester Thompson, congresswoman from St. Paul, Minnesota, took the lead. She convinced a few of the radical core to see the bigger picture, which was that more could be had in peace than in war. It took her a few years and several brushes with death. She persevered. She cleverly created a choice architecture which left holdouts no option but to take a seat at the table or be left to starve.

Thompson's ideas also gained traction thanks to federal troops, which were still the largest single force with the most powerful weapons and the best training. The Second Civil War was going to be won, as the first had been won, by the side with the ability to continuously field superior firepower. Besides, fewer and fewer of the important radicals wanted to die for their cause when they had a chance at starting over in a high position atop a remolded society. Joining the new religion made too much sense.

"Basically, we all believe the same thing!" Thompson controversially proclaimed from the steps of the Capitol, holding hands with that first group of converts. "Call it whatever you want, but our Universal Creator expects us to make peace."

A battered nation agreed by the millions. The slogan became "Peace NOW!"

When the Second Civil War began, Selman didn't want to be a target. He quit the megachurch and his fifth-string assistant pastor position, then retreated to the relatively conflict-free area of Maryland's swampy eastern shore, where he lived off his savings. Upon hearing Hester Thompson's speech, he drove to Washington, D.C. One of Thompson's staff was a friend of his from

Duke University Divinity School, where they both got their undergraduate degrees. Selman used him for an introduction to Thompson.

He presented her with his vision for a universal religion, an idea he'd toyed with during some drunken binges at Duke. The trick, he explained, was to make the new faith tangible in ways people could experience in the present. Never mind rewards in some indeterminate place like "heaven." There were promises of that type, too, including "eternal life after death in the joyful serenity of infinite oneness with our Universal Creator." It took him months to craft that phrase. Now it was chanted at the end of every Common Faith service. But more gripping than any pledge about a reward after death was a treat for the living. The bird in the hand, as it were, would bring more people into the fold than a flock chirping in the bush.

"The only way to put faith in the center of people's lives is to be the purveyor of their worldly needs," Selman said. "That means we host education and childcare. We provide healthcare. We have housing alternatives. We offer jobs for those without them and training for those who require it."

"That's quite a lot to do," Thompson remarked.

"The government had been doing it under various agencies before the war," explained Selman. "If we bring everything under the Common Faith, it will make the change much more agreeable."

"I think you mean inevitable."

She was right.

Impressed by Selman's initiative and insight, Hester Thompson assigned him to draft and coordinate the Original Doctrine, or OD, as they soon abbreviated it. He went from understudy to the star of the show. He chaired a board that included the highest-ranking religious officials in the nation. And they had to listen to him or face Thompson's wrath.

What a harrowing year that was! He dodged insults and fists, threats to his life and vows of retribution. Twice he'd been shot at, and he narrowly missed burning to death when a Molotov cocktail burst on his car. Whenever the mood got seriously vicious among his committee of elites, he called Thompson in to assert her version of authority. She was no upstart revolutionary or naïf with visions of glory. The worst offenders quietly disappeared. To where, Selman did not know, but the others learned to accept compromise.

In the end, they developed the Common Faith. With the war waning by the day, state leaders argued about the Constitutional amendment and Final Peace, as it would come to be known. While a tedious process, it happened faster than Selman himself thought possible. At the same time, it inspired him to grasp for the heights of power. Thompson let him climb the ladder a few more rungs, then stunned him by removing his name from the OD.

"If this document is truly of a divine nature, truly inspired by our Universal Creator," she said, "then no human name shall appear on it."

Irrefutable logic, Selman agreed, hiding his seething resentment. As framer of the new faith, he deserved immortal status of a sort. Didn't Saint Paul get that kind of recognition? And Moses? And Mohammed? Furthermore, he was the one who wrangled the religious animals with their stone-age sensibilities and to-the-death oaths. To get not even a footnote mention after such a heroic effort was personally offensive. She could have allowed him to use a pen name. It wasn't to be.

He bowed out for the cause. For the cause and a permanent, well-paid position. Too bad he lost the job when a few of his proclivities came to light. Thompson circled the wagons, protecting him from internal scrutiny and official sanction. She gave him a choice. Take a pension or find a place to hide. He chose Mount Carmel for its isolation. What a good choice it had been! He carved out a personal fiefdom with more freedom to enjoy all the fruits of an unsupervised territory. It was like being the king's second son: All the fun of royalty with none of the responsibility. Sadly, it was starting to bore him.

Ready to end his weekly message, Selman took a sip of water and scanned the crowd. On the right side, third row from the back, sat Denise Walsh and her son, Ian. What a pleasant surprise after last night's debacle. Apparently, the boy's mother understood the importance of his presence as it related to their future.

Buoyed by this development, Selman decided to finish early. "All rise for the Affirmation of Common Belief," he announced.

"We believe in the Universal Creator... ," began the crowd.

He let them ramble on their own. More important thoughts swirled through his mind than a droning mantra. He'd had enough of the quiet life, of handling minor details. He missed painting with a big brush. As he had in the past, Selman would make himself an indispensable servant of Hester Thompson. And when the moment was right, he would replace her, using whatever means necessary. He was the one who wrote the Original Doctrine, placing him closer to the Universal Creator than a mere congresswoman from Minnesota.

Recapturing John Carroll was merely the first step on the path to the Sanctus Chamber. In a day, perhaps two, Bartok's diligent work would have the former priest back in the dungeon. Then it would be on to step two: Compliance Specialist Zoe Whelan.

He joined the crowd, reciting, "We shall live in peace until we enjoy eternal life after death in the joyful serenity of infinite oneness in harmony with our Universal Creator."

CHAPTER 9.

"We don't nail a score, we're gonna starve," Crush said, nibbling the last bits of an apple Runt had toted from the dungeon.

"In a couple days we'll be having a feast," lied Jagger.

"On what?" asked Whip. "Cardboard and ketchup?"

Jagger let the question fade into the buckled paneling. She dreamed of derailing a train, scooping up a mountain of coal and hauling it away to Jerry Boyle for a ton of bacon and beer. But that was pure fantasy. In the first place, the train rolled slow until about four miles out of town, which meant if she rigged the track to fail, the cars might not even tip over. They'd probably squat down on the ballast rock like pack mules with busted legs. Then there was the question of a truck. She had none, nor access to one. A further complication: armed guards in the caboose who felt no compunction at shooting to kill. Not so bad if they got you in the chest or a head shot. Down you went. Goodnight. Jagger knew because she'd seen it. If they winged you in the leg, or worse, the hip, as the best of them did for sport, an infectious death ten days ahead was the guaranteed end. Thus, no great train robberies were on the docket.

On the other hand, there was a batch of prisoners due in from Graterford. Day after tomorrow, if she remembered correctly. A Common Faith rehabilitation program brought them to town. They'd come on a bus, and no doubt that bus would return empty except for the driver and one guard. Correction. The bus might not be empty. It might be carrying black-market goods the troopers had confiscated along the route, things like top-shelf liquor, pharmaceuticals, athletic shoes, and more. They could waylay the bus by putting Runt in the middle of the road. No one would suspect the kid. Soon as the guard steps out, Whip nails his skull with a well-aimed slingshot. Crush ball-bats the driver with a seasoned Louisville Slugger. All this adventure for what? For the diesel in the tank, the contents of their wallets, and the guns they had? Yes, and the black-market swag, if there was any to be had. She'd have to buy Bartok's protection with a cut of the proceeds. Then she had a bigger, better idea.

"I got it," Jagger said.

In the moment before she would have unveiled her plan to Whip and Crush, the door banged open. As if manifested by her thoughts, Randy Bartok himself stomped across the threshold. He carried Runt over his shoulder like a fireman and promptly heaved her across the room onto the couch. She landed flat on her back in the spot where Dylan died. Tough kid that she was, Runt sat up and spat at Bartok, who found her defiance hilarious.

Jagger said to Runt, "If you ain't the worst damn doorbell." To Bartok she added, "Come to pay your respects to the recently deceased?"

"Hell, no," he said. "I'm looking for John Carroll. Where is he?"

"Comes to him," Jagger answered, "we ain't the usual suspects."

"You're the only one who has the balls to bust him out."

Not wanting to accept a compliment from a former abuser, Jagger shrugged.

"Little one tells me you heard some rumors about Johnny Carroll, Man of God. Thought he might resurrect the one under that lump of dirt out there."

"Rumors I hear concern your boss Selman, and little Ian Walsh," Jagger retorted.

Bartok took one step in Jagger's direction, then drove his fist into her ear. The blow knocked her to the floor where the room spun twice then stopped when he hauled her upright and slammed her against the wall with such force that she sunk into the paneling. His right hand locked onto her neck while the left jabbed her gut.

Whip and Crush moved to opposite sides of the room, uncertain whether to risk helping their leader or make a run for it.

"Time for you and me to get reacquainted on a personal level. Show the others how we used to dance," Bartok hissed. "Sound good?"

So loud were her ears ringing that Jagger only caught a few words.

"What's the matter? Can't hear the music?"

His grip tightened on her throat. In seconds, the edge of her vision went fuzzy.

"Whisper it. Go on. Tell me. Where's Johnny Carroll?"

Jagger's bowels loosened, giving the feeling she might shit her pants and die a heap of stinking flesh in front of Runt, whose gauzy figure floated somewhere across the room.

Bartok released his grip and backed off.

Jagger fell to the floor from which she croaked, "Mike Whelan picked him up at the bridge last night."

"The bridge, eh? Another Molly execution gone wrong. My oh my, what a useless bunch of scum you are."

"Good for whatever you want."

"We'll see," Bartok said. From his pocket, he took out a key and tossed it on the floor. It clinked an inch from her nose. "Know how to drive a truck?"

"Better than you."

• • •

Claire Whelan slept the night in Zoe's room. She went home in the morning for a shower, packed a lunch, and rushed back to the clinic. She ignored the platitudes of Doctor Erbil, who assured her the amazing array of equipment would soon have Zoe on her feet. She also paid no attention to the other professionals who appeared. They murmured to each other, took notes, adjusted settings, and left after informing her a feeding tube would have to be inserted if Zoe didn't recover in the next twenty-four hours.

Restless after a day of reading and dozing in the chair, she decided to go home. She leaned close to Zoe, remembering the girl she raised, how well she'd done in school, the silly arguments they'd had. What put her on the path to become a compliance specialist, Claire would never know. That official title gave a sterile, bureaucratic connotation, but it was more inquisitor than detective.

"What got inside your head?" Claire asked aloud, almost weeping at who her daughter had become, and sadly, might still be.

In the early days of Zoe's career, Claire saw her appear on the official National News, specifically crime-buster reports. She arrested a group of Christians evangelizing in one of Philadelphia's tent villages. Then she caught another bunch hand-copying Bibles. The last one Claire watched featured Zoe in the courtroom. She wore the black robe of a prosecutor, and it was her turn to address the guilty, who had been sentenced by the tribunal to ten years' hard labor in energy production.

"My father spent his life in a coal mine," she said to the convicts. "It was honest work that made him a good man. You can do the same."

It was the last time Claire watched the news. She found the gaps between their telephone conversations growing longer and longer, until they stopped entirely. And it wasn't like they were going to exchange Christmas cards. Claire still sent a note on Zoe's birthday, but considering the unreliability of the postal service, she was never sure it arrived.

More stories of Zoe's prosecutorial zeal reached Claire through various sources, most frequently in coded notes from Father Rabek, who led Philadelphia's last group of Christians, the Surviving Few.

"Please, talk to your daughter," Rabek pleaded in a recent note.

"I suspect she has a spy among us. Yesterday, Terry Glover was taken. Surely Terry will ascend to our Holy Father before revealing secrets. For his sake, for those who have already gone, for all of us, something must be done before she catches us all. The Time of Gathering is soon."

Staring at Zoe's impassive face, Claire wondered if Rabek had sent the bomber. Perhaps not intentionally, because she'd never heard him espouse violence. Yet, his fervor often roused the less clear-thinking members, who vandalized Common Faith buildings or painted Christian graffiti in public places. It wasn't fair to speculate on blame. In fact, some raised the possibility Common Faith operatives staged occasional attacks to maintain public opinion in their favor.

For the time being, Claire only wanted her daughter to recover. The bigger issues, she trusted God to handle. She would do her part, influencing Zoe to find compassion and tolerance. If she got the chance.

Claire kissed her daughter's forehead. Taking a last look, she thought Zoe's eyelids twitched. She waited a full minute, hoping, praying for it to happen again. Nothing. She turned for the door, grabbing her purse off the chair on the way. Then she heard a cough.

Bedside again, she said, "Zoe? Can you hear me?"

Zoe's eyelids fluttered, then both eyes slowly opened, revealing her green irises. A moment passed, then another, as Claire witnessed what had to be a genuine miracle.

"Hello, Zoe. It's me, your mother."

"Mom? What are you doing here?"

CHAPTER 10.

One day sitting around her mother's house was one too many for Zoe Whelan.

"I need to get out of here today," she said, her voice barely under control. "I'm in the middle of an important case."

Why she'd been transferred from Philadelphia to Mount Carmel was beyond her comprehension. And Secretary Thompson gave the order herself! It made no sense. Not when there was better healthcare in the city. Not when she'd been closing in on the Surviving Few. Okay, maybe the doctors thought she'd be in a coma long term and there wasn't much they could do. But she was out of it now. Other than bruises, scratches, and a mild headache, she felt fine. The headache had nothing to do with surviving the explosion. It was brought on by the aggravation of arguing with people who refused to do their jobs.

"I'd like to speak with Secretary Thompson as soon as possible," insisted Zoe into the phone.

"The request has been logged, CS Whelan. Four times now," the duty officer replied. "Your orders remain in effect. If there's a change, you will be notified."

"Thank you."

Tired of wasting her time, Zoe disconnected. Her orders were to stay in Mount Carmel until Doctor Erbil pronounced her fit for duty. He insisted she rest for a week, then go to Pottsville for tests to confirm she wasn't suffering latent injuries. What was the difference if she rested here or in Philadelphia?

Onto her childhood bed, she dumped the parcel of her belongings sent by Headquarters. Several changes of clothes, her badge, a useless dress uniform, a cellphone, and her favorite boots. Handmade of full-grain leather, they were the perfect balance between ankle-high support and a lightweight comfort sole. No desk jockey, she could stand in them all day or sprint after a suspect and frequently did. Conspicuously missing was her government-issued firearm.

Downstairs she went, into the dining room where as a kid she had shared countless meals, including the interminable Sunday dinners, with her family. High on the wall she noticed a cross. Not the actual wooden Christian symbol that hung there during her childhood, but rather the shadow of it that remained. She recalled her father praying before every meal with his eyes closed. When he opened them, the first place he looked was at that cross, as if to get a nod of approval from Jesus.

"Hey. There you are."

Zoe didn't hear her mother's voice as she fixated on the wall. How many houses had she been in during the past five years where the heraldry of the past dominated? Too many. Residents of the Christian homes she raided dared to have crosses hanging in plain sight. After coming so close to dying at the hands of these people, she was more determined than ever to root them out. She'd nail the Circle and Line on their doors as a reminder of who kept the peace.

"Zoe?" Claire said.

"Why's the cross still there?"

"What cross?"

"On the wall."

Claire studied the spot a few seconds, then said, "Oh, that's just where the paint faded. How're you feeling?"

"Sore. Did Mr. Carroll visit me in the hospital?"

Startled by the question, Claire looked away before answering, "What made you think of Father Carroll?"

"Don't call him that," Zoe snapped.

"Please, Zoe. This is a small town. Out here no one cares."

"It's my job to care. When was the last time you saw him?"

"Jeez. First day out of the hospital and already chasing ghosts."

"Doing my job."

"Well, call the boss and tell her you're taking a few weeks off. You've earned it."

"When was the last time you saw Mr. Carroll?"

"Keeping track of people may be your job, but it isn't mine."

"Don't lie to me, Mom. If he's practicing Christianity, he's a criminal. Helping him makes you an accessory."

"What a paranoid thing to say."

"People like him tried to kill me. Just because they screwed up in Philadelphia doesn't mean they won't try again. And where's my gun?"

"Your gun?"

"Yes. Secretary Thompson saw to it that my things were sent here. She must have sent my gun. A grey box with a combination lock. Have you seen it?"

"Give it a rest, Zoe. Really. This isn't the big city full of gangsters."

"Don't be so sure. I heard Mr. Carroll talking in my room at the clinic. I heard him praying."

"And now you're better. Be glad. Move on."

"Wait. You still believe that dangerous crap?"

"Be careful what you don't believe, Zoe," Claire said, then went to the kitchen where she donned her coat and slammed the door on her way out.

• • •

Runt sat on the big chair, the one reserved exclusively for Jagger. It took her a long time to sort the pages, right side up and in sequence. All together they formed a hefty stack. My own book, Runt thought, but it should have a cover. The other books, what few there were in the trailer, had covers.

"Use that to spark up the fire," Crush said as she tied her shoes. "It's chilly in here."

"Nah, gonna keep it," Runt replied.

"You can't even read."

"Can, too!"

"Burn it," Jagger ordered.

"Finders keepers," protested Runt.

Jagger grabbed the pages. "Evidence, little one, is what puts you in jail. Make it disappear and you got a chance of slipping the noose. Follow me?"

Runt didn't follow but did see her book-in-the-making go into the bottom of the stove where glowing embers flared.

"Gather some kindling outside and get that fire hot until we get back."

"Why can't I go?"

"Today you guard the fort," Jagger answered. "Nobody comes in, and you don't leave the patch. Hear me?"

"Yeah." Runt ran out the door toward the trail where she already had sticks in a pile.

Seeing Whip's pouting face, Jagger asked, "What's your problem?"

"What if Bartok's setting us up?"

"Tough guy wants a score bad as we need it."

On her feet, Whip vowed, "Shit goes wrong on this, I'm gone. Taking Runt with me, too. Find a place with running water and real heat."

"Let me know where. I'll be the first to visit. Maybe stay a while, too. Now if you're done bitching, let's go. I got a truck to steal."

They exited the trailer in single file, taking the path east toward town. None of them noticed John Carroll and Claire watching from behind a group of boulders nearby.

"There's trouble on six feet," Claire commented when the Mollies were out of earshot.

"Can't be all bad," Carroll said. "They got me out of Bartok's dungeon."

"The Mollies? Seriously?"

"Was amazed myself."

Shifting her attention to Runt, who carried an armful of sticks through a stand of trees, Claire said, "She's not older than ten or eleven."

Fearing what the others would do when they found out he'd been there, Carroll said, "Maybe we can get what we came for while she's in the woods."

• • •

With the idea that she could get a temporary weapon at the Common Faith Center, Zoe walked there after the tiff with her mother. The possibility that Mom might still harbor Christian tendencies caused her a fair amount of stress. If it was true and Secretary Thompson found out, her career would stall, or more likely go into a tailspin. She'd be lucky to work security at a soup kitchen. Then she recalled her mother's attitude after her father died of injuries from an accident in the mine. Was it a year? No, closer to two that her mother withdrew from everyday life. She lost weight and hardly spoke to anyone. There was no mention of church or anything related to it. Not the actions of one accepting God's plan, Zoe reasoned. Just the same, she would be alert to clues of renewed interest.

Three blocks away, Zoe saw a line of people outside the Common Faith Center. They faced an empty table that sat about twenty feet away from a straight truck. A pair of state troopers well past retirement age stood guard.

"The Bounty of Faith," she said aloud.

In Zoe's opinion, placing all social programs under the aegis of the Common Faith had been a brilliant move. The old churches, synagogues, mosques, and temples had charities back in the day. Slicing the resources thin among the different groups made them less efficient, and more important, potentially less fair. A sole purveyor like the Common Faith was highly effective. It combined all the old systems with the resources of the federal government. Zoe understood it well. She wrote her graduate thesis on the subject, specifically showing how many pre-war ecclesiastical buildings sat empty and unused most days. Under Common Faith stewardship, the public was better served when these buildings were staffed and operated every day of the week. They became schools, vocational training centers, and homeless shelters. The ones deemed redundant were demolished, the land sold for development.

She slowed her pace, angling down a parallel block to avoid being seen. She wasn't in the mood to run into someone who knew her way back when. She wanted to get armed as soon as possible in case the Surviving Few sent someone to finish the task at which Andrew had failed.

At the next corner, she turned back for a look at the row of houses she'd passed. Not one of them showed any signs of occupation. The homes were mostly without windows and doors. Some lacked shingles on the roofs. It was as if the town was eating itself.

Curious, she climbed the stairs for a look inside one she had visited many times as a girl. This was the home of her first boyfriend, Alex Sullivan. Stepping inside the front door of what had been a comfortable middle-class home, she was stunned to find the walls had been torn open. Floorboards were missing. Jagged cuts had been made to remove electrical wires and plumbing. She ventured as far as the base of the stairs to the second floor. Looking up, she saw daylight through a hole in the roof.

Fearing a fall through the floor or something dropping from the sagging ceiling above, she picked her way back to the door. Before leaving, her gaze settled on the spot where the bay window had been in the living room. She recalled the couch that used to sit between two end tables. When Mr. Sullivan went to bed, she and Alex enjoyed some pleasant kissing on that couch. Curious about what happened to him, she checked the official database. He died in a skirmish near Nashville, fighting for the wrong side.

Putting the memory and dilapidated house in the past where they belonged, Zoe descended the stairs to the sidewalk and headed for the Common Faith Center. To her relief, the side door was open. She entered and passed down the hall, easily finding Selman's office. Zoe recognized his name from files Secretary Thompson showed her. Why he was in Mount Carmel and not Philadelphia or Washington was a mystery. It might be that he found his calling serving those who needed it most. Certainly the ones in line outside required some help.

Seeing people in worn-out shoes reminded her of the early days out of Common Faith Academy. One of the brilliant strategies during the latter part of the Second Civil War and one maintained in the early days of the peace was to limit shoe production and sales. An army traveled on its stomach, but it also walked on shoes. Without sturdy footwear, it was hard to fight. First, the government offered payments for old clothes and shoes, encouraging people to recycle unneeded garments of which there were many, due to all the deaths from fighting and disease. Then, the industry was nationalized with military supervision. Even with money, getting shoes, especially boots, was extremely difficult. Naturally a black market developed, but it was more deadly than smuggling drugs had been ages ago. A partial solution had been to offer vouchers for new shoes when a family joined the Common Faith and completed the six-month initiation program. The response overwhelmed both the initiation rolls and the voucher system.

All's well that ends well, Zoe thought. And it had ended well, with the growing ranks of the Common Faith and people learning how to get along better than ever.

She was about to knock on Selman's door when she heard voices inside. Heavy footfalls preceded the door swinging open. Denise Walsh nearly bowled Zoe over. Instead, she dodged left and dragged her son, Ian, down the hall. Zoe remembered Denise as being a few years older than her in high school, the big sister of her good friend Candy.

"The line's outside," Selman said from behind his desk, then quickly brightened his tone. "Zoe Whelan! Please, come in. Come in. Doctor Erbil said you were back on your feet."

Zoe entered as Selman came to the middle of the room to greet her.

"What an absolute pleasure to meet you! The things you've done for the Common Faith. Incredible. And so young. Oh, forgive me. How are you feeling?"

"Well," Zoe said. "Thank you."

"Marvelous. I'd love to have a chat, but I have to supervise the Bounty of Faith."

"I'll join you, but first I need some help."

"Name it."

"A gun."

Selman sucked a breath. "Oh, dear. That's quite a request." A nervous chuckle he followed with, "And we only just met."

"As a compliance specialist, I'm required to carry my weapon at all times."

"Yes, I know the regulations. Wrote many of them."

"Headquarters will be sending my originally issued sidearm in the next day or two. I need something until it arrives."

"My senior assistant, Mr. Bartok, is in charge of firearms. He's on patrol at the moment."

"All Common Faith Centers have an armory."

"We do. We do. It's just that, well, I don't deal with such things. Never touched a gun in my life, I'll have you know."

"Lead the way and I'll take care of the rest, including the paperwork," Zoe said.

"Problem solved, I suppose," agreed Selman.

The armory consisted of a tall gun safe. Selman worked the combination, swung open the door, and offered Zoe her choice of weapons. There was a lone shotgun, two revolvers, and a few boxes of ammunition.

"We're a peaceful jurisdiction," Selman commented.

"The Bounty of Faith," Zoe said, hefting one of the revolvers. She loaded the cylinder, snapped it into place and pocketed a box of bullets.

"Please keep that out of sight," he requested.

"I will."

"Good. Now let's have a chat while we help those in need."

• • •

The Mollies minus Runt regrouped in the alley. From here it was fifty yards to the Common Faith Center where the loaded truck sat parked at the curb. Randy Bartok wanted it stolen and driven out to Jerry Boyle's. Their cut was ten percent and forgiveness for busting Preacher John out of the dungeon. Hardly fair, but Jagger had zero leverage and wouldn't have any until she got a gun from the prison bus a couple days hence.

"That's a big truck," Whip said.

"Twenty-six-footer," Crush estimated.

"Not a tractor trailer. I can handle it," Jagger told them.

"I saw some troopers," Whip put in.

"With guns," added Crush.

Jagger spit to the side. The geriatrics guarding the truck couldn't run half a block. She said, "The geezers will be busy keeping an eye on anyone cutting the line. I'll come in from Fourth Street, jump in the truck, and haul ass out of there."

"Want us to make trouble in the line?" Crush asked. "Distract people?"

"Nah, then they'll know it was us. Soon as you see I'm clear, beat it out of town. We'll meet on the dirt road out to Jerry Boyle's."

Whip bit her fingernail. "Something goes wrong?"

"Bury me next to Dylan."

• • •

Zoe and Selman stood a few yards away from the tables where volunteers handed out Bounty of Faith ration boxes. So far, she hadn't bumped into anyone from her high school days. No one else in the line recognized her either, which seemed odd. Her parents had at least a dozen close friends when she was young. People who worked with them, neighbors, cousins, all were missing. She took it as a good sign. They were doing well. On the other hand, they might have died in the war or during the waves of disease. Either way, they didn't need the Bounty of Faith.

"You know," Selman said, "I was just thinking. Karl Marx was right."

Zoe coughed at the pretentious comment. "There's a loaded statement."

"Sorry. It's very rare that I have an intelligent person to converse with. I just lost myself."

"Go on," Zoe said, happy to have a distraction from the slow progress of the line.

"Well, let me rephrase that. Marx was half right. He said religion was the opiate of the masses, which of course it could be, you know, providing relief and the comfort of explaining the impossible contradictions of life."

"Okay."

"But he missed something much more important, something that could have helped his movement succeed the way we have succeeded."

Selman's statement intrigued Zoe because the Common Faith had been a resounding success to the point where other countries requested Common Faith directors like Selman to establish branches overseas.

"You see," Selman continued. "Marx despised religion and made enemies of people who could have helped him achieve his goal. We, on the other hand—that is, those of us who were in government and a few outside—realized that the religion, uh, business, for lack of a better term, needed only to manifest itself in a tangible way to be widely accepted, even by those who previously denied any possibility of a Universal Creator. The Common Faith did just that and now is a steady, guiding hand, one the masses can see and feel immediately."

"As opposed to what?" asked Zoe.

"Some magical entity not seen or heard from in thousands of years. We figured out how to… "

"Keep it in the present."

Selman gripped her shoulders. "Exactly!" he gushed. "This way, things stay more rational. I mean, look what the Christians did to you. Talk about a throwback to the old days."

"Things have changed a lot since I grew up here," reflected Zoe.

"And for the better. They still have something to believe, organized, formal, but we give them a few morsels to reinforce the point. Look how well it works. The Bounty of Faith in action."

Zoe gazed at the line. One by one they stood at the first volunteer who checked their identification. The next one gave them a pen to sign. The last one handed them a box. Soon as she was in Philadelphia, she'd recommend a study on how to improve distribution.

"Orderly. Appreciated," Selman was saying.

"This was John Carroll's church."

"Sadly, he never accepted the Common Faith, and he disappeared."

"He was in my room at the clinic."

"Unlikely, Ms. Whelan."

"He was praying."

"Dare I suggest it was a hallucination brought on by the trauma inflicted by those murderous criminals? Your reputation for prosecuting Christians is well known. Killing you would be a great achievement for them."

"Then why am I still alive?"

Suddenly there were shouts from the line. "Hey! I didn't get mine!"

"Yeah, me neither!"

"What the hell is going on?"

The truck lurched forward. The trooper seated on the back tumbled out. People in the line trampled over him in pursuit of their entitlement.

Instinctively, Zoe ran around the crowd. She surmised someone was stealing the truck, which had yet to gain any real momentum. She heard the gears grind. It was an inexperienced driver, meaning they might stall the engine. She sprinted down the street, cut to the passenger side, and leapt for the handle on the side of the cab. Just as her hand clutched the metal rail, the driver found the gear. Suddenly picking up speed, the ground rushed under her feet. In seconds she was going too fast to safely let go, yet she was barely able to hang on.

• • •

"Where do we start?" Claire asked.

The poverty of Jagger's trailer was not shocking. Father Carroll and Claire took in the sagging furniture, the stains, and the primitive, improvised solutions to restore convenience and comfort. Yet, it was no worse than at the Pads, government-operated housing at the edge of town. At least the Mollies attempted a semblance of modernity. The faucets were dry, but buckets in the kitchen and bathroom made washing and flushing possible. Drinking water, probably boiled to purify it, was contained in a line of glass jars and plastic jugs on the counter. The cast-iron stove served double duty as cooker and heater. For light, they had kerosene lamps and candles, all placed atop metal platters to reduce the risk of fire. And the home was reasonably clean. It didn't reek of fermented sweat or rotten food, nor was it messy. Things were in their places. Someone was in charge here, making rules, enforcing them.

"Where would a kid hide it?" Father Carroll said.

"Could be anywhere," Claire answered with a chuckle, pulling the curtain for a glance outside. "Hang on. We can ask her."

Through the window, Father Carroll saw Runt ambling toward the trailer, her arms laden with a bundle of twigs. He and Claire retreated toward the back bedrooms.

Moments later, the kid entered the trailer. Oblivious to the uninvited guests standing in the hallway, she toted her kindling to the stove, opened its door, and fed several pieces into the fire. Satisfied the flames would grow, she turned around, only to be stunned by the presence of Father Carroll and Claire.

"We're not going to hurt you," Father Carroll said.

Runt snatched a knife from the drain board, pointed it at him, and replied, "Stay back!"

"Put the knife down, sweetie," said Claire.

"Please," Father Carroll added. "I came to thank you for getting me out of jail."

"The boss says you let Dylan die."

"He was already dead, but with your help, we can save others."

"Liar! Fake!"

"Remember the papers you took?"

"Didn't take nothing worth nothing."

"Can I see them?"

"Too late! I burned them in the stove. Get out!"

Runt charged Father Carroll. Leading with the knife was her mistake. He sidestepped her lunge, clamped her forearm with his right hand, and spun her into a clutch. The knife dropped to the floor where Claire kicked it out of the way.

"I'm sorry!" Runt wailed. "It wasn't me. Jagger threw your stuff in the fire."

"It's okay," Carroll said.

Claire went to the stove. Opening the door, she saw the manuscript surrounded by flames. Without thinking, she reached in, only to recoil at the blistering heat. She scrambled through the kitchen drawers. Utensils clanged and spilled, until a pair of tongs slid from under a spatula. These she used to grasp the pages, which she promptly dropped into the dry sink. On the way, a streak of embers cascaded to the floor.

Father Carroll released Runt and stomped out the burning bits. Runt mimicked him until there was no danger.

"Look!" Claire shouted, her finger pointing at the sink, where flames rose from the pages. Unbelievably, the paper itself remained intact. She could see Father Carroll's neat script within the orange glow.

Runt, showing unexpected bravery, scampered to see what had frozen Claire where she stood. There was her book without a cover, wisps of fire all around, but not charred the way paper normally did in the stove.

"That's weird," she said, then casually took a rag from the counter, smothered the flames, and held the manuscript up for Father Carroll's inspection. "Don't be mad."

"I'm not angry," he said.

"It should have a cover," Runt went on. "Keep it safe."

"You're right," Father Carroll agreed.

"I could make one."

"Would you?"

"Won't be cheap. And don't try to bargain."

He took out a tall leather wallet, selected a paper dollar, the kind Jagger told her bought stuff before the war, and handed it over.

"There's a down payment."

She took the money and gave him the stack of pages. "Thanks, but you better go before the boss gets back."

"Okay. I'll see you again when the cover's finished."

"Shhh. Don't tell anyone."

Runt closed the door after they left. From the window, she saw them take a few steps then stop to talk. Their conversation drifted back to her ear pressed to the glass.

"We have to gather and share this with the others."

Father Carroll appreciated her enthusiasm. Still, he knew better than to underestimate Selman and Randy Bartok.

"The Time of Gathering is coming," Father Carroll said, "but not here."

"Where?"

"That's not for us to know."

Disappointed, Claire suggested, "Think about what we've been through out here. Fifteen years of the Common Faith. People like Randy Bartok and… and… Zoe treating us like traitors. We deserve some hope."

While against his instincts, he agreed the faithful would be emboldened by a glimpse of his testament.

"The Cathedral," he said, "five o'clock tomorrow, but only you and the other originals."

Runt had never heard of a cathedral and couldn't imagine what it was. She decided to look it up in the big book of words that was under her bed.

· · ·

Beneath her mask, Jagger couldn't help but smile. No one saw her slip into the cab. When she started the truck, they were stupidly slow to react. If she hadn't missed second gear, it would have been a perfect coup.

"Not bad, old girl," she complimented herself, shifting into third and stomping the gas pedal. A little too fast, she rounded the corner onto Fifth Street. Glancing in the mirror, she noticed an unwanted passenger, someone hanging on the side of the cab.

"Son of a bitch!"

She turned hard to the right again, then straightened her course down the center of Poplar Street, lining up for a straight shot across the bridge and out of town.

"Here we go!"

Jagger accelerated down the grade, shifting up through the gears while letting off the throttle. Her stowaway stuck it out, crouching in the slipstream as they hurtled across the bridge.

On the road out of town, Jagger swerved hard left then whipped the wheel back to the right. The truck heaved into the turns, the wheels on the lighter side coming off the pavement while the others smoked from added friction. A few boxes fell from the open rear door.

"Losing my damn profit!" Jagger hollered, noting her passenger still clung to the cab. After three more maneuvers failed to dislodge the person, she decided to go off the highway. A gravel double track led through a stretch of trees and then the over-grown fields of mine tailings. She downshifted one gear and took the turn. The grade steepened to the point where she had to down-shift again, then again. The second time she let the clutch out too soon. The truck slowed as she fought the transmission.

Suddenly the cab door popped open. Jagger was inches from a fierce woman shouting, "Stop the truck!"

Jagger slammed on the brakes, skidding to a halt while simul-taneously sending the woman into the windshield. Jagger rein-forced this battering with a wild right hook that caught her op-ponent's chin. Then she reached for the handle to bail out. She would have made it, had the woman not swung a leg off the floor and jammed a foot into her back.

Jagger's face bounced off the side window, nose blood print-ing the glass. Next came a series of punches that landed so fast it felt like she was in the ring with three boxers. Jagger tried to cover with one arm while feeling for the handle to get out. Where the hell was it? The blows came in, one after another. She twisted and ducked but they found her every time. The last jab got her ear, the same one Randy Bartok softened up during his visit.

Dazed, bleeding, trapped, Jagger slid to the floor. Through her own rasping breath, she heard, "We done here?"

CHAPTER 11.

Jagger landed in the ditch beside the truck. That was a good thing because the tall weeds made the fall from the cab less than horrible. She was beat up. Professionally beat up. There was a difference between a short rumble with a drunk at the Pleasant Corner and a thumping at the hands of Randy Bartok or this chick. A big difference. She was going to be sore for a week, probably two. If she didn't end up in the dungeon for more exercise with Bartok or some new torture fiend courtesy of the troopers. As for restarting a title bout with her present enemy, no way, not without help. Who was she, anyway? Someone sent by Bartok as part of a setup? Her quality clothes and perfect teeth indicated she was not local.

"What's your name?" Jagger asked.

"Zoe is all you need to know."

"Okay, Zoe. Call me Jagger, if it suits you."

"Whatever."

"Might take a few tries, but I can probably get the truck out of the ditch. Take us where you want to go."

"Leave it," Zoe said. "Start walking."

"Long way back to the office," Jagger went on. "Why not call Randy Bartok? Get us a ride in his jeep."

"Shut up and move it."

The instant dismissal revealed she wasn't inclined to use a cellphone or didn't have one, which meant if Jagger could get the upper hand, reinforcements would be a long time coming.

"I'm a little short of shoe leather, but I guess you don't mind putting those fancy slippers to the test."

Zoe gave Jagger a perfectly placed jab to the shoulder blade, the kind of knuckles-first punch that burned.

"Where're you from, anyway?"

"I was born here," Zoe said.

"Yeah? Ain't seen you around."

"I left years ago. I live in Philadelphia."

"No shit? Long way to go just to bust my ass. What'd you do wrong to get sent to nowhereville?"

Zoe fired another jab to the same spot, backing it up with, "I ask the questions."

"Ask away," Jagger coughed.

"What do you know about John Carroll?"

"Preacher John?"

"Preacher John, Father Carroll, whatever you call him."

"Asking in an official capacity or more like, you know, a social thing?"

"Look at me," Zoe ordered.

Jagger turned and caught a lightning-bolt slap on her right cheek. It stung like she'd been hit with a bull whip.

"Answer the question!"

"Alright. Take it easy."

"John Carroll is the subject. Tell me everything you know."

"He's around. Kind of like me. Not in public saying, 'Hey there, Mrs. Jones, how about a cup of that piss coffee?' But he shows up now and then."

"Where does he live?"

"Oh, hell, he takes up with his people here and there. Nowhere too long since that old pervert Selman's been after him. What'd he do to catch your eye?"

"He's a Christian."

"Oh, for sure he's that! Preaching to the people! Take it from me, ain't nothing special. Gave it a try. Didn't work out."

Jagger saw the next slap coming, turned her head a few degrees to catch a glancing blow. After the assault in the truck, the toss from the cab, the pokes to the back, and now the reactionary slaps, she understood her adversary. Confidence was always a good trait for an enforcer, whatever kind she was. Over-confidence, however, was a vulnerability.

They walked the next two miles to the sound of their footfalls, random birds, and not a single passing vehicle. First on gravel, then on the paved road, and finally on the streets of Mount Carmel. Zoe led from behind, nudging Jagger with a shove at appropriate turning points. By these moves and side-eyed observation, Jagger learned three things. One, she was bound for Mount Carmel's Common Faith Center. Two, Zoe knew the town and its shortcuts. Three, Zoe thought the game was over. A few clues Jagger noticed suggested otherwise.

At the corner of Fifth and Poplar, Zoe ordered, "Stop."

Jagger watched her scan the street like she was looking for something.

"Stay right there."

Jagger put her hands up. "Not going anywhere, ma'am."

Zoe jogged toward the curb and snatched her phone from the gutter.

That explained why she didn't call for help. She lost it during the ride out of town. Jagger wished she'd known. She might have made a break for it. No worries, things were about to get exciting anyway.

"Hope it ain't broke," she said.

"It's fine."

"Wow, must be a tough one. Always wanted a cellphone to stay in touch with them that matter, but who can afford it?"

"Obviously not you," Zoe answered. "Keep going. Straight ahead."

"Ahhh, now I get it," Jagger said at the next corner, which was the narrow Grape Street. "You're one of them people reels in the Jesus freaks, sends them off to jail or whatever. That's why you're asking about Preacher John."

"First thing you got right," Zoe remarked.

"Wow. I never met a serious lawman before."

"Woman," Zoe returned. "Just like you."

"Think so?"

It was a roundhouse this time, and Jagger judged it perfectly, keeping her eyes straight ahead, giving no indication she was ready. She ducked under Zoe's fist and stepped into a left uppercut of her own that caught her opponent under the jaw.

Zoe floated up on her toes until Jagger's next punch, a right cross drove her back over her heels, down on the asphalt.

"Hit like a man, don't I?" Jagger said. Not waiting for an answer, she whacked Zoe again with a jab that laid her out flat.

From behind a tarped car and around the corner of a house, the other Mollies appeared. Jagger had caught Whip trailing them as far back as the town limit. Whip had then disappeared, but showed up again, this time with Crush and Runt, who had bobbed and weaved around hedges, fences, and disused mailboxes.

"Drag her out of sight!" Jagger shouted.

Crush grabbed Zoe by her armpits, Whip got her feet, and they carried her deeper into Grape Street, dropping her between two parked cars.

"I want those boots," demanded Jagger.

"Get off me!" protested a dazed Zoe when Crush kneeled on her gut.

"Hush now, missy," Jagger said before delivering a final left jab to the face.

Whip struggled to get Zoe's boots while Crush fished out a wallet and Runt rummaged through her jacket.

"Hey, look at this," Runt said, holding up the revolver.

Everyone stopped moving, including Zoe.

The gun went off a second later. The bullet ricocheted from a fire hydrant to a nearby car's bumper to a window somewhere down the alley.

"Give me that," Jagger said, tearing the gun from Runt's hand.

Crush gave Jagger the wallet as Zoe said, "You're all going to prison."

Examining the badge and ID, Jagger replied, "Not today, Compliance Specialist Zoe Whelan. Damn, that's a mouthful. Show me the treads."

Whip held up Zoe's expensive leather boots.

"They'll fit."

"What're you going to do with her?" Crush asked.

"March her off the bridge!" Runt cheered.

"Nah. Let's be more creative."

From behind them, Father Carroll's voice came firm and even, "Give me the gun, Ashley."

Jagger spun on her heel, leveled the pistol at him, and said, "Use my name, preacher, or I'll punch another pie hole in your face."

"I baptized you Ashley Teresa."

"That was a long time ago in a church that doesn't exist anymore."

"Yet, God is still here."

Pointing the gun at her own temple, Jagger said, "Think God will save me?"

"I know He will."

She lowered her aim to Zoe. "What about her?"

"Yes."

"But she wants to arrest you. Lock you up for talking about Jesus."

"She does."

Jagger laughed. "Not for nothing, Preacher John, but click, bang, and your problem's solved."

"It'll only get worse," he assured her.

A second time she pointed the gun at him. "Then maybe I should save everyone the trouble. Send you off to meet your maker."

"He'll call me when it's my time."

"He might be expecting you today."

"I told you before. I have an important job that isn't finished. Please, give me the gun."

The weight of the gun gave Jagger the thrill of raw power. She squeezed the trigger, felt the resistance build until it tripped, then the recoil as the round fired. The bullet missed Father Carroll's sleeve by less than an inch before smashing a car's mirror behind him.

"I think I'll keep it," Jagger said, "in case we all meet in less friendly circumstances." To Zoe, she added, "Be careful, Philly Chick. This ain't the City of Brotherly Love."

The Mollies hustled down the street, turned at the first corner, and disappeared.

Father Carroll moved toward Zoe, who struggled to stand, telling him, "Stay away from me."

He stopped short, saying, "I will soon have what you came for."

The cold asphalt soaking into her socks, Zoe replied, "I came for you, Mr. Carroll."

"You are the Messenger," he informed her, "and you've come for the Next Testament."

"Let me guess. It's been foretold."

"It has. You're the one to take my Testament to the Time of Gathering."

"Excuse me, but if it's God's will," she argued, "why didn't He pick someone who already believes?"

"Because He takes pleasure in those that change their ways."

If she wasn't hurting, Zoe would have laughed at that. "Do you know how ridiculous that sounds?"

"To a doubter, yes," he answered, "but that's a temporary condition. God will make it clear. His way. Very soon."

"Really? Why not here and now?"

"Because you're not ready."

Father Carroll, like the Mollies before him, walked away with all the confidence of a man who knew exactly where he was going and why.

"I'll find you!" Zoe shouted.

"Not before you find God," he whispered.

CHAPTER 12.

"She pulled a gun on me," Zoe said.

"Sounds as if you lost control of your weapon," Selman clarified. They were in his office late the same afternoon. He sat behind the desk like a presiding judge; she stood like an innocent prisoner demanding justice.

Incensed by his disavowal, Zoe renewed her argument. "They assaulted a Common Faith officer, stole government property, withheld information about a known criminal, namely John Carroll, who you swore was long gone."

"Over the years—"

"They've been running wild for years?" interrupted Zoe. "Who's in charge here?"

Anyone else speaking to him this way would spend a month in the dungeon. Lucky for her, Zoe Whelan had the good fortune of being the key to his most desirable future. His meeting with Secretary Thompson sparked his ambition. He'd done his penance for past transgressions by flawlessly administrating his district. It was time to return to the mothership, to take his place on the Sacred Council, where he should have been all along. A brilliant play vis-à-vis Zoe Whelan was a ticket to that destination. No, Hester Thompson hadn't said as much, but she had been impressed with his rapid assessment of the situation. It was important to follow up, soon, when a return favor would be seen as a logical next step. For these reasons, Selman restrained his harsher tendencies in favor of benevolent tolerance.

"The Mollies, as they call themselves, are useful servants.

They can be a bit rambunctious, but let's not lose sight of what we're trying to accomplish."

With the confidence of an equal, Zoe sat down. "Refresh my memory," she said. "What are we trying to accomplish?"

"The eradication of these dangerous Christians. Of course, we'll catch them and let justice run its course. But we must also see to your safety," Selman began. "Based on what you've told me, it is prudent to assume John Carroll is in contact with those in Philadelphia, and therefore another assassin might be on the way. Or, they could choose to use someone already here. In any case, you're in mortal danger."

"It's not the first time. I can take care of myself."

On the contrary, Selman almost said, but caught himself before leveling another criticism. He delivered his next statement with casual certainty, knowing there was no possibility she would accept it.

"I've spoken with Headquarters and arranged for a car to take you back to Philadelphia in two hours," he said.

"No."

Selman almost clapped at how quickly she took the bait. He was overjoyed at how she ran with it.

"I intend to stay here until John Carroll is captured," she said.

"Surely you have more important work in the city. Why waste your time on him?"

"He threatened me. Personally."

Unwittingly, the Mollies had done Selman a favor. They had wounded Zoe's pride, made her angry, and therefore paved the way for his trap better than if he'd orchestrated it with them. He resolved to have Bartok go easy on them. For a little while. After all, they bungled stealing the BoF truck.

"Of course, you're welcome to join the cause."

"I'll be leading it," Zoe said.

He dripped in a little faux indignation. "That will require Doctor Erbil to certify you're fit for duty and approval from Secretary

Thompson."

"She is expecting your call."

"I see," he said with all the gravity of a chastised subordinate. Playing his part was too much fun. And so easy! But a twinge of sadness tempered his joy, brought on by how short this drama would last. By his estimate, in a week or less, Zoe Whelan would be on her way to Philadelphia. In a hearse. Bound for a hero's burial in the plaza at Common Faith Headquarters.

"Where's Bartok?" asked Zoe.

"Investigating a lead."

She was on her feet a moment later. "A lead? Good. I'll want his report immediately."

"You'll have it tomorrow. If you'll excuse me, I best call Secretary Thompson," Selman finished.

• • •

Murray Smith drew the short stick, which meant he was the lookout for the meeting at the abandoned coal breaker, formerly known as Number Four, that had been repurposed as a secret place of worship. They called it the Cathedral, and in some ways the structure resembled Europe's stone masterpieces in height and grandeur. The interior space had been emptied of the crushers and conveyors, classifiers and sorting bins, all of which were relocated to the prep plant at Number Six, Mount Carmel's current mining operation. Lattice steel columns stood in neat rows, supporting the walls and roof of the remaining hollow space. However, instead of stained glass, dust-streaked windows filtered the sunlight.

At the top of the first flight of metal stairs, Murray traversed the catwalk to the south side of the building. Ascending the next set of stairs, he looked down on the others who, like himself, were the first to join Father Carroll's underground church after the Common Faith Mandate scraped away their previous affiliations. Pamela Reed, Bill Myer, and Joe Grant stood to the side, watching Claire Whelan build a small fire.

Not a good idea, Murray thought. Smoke draws attention. He took his time climbing the next flight of stairs. Years ago, he'd broken several vertebrae while working in Number Six. Since then, every step gave him pain. Nonetheless, he accepted his duty. Welcomed it, actually, because he was tired of the bickering among his fellow Christians in town. Some thought Father Carroll was a modern prophet; others said the man was telling stories to make himself important. Murray wasn't sure what to believe. He always found the former priest to be a decent man who did whatever he could for those in need or trouble. Since he started writing this testament, however, he'd become a hermit, living somewhere out in the woods, venturing to town perhaps one night a week unless otherwise summoned.

Finally at his post three stories above the ground, Murray took a position beside a broken window that looked to the east, all the way to town. His view included the path of the railroad that served Number Four until the mine was played out. The rails themselves had been taken to the new line into Number Six. Only the bed remained, which was mostly weeds trampled by the five of them.

Leaning against the wall to his right was a sledgehammer. He recalled using it to drive errant spikes into the ties along the section of rails he was tasked to maintain into the new mine. That was just after the war, when any job was a good job, and better than being drafted by the government to work rebuilding one of the shattered cities. Then he went into the mine for the bigger paycheck and ended up half-crushed. Nothing but hard times after that. He was forced to move in with his son, Kyle, who was a janitor at the elementary school.

Murray nudged the rusty hammer with his foot. If there was cause for alarm, he'd use it to strike the nearby water tank that resonated loud as any church bell. He had the strength to swing it three or four times.

Down below, Father Carroll arrived. Murray listened closely, but kept his eyes scanning the area outside.

"The day is coming, declared the Lord, when I shall make a new covenant," Father Carroll said.

"Jesus Christ is the living covenant," the others greeted him.

Father Carroll hugged each of them then said, "Paul wrote to the Galatians, 'For freedom you were set free. Do not submit again to the yoke of slavery.'" He held up a copy of *The Common Faith Guide to Religious Harmony.* "Worldly tyrants gave us this and demanded obedience."

"At the point of a gun," Grant reminded everyone.

"Yes," Carroll agreed, "but we have something more powerful than lies and guns. We have the Word." He dropped the Common Faith Guide and raised his own manuscript for everyone to see.

"What is it?" Pam Reed asked.

"My testament and prophecy," Carroll replied. "God's Word revealed. His call for change."

Reed shook her head. "I don't understand."

"It is His plan for us to end this era of exile."

"You mean our little group?" Grant questioned. "Or everyone?"

Myer shifted nervously on his feet. "Wait a minute. You're claiming to be a prophet."

"God spoke to me while I was living in the forest and when I was in prison," Father Carroll told them. "He gave me His message for all to hear at the Time of Gathering."

"That's blasphemy," Reed said, her voice laced with anger.

Myer agreed. "No one shall add or take away. So it says in the Bible."

Before their skeptical eyes, Carroll tossed his manuscript into the fire. The flames turned white-hot, soaring high. They staggered back from the glare and heat. Fearing something had gone wrong, Claire stepped close to the fire—where she saw the pages remained unaffected.

"See for yourselves," she said. "It's not burning."

They moved to her side, shielding their faces from the blaze.

"Is this a parlor trick?" asked Myer.

"It's a miracle!" Claire beamed.

"This is God's Word revealed that we may live in the light of His world," Father Carroll explained. "His call for us to gather and renew our trust in Him and the Savior."

"You sound like a revolutionary, not a Christian," Grant chided him.

Claire expected them to be thrilled. They would be the first to hear God's message. In two thousand years such a thing hadn't happened. Instead of shouting with joy, though, only the sound of the crackling fire echoed among them as they muttered in aggravated disbelief.

To make her point, she reached into the fire, grasped the manuscript, and held it up for them to marvel. Neither her clothing nor her flesh was singed. The flames instantly dwindled to mere flickers.

"What's wrong with you?" Claire pleaded. "Father Carroll has brought us a revelation."

"All I see is some kind of fraud," Grant said.

Myer piled on. "You're a good man, Father Carroll, but this is outrageous."

"I have no idea what's going on," Reed finished, "but I'm leaving."

"Wait!" Claire shouted.

"Have you read it?" Myer asked. "Has anyone?"

"No, but—"

"We put our lives on the line to come here and you haven't even witnessed his claim?" Grant scolded.

Claire handed the pages to Father Carroll and said, "Tell us what God has planned."

For his part, Father Carroll remained circumspect. The Spirit touched each person in its own time. He took his manuscript from Claire, the handwritten pages dry and cool in his hand.

"This is God's Word as revealed to me," he repeated. "The Messenger will bring it to the world."

"The Messenger?" Myer asked. "Why not you?"

A sour-toned clang overhead startled everyone. They craned their necks toward the lookout post. The clang struck again as Murray Smith swung the hammer with all his might.

"Bartok!" he shouted down. "Coming from the east!"

"Look what you've done!" Grant shouted, an accusatory finger pointed at Father Carroll. "Set us up to be caught!"

"Shut up and run!" Reed hollered. Already she was headed for the exit on the west side. Grant and Myer followed her out.

"Take this," Father Carroll instructed Claire, pushing his testament into her hands. "Keep it safe until the Messenger is ready."

She nodded a promise then bolted for the darkness deep in the building. It was better to hide and pray Randy Bartok didn't find her than try to outrun him. Like Murray Smith up there, she'd been the lookout. There were staircases, catwalks, and ladders to countless places Bartok might be too lazy to search. She hoped Father Carroll found one, too.

• • •

The trick to driving out of the ditch was not using too much power. Jagger eased off the clutch until she felt it grab but not more. She rocked the truck back and forth several times without spinning the wheels, which would only dig them deeper into the soft dirt. Whip and Crush shoveling gravel at the tires helped gain traction, and it wasn't long before Jagger had the vehicle back on solid ground.

Runt had never ridden in a truck before. She liked it. Better than walking, that was for sure. She knelt on the seat, squeezed in between Jagger, who drove, and Whip in the middle with Crush at the passenger door. Over the broad hood she watched the road zoom by faster than she'd ever seen it go. Too bad they squeaked to a halt only ten minutes after they pulled out of the ditch.

"Welcome to the Long Foot Nation," read the majestic sign outside the double iron gate at Jerry Boyle's place. Jagger blew the horn long and loud, then slowly rolled forward for the last quarter mile into the compound. A menagerie of shipping containers, trailers, and a few school buses occupied the central area. Boyle's cabin, the original structure on the property, served as his office and living quarters. The pig pens and chicken coop were far enough away to reduce the smell, but they weren't quite out of sight.

Boyle answered to no one. Not thugs like Bartok, or the troopers that swept through every year, or that Common Faith bullshit, either. Free trade and the law of the jungle were Boyle's governing philosophies. He made money from both sides of the Second Civil War, as any clever guy with three-quarters of a brain should have. His best deal ever: carving out his estate from government land when the fighting ended. Drew up phony papers proving he was a full-blooded Lenni-Lenape American Indian, one Jerry Long Foot to be specific, army scout in personal and secret service of the generals. A fair bribe set the boundaries in stone. The Long Foot Nation was official, overseen by its president and chief, who was one-quarter Davy Crockett, judging by his appearance, three-quarters impresario by the way he did business.

"Truck and all!" Boyle greeted them with his bearded grin, not that a smile indicated he was happy. He recognized an official Bounty of Faith truck when he saw one. Possessing a stolen vehicle guaranteed ten years in prison. Fencing the contents carried another ten years. Unless it was guns. Then it was life.

"Hey! Stay where I can see you," he snapped at Whip and Crush, who had drifted toward one of the containers for a peek inside. Although the Mollies were his best partners, buyers, and sellers, it was no secret they were sometimes thieves. Didn't mean he didn't trust them, because to Jerry's way of thinking everyone stole something at sometime, whether they admitted it or not. As long as they didn't steal from him, live and let live. Otherwise, the shotgun slung over his shoulder came into play.

"Bartok's in on this," Jagger told him as they walked to the back of the truck. "Otherwise, I wouldn't have risked it."

"He's your boss, not mine," Boyle said.

"Was thinking we could get creative with the inventory," Jagger suggested as they stared at the jumble of Bounty of Faith boxes in the cargo compartment. "No telling how many fell out."

"Maybe," Boyle said. He opened a box, took out a pack of cookies, dared to bite one. Stale but a pig delicacy.

"What do you say?" prodded Jagger.

"I say the truck's a problem," Boyle said.

"We empty it, suck out the go-go juice, roll it into one of the old strip mine pits," suggested Jagger.

He appreciated the woman's ability to improvise. Truth be told, when it came to the criminally inclined, he admired her fortitude. Still, she tended to hit and run, thereby missing a big chunk of the potential upside.

"No sense throwing it away," he said. "How much fuel's in it?"

"Half a tank."

Probably three-eighths, but he wouldn't argue. Any fuel— gasoline, diesel, kerosene—was precious.

"The boxes are nothing but pig fodder."

"Bacon in the making," joked Jagger.

She was right. He'd dump them into the pens twenty at a time. His sounder of swine would gobble cardboard and all. As for the canned cheese, he'd shelve that for the winter. The truck required careful consideration. He intended to dismantle it into useful components, the final use for each to be determined later.

"Before we get into the official parlay," Boyle said, "tell me where you got the boots."

"Doesn't matter," Jagger replied.

"Nobody around here but Bartok, Selman, and the troopers have boots like that. And the miners are required by regulation to leave theirs in the locker at the end of the shift."

"Tell me something I don't know."

"For the sake of our future business," Boyle continued, "I'm telling you that walking around in fancy footwear draws attention from people less understanding than me."

"Duly noted. Now let's make a deal."

"I'll take care of Bartok when his sorry ass shows up," Boyle offered. "For you and the ladies, it's twenty pounds of deer jerky, a rack of pork chops when the pigs get the knife, and something small or shiny for each."

"Sounds a little light," Jagger said. "I'll take the chops, double the jerky, and four cases of canned veggies, couple bags each of rice and beans for a balanced diet. Ain't like we got dresses for the ball so forget the jewelry."

"Too bad," Boyle put in. "Some nice baubles in my showcase." He had a weakness for ambitious women, who he thought look best wearing gleaming metal. Under different circumstances, Jagger would have been a permanent feature in his life, as in a ring on her finger. She'd also look great wearing one of those fine gold chains and matching earrings he had locked in a treasure chest.

"And how about a couple of schoolbooks if you have them," Jagger finished. "Going to teach Runt how to read."

Hearing her name prompted Runt to pipe up with, "I can read."

"Shhh," Jagger scolded her.

"Want to bet?" Runt asked.

Cute little thing, Boyle thought. Defiant streak in her, no doubt picked up from Jagger.

"Tell you what," he proposed, "If you can read, I'll give you a box of chocolate bars."

"Let's see 'em first," Runt demanded.

The Mollies waited outside while Boyle retrieved the candy from one of his storage units. They heard three doors slam, a few chains rattle, and his cursing. Everyone's mouth watered as he set down a pack of end-of-war celebration Hershey bars, still in the wrapper with no signs of spoilage.

"Ohhhh, man," Crush groaned.

Whip was stunned silent. She couldn't remember the last time they had tasted chocolate.

In his other hand, Boyle carried a thick paperback novel. He peeled back the cover to the first page, stooped down, and held it for Runt.

"Go on," he said. "Read it to us."

While the others waited for their disappointment to be certified, Runt's eyes followed the letters across the page.

"It's okay," Jagger said, putting a hand on Runt's shoulder. "I'll start teaching you soon as we get home."

Runt shrugged off the gesture, cleared her throat, and read.

"It was the best of times. It was the worst of times."

• • •

Climbing through the old breaker, Claire debated hiding Father Carroll's manuscript. If Bartok caught her, there was a chance someone else could retrieve it. Then again, as much as she wanted to believe she could withstand the torture Selman would inflict, she knew everyone eventually broke. Therefore, the testament would still be found. She resolved to keep it, and more important, not to get caught.

After four flights of stairs, she stopped to catch her breath. Below her, Murray Smith started across the catwalk that led to the back stairs. He had almost made it when Randy Bartok called up from the ground.

"Stop right there!"

Claire knew Smith made a mistake by stopping. Had he kept running, Bartok would have had to waste precious shots on a more difficult moving target.

"Where's John Carroll?" Bartok hollered.

"Not here!" Smith replied.

"That you, Murray?" Bartok returned, softening his tone.

"Go back to your master, Bartok."

"Let's not start with the insults. Selman's given me a handful of get-out-of-jail cards for anyone with information about your beloved Preacher John. There's cash money, too, if you help."

Run, Murray! Claire almost screamed. She would have, too, as a distraction. However, she couldn't chance losing the book.

"There's no one here but me," Murray said.

"That's a lie. I heard you were having a confab, discussing some official paperwork."

"It's over for people like you! The Time of Gathering is soon!"

"Then you have nothing to worry about," Bartok called back.

Claire fought to control her panic. If she managed to escape, there was still a traitor among them. Grant? Myer? Reed? No, not them. They had as much to lose as anyone. Unless one of them was working for Selman from the beginning, in which case, there would be troopers waiting for her at home. Worse yet, Zoe would know. Was that the real reason she was sent to Mount Carmel, to arrest her own mother?

"I'm only going to ask once," Bartok said.

Reflexively, Claire peeked around a column for a clear angle on Murray. He remained in the middle of the span. Directly below was Bartok with his rifle.

"Come down before you get hurt," continued Bartok.

Murray stretched out his arms.

"I can see you're not armed," Bartok said. "Get moving before I change my mind."

Murray leaned against the handrail until he fell over the side. A few long seconds later he died instantly when his body struck the dirt at Randy Bartok's feet.

Claire buried her face into her sleeve, soaking it with tears.

She remained hidden, tucked behind a metal cabinet labeled

for electrical equipment, daring a look down at Bartok now and then. Mount Carmel's enforcer left Murray's body where it fell. He kicked dirt over the fire until it was extinguished. Then he made a cursory search of the area, popping in and out of Claire's view. She surmised Bartok came alone because at no point did she see any state troopers or Selman. Minutes later, Lenny Donovan arrived. He and Bartok loaded Murray's body into the back of the jeep. After a final look around, they both left.

Worried Bartok might have called the troopers to clear the structure, Claire scurried down the stairs. Clutching Father Carroll's testament, she ran outside, deep into the woods. There she sat on a fallen tree for a rest. She and Murray had come close to being more than friends. He had lost his wife to Red Death, and she'd been widowed when her husband, Patrick, died from severe injuries caused by an accident in Number Six soon after it opened. They shared their losses and belief in God, but for some reason never took the relationship to the next step. She was going to miss him.

Tired from climbing through the old breaker and the run, she rubbed her legs. Her sixty-sixth birthday was a few months away and she was starting to feel it. The walk home was going to require all the strength she had left. And what awaited her? Zoe with handcuffs? A squad of state troopers?

She resisted the temptation to read Father Carroll's testament. Soon it would be dark, and while she believed Zoe was not a threat, the troopers might be. There would be time to read it later. She said a prayer for Murray then set off for home, thinking where she might hide the most precious thing she ever touched.

CHAPTER 13.

The next morning Claire left the house before Zoe or Mike awoke. After what happened the day before, she needed to pray. The group's rebuke of Father Carroll. Murray's sacrifice. The responsibility of hiding the Next Testament. Her arrival home to find Zoe with new scratches and bruises from a run-in with the Mollies. It was a tangled mess of events and emotions about which she needed time to reflect.

She was most confused about Zoe. Her daughter admitted to having a confrontation with the Mollies but refused to provide any details other than that she would not be returning to Philadelphia.

"You're supposed to be taking it easy," Claire said.

"You look tired yourself, Mom," Zoe replied. "Take a rest. I'll make dinner."

Claire accepted the offer, retreating to her bedroom to ponder the meaning of her daughter remaining in Mount Carmel. Was it because she was destined to have an epiphany and accept her calling? Or was it something else? She dozed off, only to be awakened by Mike calling her to the table. They ate as a family for the first time in years, a quiet meal shared by people fearful of being openly honest.

She hardly slept, so she decided to get away from everyone before the sun rose. She had the perfect place.

When the Common Faith took over and desecrated her church with the Circle and Line, Claire converted a spring house into a personal chapel. The little stone building stood along a trail not far from where Redeemer Cemetery had been. Early settlers of the area had come here for the clean water that trickled out of the rocks into a small pool at the bottom before spilling down to the Shamokin Creek.

Anyone stumbling upon it would find only a stack of rough-hewn boards inside, as if the last person to visit meant to repair the roof. However, these were the pieces of a rudimentary kneeling bench and altar, cut and notched in such a way as to fit together easily. Claire assembled her fixtures with care. The ritual calmed her mind in preparation for prayer. When complete, she unwrapped a framed photo of Patrick and an icon she salvaged from Blessed Virgin Mary Ukrainian Church in Centralia. She hadn't been a member there; she belonged to Our Lady of Mount Carmel. Still, it broke her heart to see how the demolition crew used their machines to maul sacred objects into unrecognizable debris. This they did by order of the Common Faith Mandate. A few months after it took effect, she heard Father Carroll was forming a secret congregation. She was among the first to join. The others were Joe Grant, Murray Smith, Pam Reed, and Bill Myer. They didn't know what to call themselves because each came from different denominations. They agreed to dispense with labels and be what they were: Christians.

Yet, suddenly the others doubted Father Carroll's sincerity. Worse, they accused him of blasphemy. She had been a little skeptical herself when he first mentioned his revelation, before he was caught by Bartok. She took a wait-and-see attitude. And then, in the Mollies' trailer, when his manuscript didn't burn, she knew it was real. At the Cathedral, she'd been overcome with the Spirit's strength, plunging her hand into the flames. She felt no heat, no pain, only the cool texture of the pages. They saw her do it. Did they think she was part of a scam? The sadness in Claire's heart weighed heavier than her anger. It left her hollow, disappointed, and a little paranoid.

She knelt on the bench and bowed her head, but was interrupted by a rattling cowbell. Only followers of John Carroll knew this all-clear signal, which indicated their approach.

That they came to her before she could find them, Claire took as a bad sign. It meant they first met among themselves and made a decision. Who were they to decide anything after abandoning Father Carroll? And to think Murray Smith sacrificed himself so they could escape!

She took an inordinate amount of caution, hurriedly wrapping her objects, tucking them into her satchel, and retreating behind some nearby trees. Joe Grant led Myer and Pam. He held up the cowbell, shaking it deliberately. Behind them, she saw no one else. Relieved but still angry, she waited until they knocked on the door before revealing herself.

Loud and clear, she said, "Over here."

Startled, Joe dropped the bell.

"What do you want?" Claire asked, stomping forward, drawing them away from her cherished place.

"We came to talk," Grant said.

"About what happened yesterday," Myer clarified.

"I'm listening."

As he often did, Grant spoke for the others.

"What happened yesterday was no coincidence. How did Bartok find us? How did he know when?"

To these questions she had no answers, nor did she appreciate his insinuation.

He made it clear with, "Someone betrayed us."

"Well, I don't think Murray would have died if it was him."

"He's dead?" blurted Reed.

"Sacrificed himself so we'd have time to escape," explained Claire.

"Bartok shot him?" Grant asked.

"No," answered Claire. "Murray fell from the catwalk."

"Fell or jumped?" Myer wanted to know.

"It doesn't matter!" Claire snapped. "He died for us, so I don't think he was the traitor, which means it was one of you. Or me."

"We heard Zoe's in town," Grant said.

"Oh, I see. You're accusing me of giving her information that would put us all in prison."

"No one said that."

"No one had to. Hear it from me: Zoe knows nothing, nothing about us. And never will."

"Maybe it's Father Carroll?"

"Are you insane?" Claire blurted.

"Hear me out."

"Make it quick, because I'm about to leave, and sin that it may be, never speak to any of you again."

Grant gathered his thoughts and explained. "Father Carroll invited disaster when he left us to hide out and write his revelation or whatever that was you showed us. Then, Selman put the word out and caught him a couple weeks ago. Held him in the dungeon. Did who-knows-what to him. How many people have gone there and then disappeared?"

"Or were sent to Philadelphia," Myer put in, "for Common Faith Rehabilitation."

"What I'm trying to say," continued Grant, "is that he probably had no choice."

"No choice to do what?"

"We don't want to believe Selman broke Father Carroll," Grant admitted, "but it's the only possibility. Any one of us in his situation would have done the same thing."

"Murray didn't. Ye of little faith," Claire mocked them, "why are you afraid?"

"Have you read it?" Reed asked, her quiet voice catching their attention.

"No," Claire admitted.

"Then how can we know if it's real?" Myer insisted.

"What kind of proof do you want? Look at my coat, my hand. Are they burned?"

Next came their decision, the one Claire knew they made before coming, and the true reason for the visit.

"Give it to us. We'll read it together," said Grant.

"I don't have it," said Claire, lying by omission. She would never carry something so valuable on her person. Nonetheless, she knew where it was. She left it in a safe place with intentions to retrieve it and make copies as soon as possible. She resolved to die like Murray before revealing its location. That included at the hands of her own daughter, Compliance Specialist Zoe Whelan.

"Until we read it for ourselves, the jury's out," Grant informed her.

"Very well," Claire said. "May God be with you."

Maybe they were prudently suspicious. Perhaps one of them was the traitor. Or all of them. In any case, her trust had been broken. She left them to their doubts and plodded toward home.

• • •

The squeaking woke Zoe. It came from the far corner of her room. She sat up, squinted into the shadows, and saw a hunched figure. Her first instinct was to grab her gun, but she didn't have one.

"Who's there?" she called out.

"Who do you think?" came the reply as Mike cranked the radiator valve closed. "Hot enough to grow tomatoes in here."

More like cold as a meat locker, Zoe almost said. She had slept in her wool socks and flannels.

"Keep it down or we'll be out of coal in February."

"Hah!" she said. "This town's probably sitting on a billion tons of coal."

"Doesn't mean it's ours."

Mike always was a grumpy guy. Zoe couldn't blame him. Spent his life working in a mine, lived with his widowed mother, never found a mate. Only time he left the county was for a stint working construction following the war, but he returned after a few months, preferring the depths of the mine to the heights of skyscrapers. No wonder he lacked a sunny disposition.

At the breakfast table in the kitchen, she ate alone. Her mother left a note that she'd be home around noon. It was just as well. Zoe spent the time reviewing Bartok's report on yesterday's failure at the breaker, which Lenny Donovan hand delivered. It was impressively thorough, complete with diagrams, photos, and a neatly typed narrative. In summary, one dead, no leads. John Carroll and his tiny flock most likely scattered, hiding out in the surrounding woodland, or gone elsewhere. His conclusion: No point in wasting her time in Mount Carmel.

"Uhh, no," Zoe announced to the empty room. "I think I'll show you how it's done."

Bartok referenced a "handwritten religious document," but did not call it the Next Testament. He didn't have to. Carroll himself told her he'd written it, that she would be the one to take it to the Time of Gathering, whatever that was. The gall of Carroll to insist she would be involved in one of their rituals was as brazen as it was bizarre. At any rate, according to Bartok's unnamed informant, the purpose of John Carroll's gathering was to share this work among the group. Christians frequently claimed their scribblings were divinely inspired. This particular example's unique quality, however, was fireproof pages. Or, so said the informant.

Her training taught that the ignorant were susceptible to magic tricks. For them, perception was reality regardless of the impossibility of their fantasy. To counter this human foible, the Museum of False Truth held thousands of relics supposedly imbued with supernatural power. Exhibits exposed the fakery of each. In this case, the paper was probably treated with a substance to prevent it from burning. She looked forward to delivering John Carroll's missive to the curator, who would put a photo of her holding him in cuffs beside it in a glass case. She'd keep a page for her own trophy box.

A snappy triple-knock on the back door proceeded it opening, and to Zoe's astonishment, Jagger walked in pointing a revolver, the one she stole yesterday, deliberately at the floor.

"Don't mistake the presence of a cannon for hostile intentions," Jagger said. "Merely taking precautions. And you should lock the doors around here."

They stared at each other a long moment.

Finally, confident she wasn't about to be shot, that her unwanted visitor had another purpose, Zoe said, "Would you like some coffee?"

"Most definitely."

Zoe opened the cabinet where the coffee had always been, but it was empty. She proceeded to search the others and also the drawers. Her hand passed over several knives and a ten-inch cast-iron frying pan, both of which she briefly considered using against Jagger. Odds favored the gun. She leaned her hip against the counter, her empty hands turned palms up.

"Sorry. Don't have any."

"Shame. Thought a swanky house like this had it all. Have to make do with the usual." Jagger took a flask from her jacket, expertly spun open the cap, and swigged. Holding it out, she said, "Steve Regan's finest grog, five dollars a jar at the Pleasant Corner or a sip here and now on my account."

Such primitive customs, Zoe thought, but played along. She sipped the liquor, choking back a cough, then returned the flask.

"Now that we shared the cup, let's talk business," said Jagger.

"Help me out," Zoe replied. "What kind of business would you and I be doing?"

"Stranger in a strange land needs a local guide."

"And that's you?"

"Me and mine, your highness. Nobody knows the lay of the land better than us. Sorry you had to find that out the hard way. A smart person like yourself ought to chalk it up to verification of promises presently made. Make sense?"

"To you."

"To anyone who wants to avoid the best of the worst, which is exactly what's going to happen if you keep blundering about like a blind hog in the butcher shop."

Zoe laughed heartily at that one.

"Funny, yeah, until a fiasco or two like Randy Bartok's slip-up at the old Number Four breaker sends you to the boss's office, tail between your legs and making excuses."

Considering the source, this insight registered as remarkably astute. Hester Thompson expected results. Setbacks and mistakes were tolerated to a point. Zoe wanted to avoid that point. Simultaneously, she understood there was enormous risk engaging with Jagger.

"How do you know what happened yesterday?" asked Zoe.

"How don't matter. My awareness proves worthiness to your cause," Jagger answered. "And here's another freebie: Selman ain't on your side."

"Nice try."

"Okay. Do the deduction. Someone tipped Bartok that Preacher John was holding court yesterday, and sure as shit Bartok told Selman, who gave the okay to roll out there and do what he did."

"How'd you know where John Carroll would be?"

"Never said it was me played the rat and not important to either of us who else it might have been. What is important is Bartok flew that mission solo. Should have had a co-pilot at a minimum, namely you, especially with plenty of time before takeoff and your official capacity as specialist in the subject."

Silently, Zoe admitted she was right.

"Could have been he thought he had the jump on Preacher John and wanted to grab the glory, impress hungry mouths up the food chain, that kind of thing. But with, hypothetically speaking, the Big Man in Heaven looking after Preacher John, I'd make no assumptions as to a sneak attack being so sneaky. Or, more likely, Selman's keeping you in the dark for another reason as yet unknown. Either way, from your side of the table, that's conduct unbecoming."

It was another irrefutable conclusion. Zoe's next question was preempted.

"Yeah, why," Jagger said. "My suggestion? Find out before he finds out you're trying to find out."

"How do I know you're working with me and no one else?" Zoe asked.

"Bartok and I have a commercial relationship. Goes back to when this place had full-time electricity. That ain't going to change for quality-of-life reasons, his and mine."

"And yet, I'm supposed to trust you."

"Get what you pay for, and in the matter of you versus Preacher John, my loyalty is one hundred percent with the highest bidder. Keep that in mind on payday."

"This is ridiculous," Zoe protested. "I'm not going to be hustled."

"Okay. Here's something. It pans out, then you got proof in the pudding and I get credit at the bank."

Zoe wished she'd taken a chance with the frying pan. Listening to Jagger's patois was worse than being shot.

"Candace Walsh, she's about your age," Jagger said.

"We went to high school together."

"She's pregnant with Lenny Donovan's baby."

"That's no concern of mine."

"Come on. Tell me you'd have nothing to talk about with a secret devotee of Preacher John's with ideas of him baptizing her baby-on-the-way."

Gun still in hand, Jagger pulled out her flask for another drink then offered it to Zoe.

"Drink up. I got a ride waiting on me."

CHAPTER 14.

While Jagger parlayed with Zoe Whelan, Whip and Crush staked out the Pads, formerly known as the Lantern Motel. The slang term derived from the lily-pad green of the exterior and faded yellow flowers on the doors. Only four of the twenty units were occupied, and no one was on the premises at the moment. They set up camp a few dozen yards away, burrowed under a dense laurel that provided excellent cover.

Yesterday's score filled their bellies and renewed their confidence in Jagger. The surprise of all surprises was Runt's ability to read. No one expected that, nor the bonus candy, which they treated like gold. Emboldened by these developments, they trained their eyes and ears on Selman as he wheeled into the gravel lot.

Ten minutes later, Crush whispered, "He's just sitting there."

Whip didn't have binoculars to see what Selman was doing. "He's looking at the convict files," she guessed.

In fact, Selman waited patiently in his car, reviewing the records and photos of the two parolees about to get off the bus from Graterford Prison. The male, Otto Weber, stood more than six feet tall with a muscled build developed during his twelve years in prison for armed robbery and manslaughter. He bore the deliberately slack stare of a hardened convict that indicated disdain for the world. The female, Sara Darcy, served six years for aiding and abetting the Surviving Few, the Christian group to which Zoe Whelan's suicide bomber claimed to belong. Her vacant eyes seemed resigned to a dreadful future as long as it lasted. According to the paperwork, they cohabitated the past year as part of a required social skills program.

"How nice," Selman cooed.

Under the laurel bush, Crush nodded toward the road. "I can hear the bus."

Moments later, it rolled to a stop two hours behind schedule, which was to say spot on time. The driver and a single armed guard had made stops along the way for passengers and cargo. The sideline was strictly forbidden, but efficient corruption passed percentages up the line to prevent enforcement. No one dared accuse the troopers of working the black market.

Whip and Crush watched Selman exit his car and walk to Unit 14. This humble abode came with a job at Girard Number Six, both to have and to hold as long as they didn't violate the terms of their parole. A Second Chance at a First Life, the Common Faith called the program in which they were automatically enrolled.

"Check it out," Whip said. "Big guy and a woman."

Crush saw them stand still while the guard unlocked the former prisoners' shackles. The driver approached Selman, handing him a thin envelope.

"Skimpy payoff," said Crush.

"Maybe it's vouchers."

They both heard the driver ask, "Anything to go back?"

"Sadly, no," Selman answered.

"Have fun with the lovely couple," the driver said, whistling to his companion that they were clear to leave.

"Welcome to your new home," Selman greeted Weber and Darcy, who each carried a small bag. "Here's the key to this handsome suite, which is yours to use rent-free for the next year. Quite a reward for your good behavior. There's some canned food and other treats already in the kitchen. I encourage you to visit us at the Common Faith Center, which is a walkable distance, and well worth your time to make the journey for the Bounty of Faith."

Weber snorted the odds of him attending the weekly recognition service.

"Don't be late for work," Selman chided them. "Any other questions?"

"Where's the nearest bar?" Weber asked.

"That way," Selman replied. "The Pleasant Corner."

"How much for a ride?"

"Sorry, my vehicle is for official business only."

Selman turned for his car to the sound of Weber ordering Darcy inside Unit 14.

Pressed to the ground, Crush and Whip reviewed what they saw. Two pistols in hip holsters. No theft-worthy cargo from Selman, but possibly something already stowed in the vehicle. The bus headed into town, which meant a stop at the Pleasant Corner. They deduced plenty of time remained to set the trap on Route 61. Jagger would be happy.

"What's she want with a bus?" Whip wondered aloud.

"Drive the hell out of here," Crush speculated.

"To where?"

"How would I know?"

A breaking windowpane caught their attention. Both pairs of eyes and ears scanned for approaching danger. Next came shouting from Unit 14. The sound of a sharp slap and two more echoed through the hole in the glass.

"He's kicking the shit out of her," Whip said.

"Wish I had the gun Jagger got off that chick. Go in there—"

"And what?" interrupted Whip. "Shoot a guy dead?"

"Shoot him until I ran out of bullets."

"Then what?"

Crush didn't have a comeback.

"Let's find Jagger before you do something stupid."

•   •   •

Without a secure computer, Zoe lacked the means to research Candace Walsh, her good friend from high school. They had the usual fun together that people stuck in the same class did, but Zoe would never have considered Candy a best friend. She lacked the gumption to get out of town. Zoe, on the other hand, couldn't wait to leave, skipping her senior year for a scholarship at Common Faith Academy.

Zoe tried to use her phone, but the data service was pathetically slow. She understood the reason. People who couldn't afford shoes couldn't buy smartphones, especially not new, government-certified ones. Why provide a service that would never be used?

Because her mom was out of the house, she couldn't so much as ask how Candy was doing under the guise of catching up with a former schoolmate. The deep part of Zoe's memory recalled Candy wanted to be an elementary school teacher. If she achieved this goal, then she would be dealing with the little darlings until after three, or longer if assigned day care duties. What were the odds?

Very good, Zoe concluded.

She also remembered Candy's sister, Denise, had passed her in the hallway at the Common Faith Center. During one of their rare phone conversations, her mother told her something about Denise and her son. What was it? Oh, yeah, Ian had special needs. Specifically what they were, Zoe failed to recall. At any rate, the basic facts were relevant because they implied dependency. Denise needed someone to help with Ian; Candy was capable, and if not willing, Denise would browbeat her into service. In high school, Denise had been mean to everyone, especially her own sister.

All this in mind, Zoe broke with standard procedure that prescribed backup officers covering her moves. She ventured alone to the Beech Street address where the Walsh family lived. The walk went somewhat slower than it should have because she wore an old pair of sneakers instead of her favorite boots. Jagger had those boots, crudely disguised with duct tape around them. The thief had that gun, too. Zoe planned on recovering both, because she wasn't about to be one-upped by a petty criminal who happened to be enjoying a lucky streak.

The Walsh home was split; one half was boarded up, the other half was in exceptional condition with intact windows, a numbered door, and signs of habitation in the form of a full trash can. Zoe mounted the stairs with the idea of knocking and introducing herself to whoever answered. From there, improvise a conversation for a look inside. As soon as she reached the porch, the door flew open and Denise charged out.

"Where the hell you been!" Denise shouted. Seeing it was Zoe, she lowered her voice. "Oh, was expecting someone else. What do you want?"

"Remember me?"

"Pfft. Who wouldn't remember Zoe Whelan? Bitch like you makes an impression."

At this point, Zoe wished she came with her Compliance Team for a teachable moment. The lesson: How to show proper respect to law officers. But she was alone, unarmed, and focused on more important things.

"How are you, Denise?" Zoe asked.

"Been better. Been worse. Be on the better side you did me a favor." Denise pointed a thumb over her shoulder and said, "Keep an eye on the kid."

"Where're you going?"

"Gotta pick up his meds before Doc Erbil disappears for the day."

Denise bounded across the porch, over the rail, and leapt to the sidewalk.

"When will you be back?" Zoe shouted.

Denise ignored the question.

Inside, Zoe found an unexpectedly tidy living room. Quality furniture sat in all the right places. A large television hung on the wall. Strikingly absent was Ian. She ventured through the small dining room to the kitchen where more new fixtures awaited. She opened a cabinet to find it stocked completely full—coffee, powdered milk, cereal. Enough for a month if it was eaten every day. Her mother's cabinets were practically empty.

"Ian," she called out. "Where are you, Ian?"

Getting no response, she returned to the living room, where a flight of stairs led to the second floor.

"Are you up there, Ian?"

On the stairs, Zoe wondered if Denise was playing a joke on her. If she was, the unintended consequence was free rein to search the premises, not that a compliance specialist needed a warrant.

Consistent with the first level, the second was similarly furnished and decorated. The front bedroom smelled of fresh paint. The hall bathroom featured new tile. Combined with the rest of the house, it was more than an elementary school teacher's salary bought. In fact, it was more than Zoe's salary afforded, even with a government-provided, zero-interest mortgage.

Finally, she found Ian in the back bedroom. He sat cross-legged on the floor facing the corner. His hand moved across a large artist's pad on his lap.

"Hey, Ian," she said.

No response.

Moving closer, she asked, "What're you working on?"

He turned his head, revealing a bruised cheek. Above the purple flesh his eyes gaped wide in pure terror. From his mouth came the most horrible screech Zoe ever heard.

"I'm not going to hurt you," she said.

He screamed again, twisting against the wall like a wounded mouse.

Zoe took out her badge. "Look. I'm an officer of the Common Faith."

His pitch increased to a blinding shriek. For Zoe it was like standing next to a jet engine. Reflexively, she covered her ears.

Ian wasn't finished. Still screaming, he grabbed his drawing and bolted from the room.

"Stop!" she hollered, not sure he heard her over his own cries.

His head start enabled him to get to the hall closet where he ducked inside and slammed the door closed a full second before Zoe got to it. She yanked on the knob to no avail. She banged into it with her shoulder then pulled again. One more hit warped the thin wood enough to pop the lock. She hauled open the door to find the space empty.

"Where did… "

Nothing disappears without a logical explanation, she told herself. She found it on her hands and knees. A thin sheet of plywood covered an opening in the back of the closet. She kicked it out of the way and stuck her head through. A few seconds passed until she realized she was looking at the gutted second floor of the twin next door. Ian cowered beneath one of the broken windows.

That instant she remembered that Ian was deaf and unable to speak. His classmates and others must have bullied him to no end. He had probably developed Post Traumatic Stress Disorder. It explained why he panicked at the sight of a stranger bigger than him and why he wasn't in school.

Zoe lowered herself to the floor, gradually moving closer to him until she was able to put a hand on his shoulder. He jumped at her touch, but she gently held on. After a while, he stopped shaking. The drawing pad slipped from his hand, and soon after he seemed to fall asleep.

Zoe got to her knees. She paused for a look at his sketch. A pencil-line dragon, stabbed in the chest by a lance, roared at the upper corner of the page. The lower right corner contained a smaller, less-detailed figure. Ian's talent showed in every stroke. The finished work was sure to be photorealistic. It was nothing compared to what she found painted on the wall behind her.

Like his drawing, the images were created with stark black lines shaded in greys. In the center hung Jesus on the cross. On both sides, saints floated atop broken plaster. Distant hills fringed the work in progress. It was the kind of mural she saw behind altars. No doubt about it, the style belonged to Ian.

The question, as Jagger would have put it, was, "What're you going to do about it?"

. . .

Duplicating Father Carroll's manuscript was the best way to preserve it. Claire had enough pens to hand copy the missive several times, but paper was expensive and in short supply. Plus, she worried the others would dismiss anything she'd written as an attempt at perpetuating a fraud. Any duplicate must be an exact replica for their group, and the world, to see for themselves. Therefore, she had two choices: photography or a copy machine. Both were problematic.

A digital camera wasn't the answer because the images still had to be printed or shared electronically. That type of sharing would be caught by Common Faith internet censors and their all-powerful algorithms. If she went the photo route, she'd have to do it the old way, with film and chemicals. Who had such equipment and skills? Jerry Boyle might know someone, but then he would be curious and exact a fee for the connection. It was the safer way but would take an eternity. Did she have that much time? Not if there was a traitor among them.

The fastest and simplest method was to commandeer a copy machine. It was also the most dangerous. Using a copy machine to disseminate religious concepts earned a twenty-year prison sentence, and for a good reason. Prior to and during the first part of the Second Civil War, warring factions used social media to rally their sympathizers and troops. The federal government shut down the internet, then jammed broadcast television and radio all the way to the old citizen band frequencies to disrupt communication. Left with nothing else to spread their messages, copy machines became as critical as rifles, toner and paper more valuable than bullets.

Since the war ended, internet, television, and radio had been restored under a carefully regulated system monitored by Common Faith officials and artificial intelligence. Copy machines required three permits: one to own, another to operate, and a third to purchase supplies. Paper was expensive, but toner cost a fortune. It was produced under government license and had supervised distribution the same way as the national currency.

Twenty years in prison wasn't Claire's greatest concern. Her worst fear was losing the manuscript to Selman or one of his people, including Zoe. It was safe for the time being but did no good hidden away.

The copy machine in Selman's office—now that was a fun thought. Every local Common Faith Center was given one as part of its standard equipment. Claire guessed it required a passcode, not to mention an opportunity when the building was completely empty.

The other possibility sat in Alvin Filner's office at Girard Number Six. Less security made it tempting. Unlike the miners, the office worked a single shift. The rest of the time, it was vacant except for an old guard, Herb Gunther. Judging by his sad posture, she guessed he slept in a chair most of the night. His ancient ears and eyes presented no danger compared to Randy Bartok.

Claire felt a rush of excitement at being part of something incredible. It was vain to compare herself to any of the church founders, but she wondered if this was how Timothy felt when he traveled with Paul. She vowed to live that way, a reliable companion to Father Carroll, one committed to helping him through the trouble ahead, dedicated to the new beginning his message brought.

Such were her thoughts as she arrived home. Buoyed by confidence in a difficult but workable solution, she entered via the side door to the kitchen where she found Zoe opening a package.

"Hey, Mom," Zoe greeted her. "Missed you at breakfast."

"Sorry," Claire said, pleased that her daughter sounded sincerely unantagonistic for the first time since she got to Mount Carmel. "Went to see some ladies I know."

"Yeah, who?"

"People you wouldn't remember."

"Too bad," Zoe said, peeling the paper away from a sturdy plastic box embossed with the Common Faith's Circle and Line. "Been thinking about my high school friends."

"That's great. I'm sure a few live in town or nearby. Why not visit them before you go back to Philly?"

"I did, but they weren't home," Zoe confirmed as she opened the box, revealing a brand-new nine-millimeter automatic with three spare magazines already loaded. Once again, Headquarters had supported her with the Bounty of Faith.

• • •

The bus driver and guard pulled away from the Pleasant Corner with just enough time to make Pottsville before dark. They each drank six jars of vile grog, which provided in effect what it lacked in taste. Their entertainment was limited to drinking due to the absence of suitable female company. Last time they scored a couple of miners' widows eager for a possible one-way trip out of town. Stories of promises made and broken might have been spread by that pair. The disappointment was tempered by other options down the road. Their schedule called for an overnight in a bunkroom at Pottsville where new convicts awaited transport to Graterford. What they missed today, they would have tomorrow on the final leg, during which additional stops for bonus cargo and a fun snuggle awaited.

Relaxed and half asleep, the guard rode in the front seat with his feet propped across the aisle. It was only nineteen miles to Pottsville, but on climbing, winding roads that limited their speed. He paid no attention to the scenery of endless trees.

"Check this out," the driver said, letting off the throttle.

"What?" the guard said, not bothering to open his eyes.

"Looks like a kid."

Annoyed, the guard sat up, peered through the window, and saw a girl standing in the middle of the road waving her arms. "Give her the horn," he said.

The driver blasted the horn three long times as the bus lost speed. "She's not moving."

"Go around."

The driver downshifted and eased the bus into the oncoming lane. The girl stepped toward his path. He jammed the breaks then swerved right, waiting for the thump of impact.

"Must have missed her," the guard said, turning to the side window. From the corner of his eye he saw a woman sitting in the fourth seat. She was pointing a gun at his face.

"Damn lucky you did," Jagger said.

She had spent the whole day waiting for them, revising her plan on the fly. After the confab with Philly Chick Zoe Whelan, she lolled about town, checking in with Crush and Whip. Then she lingered near the Pleasant Corner before slipping aboard the bus and tucking herself under a seat.

At the sound of a strange voice, the driver glanced in the mirror, saw his partner at gunpoint, and said, "They'll come looking if we're late to Pottsville."

"Going to be right on time," Jagger assured him. "Pull over!"

"Kiss my ass!" The driver accelerated into the next turn. "Take care of her, would you?" he told his partner.

The guard made the mistake of chuckling at Jagger, saying, "Stupid bitch. Give me that before you hurt yourself."

"Okay," Jagger agreed, moving forward. She twirled the gun, took it by the barrel, and extended it to the guard. When he hesitated, she asked, "What's the matter?"

"Don't play games," he snarled.

"Just following orders. Was hoping for a date with you fine gentlemen."

He shifted on the seat, reaching out with one hand while putting the other on his own holstered weapon.

Jagger gave him her best "I'm sorry" blink, waiting until his fingers were an inch away, then she leaned into a right cross that caught the left side of his face. Had it been a bare fist that landed, the punch might have merely angered the guard. But the weight and edge of her brass knuckles crushed his cheekbone. Jagger followed up with two more strikes, one of which broke his nose. He was down for the count, slumped on the floor, losing consciousness.

She pocketed the brass knuckles then ripped the guard's gun from its holster, giving him a stomp on the shin for good measure. Now with pistols in both hands, she loomed over the driver.

"Hammer down," she whispered, pressing the barrels into the side of his neck. "Let's go off the cliff together."

The driver brought the bus to a smooth stop on Merriam Street, which was nothing more than an unfinished lane near the highway into a grid of asphalt streets that might have become a town but never did because of the war.

"What do you want?" asked the driver.

"Shut up and open the door," Jagger ordered.

The driver obeyed, swinging the lever to release the doors.

"Drag him out," she said.

The driver struggled with his dazed partner. It took several tries to maneuver him down the three steps. Outside, the driver's foot slipped in the loose gravel. He fell to the ground, the guard landing atop his legs.

Whip and Crush ran in from the highway.

"Take this," Jagger said, handing the guard's weapon to Crush.

"Going to be a hundred state troopers picking through these woods," the driver said as Whip disarmed him. "Only chance you'll get is if I put in a good word for you."

"Yeah? How's that go?"

"I'll say it was someone else. They got the jump on us, but we fought them off and managed to escape."

"Who were these villains?" Jagger queried.

"The Jesus freaks. They're always making trouble."

"Jesus freaks ain't big on guns."

"Still a good story. Get my phone on the console. I'll make the call while you beat it out of here."

Jagger nodded to Whip, who retrieved the device.

The driver said, "This is all going to work out. You'll see."

"Where's the cargo?" demanded Jagger.

"Selman didn't have any."

"You made stops before you got here."

"Only drop-offs, no pickups."

Whip showed the phone to Jagger then put it in her pocket.

"Give me that! If I don't call in, they'll send a squad to find us," insisted the driver.

"On your feet," Jagger said. "Strip."

"Seriously?"

"Take his arms," she told Crush, slipping the fingers of her empty hand into the brass knuckles and displaying them for the driver.

"Alright. Alright."

As the driver disrobed, Runt scampered in from the highway.

"Help Whip search the bus," Jagger told the youngest Molly.

"What're we looking for?" asked Runt.

"She'll tell you what," snapped Jagger.

As Whip led Runt to the bus, the guard stirred on the ground. "What the hell's going on?" he muttered.

"The princess wants a free show," answered the driver.

"Damn right, I do. Help him out of his uniform," Jagger said.

"No."

A nod from Jagger prompted Crush to kick the guard's ribs. He rolled and howled in pain.

"Nasty bitch you are," said the driver.

"Get your pal out of that uniform or you'll feel worse."

Helping the guard remove his shirt, the driver explained, "They're tracking my phone. They'll see we stopped here and wonder what's going on."

"No one's tracking your phone or the bus."

"I swear!"

"They tracked your stops along the way from Philly, logged Selman's payoff at the Pads, then to the Pleasant Corner where you sucked grog all afternoon, trying to play grab ass with a few hags who ain't heard your lies. Is that what you're telling me?"

"We look out for our own is what I'm saying," he answered, tugging off his partner's boots.

"And sure as hell not for anyone else," returned Jagger. She didn't say another word until the guard's pants were off, then she told the driver, "Help him up."

"Pack of mongrels is what you are," the driver said. "Skinny one, fat one, crazy one. Whose kid is that? Eh? One of you a breeder? Let me guess. Eeny, meeny, miny, HOE!"

"That the best you got?" Jagger asked.

"Not hardly," he continued. "The troopers are going to have a party after they hunt you down. One hundred percent guarantee they are. Everyone gets a turn, some more than one. Knowing old Selman, he'll take the little one. Likes them young, he does."

"Shut up and on your feet," Jagger said.

The driver stood then hurled a fist-sized rock at Jagger, hitting her in the chest. Startled, she stumbled back, giving him a split second to lunge for her legs. Down they went, landing with a thump.

The guard took his chance, too. He tossed a handful of gravel at Crush then scrambled toward her. She ducked the flying mess, righted herself, and leveled his own pistol at him. He froze in the crouching position.

"Stay back!"

"Or what?" he dared her, rising to his full height.

Crush glanced at Jagger and the driver wrestling on the ground.

The guard took a step toward her before stopping again when she pointed the barrel at his face.

In the long moment that passed next, the sound of grunting from Jagger and the driver as they struggled for control and her own heavy breathing was all Crush could hear. She locked eyes with the guard who risked a swat at the gun. She squeezed the trigger, but nothing happened. Momentarily confused, she stepped back.

The guard snorted through his bloody nose, released a wicked laugh, then said, "Pathetic and probably too stupid to know what the word means."

This time, he lurched forward to tackle Crush when the sound of her thumb flicking off the safety reached his ears. Next came the shot that killed him. He fell flat to the ground, the hole in his forehead leaking blood into the soil. A second, muffled shot followed from Jagger's gun, which had been pressed between her and the driver. She slid from under him, noting the gaping exit wound in his back.

CHAPTER 15.

From where Father Carroll walked in the woods, the first gunshot sounded like a distant whip-crack. It was the shorter, popping report of a handgun as opposed to the deeper boom of a rifle. The second was oddly less distinct, but unmistakable as to what it was. He waited in the fading dusk, listening for signs of anyone moving in his direction. As for who fired the shots, the list was short: Bartok, a trooper, or that rare person who dared to possess a firearm. That more didn't follow meant the target was hit or was gone. Silence gave him no relief, especially after Bartok's surprise at the Cathedral. There was a weapon out there in the hands of someone inclined to use it. Perhaps more than one.

He picked his way around thickets and under low branches, careful not to leave signs of his passing. An hour later, he emerged behind the high school. Under the awning of the service entrance, he rested, listening for anyone who might be tracking him. Hearing nothing, he started for the north side of town, with Claire Whelan's home his intended destination. He hoped to retrieve a package of food to last him several days. Claire was always generous, even when necessities were scarce.

Disappearing in a crowded city was much easier than a deserted town. Instead of one face in thousands, he was alone on an empty sidewalk. Thankfully, the troopers limited their patrols to random days, amounting to less than once per week. Randy Bartok, with the help of Lenny Donovan when needed, took care of the rest. Since all the old scores had been settled, there were no more cases of neighbor accusing neighbor for real or imagined transgressions. He was the only big catch, worth ten thousand dollars, according to rumors.

At the corner of Third and Hickory, he spotted a good reason to change direction. On the rusted mailbox outside the disused Post Office building, there was a chalk mark in shape of a fishing hook. It was one of the several symbols he worked out to communicate with his followers when he stopped attending regular services to write his testament. A halo was for someone gravely ill. A waterdrop indicated a baptism. Interlocking circles announced a pending marriage. The rudimentary system worked well. People made the appropriate mark for Father Carroll and other believers to see. Word passed among their tight-knit group rapidly enough for a timely response.

Tonight's fishhook meant a meeting was to be held. Father Carroll guessed the subject was his testament and what ultimately happened at the Cathedral, the details of which hadn't yet reached him. He was eager to know if they had all escaped, not to mention the reaction to what they'd seen.

At the risk of drawing attention, he broke into a steady jog. The meeting began in less than an hour. Fifteen minutes before the start time, a lookout would be posted. He rushed to beat that person's arrival. A dog barked from the back yard of a house near Apple Street. He diverted to Fourth, continuing east, crossing Market where the only streetlights in town lit his progress.

The next eight blocks, all the way to Almond Street, were comfortably dark. He caught his breath before walking toward a brick building that had been a sewing mill then a machine shop and finally a warehouse. Now it was vacant. As if he was bound anywhere else, he passed the entrance on Almond, glimpsed the door on the north side, and continued around the block.

The second time around, he heard a giggle followed by a quick, "Shhh." Carroll dropped to a crouch. Footfalls and clothing rustled behind a shed in the next yard to his left. He took cover at the base of a wooden fence, from which he recognized the whispers of Candy Walsh and Kyle Smith.

"My dad's dead," Kyle said.

"Oh, my God!" Candy hissed. "What happened?"

"He was lookout for a meeting at the Cathedral. Somebody tipped Bartok."

This was the first Father Carroll heard what had happened to Murray Smith. Of all the revelations given for his testament, this had not been one. It left him wondering why, and concerned for the others. He'd done his best to guide them through the current era of hardship. To their credit, they were sincere, devoted followers. Since he began his testament, however, he left them mostly without counsel. Perhaps he should have divided his time differently.

If there was a traitor among them, there was a chance he could be recaptured. He resolved to eavesdrop on the meeting instead of speaking to them directly. Depending on their sentiment, he might be safer returning to the forest without a word.

At the moment, he caught snippets of Candy and Kyle, who weren't ten yards away.

"We have to get out of here. I'm going to apply for a transfer," Candy offered.

"Not until I get Bartok."

"He'll get his in hell," said Candy.

"Which is where I'm going to send him."

"It's too dangerous. We have a baby on the way."

Another secret revealed: Kyle Smith was the father of Candy's child, not Lenny Donovan. Good for you, Father Carroll thought. Kyle was better husband material. That is, if he avoided a tangle with Randy Bartok over the death of his father.

"Come on," Kyle said. "We'll be late for the meeting."

"Plenty of time. Kiss me."

Father Carroll left them for the door to the meeting hall. The fishhook was on the bricks to the right of the handle. He knew the members would meet in the basement, which had separate fire exits to Almond Street and the empty lot to the north. In the event of a raid, they would split up and use these options to flee. Guided by a tiny flashlight, he took the stairs to the second floor. Like a stowaway aboard a ship, he hid himself behind stacks of wooden pallets. He switched off his light and waited for the lookout to arrive.

"Thieves and vandals beware! The night watchman is here!"

Carroll recognized the voice of Brad Sawyer, who had been an altar boy at Holy Redeemer before the Common Faith took over. Now Brad was in his late thirties and worked at Number Six's coal processing plant.

"Come out, come out, wherever you are!"

The idea behind being loud was that anyone, including the authorities, would mistake them for someone who belonged there as opposed to someone engaged in the illicit activity of Christian worship. The method worked, too, because last year a lookout ran into a plumber fixing a leak. In that case, he lent the guy a hand doing the job and prevented certain capture and future suspicion.

Sawyer plodded up the stairs, scanned the area with a bright light, and shouted, "I can see you!"

Lying on the floor, Carroll would have grinned at the pretense had he not been mourning Murray's death.

Seeing nothing, Sawyer said, "Until next time," and went downstairs to take his post at the entrance.

Soon after, in ones and twos, Mount Carmel's few remaining Christians entered the building. It pained Carroll to recall the boisterous greetings before and after his church services—plans for Sunday dinners, family outings, and a good game on TV. Now they were reduced to silent gestures. In his mind, he saw them making the sign of the cross, first to Brad Sawyer, then to each other before descending the stairs to the basement. He eased out of his hiding spot and padded down the stairs to ground level where he was able to hear the proceedings.

Joe Grant said, "Amen," bringing the meeting to order.

"Yesterday my father was killed!" Kyle blurted.

This news caused all to break the rules as loud whispers rose up from the group.

"Shhhhh."

"Please, quiet."

"What're we going to do about it?" demanded Kyle.

"First, tell us what happened."

"Claire called for a meeting at the Cathedral," Grant explained. "Father Carroll was there. He showed us something he'd written."

An indiscernible voice interrupted.

"No, we didn't read it. We were told that it was his testament. A message from God Himself."

A ripple of murmurs spread through the group.

"There was a moment of truth so to speak. Or not. It's hard to say. Father Carroll dropped his papers into a fire, and they did not burn. Claire put her hand in to take it out, and she was not harmed, either."

More whispers until another harsh, "Shhhh."

"We're all believers. We trust in God. But I have my doubts about this and for good reason. Only us and Father Carroll knew the time and place of the meeting. Unfortunately, Randy Bartok showed up at the Cathedral, too. How did he know we were going to be there? The answer is critical, because Murray Smith gave his life for us."

Pure silence.

"Where's Claire?" someone asked.

"I don't know, and I'm sad she is not here to explain her side. Let me give you mine. Father Carroll was in Selman's custody. That means torture and deprivation. I fear he's been compromised. His testament, as he's calling it, is surely sincere, but a revelation from God? Who knows? Maybe he wrote it to buy his way out of Selman's dungeon and lure us into the open. Or, one of us is a Judas Iscariot. Strong words, I know, but what else explains it?"

A jumble of voices, then, "What if Father Carroll has brought us a message from God?"

Followed by, "If we chase him away, aren't we deniers?"

And, "I want to see it."

"Me, too."

"We know what the Bible says about false prophets."

"Doesn't mean Father Carroll is a liar. Maybe it's real."

"Shhhh."

"Claire has it," Grant said.

"Let's find her."

"I saw her this morning."

"Where?"

"Who cares? She's not here now when we need her. She could be the—"

"Shhhh."

"Claire is one of us," Grant told them. "Never forget she brought us together when Selman purged the churches."

"So you're saying it's Father Carroll."

"I'm saying, until he shows himself to explain," Grant replied, "we're all in danger."

"If it's real, he wouldn't hide from us."

"Unless someone else is the rat."

"Like who?"

"Please! Let's not argue about things we haven't seen or can't prove," Grant pleaded. "We must stay united. For the time being, we worship in private. No gatherings. As your humble servants, myself, Bill Myer, and Pam Reed will investigate. When this is sorted out, we'll celebrate. Anyone opposed?"

Silence.

"It is agreed. Amen."

"Amen."

"Doesn't anyone care about my father?" Kyle asked. "Anyone?"

Father Carroll felt the strain in Kyle's voice, the hopeless frustration.

"We'll help you bury him," someone said.

"I'll do it myself!" shouted Kyle. "You're all cowards!"

Gasps preceded the thumps of Kyle's feet on the stairs.

Father Carroll retreated to the second floor where he again took cover. He understood their paranoia. He accepted their reasonable doubts. In this age, skepticism was a reliable survival tactic. For everyone, himself included, the test was coming. No more secret signs on the street. No more hiding in basements. And there would be justice for Murray Smith.

• • •

The tunnel itself was a test shaft, dug a long time ago to assess the quantity of coal in the mountain. Abandoned by the prospectors who found worthless slate instead of anthracite, it grew moss ever since. The Mollies camped here once in a while, especially when the troopers were on the prowl, tossing everyone's place in search of contraband and guns, or when Joannie T was out of town. It was tricky driving up the overgrown road, but Jagger managed, which was impressive in the dark. Crush and Whip finished stashing the bus inside by pushing over a few smaller trees to obscure the entrance. They made it look natural, as if they'd fallen in a storm. The camouflage was just enough to avoid close scrutiny. Pending rain would make the tire tracks seem old, that and Runt's dancing. Her little feet trampled the clearest of them.

It was an hour walk to their trailer, and Whip lagged behind. Not because she was out of shape, either. Or afraid of the dark. She was the fastest of them. Her cat's eyes missed nothing. Crush knew the reason. She didn't want to deal with it. Personnel matters were for the boss.

"Better have a talk with Whip," Crush said. "I'll keep an eye on Runt."

Contemplating how to handle the issue, Jagger adjusted her pace, letting Crush and Runt stretch out ahead. She expected

Whip to play the cry baby. She was the sensitive one, and events did take a dramatic turn when the driver and guard resisted.

Jagger broke the ice with, "Can't wait for them pork chops Jerry's got for us, eh?"

Whip pounded along the trail.

"Don't it make you hungry just thinking about them?"

"Crush shot that guy in the face," Whip said incongruously. "I saw him dead on the ground."

"Beat me to the punch," replied Jagger.

The guard died instantly. The driver bled out nearby. After hearing the shots, Whip ran from the bus, saw the bodies, and bolted back to intercept Runt before she witnessed the death scene. There she remained until Crush and Jagger emerged from the woods having left the carcasses as a feast to be found by scavenging animals. They gathered the uniforms into a bundle, including the boots which were almost more valuable than the guns.

"The bus was empty, too," continued Whip. "It's going to be the end of us."

"How do you figure?"

"Like the driver said, the troopers are going to come looking."

"Even if they find the bus and whatever's left of them two, what're they going to think? Huh?"

Whip didn't answer.

"They're going to think it was a double cross by one of the scumbags they hustled on the side for stolen cargo. Bet it happens all the time."

As much sense as that made, Whip remained unconvinced. "They'll station troopers to keep an eye on things," Whip said. "We'll be trapped. And that pile of deer jerky ain't going to last the winter."

"Pork chops on the way," Jagger quipped.

Whip poured on the speed, but Jagger was no slug. At the next rise, she hauled her underling to a stop with a firm hand on the shoulder.

"What're you afraid of?" Jagger asked.

"Not knowing what the hell's going on," Whip retorted. "Why steal a prison bus? Why kill those guys?"

"Because when the time comes, that bus is a free ride out of here."

"When the times comes? And to where? The next checkpoint?"

"To be determined."

"You're so full of shit!"

Jagger understood the need to vent. She also welcomed the opportunity to take disciplinary action. To that end, she tackled Whip in a patch of leaves and pinned her face down.

"Couple days ago you were complaining about being hungry. Now your belly's full, and the larder's stocked to the gills. Last year it was no shoes. Who got the first decent pair? You. How many wishes got to come true before you quit being a pain in the ass?"

Whip stopped struggling.

"And ponder this between your scrawny ears. The worst possible scenario. Randy Bartok or the big bad troopers catch one of us. Drags you, or Crush, or even me, off to the dungeon, maybe down to Pottsville and shoves a live wire up your ass until your lips are flapping a hundred miles an hour. What're they going to hear?"

On her life, Whip had no idea.

"That's right. Nothing. Because you or Crush don't know nothing. Hell, I haven't the faintest clue where the wind's gonna push our sails. Spontaneity's a good thing. No way to rat each other out if you don't know."

"I'd never tell them shit."

"Never's forever when they got their hands on you, dear, or did you forget Bartok gave me the honeymoon suite for a week and that wasn't the first time."

"And now you're dealing with him."

"Damn right I am," Jagger took out Zoe's borrowed pistol and pressed it on the ground next to Whip's face. "And he has to deal with me. Don't he?"

The gun gleamed in the starlight.

"Any dancing or romancing will be at the sole discretion of those so inclined, who reserve the right to say, 'No,' should they not be in the mood or have a lesser reason."

Whip recognized the weapon's power was undeniable.

"All of them, Bartok, the troopers, even that sack of filth Selman, are counting on a silly girl who can't pull the trigger. Surprise them."

The driver's gun she'd taken a few hours earlier weighed heavy in Whip's jacket as Jagger leaned close to whisper her final advice.

"Just be damn sure to save a bullet. That way, if the moment goes sour and there's no way out, the final decision's yours."

CHAPTER 16.

The next morning, Mike Whelan and his gang donned their gear like knights preparing for battle. Thick coveralls and heavy boots. Helmets and gloves. The clanking of tools and lunch boxes. Groans of aches and pains from unhealed injuries, old age, and a bad night's sleep. Like combat, Girard Number Six did its share of killing. Collapse, methane, electrocution, and drowning were most often the causes. Distraction was another, because a miner who lost focus was likely to lose his life or cost the lives of his fellows.

Such were Mike's thoughts when he saw the convicts standing at the end of the locker room with Superintendent Filner.

"Since your team is short several men," Filner said to him, "give a warm welcome to Graterford graduates Otto Weber and Sara Darcy."

Two of the most unlikely miners stared at Mike, the overalls too tight on Weber's gigantic frame and too big on Darcy's much smaller one. The last thing he wanted was a pair of felons down the hole when already his men were on edge about Rat's prediction of a collapse. However, he didn't argue. Their presence would neither hold up the ceiling nor bring it down. And if it fell on them, it would fall on everyone.

"Today it won't be me," he said to himself as he led them and his crew to the lift, pulled the gate closed, and rang the bell for the operator to send them down.

The men eyed Sara Darcy, novelty that she was, and the bruises on her face. They also sized up Weber. Each of them sensed trouble at hand. The recently paroled never lasted more than a year, due to injury, death (usually suicide but sometimes by accident), or escape. The convicts were often found starved or frozen along the highway, the winter being a better natural boundary than any fence. Randy Bartok found a gnawed skeleton once. A mountain lion or a wolf got that guy.

The men's instincts led them to avoid the criminals. Today, a few contemplated a pass at Darcy, but thought better of it, and not because they feared Weber. Tough as he was, they were no box of tulips to be plucked, nor a punching bag like Darcy. No, this group of miners shielded their good luck from all manner of dilution, and nothing wiped out nature's providence like a couple of people recently out of prison. History proved the fact.

At the bottom, the gang ending its shift immediately noticed Sara Darcy exiting the lift.

"Mike finally got a date," someone said.

"What's she wearing under there?"

"Yeah, give us a peek, sweetie!"

There were whistles and shouts until foreman George Nash punched one of his guys in the mouth for delaying the ride up.

Mike's men moved fast, following the long conveyor that led into the tunnel ahead. Mike walked at his regular pace, with Weber at his side and Darcy a step behind.

"Where the hell are the lights?" Weber asked.

"Only the face is lit," Mike answered. "See the reflectors on the side? Follow them in and out."

They splashed through shallow puddles and over lumps of rock deeper into the tunnel. The reflectors beckoned like buoys in a river.

"This is the extraction conveyor," Mike explained. "It leads back to the discharge unit that takes the coal to the surface. We're headed the other way, to the face where we cut the coal out of the earth."

"Looks like coal all around," Weber said.

"This is a room-and-pillar mine," Mike told him. "Think of it like a checkerboard. We took the coal out of the red spaces and left the black ones to hold up the roof."

Weber nervously looked up, the light on his helmet revealing steel mesh bolted into the rock above.

"That'll hold as long as we leave the pillars in."

They came to a low-slung, four-wheeled machine resembling a giant wheelbarrow.

"This is a shuttle car. It carries the coal from the mining machine at the face to the extraction conveyor."

"I can drive anything," Weber said.

"Tony drives that one."

At last they stopped at another machine. It squatted over tracks with a cutting wheel spanning hydraulic arms at the front. Below was what appeared to be an enormous shovel where two more hydraulic arms raked in coal falling from the cutting wheel, shoving it into a steel gullet from which a short conveyor carried it to the rear of the unit. Back there, Tony parked the shuttle car for loading. Several pairs of these machines worked removing coal from Girard Number Six.

"What a beast," Weber commented.

"It's called a continuous miner. It does most of the work down here. The cutting head chews into the coal."

A cable-tethered remote-control box, about the size of a small laptop, allowed an operator to stand several yards away from the machine while it was in operation. The box featured joysticks, one that raised and lowered the cutting head and another that walked it in any direction. Buttons activated the cutting head, the arms raking coal into the gullet and the discharge conveyor.

Sheldon Hunter appeared from the far side of the machine. Having completed his safety checks, he took the remote-control from the track, slinging its strap over his shoulders. His thumb nudged a joystick and the machine forward. A press of a button and the cutter head began to rotate. He gave Mike a wary wave and turned toward the coal face.

"It's about to get loud," Mike said. "Let's go." He ushered Weber and Darcy back through the tunnel to a crosscut that led to another face with the same set of equipment. Rat Durkin was about to start work.

"Thanks for the show and tell," Weber remarked. "The woman and I are headed back to the elevator."

"I'm staying to do my job," Darcy said. "Whatever it is."

Her statement caught both Mike and Weber off guard. A second later, Weber yanked Darcy's arm as he turned for the lift. She stomped her boot into his calf and twisted free with a satisfied grin that he was down on one knee and howling curses. He pounded after her, his longer stride quickly putting him in striking distance. Darcy tripped over a rock, landing flat on her belly in a deep puddle.

Weber pulled up short, cackling at her misfortune. Then he fell flat on his face. The convict would find out later that Mike hit him with a hammer handle. It was a glancing blow to the back of his thick skull, the right place to knock a man out cold. Mike had done it before, when Rich Donnelly lost his nerve and wouldn't settle down until the shift ended.

At present, Sara Darcy crawled out of the puddle. Seeing Weber fall was satisfying, albeit at an undetermined cost to be paid in the future.

"Help me tie him up," Mike said to Rat. "We have a quota to make."

• • •

"Oh my God! It's really you!" Candace Walsh said. "Sorry, not supposed to say that. Old habits, you know."

"How are you, Candy?" Zoe replied.

"Okay. Teaching. It's something I always wanted to do."

They stood in the hallway outside her third-grade classroom.

A banner hung over the door. "PA's TOP TEACHER," it read. Another sign announced, "Best Students in the County!"

Zoe purposely met her classmate at the school for two reasons. First, it was inside Candy's comfort zone. Second, the location gave her leverage. Candy wasn't going to make a scene in front of her supervisor or the children.

"Hey, do me a favor," Candy said. "Come in and meet the kids. They'll love it."

"Sure," Zoe agreed.

In the room, it felt like Zoe went back in time. Thirty youngsters sat at scaled-down tables, sharing one book between five of them. There was an actual chalkboard on the wall instead of a digital screen. In fact, she saw none of the technology found in Philadelphia classrooms, not a single computer or tablet. Maybe it was a social experiment, a technique to teach sharing and fairness.

"This is an old friend of mine," Candy announced. "We went to school together just like you. Meet Zoe Whelan."

"Hello, Ms. Whelan," the children replied in unison.

"Hi, there," Zoe said, feeling too tall and suddenly shy.

"Are you a cop?" a boy in the front row asked.

"Uh, yes. How did you know?"

"I can see your gun," he said, pointing to her hip.

The door opened and Principal Wachowski entered.

"Alright everyone, let's settle down. While I catch up with my friend, Mr. Wachowski will help you with lesson eight."

"See you later," Zoe said to the room.

"Bang bang," the boy in the front mouthed at her, displaying finger pistols.

On the way to the break room Candy apologized. "Darn kids don't miss a thing," she said.

"No worries."

"I heard about what happened in Philly," Candy rambled on. "Close call, eh?"

"It was."

"I told Lenny it's safer working in Number Six than with the Compliance Division."

"You mean Lenny Donovan?"

"Yeah, he's a guard at the prison in Pottsville most days. Other days, he helps Randy Bartok around town. Lenny and I have a unity pact. Jeez. Sounds weird to say that. Like being married was, is, whatever. Common Faith lingo we're supposed to use. But listen, it's just for the benefits. He gets more out of it than me. That's life, right? Nothing's fair. And with one on the way, have to get ready."

"You're pregnant?" Zoe asked as if she didn't know.

Candy nodded an exuberant yes.

"Congratulations."

"Oh, thanks. Hope it's a girl. Always wanted a girl."

Zoe couldn't imagine having a child, not with how things were in the country.

"Everyone always said you'd be a winner. I guess they were right," Candy said.

Entering the break room, they met Kyle Smith in his janitor's coveralls, mopping the floor. Candy pretended not to know him, and he followed her lead.

"I'll finish in here later," he said.

"Thanks," Candy said.

When he was gone, Zoe placed her bag on a round table and took a seat opposite her old friend. The setting brought to mind a favorite instructor at the Common Faith Academy. He taught advanced interrogation techniques. During the first lesson, he noted how any number of factors stood between the person asking the questions and the person answering them. A professional, he warned, must never lose sight of the goal, which is to get information. The key was recognizing the interceding factors and overcoming them. They included one's sympathies, prejudices, fears, and delusions.

Looking up from her bag, Zoe realized she was about to manipulate a person who once trusted her with the kind of pre-teen secrets that today would make her blush. Furthermore, she understood Candy herself was not a major threat to the Common Faith. At worst, she was a misguided dabbler in forbidden things. None of this negated the circumstances that placed her on the trail to John Carroll and perhaps others who were dangerous, who created social turmoil that lit the fire of civil unrest. It was Zoe's job to stop those people, thereby ensuring a lasting peace. If that meant giving a childhood companion a rough time, so be it.

"I was at your house yesterday," Zoe began.

Like one of her pupils who was about to be scolded, Candy sat up straight. "You were? Denise didn't say anything."

"In the afternoon. I spoke with her and met Ian. He's very creative."

"Oh, for sure. He likes to draw. Helps with his, uh, seizures."

"I found this in your room," Zoe said as she removed a Bible from her bag, placing it on the table.

"You searched my room?" protested Candy. "What the hell?"

"Doing my job. Lucky for you it was me and not someone else who might not be as understanding. What're you doing with a Bible?"

"That's... that's... not mine. That was my mom's, you know, from way back when."

"It was in your room," Zoe repeated, adding, "along with these." She took out several sheets of Ian's drawings. They were studies of the figures and scene she found on the second-floor wall: Jesus on the cross; a woman holding a scroll, her face strangely absent.

"He's a kid, Zoe. He has an imagination."

"Naturally. You have to know possession of a Bible is against the law. Influencing a child with religious propaganda is, too. A serious offense."

Candy sat perfectly still.

"I've been told you intend to have your baby baptized by Father Carroll."

"People lie about each other around here. Always did; always will."

"But if you tell me the truth," Zoe said, "there's nothing to worry about."

• • •

Mike's plan was to rob out the pillars of coal holding up the roof in the deepest part of the mine. It was the only way to meet the quota. As they backed out, his gang would remove supports in a logical pattern, thus deliberately allowing the rock overhead to collapse in a controlled manner. What didn't fall, they would blast.

Mother Nature intervened.

Having completed a pillar, Rat crawled his continuous mining machine toward the next one. Sara Darcy used all her strength to drag the heavy power supply cable out of his way. It was supposed to be on a reel but that was broken. Fellow convict Otto Weber was unavailable to help because he was sitting a hundred feet away with bound hands and feet.

Rat guided his machine to the next starting point, then shut everything off. He stared at the shiny black coal, listening for the faint sounds of shifting earth. Sara approached him, only to be stopped by Mike.

Very deliberately, Rat ducked out of the remote box's sling, set it on the track of his machine, and retreated from the coal. Step by step, he placed his feet carefully, eyes never leaving the same spot. He was ten feet away when bell dropped out of the roof, crashing to the floor on his right. It was called a bell because the shape of the falling rock was roughly the same. Some geologists speculated they were the ossified remnants of ancient tree stumps. In any case, had that been all that fell, it would have been another fortunate day. But there was more to come, and Rat knew it.

He turned and ran, joining Mike and Sara already rushing

for safety. A hissing crack followed by a horrible roar chased after them. Massive chunks of rock dropped into the chamber, sending a plume of dust in every direction.

Rat and Sara didn't slow as they passed Weber, who shouted, "Don't leave me here!"

Mike drew a folding knife from his belt and cut the rope binding Weber's hands and feet. Glancing back down the tunnel, he saw the giant apparatus of the continuous miner disappear under the falling debris. On the move again, dust obscured his view. He lost track of Weber and the others.

At the next crosscut, Mike stopped running. He dropped to his knees, fumbling with the canister on his belt that held an emergency respirator mask. His first thought was to find Rat and Sara. They were ahead of him and should be okay. However, the dust thickened around him like swirling ink. His helmet light hardly reached his feet.

"Rat!" he hollered, before donning the mask that covered his mouth.

No response didn't mean bad news. Mike took it as a good sign that his friend and Sara, and even that thug Weber, were in the clear. Still in the thick of the dust, he ventured a few feet down the tunnel, drawing deep breaths of filtered air. He spotted a reflector that assured him he was going the right way. No need for a rescue party, he thought; I'm walking out.

At the next reflector, he was struck by a solid blow to the side of his helmet. It was powerful enough to knock him down. Landing on his side, he was nearly overcome with fear that the collapse was running like a zipper along the tunnel. He saw a light flick on, one atop Weber's head, and realized he'd been punched by the convict.

Weber hurled a melon-sized rock at Mike, who rolled to avoid it. Angry at having missed, Weber leapt atop him, fists aiming for his face.

Mike's helmet twisted askew, its light now pointing uselessly to the side. Weber's next hit struck Mike's cheek, knocking his respirator off. The one that followed caught his gut. Mike wedged his foot into the convict's crotch and shoved him off.

"You'll never find your way out," Mike said as they squared off.

"Take my chances," Weber replied. "Soon as I'm done with you."

Mike anticipated the roundhouse, ducked under it, then drove a hard right into Weber's midsection. The convict staggered before throwing several wild punches that forced Mike to cover and dodge. Next came a kick that knocked the wind out of him. His strength faded as he dropped to the ground, coughing in the dust-filled air. Weber aimed carefully, hitting him just below the right eye.

Flat on his back, on the verge of passing out, Mike felt Weber tugging at his belt. He saw his own knife in Weber's hand, watched him open it, heard his comment.

"Nice blade."

Weber flipped it expertly into the hammer-grip position.

Mike found the situation almost comical, that within minutes he would survive a catastrophic collapse only to be murdered by a criminal whose life he just saved.

Weber raised his arm in preparation for the death blow. But something whooshed through the dusty air and whacked his helmet. He tumbled away from Mike, landing on his back. There was a second slash, followed by an almost simultaneous crunching of cartilage and a hearty grunt.

Mike adjusted his helmet, directing the light toward Weber. In the haze, he saw Sara Darcy crouched over him. She'd driven a slab of rock into Weber's throat.

She looked over her shoulder and said, "We're even."

• • •

Was news of a calamity at Number Six ever good? No, Claire told herself. It was always a tragedy. The collapse this afternoon claimed a man's life. That he'd been a criminal mattered little to her. She prayed for him, asked God to forgive his worldly sin. She was also grateful for those who lived. Mike, his men, and the other convict, the woman, survived with minor injuries. For this and all her blessings, Claire thanked God. She quietly included the opportunity to use the copy machine at the mine office. To-morrow was the day.

Criminal or not, any miner's funeral was a big deal in Mount Carmel. Selman passed out the treats afterward, an extra Bounty of Faith box, and the death benefit to the deceased's next of kin. If for no other reason, people came to the service for the goodies. Claire didn't blame them. Most traded the contents to Jerry Boyle for something they needed. More important, Alvin Filner and the office staff attended, leaving behind Herb Gunther to sleep unmo-lested. It was the perfect time to commandeer the copy machine.

"I could use that cloth," Mike said from his seat at the kitchen table.

Claire refocused her attention on him. "Sure you don't want to go to the clinic?"

He raised an eyebrow.

"I know, I know, but what if something's broken?"

Zoe came through the back door, startled at the sight of her bruised and cut brother. "What happened to you?" she asked.

"There was a collapse at the mine," Claire snapped. "A man was killed."

Zoe flushed with embarrassment. If she'd seen one of her col-leagues in a similar state, she would have assumed it happened on the job. What did she think her brother was up to, a brawl at the Pleasant Corner?

"Sorry. I hope you're okay," Zoe said. "Anything I can do to help?"

"Tell the big shots in Philadelphia how unsafe it is supplying them with coal," Claire said, using a freshly rinsed cloth to clean a nasty scrape on Mike's shoulder.

"The coal isn't for Philadelphia, Mom. It's for the whole country." Zoe accepted that her mother would never understand the intricacies of putting a nation back together after a civil war, that a debt had to be paid by whatever means necessary to restore international credibility. The Chinese loaned the U.S. the money and it was paid back, in part, by coal, oil, and natural gas.

"Then make a trip to Washington. Tell them."

"What about the guy who died?" Zoe asked. "Did you know him?"

"No. Was his first day on the job."

"Terrible. I feel bad for his family."

Mike laughed and took the cloth from Claire.

"Did I miss something?" Zoe queried.

Getting up from the table with obvious pain, Mike shook his head.

When he was out of the room, Claire said, "I'd appreciate it if you would go to the clinic. We could use some ointment and bandages. They might give them to you."

"Medical supplies are part of the Bounty of Faith," Zoe said. "They have to give them to anyone in need."

"Oh, right."

As Zoe pulled the door closed, Claire noticed her daughter wore old sneakers. She found it odd, given the clothes sent from Philadelphia included a pair of fine leather boots. She thought perhaps Zoe didn't want to show off such an extravagance. But if she had found the sneakers in the basement, she might have rummaged through other things.

In a mild panic, Claire raced down the stairs, going to shelves of family albums and boxes of memorabilia. Scanning the shelves, she stopped where the dust on some books had been disturbed. They were yearbooks from Claire's time in high school. Her senior year was in the wrong place. It was first instead of fourth.

Why would Zoe have been interested in it?

Claire paged through, fondly recalling the silliness of being eighteen. Seeing herself nearly fifty years younger was almost too much. She flipped to a page for the class play. She stood next to Patrick, that gangly boy who could have gone to Broadway. He was in love with her, which was wonderful, but being an actor was no way to support a family. She let the tears come. It hurt less to cry than to fight the sadness. They were married a year after graduation.

Claire wiped her cheeks, put the yearbook where Zoe had left it, and went down the shelf to the family photo albums. They were much thinner than the ones belonging to her own parents, which were made when photography was done on paper exclusively. Digital images, kept on people's phones or on their computers, rendered printed images obsolete. Still, Claire preferred the albums. Digital images were subject to automatic scanning by facial recognition software that constantly surfed the internet. She preferred to remain hidden from that type of attention.

Flipping the pages, Claire found blank spots. The bride and groom photo with Father Carroll. One of him at the wedding reception. Another with him and Patrick visiting the mine. Zoe's baptism. Father Carroll praying at the mine while families waited for news of those missing in the explosion that mortally wounded Patrick. Incriminating evidence, it was now called. Zoe had taken them all, protecting herself should she ever be the subject of scrutiny by the Compliance Division. So be it, Claire decided, putting the albums back in their place.

Despondent as she was, Claire felt a measure of relief that other boxes remained undisturbed, especially the one full of old cookbooks. To it she went but hesitated to open the lid. She started to laugh. What did she expect? Golden rays of sunshine? Angels to fly out? She slid out a large binder, and found in the center where she once kept church recipes, the stack of neatly written pages that did not burn.

While she promised to wait for the others, the lines of potentially sacred words were too much to resist. Twice she turned her head, pinching her eyes shut, only to laugh again. If it's God's message for the world, then no harm will come.

But what if it's not? What if Father Carroll had gone insane under Selman's torture? What if he wrote meaningless lines on special paper as part of a trap?

She dared to peek.

"The chains of this world are of this world and have no power to bind us."

Upstairs, she heard feet on the floor. Not the solid gait of Mike, but Zoe's lighter tread. She closed the binder, stuffed it in with the others, and headed for the stairs.

CHAPTER 17.

Well-rested but sore the next morning, Mike left his room at the back of the house for the kitchen table. There he found a note from Claire. She was out to see her old friend Lena. Mike also had plans to do some visiting, in his case with someone he recently met, Mount Carmel's newly minted widow. Eating alone gave him time to consider whether or not it was a good idea. He concluded it was.

Equipped with two shovels, Mike walked to the west side of town, beyond what had been the borough limit. He passed a few people he knew, all of whom mentioned his good luck to survive the collapse yesterday. Was he going to the convict's funeral? Did he hear anything about a bonus box from Selman? Yes and no were his answers. There was no comment regarding the shovels. He was glad for their lack of interest. One way or another, the gossip was bound to start within the hour.

He knocked on the door at Unit 14. The curtain fluttered at the window and a moment later, Sara Darcy opened the door.

"I told you we're even," she said.

"Hear me out," he replied.

They went to the new cemetery, the one Selman inaugurated when he took over the district. The Common Faith Circle and Line hung at the gate. Already rusty, it left a stain on the ground. In the patch of earth reserved for miners, Mike cut a neat rectangle in the dead grass. Then he dug the first shovelful of dirt.

One-on-one was never his strong suit. He preferred a group, as in giving simple orders to his men. There was a job to be done and a right way to do it. He led by example; most followed. Encouragement or discipline wrangled the recalcitrant. This morning was not like that, nor was it the same as an afternoon at the Pleasant Corner, where he sat in his regular seat surrounded by stories often told, nodding when appropriate and otherwise tending his own quiet thoughts.

Sara watched and listened until he was knee-deep in the hole. What he said made too much sense to deny or ignore. Liking it or not was another matter. She endured worse. She remembered much better.

"You can live in our house," Mike said. "Have your own room. Eat at the table. Chip in for the budget and do some chores to keep it honest and fair."

"Or stay on my own."

"If you want. I advise against it."

At that point she picked up the other shovel and took her turn.

"People will think we're a couple," continued Mike. "Doesn't mean we are or have to be."

"That's very accommodating."

"The men won't bother you unless that's the kind of attention you want, which is your choice, and I won't get in the way."

"Being under your roof limits my options, doesn't it?"

"It does."

Mike dug the last two feet. Not because it mattered but because he did things the way they were supposed to be done, he shaved the sides of the hole to a level floor at the bottom. When his time came, he hoped someone took as much care. Finally, he climbed out.

"We expected to finish this job?" Sara asked.

"Somebody has to," replied Mike.

"I'll make up my mind then," she told him. "See you at the service or whatever it's called."

He jammed the shovels into the pile of dirt for use later. There he left them, because no one stole shovels.

• • •

Claire had slipped out of the house just before dawn. In her purse, she carried a letter she wrote the night before.

"Dear Superintendent Filner," it began.

After three drafts she settled on the tone. Sincere, well-reasoned, honest. She limited the length to a single page with her signature on the bottom. She didn't expect any results from the effort, but if she was caught in the office it justified her presence. Or so she hoped.

In a canvas satchel, she toted the manuscript-containing cookbook with two others like it. Anyone making a cursory search of the bag might not deign to open them for closer inspection.

"Taking them to an old friend," she planned to answer when asked.

"Who?"

"My friend Lena. Don't tell her; it's a surprise."

She rehearsed the exchange aloud as she traversed the deserted streets.

How much had she walked the past year? Too much, and she was starting to notice. Her knees and right hip ached. Thankfully, she was fortified by a powerful sense of purpose. It was her duty to copy Father Carroll's testament. She brought another satchel to contain the copies for the walk back.

Then it struck her how dangerous the return journey would be. Not just the cookbooks, but also the weight of the copies would be on her shoulders. They couldn't be explained away as the subject of conversation with an old friend. Completely preoccupied with the first part of the mission, she had neglected to plan for the second.

Crossing the Poplar Street Bridge she settled on a solution: hide them somewhere along the route. Come back and get them later. The original? Do the same. She recalled the *Book of Kells,* an illuminated manuscript of the Gospels, had been hidden under a rock for centuries. It had survived.

The next hour passed with mild discomfort but quickly enough. She recited Psalm 23 to distract herself from thoughts of Joe Grant. She was still cross with him. He was first on the list for a copy. She wanted to hear him read it aloud. See the look in his eyes when he realized how foolish he was. Or, maybe she'd give the first copy to Candy Walsh. She had a baby on the way. Knowing there were good things coming would be a big boost for a mother-to-be.

Ahead she saw the breaker at Number Six. She detoured into the woods for a rest and sip of water. Leaning against a thick oak, she looked skyward and prayed for the courage to continue. So far, nothing had been more difficult than putting one foot in front of another. Next came the fence, possibly locked doors, perhaps a more-alert guard.

A noisy truck caught her attention. There used to be hundreds of them coming and going from Number Six. Now the coal left only by train on the new line built by the government. Supplies and machinery arrived by truck less than once a month. She scooted behind the tree. Looking out, she spotted a personnel carrier driving away from town. The grey body with a blue stripe were the unmistakable colors of the state troopers.

At least they're headed out of town, Claire thought. Time to get moving.

She picked her way through the woods, the whole time using the six-story breaker as a landmark. Getting over the fence was hardly a challenge. More than one tree had fallen across it, probably during one of the winter storms that barreled through every year. She walked to a convenient one and tread on its knobby bark until she was inside the compound. The squat office building was directly ahead.

So was Herb Gunther.

Claire recognized Gunther's hunched figure, his back the shape of a broken pretzel. He was the Pleasant Corner's bartender before owner Steve Regan fired him for stealing from the till. Was he the only one on site? She answered the question with a question. If they didn't bother to fix the fence, why would they hire more guards?

Gunther stood at the front door for a few seconds then plodded toward the main gate, which was down a gravel road about a quarter-mile long. His pace was consistent with his crooked back.

"Now or never," Claire whispered as soon as Gunther was a fair distance away. She jogged toward the rear corner of the building, putting it between herself and him. Her feet suddenly seemed to make a racket that went on for only seconds but felt like an hour. She tagged the corner with her hand and continued to the front door, yanked it open, and darted inside.

Like every office, there was a reception area. She wasted no time, going directly upstairs where another desk sat outside a pair of double doors bearing the stenciled word SUPERINTEN-DENT. She tried the knob. Locked. The gap between the door slabs was a quarter inch.

Claire rushed to the window, which opened onto the parking area and road to the main gate. Gunther was a tiny figure still headed in that direction. Depending on the machine's output, she estimated he'd be gone long enough to make five copies.

She sat at the desk, pulled open the center drawer, and found a metal ruler. She inserted it in the gap between the doors, wedging it against the bolt. Jiggling the doors back and forth, she managed to work the ruler along the strikeplate until, Voilà!

The doors swung open on a magnificent personal office. A massive desk, leather chairs, well-tended plants, framed photos of giant equipment, and that glorious copy machine all occupied the usual places.

"Oh, thank God," Claire sighed.

She noticed there was a key inserted into the control panel. A twist of her wrist and the machine came to life. Pulling open the drawers she found plenty of paper. Carefully, she took Father

Carroll's testament from inside the cookbook. That it had been untouched by the flames amazed her. After fanning the pages several times, she placed them in the automatic feeder.

"Here goes," she said aloud and pressed COPY.

While the machine hummed, she took another peek from the window. Gunther was out of sight. She paced a few circuits around the room, looked again, then checked the copies. Every page was blank.

"Darn it!"

She recycled the paper into the supply drawer then examined the feeder closely. Perhaps she put the pages in the wrong way. She turned them over and again pushed COPY.

Blanks exited onto the finish tray.

Perplexed, she opened the doors to the machine. Yes, there was plenty of toner in the reservoir. Yes, she put the pages in the correct way. What could be wrong? She went to Filner's desk where she grabbed an old magazine. She placed it on the glass deck, closed the lid, pressed COPY.

Out came a perfect image of the page.

Next, she took the first page of the manuscript. She read the first line, "*The chains of this world are of this world and therefore have no power to bind us.*" Face down on the glass it went. COPY.

Another blank page.

Her only regret was not bringing someone along to witness what happened.

• • •

Martin Selman loved a ceremony and Otto Weber gave him good cause for one. Selman expected it would be at least a month before a miner's funeral, either for Weber or someone else. But in forty-eight hours? It was unprecedented. Furthermore, Doctor Erbil's perfunctory exam revealed Weber's death was consistent with a mine collapse: crushed windpipe, broken vertebrae, various severe contusions, including one on the cranium. Selman never expected that set of facts, not when convicts sent to Mount Carmel usually died of violence or exposure attempting to escape. Top it off with Sara Darcy digging the grave herself, assisted by none other than Mike Whelan, and Selman had himself a genuine hero to be celebrated. If only a camera crew were there to record the event!

He addressed a standing-room-only crowd at the Common Faith Center, including State Police Colonel Stewart. Some in attendance came for the extra Bounty of Faith boxes. The good colonel and twenty troopers were on hand to ensure delivery and deal with anyone who might try to steal the truck.

"Beloved Otto Weber," Selman said from the podium. "A man who made his mistakes, paid his debt to society, and began anew. Through the Common Faith, he came here. Blessed we were to have him, if only for a short time. Otto's difficult life proves to us that no matter how lost we are, the Common Faith shows the way home, guided by the Universal Creator's benevolence to the Bounty of Faith. Otto departed the path of self-destruction, gave up violence and hatred. He made a unity pact with another lost soul."

Selman gestured for Sara to stand.

"Allow me to introduce you all to Sara Darcy."

The crowd eyed her and Mike Whelan, who hadn't been seen in the Common Faith Center since it was still known as Our Lady of Mount Carmel, the occasion being another funeral, the one for his father.

"A unity pact brought them together in the Common Faith, two halves made a whole, and surely the Universal Creator will continue to bestow upon them the Bounty of Faith, in this world for Sara, and in the next for Otto. Open your hearts and minds. Let us learn from them that we may be better people ourselves."

He would have gone longer, but Colonel Stewart looked anxious. Thus, Selman ended the service with the promise of renewal from the Bounty of Faith, meaning all were requested to line up outside for an extra measure to assuage their sadness.

"One lucky person will get a ten-gallon gas voucher," he said. Hearing that created a mad dash for the door.

• • •

In Selman's office, Colonel Stewart got to the point.

"The bus that brought those two scumbags from Graterford never returned."

"Oh, my," Selman gasped. "That's bad news."

"Save the dramatics for your congregation," Stewart grumbled. "My recon platoon has begun a search. They'll be in the area for as long as it takes."

"Be my guest," Selman said. "A crack team like yours, who knows what they'll turn up."

"Any southbound cargo from you that could have invited trouble?"

"None."

"Unlikely someone jacked an empty bus. No point to it."

"How different our world would be if what people did made sense," Selman said, smiling at Stewart's failure to grasp the irrational nature of human behavior.

"Let Bartok know my men are out there."

"Of course," Selman agreed, holding up an envelope. "If you'll excuse me, I must deliver this at the interment."

"Convicts get the death benefit?" Stewart questioned on the way out.

"One thousand dollars."

"I thought it was two?"

"Sadly, budget cuts force us all to make do with less."

"Tell me about it," Steward said.

When the colonel was gone, Selman removed half the money, which he put into his pocket. What did an ex-con-turned-miner need with another thousand dollars?

• • •

Claire ran out of Filner's office like it was on fire. At the bottom of the stairs she realized she left the door open. Up she went again, this time tripping on the top step, landing on her face. The doors properly closed, she retreated to ground level, where she turned down the corridor toward the rear of the building and exited.

Outside, she stuck close to the wall, peering around the corner. Gunther was still out of sight. She ran for the fence, tears dripping off her cheeks. She lost her balance on the fallen tree, scraping her hands and arm when she slipped. For a few minutes she lay on the ground, crying like she did when Patrick was killed.

You can't float home on tears, Claire told herself, getting up, checking her satchel.

Anger at herself powered her through the woods, dulling the pain in her knees and hip. She should have gone to the meeting. Should have held the manuscript up for all to see. Should have read it to them, passed the pages around. But no. She wanted to make copies. Yes, it was a good idea because duplicates improved the odds of the Word spreading. Still, she should have anticipated that the holy nature of the writing might present a challenge. And what if Bartok had raided the meeting? Then all would have been lost.

She left the woods and turned toward town. Walking steadily, she resolved to involve the others by revealing Father Carroll's work at the next meeting of her co-believers. She would read it aloud to them. In the meantime, the manuscript was safe with her. In fact, Zoe's presence in her house made it the safest place to hide anything. Bartok wouldn't offend a compliance specialist by searching her home.

She stopped for a drink of water. Sitting on the berm, she again heard the trooper personnel carrier coming. This time they were moving fast. She scrambled up the embankment more out of fear of being hit than being seen. They whizzed by without slowing, which made her think what reckless idiots they were. Then the brake lights came on.

No point in running. In good shape but no match for trained men, she returned to the road and walked directly at them. Her story was the truth and thus the best defense.

A two-man team barely old enough to shave met her at their vehicle.

"Hands up," one said.

She complied, saying, "I'm on my way home."

"Keep 'em up. Follow me."

Claire followed him, aware of the other trooper behind her.

A sergeant took over. "Why are you walking this far from town?"

"To deliver a letter," Claire answered. "To Superintendent Filner."

The sergeant smirked at her serious tone. "Must have been important. Sound a little upset."

"There was a collapse yesterday that killed a man and injured a member of my family. I wanted to lodge a complaint with Mr. Filner about the terrible conditions."

"Yeah? What'd he say?"

"No one was there."

"Sorry to hear that," the sergeant said, a touch of empathy entering his tone.

"If that's all, I'd like to go home."

"We'll give you a ride."

"Thank you, officer. I appreciate the kindness."

"Sit up front with me," he said, holding the door.

Just as Claire put her foot on the step to climb in, the sergeant took her arm.

"Hang on a second. Show me that letter," he said.

Using her free hand, Claire took the envelope from her satchel.

The sergeant read her letter then returned it, asking, "What else is in the bag?"

Without hesitation, Claire took out one of the binders for all to see. "Cookbooks for my friend Lena. She has sugar vouchers."

"Load up!" the sergeant shouted at his men. "We'll drop this lady in town and move south."

•   •   •

With school closed for Otto Weber's funeral, Zoe took the opportunity to press Candy into service. She watched the house until Denise and Ian exited from the rear. Confident any self-respecting Christian was staying away from an official Common Faith event, she went to the back door, where a look in the window revealed Candy seated at the breakfast bar, sipping coffee.

Uninvited, Zoe entered, saying, "Does anyone lock their doors around here?"

"Wouldn't stop you," a sullen Candy greeted her. "So why bother?"

"Cheer up," advised Zoe. "Today's the day things start to get better."

"Look around. Things are pretty good."

"Yeah, tell me, how does a schoolteacher and an unemployed single mom pay for all this?"

"Ask Denise. She has rich friends."

"I will. Later." Zoe poured herself a cup of coffee like she lived there, tasted it, and moaned with delight. "Good stuff."

"Get to it, okay?" Candy said, not hiding her bitterness.

Zoe used bait to hide the hook. She played the easygoing friend with a difficult job.

"First thing I want you to know," Zoe began, "is that I'm not going to wreck your life."

"No, just lock up everyone I ever talked to."

"I'm going to bend the rules, which I can do when someone helps me."

Candy stirred her coffee a long moment. She said, "If I don't help, you're going to send me to jail, right? I'll go to Graterford, lose my baby, and end up like that lady who almost died yesterday in the mine."

"Maybe."

"Definitely, so let's keep this real," Candy affirmed. "If I'm going to rat out people I've known all my life, what do I get? Huh? Nothing in this house is mine. That coffee isn't mine."

"And you'd like something of your own?"

"Not for me. For my little girl when she comes."

Candy's wet eyes and runny nose begged for a hug, but Zoe resisted. This early in the negotiation was not the time for acts of comfort but rather a taste of future generosity. She placed a book of gas vouchers on the counter.

"Wow," Candy said. "I've never seen a whole stack of them."

"And not what you really want, either," Zoe continued. "Not a year's worth of gas to ride around, or a new house. Let's talk about the big picture. A job teaching in a Philadelphia school where you'll have at least two assistants, and a classroom packed with so much tech you'll think it's a spaceship. Imagine an apartment in a great neighborhood like the one where I live. We might end up neighbors. For the rest of your pregnancy, see the best doctors and deliver under their care. Take six months off to nurture your baby. Then get back to work at that school, where the day care is onsite, where you're the star of the show. That's what you really want, isn't it, Candy?"

"It would be nice."

"And I'll make it even easier for you. I'm not interested in your friends, or the other people who, let's face it, are breaking the law, but don't really count for much. I'm interested in John Carroll."

At the sound of his name, Candy shifted her gaze to the window. "Give me something upfront," she said. "Proof that I can trust you."

Zoe leaned back and sipped her coffee. She appreciated the challenge of betrayal. She understood how an individual weighed the ramifications, which was why the offer went straight to the top. Or so it seemed. In reality, transferring a teacher, arranging for an apartment, and finding an obstetrician was an hour's worth of phone calls, a task Zoe would hand off to an assistant. She gambled Candy didn't know that.

Zoe also gambled that John Carroll was no backwater, one-eyed preacher leading a blind flock. He was the architect of a movement. This she deduced by connecting the dots that he was known among the Surviving Few in Philadelphia yet remained free to finish his testament as far away as Mount Carmel. Capturing someone like him was the kind of achievement that would make her Secretary Thompson's favorite. She took the book of gas vouchers from the counter and tossed them onto the table.

"How's that?" Zoe said, watching Candy page through them, carefully examining the validation stamp. "Now let's hear it."

"Father Carroll was writing this thing, like a prophecy, or a revelation," Candy said. "I'm not sure exactly, but they said it was God's message to inspire change in the world."

"Before you go on," Zoe put in, "let me say, you'll love it in Philly."

"Anyway, he was in the middle of writing it when Selman caught him."

• • •

A grumpy Randy Bartok leaned on the cemetery gate. A minute ago, he dumped Weber's canvas-wrapped body graveside with the same care he gave bagged coal as a teenager. The trooper platoon searching for the prison bus pissed him off, and not because they were doing his job. They had the gall to interrupt regular commerce, exacting tolls on trucks taking a shortcut on Route 54. That was his money down the drain, his cut of it minus the portion kicked up to Selman. Worse, it debased his authority. With regard to finding the bus, they hardly got their boots dirty, unless he counted the vomit they heaved on each other after a long night at the Pleasant Corner.

In the interest of sending them back to Pottsville as soon as possible, Bartok took it upon himself to locate the bus. He poked his jeep into so many dead ends that he almost ran out of gas. He put the squeeze on Jerry Boyle, who had the skills and tools to dismantle the vehicle. However, he was too busy tearing apart the stolen BoF truck Jagger boosted. Bartok's short list was down to the Mollies taking a second bite at the apple or some new actor, and he hadn't seen any strangers in town except for Zoe Whelan.

Did hijacking a BoF truck give Jagger the idea to go for the prison bus? Initially, Bartok thought it did not. A couple of grand-father-aged troopers was an easy hurdle to jump for a broad with balls the size of Jagger's. Taking out better-armed, better-trained prison guards was a much taller order. Then again, like the troop-ers, the guards sucked down their fair share of the Pleasant Cor-ner's house juice. And, Jagger had lifted Zoe Whelan's gun. Did one and two make three? If so, then the Mollies had upped their game, because the guards had to be dead.

He played the scenario another step, assuming the Mollies jacked the bus. Why? They couldn't unload it on Boyle. A full tank of diesel gave them a three-hundred-mile range. Too bad the first checkpoint was twenty-five in any direction. Unless they had help from someone up the food chain, they were corralled like unbro-ken broncos. A Selman subterfuge done on the sly? Only if it connected to Jesus-freak John Carroll, Bartok concluded, which was a long shot, given the Mollies were not in direct contact with the local Common Faith director. Not that Bartok knew, anyway. No, there was something else going on.

The arrival of Selman's sedan interrupted Bartok's rumina-tions. Bereaved widow Sara Darcy and Mike Whelan got out of the back seat. Lenny Donovan and Selman from the front. Bartok met them at the grave.

"To the earth we commend the departed," Selman said. "May he enjoy eternal life after death in the joyful serenity of infinite oneness in harmony with our Universal Creator."

When it came to body disposal, Bartok preferred rolling them in ditches. This being an official proceeding, he assisted with the ropes. When Weber touched the bottom, Bartok released his line, leaving Lenny Donovan to pull it out.

"The Bounty of Faith," Selman said, presenting the envelope to Sara Darcy, who accepted it without comment.

Whatever their relationship had been like, Bartok noticed Darcy shovel dirt on Weber like he deserved it. From the front seat of his jeep, he watched her and Whelan whittle the pile to nothing. They went so far as to smooth the filled grave to a tidy patch of brown. Their connection was another odd development. Darcy must have been a lovely woman before prison and Weber ground her down. She still wasn't bad. Maybe he'd give her a twirl. Appearance alone, though, didn't explain Whelan's presence. A foreman, he ranked near the top of the earnings scale in Mount Carmel, and he wasn't ugly either. More attractive women, both younger and older, played for him with zero results. Why this one? Why on the second day? Was she the first willing to dig coal? Everybody had their idea of desirable, Bartok chuckled.

Cheered by all this intrigue, Bartok fired up the jeep and wheeled around to Darcy and Whelan, who were closing the gate.

"Need a ride?" Bartok offered.

"No, thanks," Darcy answered, handing him the key to Unit 14 at the Pads. "Give that to Selman."

Bartok palmed the key then coasted down the drive to Fifth Street. In the rearview mirror he caught a glimpse of Darcy and Whelan turning the corner at Apple.

CHAPTER 18.

A modern prophet writing a message from God. Blah, blah, blah. Zoe had heard it all before, but she listened patiently while Candy rambled, and not because they'd once been friends. Rather, it was a specific term Candy used in the middle of their conversation that garnered Zoe's attention.

"It's the Next Testament," she said with conviction. "Father Rabek sent a message that the Time of Gathering is soon. We're all supposed to hear God's word, and I think this is it."

Zoe flashed back to the moment at Common Faith Headquarters when Andrew said, "To get the Next Testament." While the term "testament" figured prominently in Christian lore, what were the odds of two people as far apart as Candy and Andrew using the same phrase, in the same week, to the same person? Better than one might have thought. Both adhered to the same religious philosophy. Both belonged to groups that probably communicated through underground networks.

Another one of Andrew's comments haunted her. "Because your journey begins here," she heard him say. His voice repeated over and over in her mind.

"Am I going too fast?" Candy asked.

"Sorry," Zoe said, snapping into the present. "Give me a minute to process what you said."

She went to the coffee machine for an excuse to reanalyze what had happened at Headquarters. What if Andrew had been telling the truth? Had he been the first part of an elaborate ploy? After all, if they wanted her dead as simple revenge, the explosives would have done the job. Or, they could have ambushed her on the street. But what would murdering her do for them? Hurt their cause. The public had no sympathy for homicidal radicals, not after the Second Civil War took someone from everyone. Then a more sinister notion came to her. What if they wanted to ruin her? And not just her—the entire Compliance Division. The best way to do that? Make it look like she was one of them. A mole. Possibly one of many. The ensuing chaos of sorting good people from bad would disrupt operations for a year or longer and unnecessarily purge the ranks.

"To get the Next Testament."

And here she stood in the kitchen of a person with direct links to the author of said Next Testament. Well done, she admitted. Very well done. The explosion almost backfired. Literally. However, she survived the coma, and was sent where? Very predictably, home to recuperate. Surprise! Your old friend Candy happens to have some key information. And who put her on to Candy? A local bandit keen on helping. For a price.

Bravo.

Not quite. There was a hole in the story. Candy specifically said that John Carroll had been captured. If that was true, then he would be in custody, which was not the case unless Selman stashed him somewhere. Zoe doubted Selman would take the chance when he had too much to gain by delivering a man of Carroll's status.

But, there was an alternative.

A steaming fresh cup of coffee in hand, Zoe returned to the table, asking, "How did Carroll escape?"

"God must have helped him," Candy answered, "because no one gets out of Selman's dungeon on their own."

Zoe suspected worldly intervention. Had the chatterbox co-opted Lenny? Her unity pact with him certainly put her in a good position to that end.

"Lenny was furious. Cost him the reward. Was Lenny who spotted Father Carroll going into Connie Flynn's house. Bartok nabbed him there while he was giving her the last rites. But unless Father Carroll's caught again in the next couple days, Lenny gets zilch, which isn't fair."

Unless he enabled the breakout, Zoe thought. "You have no idea where he is now?"

"Lenny's with Selman at the funeral for that convict miner."

"I meant Father Carroll."

"Oh, sorry. Nobody knows where he is until he shows up, and he doesn't show up often. Not since he started writing."

"People wait for him?"

"Heck, yeah, they do," Candy answered. "Father Carroll's been talking to God. Wouldn't you want to hear what he has to say?"

"Absolutely," Zoe replied, catching an undertone in her classmate's voice. "You sound worried."

"I am." Candy cleared her throat. "For you."

Zoe put her mug in the sink, then gave instructions. "Make a list, handwritten, of the five people closest to Father Carroll."

"I knew you were lying, that you'd take us all."

"Only if you stop cooperating or make them aware of our deal."

"Oh, we still have a deal? Or are you going to bail on that, too?"

"Make the list. I'll pick it up at school tomorrow morning."

On the way home, Zoe passed Abbonizio's Shoe Shop. She expected it to be closed, but was more disappointed by the empty window display. Maybe he locked away the merchandise during off hours. Shoes were still extremely expensive and frequently stolen. Nonetheless, she wasn't going to wait any longer for better footwear. In her report to Secretary Thompson, she would requisition at least three pairs of boots, including one suitable for winter. Yes, she expected to be in Mount Carmel not only until John Carroll was caught, but as long as it took to roll up his network. Then she might stick around to clean house around Selman, who clearly had a mess on his hands. She would be careful in that endeavor. He and Thompson went all the way back to the Common Faith launch ceremony. Finally, the Mollies. Then maybe a week or two vacation somewhere warm.

She entered her house through the back door, eager to pre-pare her report. Not two steps in, she drew her gun and pointed it across the room at someone she immediately recognized, a per-son who had no business reaching for anything in her mother's cabinet.

"On the floor!"

Sara Darcy raised her hands. Very slowly she lowered to her knees.

CHAPTER 19.

"What the hell! Put the gun away!"

"She's a criminal, Mike," Zoe retorted, keeping a bead on Sara. "I sent her to jail years ago."

"And she served every day," her brother said. "Now put the gun down."

"She's part of the same group that tried to murder me. They call themselves the Surviving Few."

"I was a church secretary," Sara Darcy said from the kneeling position.

"Quiet!" Zoe shouted. "You provided logistical support to a terrorist organization. I proved it in court."

"So what?" Mike said. "She works in the mine now. Almost died yesterday with the rest of us."

"Why's she here?"

"I asked her to move in."

"She's using you. Manipulating your sympathy."

Mike laughed. "For what? A better job five hundred feet down the hole?"

Offended by his flippant remark, Zoe replied, "To get at me."

"I had no idea you were related," Sara said.

"Relax, okay? We've all been through a lot the past couple days, including Sara," Mike said. "Put the gun down and let's talk."

"There's no telling who she associated with in prison," Zoe continued.

"Mostly one guy. He did twelve years for armed robbery and murder," Mike said. "Far as anybody knows, he didn't belong to a church. We buried him an hour ago."

Angling her aim to the side, Zoe said, "She can speak for herself."

Sara stood and faced the compliance specialist who had denounced her in court six years ago, who had destroyed the modest life she once lived. "No hard feelings," she said. "Life's too short for grudges."

• • •

Whip heard their laughter long before she saw them. Three troopers busting each other's balls and sharing filthy jokes. Wasn't like they had anything to be afraid of, not with machine guns, and radios to call for backup. Fortunately, they stuck to the trail, giving her a clear run along the bluff. She shadowed them for fifteen minutes, while constantly checking her rear and flanks for a trap. She learned the technique from a war movie they watched. It was stuck in a DVD player they found on one of her first missions with Jagger.

The gun in her jacket was the problem. Both an asset and a liability, she didn't want to lose it or be caught with it. Under a rock was a bad hiding place. Dirt and damp were bad for guns, according to the same movie. She came to a broad maple tree that had plenty of thick branches. Taking a running leap, she grasped the lowest one, then climbed to the next. She found a wide fork where the trunk split in two. There she nestled the pistol. It might get some rain, but it was the best she could do.

On the ground again, Whip took bearings on the tree for later reference. Half a hand from the outcrop on Bear Mountain. Two hands from the peak at Crossly Point. She counted her strides back to the trail, too. The troopers were far ahead, nearly out of range to the west.

In sight of the trailer, Whip slowed to a casual pace. She took deep breaths and rehearsed what she was going to say to Jagger.

Her proposal: forget the prison bus. Sell the fuel to Jerry Boyle. Plenty of cash to bribe Bartok for travel passes and a ride to Hazleton. Cold as hell there, but second cousins might have central heat and running water. Put Runt in school. Find jobs, maybe at the official shoe factory the government opened. It was worth a try and had better odds than another winter in the trailer.

Yanking open the door, Whip had her mouth ready to spill all that. However, she stepped into a living room packed with a sergeant, four troopers, Jagger, Crush, and Runt. There was barely space for a fart.

"Welcome to the party," the sergeant greeted her.

Whip took in the scene. A trooper whose name badge read KEDRON kneeled over Crush, who was face down on the floor. Against the back wall, another propped the barrel of his gun under Jagger's chin. The third one head-locked Runt.

"Close the door and frisk her," the sergeant ordered.

The fourth trooper felt every part of her, lingering on the softer and warmer areas.

"Nothing."

"Tell me about your bus ride," the sergeant prodded. "I think these two left out some details."

All of a sudden, Whip noticed a smell in the room. It was piss. Instantly, her eyes darted to Runt, but her pants were dry. Sadly, Crush had a spot that stretched to her knees.

"Give her another one," the sergeant said.

Kedron hit Crush with an expertly placed jab to the right kidney.

The sergeant snapped his fingers at Whip. "I'm listening."

Whip never thought she'd feel the kind of rage Jagger and Crush spouted. Yet at that moment, she understood it. Yes, what they did was wrong. They were thieves and had recently become killers. No, not because they had to be. They could have found work of some kind, maybe at Number Six, or gone away to rebuild cities wrecked by the war, or in that shoe factory in Hazleton. No, they were who they were because men like these took too much from people like them. The bribes and kickbacks and perks, all that plus a salary wasn't enough. They wanted total submission. By the look of Crush's piss-stained pants, the tears and slobber dribbling off her face, they were getting it, too. Once they reduced someone to that, it was just like the movie: a guerrilla war.

"Another."

The trooper smashed his fist into Crush.

"We haven't been on a bus since a trip to Frackville last year."

"Another."

Crush spewed a stream of bile.

"Where's the guard? The driver?"

"Only guard I know is Lenny Donovan. He works at the prison in Pottsville when he ain't helping Randy Bartok keep order in town."

"Another."

Kedron's next blow landed between Crush's shoulder blades with a sickening thud. She passed out cold.

Runt fell limp at the sight of Crush's eyes rolling up in her head.

"Tell me, or you're next!" barked the sergeant.

"Nothing to tell," Whip insisted.

Everyone's attention shifted to the opening door. Randy Bartok stood there, holding his shotgun one-handed.

"Gentlemen," he said, "there's no reason to mistreat my friends."

• • •

It was her third big test of the day.

First came the disappointment of the copier. Then the shock of not only dodging the troopers, but also getting a ride from them. Finally, Claire was treated to the sight of her daughter, gun drawn, in the kitchen with her son and another woman.

"I won't have you threatening people in our house," she said to Zoe. "Put the gun away and tell me what's going on."

Zoe lowered her weapon, informing her brother and Sara Darcy, "We'll continue our discussion after I explain a few things to my mother."

"We're not going anywhere," Mike replied.

Zoe and Claire moved into the living room while Sara and Mike sat outside on the back porch.

"I'd be sad to see you leave," Claire said, "but maybe it's best if you go back to Philadelphia. Following up with a good doctor there is ten times better than what we have here."

"You're kicking me out for a convict?"

"Making a suggestion."

"Well, I can't leave," replied Zoe. "For professional reasons."

"What does that mean?"

"Not something I can discuss."

"I'm your mother, Zoe. We can talk about anything."

"Okay, let's talk about Mike's decision to ask an ex-con to move in. Did he mention that to you?"

"No, but he's a good judge of people."

"I sent her to prison, Mom! We can't live in the same house."

"Her alternatives might not be as comfortable as yours."

Zoe shook her head in disbelief. Her mother was arguing in favor of a felon.

"You're welcome to stay. There's plenty of room for everyone here. But no guns."

"Mom, please, put yourself in my position."

"The Common Faith is all about inclusion, isn't it? Someone in your position should lead by example and take the opportunity to accept a person who paid dearly for their mistakes. Give her a chance. Maybe you'll become friends."

The coincidences and bizarre circumstances of the past few days had driven Zoe into a state of paranoia. She couldn't decide if her mother was sincere or if she was using reverse psychology. Maybe the explosion at HQ had scrambled Zoe's brain. Nothing made sense.

"Let's have a nice lunch," Claire said. "Everyone around the table. What do you say?"

Watching her mother walk toward the kitchen, Zoe's gaze was drawn to the spot on the dining room wall where she'd seen the outline of where the cross had once hung. It was still there, perhaps even more noticeable. She coughed, wiped her eyes, and it was gone.

"Are you coming?" her mother asked.

"I'm going to get some fresh air," Zoe answered. She went out the front door. Tomorrow she was going to paint that wall. More like the whole damn room. And Sara Darcy was going to help.

• • •

"The troopers have to go," Bartok said, leaning his shotgun against Selman's desk.

"How bad is it?" Selman asked.

"I got one in the clinic and two on the warpath," Bartok answered. "The little one shocked but fire in her belly."

"Then it wasn't the Mollies who took the bus."

Bartok grinned. "The troopers found no evidence they did. No guns, nothing from the guard or driver, and no confessions under a wicked dose of persuasion."

"Your opinion?"

"Outside Jagger's profile. That said, things aren't what they used to be around here. I suggest we restore order before cooler heads no longer prevail."

"I'll make an appeal to Colonel Stewart," Selman said. "On to more pressing matters. Our local Christian faction as they relate to Compliance Specialist Zoe Whelan."

"They're spooked. Gone to ground since John Carroll slipped the noose."

"Perhaps the Mollies can pinch hit. I'm in a generous mood for impressive results."

"They got troopers on the brain."

"Secretary Thompson does not accept failure," warned Selman. "Give me alternatives."

"Kyle Smith," Bartok suggested.

"But it wasn't Zoe Whelan who killed his father. That honor belongs to you."

"For the record and as per my report, his dad took the plunge of his own volition. Kyle's a sissy but point him in the direction of the real enemy and he could do the job. If we can link him to the bus, then we get bonus points from the colonel."

A knock on the door punctuated Selman's smile of satisfaction, which was more than appropriate when Zoe Whelan entered.

"We were just talking about you," he said. "Hope you're on the mend?"

"Doing well, thanks. I'd like to conference with Secretary Thompson."

"Dare I get a preview of the subject matter?"

"My request for emergency authority over this district."

A demotion, no matter how temporary, spoke ill of his career future. If it came to pass, Selman would accept it as the price of bigger gains that were close at hand. Zoe's assumption of command and subsequent horrible demise would absolve him of all managerial responsibility. Simultaneously, he would be positioned for accolades when he solved the crisis.

While pacifying rebellious upstarts might earn him a speaking tour to regional directors like himself, it was not enough to secure him a position at Headquarters. For that kind of elevation, he needed a trophy. John Carroll and his Next Testament were just the thing. He chafed at the thought of having lost the prize. Recovering it required more than the devious capabilities of Randy Bartok. This task demanded his personal attention.

"I'm willing to accept the decision of Secretary Thompson," Selman said to Zoe.

• • •

Without Bartok's help, Crush never would have made it to the clinic. Jagger and Whip loaded her into the jeep. Then all of them piled in around her for the ride to town. His assistance ended at the front door, where Nurse Porter took over. She produced a squeaky old wheelchair to transport Crush to the examining room, where Doctor Erbil had a look.

Later, they washed Crush from head to toe in a private room. Jagger did the heavy lifting. Whip steered the sudsy cloth. Runt turned valves. They drained the tub, refilled it with clean, warm water, and let Crush soak. Trooper Kedron had spared her face, which hung pale and slack on the porcelain edge. From the neck down, her flesh bore the blooming harvest of an expert boxer. Doctor Erbil diagnosed unspecific internal injuries, not that they were a mystery. The damage within manifested itself in a blood-tinged urine streak for all to see.

Whip dried her hands, took her jacket, and headed for the door. Jagger caught up with her in the hallway.

"Where're you going?"

"A private party," Whip answered.

"The next room's empty. Hit the shower before you leave."

"What's the point?" Whip asked.

"Whatever you're going to do, start clean."

The power of suggestion put Whip under the nozzle. Hot, running water was the rarest of luxuries. Afterward, she felt less refreshed than prepared to do what had to be done.

Whip didn't care about time burned on a detour to the Pleasant Corner. She sidestepped to the open rear door from which emanated a nonstop blast of profanity-laced bragging. She recognized their voices; it was the sergeant, the two from the trail, and the one who did the punching. Kedron.

"So Sarge says, 'Another,' and I knuckle-punched that fat bitch right above the ass cheek. Thwack! Blaaaaaargh, she pukes all over the floor. Missed Sarge's boots by less than an inch."

Laughter all around.

"You first," Whip whispered, her anger sufficiently stoked to follow through on a vow made the moment she saw Crush on the floor.

A three-quarter moon lit the way to the trailer, where she took her time setting the place to rights. There was no hurry. Already stupid drunk, the troopers would be blotto in two more hours. She tossed out the rug and mopped the floor underneath. When she was finished, their home looked pleasantly presentable. An added touch: fifteen minutes burning a vanilla-scented candle that was part of a score from an abandoned house in nearby Locust Gap.

On the move again, the trek along the darkened trail tested her night vision. She stumbled but avoided the worst hazards. Finding the maple was easy, too. Bear Mountain loomed black against a few distant clouds; same for Crossly Point. She counted her steps off the trail and walked straight to the tree.

High in the branches, she recovered the pistol. As she saw in the movie, she ejected the magazine and counted the bullets. Racking the slide exposed a round in the chamber. Fifteen total. She pointed it at the sky until the front sight blocked a bright star. Fourteen for you, one for me, she thought. Or maybe one for me here and now. No, because then they won without paying a price. She was determined to make them earn it.

A familiar voice to the right surprised her.

"Mind if I walk with you?" Father Carroll asked.

Whip gripped the pistol's handle, but kept it in her pocket. "Long as you don't slow me down," she quipped.

And he didn't. Father Carroll matched Whip stride for stride. He increased the pace, too, challenging her to practically run. He never lost his footing, either, dodging rocks and roots with goat-like alacrity.

They finally took a break outside the trailer, sitting on the stumps where Crush chopped wood. Father Carroll set a pill bottle beside her.

"For your friend. They'll help with the pain. One every four hours," he said.

The pallor of Crush's face, her eyes rolled up, the inability to hold her water, the blood seeping out of her, the bruises already turning black. Whip understood what that meant. Soon her sister would be next to Dylan.

Overwhelmed by the certainty of Crush's death, Whip dropped her head into her lap and wept. Not only for Crush, but for all of them, she sobbed until her shirt was damp. The troopers, minus a few if she was lucky, would still be there. And Selman. And Randy Bartok, who helped them this time, but his favors were always repaid in triplicate.

Whip was prepared for her fate. Jagger also accepted what the world dumped on her. Runt? A girl of maybe ten? It wasn't that she would lose anything, that tormented Whip. It was that she would never have anything to lose.

Whip sat up straight, coughed loudly, and wiped her face. Embarrassed at losing control in front of Carroll, she refused to look at him.

"I don't want to die," she said.

"Then choose life," he replied.

"That ain't so easy."

"Don't be like the ones you despise," he said. "The blind can't lead the blind."

"What does that mean?" she grumbled.

"If you do what was done to you, there is no change."

"I can change everything for that bastard who made Crush his punching bag. Damn right I can."

"And then the troopers kill you. Jagger kills them. They kill her. On and on it goes. Try something different."

"Try? Try! This ain't no football game. Try harder. Do better next time. Crush is dying, and they're having a party!"

"Kill a trooper and no one will be on your side," Carroll explained. "The people in town will also be your enemies."

"Hey, in case you haven't noticed, nobody likes the troopers or Selman."

"Don't give them a reason to switch sides. Give them a reason, a darn good one, to take your side. Then you are stronger."

"Wow," Whip sighed. "You really believe that shit."

"Because it's true. The Romans conquered the world. They were the most powerful empire of their time. They killed Christians for sport. Then a strange thing happened. A few hundred years later, the Romans became Christians, and not because the Christians had a better army."

"A few hundred years! I'll be lucky to make it through the winter."

"Then best do something worthwhile."

Whip had heard enough. She had a gun and the courage to use it. John Carroll was welcome to give his theories a whirl after she was gone, but she wasn't leaving this world with an unsettled score.

"Don't forget these, Elizabeth Marie."

Whip spun at the sound of her real name, catching the pill bottle against her chest. John Carroll was no longer there—not seated on the stump, not walking away, nowhere.

Angry that she had wasted time talking, Whip jogged to town. She beelined for the Pleasant Corner, taking Fifth Street instead of the back alleys. Two blocks away, she slowed to calm her nerves. For the last time, she recalled that stupid war movie, how the men kissed pictures of their wives and rubbed lucky charms before going into battle. She felt no need.

Ahead, a crowd filled the street. They were shouting and pointing in every direction. She couldn't imagine a reason for them to be after her, but she clutched the pistol tighter, her thumb ready to flip the safety. Then a burst of machine gun fire echoed down the block. The crowd split, half rushing away, the other crouching behind whatever cover was available. Another volley of gunfire erupted.

People running her way nearly bowled Whip over. She pressed into a doorway then darted between two groups before making the corner where she saw the action. It was a full-blown street brawl. She recognized George Nash and his co-workers trading blows with the troopers. Behind them, the sergeant stood atop the personnel carrier. He fired his automatic rifle in the air. Nash and his men ducked but didn't run away. They pressed closer. In the background, here and there, men with baseball bats, pry bars, and shiny wrenches broke through the crowd. The troopers were surrounded.

Then Whip saw the trooper who battered Crush. Kedron was flat on his back outside Pleasant Corner's front door. Steve Regan came out and helped him stagger toward the personnel carrier. They made it just before Randy Bartok skidded to a halt across the street. He and Lenny Donovan hopped out of the jeep.

Bartok strutted directly into the fracas, using his shotgun's stock as a club and battering ram. He knocked out a trooper, bashed one miner, and kicked a second in the crotch. Donovan backed him up with a two-handed pistol grip that warded off secondary sneak attacks. Bartok pointed his shotgun skyward and let loose.

KABOOM!

Relative silence followed.

Whip knelt, her eyes scanning for anyone headed her way. So far, so good.

"Everybody out of the street!" Bartok hollered. "Go home!"

"That asshole," Nash said pointing at Crush's assailant now being helped by two troopers, "grabbed my wife."

"Consider it a compliment," Bartok said.

Nash wiped the blood from his mouth and asked, "They got you on the payroll now, Randy?"

"Go home, George."

"Trouble tomorrow if they're still here," the miner said. "For you, too, old buddy."

A hand on Whip's shoulder startled her white.

"Hah! It's me," Jagger said, clearly delighted by the melee. "Looks like you kicked some ass."

"Yeah. How's Crush?"

"We have to get her out of there. Clinic's gonna be full of shit-head miners in no time."

They raced each other to the clinic. Whip won, but not by much.

CHAPTER 20.

"When did John Carroll escape your custody?"

Of all the questions Selman expected the next morning, this one was not on the list. He had one of his own, too. Who told Secretary Thompson that nugget of political gold? Not Randy Bartok nor Lenny Donovan nor some random Christian devotee who called the Intolerance Hotline as payback for his capturing the former priest and alleged modern-day prophet. The only person able to get the Secretary herself out of bed early enough to be in Mount Carmel before nine was Zoe Whelan. And that particular compliance specialist stood to the side of his desk, her arms folded confidently, and both eyes boring into the hole she blasted through him.

"John Carroll was never in my custody," Selman answered, his own gaze not wavering from the Secretary, who occupied his chair.

Thompson's pause before speaking hinted at a scintilla of doubt in her star's revelation. It also set the trap for him to undermine a solid lie with desperate chatter. Instead, Selman let the silence build. He hardened his face, displaying a measure of indignation for the ambush.

Thompson lifted a sheet of paper from her open case on the floor and read the first line. "Application to release funds. Purpose: Reward for the capture of John Carroll, indicted in absentia for subversion… blah, blah, blah." She dropped the sheet on his desk and said, "That's your authorization code, isn't it?"

"It is, Madam Secretary, and if you'll notice the reward

recipient's name is blank."

Zoe glanced at the page then at Secretary Thompson who appeared less pleased than a moment ago.

"I filed the application to facilitate John Carroll's capture. We had been monitoring his activities, and I believed very soon he would be caught. Nothing encourages the public's continued cooperation like a speedy reward."

As it happened, John Carroll was in the dungeon when the paperwork was filed. Carroll's arrest came after Selman got a tip from his reliable source, who was one of the few remaining Christians in Mount Carmel. This person had an odd sense of piety in the vein of, *"Render unto Caesar the things that are Caesar's."* In other words, he accepted the government's authority and encouraged other believers to pay the unofficial fine when Bartok came to collect it. In exchange, Selman permitted Christian activities to continue as long as they remained out of sight. No evangelizing. No preparations for violence. No frothy talk about the Second Coming or the Apocalypse. It was a fair deal in that the faithful expressed themselves with minimal harassment and Selman augmented his pension. The arrangement had worked very well until John Carroll started talking about his testament. As always, there were some thirsty for the mysterious and unprovable. Selman couldn't have that in his district, or worse, spreading beyond its boundaries. His informer felt the same way. Hence, the tip and John Carroll's incarceration.

But Selman couldn't reveal the identity of his informant by putting his name on the reward application. Therefore, he left that space blank, promising Lenny Donovan a portion of the reward after the former priest was sent to prison. Unfortunately for Donovan, Carroll's escape voided the agreement.

Selman continued his explanation to the Secretary. "In fact, we cornered Mr. Carroll and a few of his followers, but tragically, one of them committed suicide, which led to Carroll and the others getting away. Just as Ms. Whelan did not expect the Christian in Philadelphia to detonate his explosives, I did not think a Christian here would defy their prohibition against taking one's own life. Had we known of their, ahem, philosophical pivot, I'm sure we both would have taken alternate measures."

"That's a fancy way of admitting Carroll escaped."

"Not to argue semantics, but I prefer to see it as Carroll evaded us."

Zoe reacted with a grunt.

Sliding forward in her chair, Thompson tapped the application on the blotter then said, "I'm struggling to see you in the best light, Martin. The riot last night shows a lack of respect for your authority."

"The incident was nothing more than a mixture of too much alcohol and testosterone," Selman said.

"In the interest of social tranquility, perhaps the Common Faith should open a brothel for them to relieve themselves of the masculine burden," she suggested.

It wasn't the worst idea he'd heard, one worth exploring when the current situation was tamped down. Selman kept it to himself and explained, "With respect to Colonel Stewart and his men, their heavy hand provoked the citizens. Prior to the brawl, they assaulted several young women, one of whom was taken to the clinic with severe injuries."

"She's a thief," Zoe interjected.

"As well as an informer. Part of a network that provides valuable intelligence," clarified Selman. "She did nothing to deserve such abuse. I would have overlooked it as excessive enthusiasm on the part of a random trooper, but I'm told they were also quite fresh with the miners' wives. It was the last straw."

Thompson leaned her bulk against the chair. A glance at Zoe revealed the two had prepared for an easy kill as opposed to a robust defense. Still, it seemed she was staying the course.

"Social order is the responsibility of the local Common Faith director, is it not?"

"Of course," Selman answered.

"Share your passwords and keys with Ms. Whelan," Thompson said. "She will serve as acting director for the next six months and take command of the John Carroll investigation. You will continue leading Common Faith services and manage outreach programs."

Selman wondered if Thompson had played him from the very beginning. It wasn't beyond the realm of possibility that she set him up as a career stepping-stone for one of her most ambitious operatives. Only in town a few days, Zoe Whelan showed a remarkable ability to ferret out compromising details, and that gave him cause for worry. If John Carroll was captured on her watch, it would be Zoe Whelan celebrated as keeper of the peace, not Mount Carmel's dutiful Common Faith director. He would be seen as incompetent, giving Secretary Thompson good reason to demote and relocate him.

Furthermore, without any official authority, Selman would have nothing but his informal alliance with Colonel Stewart and the loyal Randy Bartok to continue his pursuit of the trouble-making former priest. While Bartok was very capable, the colonel and his troopers were less predictable, especially considering the previous night's episode.

A committed cynic who believed in nothing but what he could touch and feel, Selman refused to rely on hope and prayer to the Universal Creator.

"I'll do whatever I can to help the cause," he said.

• • •

Between them, Nash and his men had more broken fingers and noses, bruises and loose teeth than a championship-losing rugby team. They'd fought before with strangers, and each other, over a litany of offenses, but when the biggest trooper grabbed Nash's wife by the ass and dragged her close for a tongue kiss, the fuse was lit. It might have passed as the stupid move of a drunken fool, which normally was forgiven at the cost of an apology and round of grog. Not this guy. He made the mistake of taking it two steps further. First, the oaf palmed the crotch of her jeans. Second, he asked, "What're you going to do about it?" Every uniform in the bar became a target for the ensuing barrage.

Bottles and glasses, stools and chairs, anything at hand flew across the room. A wave of fists and feet followed close behind. Nash and his men were no gaggle of unruly teenagers. They wrangled heavy machinery and worked together daily as well as any military unit. The troopers quickly discovered they were not cowards, either. Not one of the miners backed down, not even outside when the sergeant unleashed an arc of bullets across the sky.

If Randy Bartok hadn't intervened, a dozen bodies would have bled in the street. Most would have been shot dead, but a few more, the ones in uniform, would have had broken necks and caved-in skulls. As it ended, the troopers withdrew to Pottsville when a rumor spread about the miners launching another attack.

There was more to the situation than a lecherous advance. It was the trigger, but the issue of returning to the depths of Number Six had every miner on edge. While it relieved the overhead stress at one specific point, the collapse did not change the fundamental problem of robbing out the columns. Not a professional geologist but a man with twenty years of experience gouging coal out of the earth, Rat Durkin explained it in simple terms.

"It's soft under and over them columns. Old clay can't hold up the weight," he said, and he was right.

George Nash agreed and was ready to do something about it. His cracked lip, black eyes, and taped hand lent an air of desperate sincerity to his case. He clambered atop a bench at the end of the locker room the next morning, getting everyone's attention.

"I'm calling a strike," he announced. "No one goes down the hole until the government gives up on the quota and we get better conditions."

"And pay!" someone shouted.

"Yeah!"

Mike finished tying his boots, shrugged into his jacket, and took his helmet off the rack. Beside him, Sara did the same. Rat Durkin and the others waited to see what happened.

"A man died down there," Nash continued. "Doesn't matter that he was a convict. Could have been one of us. Could have been you, Rat. Or you, Mike."

A round of shouting drove home the point.

Too bad it was a lost cause. As essential employees of the Department of Energy, a strike was illegal. When the department first took over, the miners tested the government's mettle, throwing a strike over the end of profit sharing and the use of convict labor. It got them less than nothing. The government transferred workers in from West Virginia and paid them more. Broke and unable to travel themselves because all the mines were nationalized, they returned to work at a ten-percent-reduced wage.

"And if they send scabs from somewhere else, we'll kick their asses like we did the troopers last night!"

More whoops rattled the locker doors.

"You with us or against us, Mike?"

Mike knew better than to confuse a street fight victory with the odds of beating the federal government.

"I talk to you alone a minute?" Mike proposed.

Nash jumped off the bench and powered his way the length of the room. "Anything you say to me, you say to everyone," he demanded.

The danger below them was nothing to be ignored, but Mike believed it could be mitigated. There was no point explaining how, not to men high on adrenaline and delusions.

"There's a quota," Mike said. "We'll make it, or we won't get paid. Worse, a strike gets former rebel soldiers, like many of you, a one-way ticket to prison camp."

"We got the right of appeal under extenuating circumstances.

Says so in the contract. And that includes ex-soldiers, too."

"Guaranteed denial like all the others, and a paycheck for no one while it's under review."

"We got money saved, enough to last the winter if it comes to that."

Mike doubted the claim. No one had money in the bank or under the mattress. Even if they did, the government had ways of making things unbearable. Checkpoints would hold up deliveries to the grocery store until the cargo rotted. And mere gossip about a checkpoint delay would send people rushing to get whatever they could, thereby emptying the shelves and creating a panic. It happened during the previous strike. It would happen again.

"Try buying some brains," Mike said.

"We're on the picket line, every one of us," insisted Nash.

"Do what you want. I was the last one out, and I'll be the first one back in."

Blocking Mike's way, Nash said, "What's with you? Your mommy got you convinced you'll go to heaven?"

Mike laughed at that.

"Damn it if maybe you want to die."

"I want to eat," Mike said, then adjusted his helmet and headed for the lift.

Nash let him walk away. He'd known Mike Whelan since childhood, known him to be a quiet guy, reliable, and tough in the sense that he never complained. Still, something clicked in the man the other day when that woman arrived in town. To Nash's way of thinking, she should have given him a reason to live. But she seemed to have the opposite effect, which was bad news for everyone, because if Mike Whelan went down the hole, the rest would follow.

"What about you?" Nash asked Sara. "You want to die, too?"

"I'm already dead," she replied, then led Rat and the others after Mike.

CHAPTER 21.

Bartok was on his way to the clinic when Hester Thompson's car passed him on Market Street. He was glad to avoid a pow-wow with the Big Lady. His patron, Selman, was sure to get the boot, especially after last night. Best case, it was the temporary suspension for which they planned. During the hiatus, their destiny was in his hands. Catch John Carroll with his book of bullshit and it was good times again, including a bonus, which he'd take in travel passes to the Florida sunshine. He always wanted to shoot gators. Worst case, Zoe Whelan got Carroll, which meant he'd be reassigned to a metropolitan district where he'd be another grunt with a gun. He'd rather eat a bullet than roam the concrete canyons.

Sufficiently motivated by self-preservation, Bartok went to the basement of the clinic, where Murray Smith's corpse lay on a slab. As instructed, Doctor Erbil called to say Kyle was there to claim his father's remains for burial. Bartok kept one hand on the pistol tucked in his belt as he entered the morgue. Head bowed, Kyle was praying over his dead father.

"Sorry for your loss," Bartok said.

"Come to gloat over your handiwork?" Kyle asked. "Or arrest me for saying a prayer?"

"Neither."

"A killer is what you are. Murdered my father in cold blood."

"He was stupid and jumped. I'm here to give you a chance to be smart and get even."

Kyle shook his head. "Vengeance is mine, so sayeth the Lord."

"Then prepare for more of it, but not from me."

"Another lie."

"Fact is," Bartok continued, "you and the Jesus freaks had it pretty good around here. No one harassed you. Not me, anyway. It was live and let live, wasn't it?"

Kyle admitted the truth with a shrug and said, "As long as we paid your bullshit fine."

"Forget the pennies. Then a compliance specialist big shot showed up from Philadelphia, looking to make her name. Boom, Dad's dead. See what I'm saying?"

"You, her, Selman, all evil scum to me."

The kid was thick, but Bartok figured that was to his advantage. Once the message sunk in, the dolt would be single-minded about getting the job done.

"Big difference between me and the rest," Bartok said. "Pay attention before you get a spot next to your old man."

"Bring it on. I'll choke you out with my bare hands."

This from a twerp too weak to strangle a squirrel. Bartok resisted a chuckle, and warned, "Stick to the plan," as he took his revolver, snapped open the empty cylinder, and dropped a bullet into one of the chambers, then extended the gun to Kyle.

"You got one bullet. Use it to shoot me or the person who really did this."

"Just 'cause I'm a janitor don't mean I got to do your dirty work."

"Zoe Whelan's more your problem than mine."

Kyle eyed the gun, then Bartok's face. "When?"

"Make it soon, because I'm taking that back, and I'd prefer it be used on someone other than you."

"No, thanks," Kyle said. "I'll find another way."

• • •

A wheelbarrow stolen from an unlocked shed was how they transported Crush home. Jagger took one handle, Whip the other.

Runt ran point. The worst part was wheeling her past Dylan's burial plot. Thankfully, darkness kept it hidden. They humped her into the trailer for a night on the couch.

In the morning, Runt was the first awake. Church-mouse quiet, she picked through one of the boxes from Jerry Boyle. She found brightly colored oatmeal packets among the canned soup, dried beans, and bags of rice. The picture showed the prepared dish with strawberries on top. She never tasted strawberries but had one last apple she'd been saving. Her small feet padded back and forth as she built a fire in the stove and boiled a pot of water. Minutes later, the aroma filled the room.

"Smells good," Crush said from the couch.

Runt filled two bowls then started making another portion because Whip and Jagger appeared from the back.

"Take one of these," Whip said, handing the pill bottle to Crush. "They kill the pain."

"Nice score," Jagger said. "Get anything else from the clinic?"

"No," Whip answered, not mentioning from whom she got the painkillers.

Crush downed the medicine with a gulp of oatmeal.

"The prick that worked you over got his," Jagger went on. "Tell her, Whip."

"Laid out on the sidewalk by one of the miners."

"Steve Regan had to carry him to the trooper wagon," Jagger put in.

"Yeah?" Crush said, uninterested. She extended her bowl to Jagger. "I can't eat. Give it to the kid."

Jagger didn't push the issue. She'd taken her share of beatings. She'd wait a day or so then force feed her, because the only way to get strong was to fill up big-time.

"Hey," Runt said from the kitchen. "It's that lady we rolled."

Jagger leapt to the window for a peek. Zoe Whelan approached from Selman's sedan. The man himself was nowhere to be seen, which meant something odd was afoot. No one drove that car but

Selman unless it needed service, and then it was Lenny Donovan at the wheel.

"I can't run," Crush sighed.

"Relax," Jagger told her. "Let's see what she wants."

They waited for the knock, then Whip opened the door and Zoe came in like she'd been lifelong friends with all of them.

"How's everyone doing this morning?" she asked.

"One of us a bit under the weather," Jagger replied. "The rest curious why you give a shit to ask."

"My apologies for what happened yesterday."

"I feel better already," Crush muttered.

"Take a few minutes to get ready, and I'll drive you in my car to the Pottsville Hospital."

"No thanks," Crush said.

"Your car?" Jagger asked. "Lady, those wheels ride under Selman's crooked ass or they don't spin."

"I'm acting director now and come with an honest offer."

"If we're going to deal, let's go to my office," Jagger said, tying off boots that had been Zoe's. She grabbed her jacket from the peg and went outside.

At the woodpile, Jagger sat with one eye scanning the forest, the other on Zoe Whelan to see if she meant what she said or if she was bullshitting to disguise another purpose.

"You offered to help find John Carroll," Zoe began.

"Given what happened to my colleague," Jagger said, "the price has gone up. And I don't help. I do it, or I don't do it, whatever it may be."

"We never discussed a price."

"Reward was ten grand."

"That's fair."

"Hah! As if I'd settle for the advertised price when I know there's more where that came from."

"I'm not going to negotiate against myself. Give me a number."

"See, somebody once said, 'Money's not everything, it's the

only thing.' That was before the war, when going here, there, and everywhere was a matter of following the road you chose."

"There's a point to all the prattle, right?" interrupted Zoe.

"The point is, I'd like to pull up stakes and disappear like I was never born and be reborn someone who wasn't born me. Understand?"

Zoe did, but let Jagger ramble on, which was almost as bad as listening to Candy.

"Twenty grand and plastic for us four, as in official ID with names, numbers, and nothing in the past. Unrestricted travel through the Reunited States of America, which is what some are calling the nifty fifty these days."

"I was thinking ten thousand and amnesty for crimes committed."

"You thought wrong," Jagger said. "Wander around the woods a while. Maybe you'll stumble into a rabbit hole and find Preacher John. Or, maybe you'll go missing forever."

Zoe leaned close, the edge in her voice cutting the cold morning air. "Don't threaten me, you piece of shit."

"Damn, if you ain't the dumbest city chick to lose her shoes," Jagger mocked her. "Whatever went down between you and Selman that put you in the driver's seat only lit a fire under him. Unlike me, he's rather one-dimensional about the people who screw him over."

"Nice try at divide and conquer."

"Awww, how cute. You're learning the lingo," Jagger scoffed. "Ain't nothing unified about you and Selman, as previous warnings from yours truly rang loud and clear. Without me and mine, you're on your own. Call in reinforcements from Philadelphia, or pay the piper. What's it gonna be?"

There was a third option: Candy Walsh. However, Zoe didn't want to make her the only avenue to John Carroll, which is why she'd come to Jagger. Still, she refused to strike a deal without demanding a token in return.

"Okay. Twenty thousand, identification, and travel passes, but give me more than a promise or I'll send you to Graterford right now."

Jagger bobbed her head in respect for her opponent's tenacity. She pulled out the gun she'd taken on the day they scuffled in the alley, held it by the barrel, and presented it to Zoe.

Zoe took the weapon with no assumption that Jagger was completely disarmed.

"Now you got me," Jagger said smirking, hands in the air. "To show a little appreciation for the kindness extended toward my wounded comrade, you're welcome to join us at the breakfast table."

"Thank you. I've already eaten."

• • •

There was a trick to getting a message to the locomotive engineer and it required perfect timing. The railroad made a bend along the Shamokin Creek as it crossed the borough line. When the locomotives entered the straightaway after the turn, the caboose was still out of sight around the bend. Because an empty train was not a target for theft, the troopers remained in the caboose, sleeping, playing cards, or drinking grog. At this exact point in the journey it was impossible for them to see the locomotives at the front, which was why Claire waited in the nearby woods.

At breakfast, Mike had assured her that despite the collapse and two days' lost production, there was still enough stockpiled coal to load the train. He didn't ask why she was curious. He seemed preoccupied with what awaited him in the bowels of Number Six. Claire tried to make conversation with Sara. While the newcomer was polite, her short answers revealed little, which was a shame because Claire hoped they'd become friends. Another woman in the house, one who didn't carry a gun, was refreshing. She prayed for both and everyone else who went underground.

About ten thirty, Claire noticed the coin on the rail start to quiver. It was an old game, one learned as a little girl when she and friends put a penny on the track to be squashed flat by the train's heavy wheels. More recently she learned to interpret the coin's movement, accurately calculating when to snatch it away and prepare to toss her message to the engineer who would have his side window open.

She wrote her note in the simple code of their group, a series of Bible passages. Interpreting the message required an understanding of the references. The small square of paper she inserted into an old tennis ball that she now squeezed to relieve the stress of waiting.

The shiny quarter slipped off the rail. Claire darted out from the woods, grabbed the coin, and looked toward the bend. The locomotive's light swung into view. She started walking along the tracks, a safe fifteen feet to the side, but also an easy toss of the ball. Behind her, the thrum of the engines grew louder and lower in pitch as the train slowed for the curve and ultimately its destination just a few miles away.

The ground vibrated beneath her feet. The time had come. She glanced to the right as the front of the lead locomotive passed her. As always, the cab window was wide open. Like nothing at all, she lobbed the ball with a gentle underhand toss. A hole in one! She saw the engineer catch it and the lazy salute he gave her in return.

Relieved she accomplished her task, Claire turned into the woods, retracing her steps toward town. For the sake of Father Carroll and all of them, she prayed the message found its recipient. If not, they were on their own.

She was about to exit the woods at the end of West Street when she spotted Joe Grant waiting for her.

"I saw what you did," he said.

· · ·

"He's good at this?" Sara asked.

"Never been wrong," Mike answered.

"That's reassuring."

Like a platoon of soldiers, Mike's gang came to attention when Rat's light appeared in the distance. Much of their shift had been spent clearing debris from the collapse, fixing the conveyor, and repositioning equipment close to the face. They were ready to mine coal as soon as Rat gave the all clear. He appeared with his verdict.

"Hear anything?" someone asked.

"Come on, Rat, we ain't got all day."

"Shut up. Let him talk."

Rat said, "I don't know."

"Awww, for Christ's sake!"

"Things ain't totally settled," Rat went on, "but seems okay for now."

Sara made the sign of the cross and said, "I'm going in."

Brave or stupid? The men couldn't decide. They looked to one another first, then at Mike, who seemed as confused as they were. The silent calculation among them was that either she had used up her good luck or was, like Rat, their good luck charm. After all, the thug who came with her was dispatched in short order, but she came out of the collapse practically unscathed. Did that mean there was something to her Christian beliefs, as in God looking out for her? A few thought it might be true, and thus staying close to her meant going home at the end of the day, as it had for Rat and Mike when the roof fell. Others put no stock in religion, but in the reality of their situation, which was that sooner or later they had to send coal to the surface or go to prison camp. One guy kept it simple. He refused to be shown up by a woman.

"Find a spot for lunch," Mike said. "Then we dig."

Therefore, each for his own reasons, Mike included, they followed Sara into the darkness.

"Looks like we got a church of our own," Rat joked, his

helmet light shining up at the vaulted rock above.

Sara found a dry patch where she sat down to eat. Mike joined her. The other miners chose to stay closer to Rat, not because they had anything against her but rather saw him as an early-warning beacon if the earth started to move.

"How many years you spend in prison?" Mike asked.

Sara took her time answering. "Six, courtesy of your sister. But, that included ten months of SR with Otto."

"SR?"

"Social Rehabilitation," she replied. "Speed dating for convicts. They send you to an honor farm with your chosen partner, you play house, pretend to accept the Common Faith, and train for a new career."

"Otto was the pick of the litter, eh?"

"Rather take a weekly beating from one then get raped daily by the rest."

"Makes my twenty years in the dark sound pleasant."

"From what I've seen so far, it is."

Mike gulped his cold tea, poured himself more from the thermos. "Don't expect to lose your life down here," he said, "and you won't."

"Otto beat the expectations out of me."

"But not what you believe," Mike commented.

"God didn't give up on me; I'm not giving up on Him."

"Sounds optimistic, given what you been through."

"A guy who spent twenty years underground appreciates the sun, right?"

Mike raised an eyebrow at her statement.

"At least you're not afraid of the dark," Sara said, "or you wouldn't have asked me to move in."

"Think my sister's going to haul me off to jail for helping the enemy?"

"Given a reason? Yeah, she will."

Mike often wondered how Zoe might deal with their mother's

faith and association with Father Carroll. Conflict never came, however, because they both did their thing a hundred miles apart without ever crossing paths.

"Want me to find us another place?" Mike asked.

"No need. Zoe will be gone soon."

After what happened to Otto Weber, he considered his sister might have been correct in her snap assessment of Sara.

"She has bigger things to do than poke around a small town."

Relieved, Mike started his second sandwich.

"But we have to paint the dining room wall before that shadow of a cross drives her crazy," Sara finished.

"We'll do it tonight."

• • •

While the class played at recess, Candy sat in the empty classroom, grading a spelling test. She giggled at their creative answers written in blocky letters. Despite Zoe's promise of a high-tech environment in Philadelphia, Candy wanted her child to start with a crayon, then hold a pencil, and finally a pen. There was something artificial about a touch screen. Sure, it was supposed to be good for the environment, eliminating paper, saving trees and whatnot, but in a flash the content disappeared. She couldn't put her daughter's creations in a box to reminisce later or pin them on the refrigerator the way her mother had.

She'd been to Philadelphia for her Teacher of the Year award. The crowds and high prices were unappealing. Living in a building with hundreds of other people, some of whom might call the Intolerance Hotline at the sound of a whispered prayer, frightened her. However, if she could connect with the Surviving Few, she might ultimately make a home with them. Then there was Kyle. She hadn't told him about Zoe trapping her.

"Pssst."

And there Kyle was, at the door in his janitor's uniform. She waved him in, eager to spend a few moments together before the kids returned.

"I'm burying my dad this afternoon," he told her.

"It's terrible what happened," Candy said.

"All part of God's plan."

His reply sounded stronger than she might have expected for the circumstances. Perhaps he was overcompensating for the pain he felt. Kyle never was a tough guy, not like the miners or the other men Candy dated, and that's what she liked about him. She hoped his father's death wouldn't turn him into one of them with their angry attitudes and sarcastic jokes.

"What time?" she asked.

"Better you stay home," he said. "With Bartok and Zoe Whelan around, it could get rough."

She picked up on his anger, felt it herself. "Someone has to help you," she offered by way of distraction.

"Worry about our baby, okay?" He gave her a hug then asked, "Is Zoe making trouble for you?"

"No," Candy lied, "just catching up after all these years."

"She should have stayed in the big city."

"Her family's here."

"Yeah, and that's a problem, too. Joe thinks Claire—"

"Don't say it," interrupted Candy. "Claire's one of us, Kyle. I swear she is."

"Maybe Zoe got something on her," Kyle speculated. "Why else is she holding back Father Carroll's testament?"

"Stop it!" The words came out in her teacher's voice. As soon as they did, Candy wished she'd let him babble instead of being a scold. "I'm sorry," she said, embracing him. "Bury your father. We'll meet later."

"See you then," he agreed, and kissed her cheek.

She watched him go out the door, then turned toward the window. In the parking lot outside, she saw Zoe getting out of Selman's car.

. . .

"You should know better than to send a message," Grant admonished Claire. "Anyone could have seen you."

"Why watch the tracks, Joe?" she retorted, increasing her pace, forcing him to hurry alongside her.

"As rector, messages go through me," Grant insisted. "Or, are you taking over?"

"I'm doing what is necessary to protect Father Carroll and his testament."

"Then share it with us."

Claire stopped short. "I tried," she said. "Yesterday, during the funeral, I went to the mine office where I was going to make copies. Guess what?"

"You almost got caught?"

"Hah! I put the pages in the copy machine and only blanks came out."

"Absurd."

"No. It's proof Father Carroll's testament is special." Seeing the disbelief on his face, Claire walked away from him.

Catching up again, Grant said, "If it's real, then why not let us see it?"

"Because I don't trust you, Joe. Not you or anyone."

"It's your daughter who is a compliance specialist, who sentences us to years in prison, and sometimes worse."

"If I was working with Zoe, wouldn't I have given her the testament already?"

"Maybe you have. The last anyone saw it was at our Cathedral."

"And no one else will until the Time of Gathering."

"Because you're now keeper of the Word? The only one worthy?"

Of her flaws, arrogance was not on the list. She would never claim to be the only one worthy, but she surely was among them. When her hand came out of the fire unscathed, she recognized the power of the Spirit. She also accepted it as a sign of God's intent. She'd been assigned a mission.

Claire stopped again, saying, "The testament is the one thing keeping me alive."

If her statement caught him off guard, he was stunned by her next.

"I know where it is and nobody else. Not even Father Carroll. Whatever harm anyone may wish upon me, or him, remember that."

"It's against all we believe, our way of life. Don't accuse us of evil."

"God knows better what's in someone's heart than I ever will," she said. "And let me promise you this: the testament, like the Scriptures, will spread among the people. I suggest you prepare for the Time of Gathering."

• • •

Much to Jagger's relief, the state troopers left town. From a perch in the woods, she and Whip saw the armored personnel carriers roll past on Route 61.

"Think they'll be back?" asked Whip.

"Ain't sure," replied Jagger.

She guessed the troopers weren't keen on religious hunts because it wasn't their primary job and lacked much in the way of extorting bonus cash. Therefore, when it came to the competition in pursuit of John Carroll, it was a three-way tie between Randy Bartok, big shot from the city Zoe Whelan, and Jagger's own Mollies. To some extent they were working together, and at the same time, for themselves.

Now that Zoe had Selman's position, her strongest play was the cash reward. Citizens looking to collect might bring Carroll to her. Ten grand announced on posters drew a lot of eyes, including those that might previously have looked the other way in defiance of Selman, who was no one's friend. However, Zoe was on a tangent with Candy Walsh, who talked too much and rarely said anything important. Jagger had a good laugh about Zoe's eagerness to jump at that treat. Similarly, the wicked compliance specialist knew zero about the countryside and didn't seem inclined to get her shoes dirty.

Bartok, on the other hand, was willing to walk barefoot over a mile of broken glass to grab Carroll and put himself back on the left hand of Selman's throne. He also drove a jeep, giving him a quick response time to reports from his own gaggle of spies, most of whom were degenerate friends of Lenny Donovan. While he was technically an unofficial operator at this point, anyone with three brain cells not drowned in grog knew Zoe Whelan's elevation was temporary. If Bartok put the press on, they would cooperate. Doubters need only recall his dive into the brawl between the miners and the troopers to see he wielded authority on the street.

That left Jagger in Zoe's comfortable boots. She was grateful for them, because she'd be covering a lot of ground searching for Preacher John's hideout. Since Crush was on the disabled list with Runt attending, she was down to herself and Whip. Her confidence in Whip stood at less than a hundred percent, but that trooper lying on the ground gave her skinny, fleet-footed cousin a taste of revenge courtesy of the miners, yet just as delicious.

Jagger offered another incentive, and not just for Whip, but for all of them. Maybe the idea lurked in her subconscious when she hijacked the bus. Or, it could have been in there as far back as when she grabbed the gun from Zoe Whelan. On purpose or by accident didn't matter. One way or another, she was accumulating the means to get out of Mount Carmel. All she had to do was get Preacher John, and the fantasy was reality.

As was her manner, Jagger planted the seed in too many words but where it was still plain to see.

"Remember your mom and dad?" she began.

"Not much," Whip admitted.

"Tell me something. Anything."

"Uhhh… they would dance on the porch at night. I'd lay on the floor in the living room by the sliding glass door, watching them, wondering why I couldn't hear the music. One time, I slid the door open just a crack. Wasn't any music. Just them singing to each other real quiet."

"Nice. Think you could dance with someone?"

"Seriously?"

"Say you were at the Pleasant Corner tonight. Guy comes up and says, 'Wanna dance?'" Think you could do it?"

"Yeah and look like an idiot," scoffed Whip.

"Bet them long legs of yours would figure it out," Jagger assured her.

"What do you remember?" Whip asked.

"Playing in the sand."

"Around here?"

"Nah. This was right before the country blew up. I was maybe seven, Dylan barely a peanut. My mom and dad were arguing all the time about shit I didn't get. They had an epic fight. I guess Dad felt bad about it, because the next morning we were all in the car driving. Man, we drove and drove and drove. Stopped twice to pee. Next thing I knew, we were looking at the ocean. Smells weird by the ocean."

"Like bad?"

"Not bad. Just weird. I played in the sand. Had a ton of fun chasing the waves. We were there a couple days then drove home. I slept the whole way. Dad left a week later. I thought he was going to work, same as always. Never saw him again."

"That sucks."

"Fought for the losing side, my dad did. Mom told me he died in a federal prison camp somewhere near Baltimore."

"That why you killed those prison guards on the bus?"

Jagger spent a few seconds rolling the question around inside her head. "No," she finally answered. "I did what had to be done."

"Had to be done about what?" Whip queried.

"Stick with me and find out," Jagger replied. "I promise when it's over we'll be dancing on the beach."

CHAPTER 22.

When it came to Candy, Zoe couldn't decide if she was deliberately obtuse or simply stupid. Ten minutes of questions yielded nothing worthwhile, not even the list of names she was supposed to prepare.

"You asked for the people closest to Father Carroll," Candy whined. "I'm trying to figure out who they are."

"Every group has a hierarchy," prompted Zoe, slamming a pencil down on the desk. "John Carroll's at the top. Who's next?"

"God's at the top."

"Don't give me that crap about you all being equal in God's eyes."

"It's true. The Common Faith says the same thing."

"In the abstract! But there's Secretary Thompson, the Sacred Council, people like me, and so on down the line. Churches, religious groups organize that way. Stop stalling and make the list."

"We're different. There's God and then… and then… just us."

Zoe threw the pencil across the room, grabbed Candy by the shirt, and leaned in close.

"Five names will be on that paper or you'll be under arrest."

"Please," Candy begged. "Listen to me—"

Zoe slapped her once to stop her from speaking, a second time to remind her who was in charge, and a third to prove she was willing to keep going.

Suddenly, the door flew open. A scruffy boy darted in from the playground. Seconds later, two dozen more kids followed.

As the children took their seats, Zoe ordered, "The list. Now."

Candy took her red grading pen in hand. She dared to think a moment, tapping the pen against her lips, not shrinking from Zoe's glare. At last, she wrote five names, folded the sheet, and handed it over.

"Thank you," Zoe said, then looked at the list. Her face clouded with rage. She stuffed the paper into her pocket and stormed from the room.

On the way out the door, the kid who was first in the room pointed his finger at her. "Bang bang," he mouthed.

• • •

After fifteen minutes of Filner bending Bartok's ear about unauthorized copy machine use, the superintendent finally got to the point.

"There's rumors of a strike," he said.

Bartok cared as much about a strike as he did about the ream of blank paper run through Filner's copier. He knew the miners didn't stand a chance.

"If Selman passes out some goodies," suggested the superintendent, "we might be able to avoid a full-fledged fiasco."

"I'll mention it," Bartok said. "Anything else?"

"A sense of urgency, if you please."

Bartok plopped his hat on and left. He was about to get in his jeep when a voice called to him from a few parking spaces away.

"Hey, Bartok!"

He turned just in time to catch a tennis ball arcing in his direction.

"What's that worth?"

Bartok squeezed the ball before replying, "Since my dog died a while back, I'd say nothing."

"Then give it back."

He knew the engineer wouldn't have asked the value without a reason. "Maybe I'll get another dog," he said.

"Pay up or I'll take it back to Philadelphia."

It took Bartok a second to recognize the guy as an apprentice, not the regular engineer, who was at least twice his age.

"What happened to the old guy? He retire?"

"They arrested him yesterday."

"They" could mean anyone from the state troopers to a compliance specialist to the local cops in some town along the line. A patient man, Bartok played along.

"Smuggling people or property?" he guessed.

"Information," the rookie answered.

"Is that right?"

"Had all kinds of things to say about you, too. Three years I listened to him tell me about big bad Randy Bartok. Bartok killed two men with one knife. Bartok blew someone's head off with a shotgun. Be damn careful around Randy Bartok. He warned me a thousand times."

"Sound advice."

"Yeah. Trouble was, the fool never thought someone like me might not be someone like him."

"Meaning?"

"He was a Southern Baptist in Common Faith clothes," the rookie replied. "Took me a year to gain his confidence at the controls and with his beliefs. Kept a Bible hidden in the cab. Read it on the boring stretches. Thought he converted me."

"How much was the reward?" Bartok asked.

"Five grand and his job."

Still not sure what the tennis ball had to do with it, Bartok said, "Want reward money for a local apprehension or have something else in mind?"

"No future driving trains. Fixed salary. Lousy schedule. Then again, there might be a way to make it worth the effort. If there's anyone who could make that happen, it would be the baddest of them all, Randy Bartok."

"Thanks for thinking of me."

Pointing to the tennis ball, the rookie said, "Put that to good use, and keep me in the loop for anything moving along the rails."

"Will do."

The engineer plodded away toward his train, leaving Bartok feeling like the drive over to Number Six hadn't been a waste after all.

• • •

Zoe went directly to her mother's basement. She thrashed a rack of winter clothes. She kicked a stack of empty five-gallon pails. She knocked over boxes, spilling a bunch of cookbooks. At the sight of these she stopped to wonder what her mother wanted with hundreds of recipes when the cupboards were practically bare. She nudged the nearest one open with the edge of her shoe, revealing a faded magazine page that featured a spectacular chocolate cake on a glass stand. To Zoe's knowledge, her mother had no ration books for sugar or chocolate. Clinging to the glorious past instead of embracing the brighter future, Zoe assumed, before continuing the hunt for her father's tools. She found them under the stairs. She dug among the wrenches and ratchets, saws and screwdrivers. Finally, under a tray of miscellaneous pliers, she grabbed what she sought.

A hatchet.

She slid the handle through her belt, grabbed a step ladder, and returned to the dining room, where the dusty outline of the cross on the wall had menaced her from the moment she arrived. Well, not anymore, she thought, pushing the dining room table and chairs out of the way.

Not for a moment did Zoe pause to consider how she might be overacting to the names on Candy's list. In the first place, she didn't believe the list was real. Candy was stalling, hiding behind the schoolchildren. As if that wasn't infuriating enough, Candy taunted her with a name sure to provoke a hostile reaction. And it was at the top in red capital letters.

CLAIRE WHELAN.

Very funny, Zoe had almost said, before unleashing some advanced physical techniques that would have left Candy begging for mercy. However, with children in the room, that wouldn't have been a good idea. Very well. Punishment delayed was punishment intensified. She'd give Candy a day, then have her sent to Philadelphia, where the interrogators would not be patient.

In the meantime, Zoe was going to get some work done, starting with chopping the cross out of the dining room wall. An imprecise instrument, the hatchet blade shattered the plaster, which was exactly the effect she wanted. She swung it again and again, hacking a rough square through the lathing. Chunks of debris dropped to the floor as the room filled with dust.

"Zoe!"

She continued until a gaping hole opened in the wall cavity.

"Zoe!"

As she reared back for another swing, her arm was suddenly frozen.

"Zoe! Stop it!"

Bits of plaster stuck in her hair, she turned to her confused mother, who had both hands around her wrist.

"What are you doing?" her mother demanded.

"Remodeling."

Zoe twisted free then tossed the hatchet on the floor. Heading for the kitchen, she said, "Follow me," then ordered her mother to take a seat.

"What's going on?"

"Sit down, Mom," insisted Zoe, who remained standing. She moved to her mother's side, took out Candy's list, and set it on the table.

Claire glanced at the names.

"You know what we call that?" Zoe asked in her official voice.

A blank stare was Claire's answer.

"Evidence. It's all I need to open a case, to arrest someone, to lock them up indefinitely while I dig into every aspect of their life."

All of a sudden, Zoe's face and arms itched from the plaster stuck to her. She went to the sink, opened the tap, and wet a cloth. Wiping her face cooled the anger that had boiled over minutes ago. She almost laughed at the hole she'd made in the wall, but the stakes were too high.

"I'm not sure what do with that," Zoe said, sitting down at the opposite end of the table.

"Do your duty, officer," Claire stated. "Arrest your mother."

CHAPTER 23.

Bartok found Denise Walsh on her back porch, where she sat beside an overflowing ashtray. In other words, Selman had been inside a long time, which could be good or bad. At least he had interesting news for the boss, something to pull the man out of his funk, if not cheer him up outright.

"No smokes?" Denise said as he mounted the stairs.

He tossed her a carton of pre-war Marlboros, probably Sahara-desert dry, but he wasn't going to waste quality Amish tobacco on someone incapable of rolling her own cigarettes.

"Make some noise when you go in," she advised. "Nobody likes surprises."

He rattled the door and wasn't quiet about closing it either. Turned out to be unnecessary, as Selman was sulking on the couch in the living room, staring at the television, while Ian faced the corner, drawing on his tablet.

"Look at this," Selman greeted Bartok.

On TV, Jesse Young reported, "Another terror plot foiled here in Philadelphia. Compliance specialists backed by federal troops swooped in on a bomb-making facility in the First Ward. Early reports indicate five people were arrested, all members of the Surviving Few. Common Faith Secretary Hester Thompson praised the work of all first responders in preventing a greater tragedy."

The screen cut to an interview with her, which interested Bartok less than how many cigarettes Denise smoked every day.

"That should be us," Selman said.

You, Bartok wanted to correct him, but let it pass. He held up the tennis ball.

"Not my sport," reflected Selman.

"Take a closer look."

Selman caught the ball, turned it around several times, then noticed the cut. He squeezed it, forcing the gap open, and wiggled in a finger. The paper inside transformed his sour puss to a grin, which grew into a broad smile. He unrolled the slip, carefully examining the lines written on it. They were appropriately labeled Bible verses. For a moment, he flashed back to his days as an assistant minister at the megachurch, when between the singing and hour-long sermon by the founder, he read scripture to pass the time.

Now with an audience of two, only one of whom could hear, Selman delivered the message aloud, starting with, "Hebrews 12:25, *'See to it that you do not refuse Him who is speaking, for if those did not escape when they refused Him who warned them on earth, much less will we escape who turn away from Him who warns from heaven.'*"

The message was lost on Bartok, who understood only that it was code.

"Isaiah 6:8, *'Then I heard the voice of the Lord, saying, "Whom shall I send, and who will go for us?" Then I said, "Here am I. Send me!"'*"

"Whatever," Bartok remarked.

"Stay with me," Selman told him. "Deuteronomy 40:4, *'If your outcasts are at the ends of the earth, from there the Lord your God will gather you, and from there He will bring you back.'*"

"Sounds like someone's planning a party," Bartok translated.

Selman added, "And the host is to expect a gift for his efforts."

"John Carroll's scribbling," guessed Bartok.

"A safe assumption. Let's take a ride to Pottsville for a meeting with Colonel Stewart."

It was one thing to stand up to the troopers on his turf, quite another to venture into theirs. For that reason, Bartok suggested, "After what happened at the Pleasant Corner, it's better if I stay here."

"Very well," agreed Selman. "But I'll need your vehicle, since Ms. Whelan has availed herself of mine."

Bartok tossed him the keys.

"Find the Mollies. Do what it takes to get them on our side."

"That'll be expensive."

"And worth it."

• • •

Zoe convinced herself that covering up her mother's Christianity was a temporary and erasable offense. If her mother stopped today, this very minute, then no one needed to know. It would be as if she'd never done anything wrong.

"You're going to stop," she told her mother. "Now."

"Stop what?" Claire asked.

"Practicing Christianity."

"Why?"

"You need another reason besides breaking the law?"

"Yes."

Zoe took a deep breath. Where to begin? With logic? Reason? A plea for self-preservation? She settled on the facts.

"We fought a civil war over it," she began.

"Not over Christianity," argued Claire.

"What was it then?" snapped Zoe.

"Some people's… unwillingness to accept others."

"Oh, how quaint, Mom. Millions died over this nonsense. Tens of millions. The country is still being rebuilt and will be for another fifty years. We have to change. It's why we all accepted the Common Faith."

"Not all of us."

"Your God is better than my God? Is that what you're saying?

Because that's how the problem started."

"The Common Faith is humanity's creation, not God's."

"Why's that? Come on, explain it to me."

If only you'd seen my hand in the fire, Claire thought. Or, if it had been your own hand that came out unscathed.

"Let me help," Zoe volunteered. "God inspired a bunch of guys thousands of years ago. They wrote it all down, crossed their T's dotted their I's, and that's it until kingdom come. Am I on the right track?"

"No."

"Ahh, so there's some room for interpretation?"

"Of course there is. People are inspired by God every day."

"But not the people who created the Common Faith? It's not possible they were inspired by God, as you call Him, or Yahweh, or Allah, or any of the other deities that are incredibly similar yet claimed to be completely different?"

"Anyone who opens their heart to God can hear His message."

"That's what I'm saying, Mom! The top religious leaders of the country sat in the same room and made peace. If that's not God's work, then what is?"

Claire felt genuine pity for her daughter. Simultaneously, she blamed herself for not doing more to show her the path to God's love. She'd let her child slip away, at first for the opportunity of an education, and later out of cowardice. She'd always been afraid of what might happen, and now it had come to pass.

"What difference does it make if we say Universal Creator or God?" continued Zoe. "The Common Faith is something we can all believe in."

"And what have you done with it?" asked Claire. "This marvelous creation of yours has its own police, its own courts, its own prisons. Are they all part of your Universal Creator's plan? Is hunting people like Father Carroll your idea of a good deed?"

"Yes," Zoe replied with complete confidence. "People like him give us reasons to hate one another."

Claire was stunned silent.

"People like him stirred the pot until we were shooting at each other from ten different sides. It's a fact of history. It's my job to prevent that from happening again. I'm trying to protect you, Mom."

"Who's going to protect you, Zoe?"

• • •

"Dead men wear no clothes," Jerry Boyle once joked as he dumped a truckload of garments at a fiber recycling plant in Harrisburg. That was during the latter half of the Second Civil War, when the government had initiated a buyback program to put money in people's pockets. Heaping piles of jeans and shirts, an acre of them, spoke to the number of dead. Shoes, too. Lots of shoes.

Understanding the law of supply and demand as he did, Boyle retained the best of what he collected. Sooner or later, he accurately predicted, there would be a shortage. Selling to underground retailers earned him solid profits in the following years until he liquidated the majority of his stock. Most of it had been the standard stuff of working people, but there had been some higher-class items that never sold. Of the multitude of goods pilfered, bartered, and paid for, he rarely came across anyone looking for quality women's clothing, like dresses and pantsuits. Yet today Jagger showed up looking for exactly that, which left him puzzled because she and hers weren't the kind to dress fancy.

"You got nothing but ditch-digging duds and not much of that," she commented. "Where's the good stuff?"

"Like what?"

"The kind of clothes requiring a decent haircut."

"Got a new job in an office somewhere?" he asked.

"Not yet," Jagger answered.

"In that case, I could use some help around here," he continued.

Diversified as he was, Boyle's operation encompassed several enterprises, from distilling grog to trading car parts. His expansion had been limited by his inability to retain employees, all of whom eventually stole from him and disappeared. Although the Mollies were born thieves, they demonstrated extreme loyalty in their dealings and he believed them better qualified.

"Set my sights higher than feeding pigs and stoking the still."

"Wouldn't waste your talent on that," Boyle said. "Could deliver grog to the Pleasant Corner and a few other stops. Not like you don't know how to drive a truck, and with them other two helping, you could make a couple runs a day."

"Thanks, but no thanks," Jagger replied. "Guess I'll have to look elsewhere for new threads."

"This way," a disappointed Boyle waved.

He led Jagger and Whip to a blue shipping container at the end of a row. The interior was like an entire department store compressed into several closets. The clothing hung on racks three levels high. Stacks of boxed shoes covered the back wall. Everything was organized by type and size.

"How were you ladies planning on paying?" Boyle dared to ask.

"Lay away," Jagger answered, marveling at what sparked memories of her mother.

"Enjoy your shopping experience, but nothing leaves until paid in full."

"Wouldn't have it any other way," Jagger agreed, stepping inside to make her selections.

"It's not like we're naked," Whip protested when Jerry was out of earshot. "And we ain't got the money for anything here."

"We'll have it soon enough," Jagger said, paging through the rack. "Pick out three ensembles and a bikini for the beach if you can find one."

"You're crazy."

"I'm preparing for departure."

Whip remained unconvinced. "I appreciate the happy talk,

but we don't have travel passes to get beyond Hazleton or Potts-ville, and people like us don't dress like this."

"Because we're not going to be people like us much longer."

"Oh, yeah? Who're we going to be?"

"Better."

They spent the next fifteen minutes weeding through the racks until Boyle's sharp whistle got Jagger's attention. She stuck her head out of the container to see him approaching with Randy Bartok at his side.

"Pick out the best that fits," Jagger told Whip, then exited to deal with Bartok.

"Spending money you don't have?" he greeted her.

"Want to look good at your funeral," Jagger quipped.

Wisecracks earned a double-slap minimum, but Bartok re-strained himself in the interest of productive negotiations.

"Because you did good with the BoF truck," he began, "I got another job for you."

"Might not be time in my busy schedule, but let's hear it."

"John Carroll."

A second bidder put her in a position to up the price. None-theless, Jagger wanted clarification. "Dead or alive?"

"Doesn't matter to me, but no payday without the paperwork," Bartok informed her.

"His Holy Book of Horseshit?"

"The original. No copies."

A treasure hunt complicated the manhunt. Zoe Whelan hadn't mentioned the man's writing, which meant Jagger might still get a prize if the job went half done.

"Ten grand and a look the other way for killing the two guards," Bartok said. "Keep whatever Jerry pays for the bus."

Repressing any hint of guilt in her voice, Jagger countered with, "What bus would that be?"

"The one you scored and stashed up a bull's ass."

"Don't conflate fantasy with facts."

"Tell it to the troopers, if they don't kill you all first."

"Us dead helps you how?"

"Better help yourself, sweetheart. No one else will."

To argue for more would have been pointless. Besides, Philly Chick Zoe Whelan offered more, and whether Bartok knew that or not, Jagger didn't care. Plus, she suspected Bartok would double-cross her at the end of the game. Nothing was for nothing with him. He hadn't intervened with the troopers out of the kindness of his heart. He did it for the favor to be repaid.

"Do what I can when the opportunity comes along," she said. "Now if you don't mind, I'd like to finish my shopping."

• • •

Never had Claire been as worried for her daughter as when they parted ways that afternoon. Zoe demanded she convert to the Common Faith, promising to ignore the other names on the list if she did. With regards to Father Carroll and his testament, Zoe was willing to recommend house arrest, but only if he surrendered within forty-eight hours. There was more, too.

"I want you to move to Philadelphia. You can live in my apartment until we find a nice place nearby."

"And your brother and Sara?"

Zoe had it all figured out. "They can stay here if that's what they want, or I can see about jobs in the city."

"A compliance specialist can do it all," remarked Claire.

"And more. Be grateful, Mom."

Claire was grateful for many things, but not these horrible overtures.

"I'll think about it," was the best she could say without lying.

She retreated to her chapel, where she prayed aloud with her eyes open. Someone watching might have thought she was a lunatic talking to herself or the wall. She saw it as much a conversation with God as with anyone born of the world. And she needed a talk with God more than ever.

She expressed her thankfulness for escaping the troopers and being chosen to shelter Father Carroll's testament. She vowed to protect it until the Time of Gathering came. Next, she prayed for the safety of all the miners in Number Six, especially Sara Darcy who was new to that environment. Finally, she asked that Zoe be shown the light of grace, that she find mercy in her heart for all those who believed.

"Amen."

"Amen," another voice repeated outside.

Surprised but not frightened, because she recognized the person, Claire said, "Come in, Candy."

Candy ducked her head through the doorway, allowing her eyes to adjust to the dim interior. "Sorry to intrude," she said, "but I knew we'd be alone here."

"You sound worried."

Candy collapsed to her knees, sobbing uncontrollably. Claire knelt beside her, pulling her close, squeezing her shoulders.

A few minutes later, Candy recovered and propped herself against the stone wall.

"I did something terrible," she confessed. "I was mad as hell and wasn't thinking."

Claire sat on her prayer bench and said, "I know."

"Zoe told you?"

"She showed me the list."

Candy almost broke down again, but then her face clouded behind an accusation. "It's true. You told Bartok about the meeting. Murray's dead because of you!"

"Please, listen," Claire replied. "Zoe's my daughter and always will be. But I would never betray us to her. Never. She's after Father Carroll, and I'm going to find a way to change her mind."

"How? She's a compliance specialist," whined Candy.

"That's my problem. In the meantime, let's deal with your troubles."

"I need help leaving town."

"Why?"

"Everyone's going to hate me for giving Zoe the list!" blurted Candy.

"They'll forgive you. I promise they will."

"She's going to arrest them any minute. She might have arrested them already."

"She has not, and she will not," advised Claire. "Zoe's ambitious, too ambitious for her own good. She always goes for the big prize. Besides, her boss in Philadelphia would never accept a couple of small fish."

"They want us all, Mrs. Whelan," whispered Candy.

"There's not enough prisons. The best thing to do is go to work, do a good job, and let all this sort itself out."

Candy rolled onto her side and laughed hysterically. Then she stood and said, "Zoe was furious that I put your name on the list, Mrs. Whelan. She expects me to cooperate, and if I don't, my baby's going to be born in prison. She'll be put up for adoption or raised at one of the war orphanages."

"Running away is not the right thing to do."

"Why? I can jump the coal train to Philadelphia. Hook up with the Surviving Few. They'll help me."

"Candy, that's incredibly dangerous. The guards on the train shoot to kill."

"I'll take my chances."

"You're five months pregnant!" shouted Claire. Lowering her voice, she added, "In a few days, Zoe will be gone."

"Gone? How do you know?"

"Father Carroll told me."

• • •

Runt trotted along the path, gathering kindling, stuffing it into her satchel. She'd rather be making a cover for Preacher

John's book. He paid a dollar. It was only right she do the work. But Crush was cold, which was strange because she was sweating. When Runt's bag was full, she darted around the turns of the trail, wasting no time looking for shiny stones.

Entering the trailer, she saw Crush hadn't moved from the big chair in the corner.

"Warm in a few minutes," she said, but got only a bobbed-head reply.

Runt carefully cleared the belly of the stove. She built a proper fire, from the paper on the bottom all the way to the larger sticks on top. To light it, she used one of the long wooden matches, sure to touch five different spots. Soon as the flames licked the dry twigs, she closed the door and adjusted the vent.

"Be a good kid and help me up," Crush groaned.

Runt was strong for her size. Gathering firewood, hauling buckets of water, and running away from Bartok worked her muscles better than any exercise regimen. Still, Crush was practically dead weight. Prying her out of the chair was not going to happen.

"I'll find help," Runt said.

"No. Just give me a sec to wind up."

However, Crush's head rolled back, and she let out a long sigh. Her body settled deeper into the chair. Runt got a cloth from the kitchen, wiped her friend's face, then touched her forehead. It was like brushing against the stove after boiling bath water.

Suddenly, Crush's eyes sprung open. "Okay. Here we go."

She slid to the edge of the chair, and with a solid tug from Runt, was on her feet.

"Yay!" cheered Runt.

"Stay with me."

Her first wobbly steps settled into a rhythm of short strides balanced first on Runt, then Jagger's chair, and finally against the far wall. There the trip ended when her knees buckled. She slid down the paneling, thumping on the floor like a fallen rock.

Runt heaved with her little arms until she rolled Crush onto her back.

"Go outside a while," Crush whispered.

"I better stay here like Jagger said."

"She won't be mad. Wait out by the wood pile, okay?"

Runt wasn't sure what to do. Jagger gave the orders, but when she wasn't around, Whip and Crush did. Not the same way, they were a lot nicer, but they told her what to do.

"Please, Runt," Crush begged. "Take a little walk."

Runt stepped back, noticing the growing wet spot on the floor near Crush. The liquid was dark and oily, and it stank. She felt the sudden urge to cry but held the cloth over her eyes instead. Taking it away, she saw her friend's left eye close in a lazy wink. She almost laughed, but then Crush raised one hand to wave goodbye.

Runt raced for the door, yanked it open, and hurtled into the cold afternoon. She leapt over the newly cut firewood and around the big tree near the start of the trail. She ran as fast as she could, picking up speed going downgrade until a misplaced foot slid on a patch of moss. She tumbled over her own shoulders, landing in a ball of tucked arms and messy hair.

"Are you okay?"

Pushing her hair back, Runt saw Father Carroll standing over her, his heavy coat hanging open.

"That was a heck of a fall," he said.

"Can you help my friend?" Runt asked.

They rushed to the trailer where Crush remained flat on the floor. Runt watched Father Carroll take her pulse at the neck then gently pat her face.

"A glass of water," he requested.

Runt tapped the clean jug on the kitchen counter. She returned with the full glass and waited as Father Carroll poured it over Crush's forehead as he smoothed her hair back.

"Fetch another," he said.

Runt did as she was told. When that glass was empty, Crush stirred, let out a quiet moan, and opened her eyes.

"Ah, there you are," Father Carroll said.

"Not for long."

"You're going to be alright," he assured her.

"You can't save me, Father. I killed somebody."

CHAPTER 24.

Their twelve-hour shift ended with no casualties. Mike, Sara, Rat, and the others trudged to the lift. The cage wasn't waiting, which elicited a collective groan. Mike leaned on the call bell as the rest of his crew found places to sit. After a few minutes with no response, he pressed it again.

"Think it shorted out?" Rat asked.

"Nah, probably someone late for work," Mike replied.

Finally, they heard the lift descending. Exhausted from a hard day's work, no one bothered to get up until it lowered into view.

George Nash stayed behind while his crew fanned out to their positions. He took Mike on the side for a private chat, the eyes of the men in the lift glaring at them.

"Things got to change," Nash began. "No offense to your new lady friend, but I don't give a shit about that convict catching a rock with his head. Doesn't mean any of us should die to meet the quota."

"What choice do we have?" Mike asked.

"That's the point. They don't give us one. We have to do what's good for us by making our own choices."

"Many of the men are ex-soldiers from the wrong side," Mike said. "They can't strike, or it's back to prison camp."

"What about the others? Eh?"

"I'll bet they don't want to be starved out."

"Come the day we'll all have to take sides again," Nash warned. "Have some fun with your lady then give that some thought."

Mike entered the cage and rang the bell.

"Buy you and Sara a round of grog?" Rat offered.

"Thanks," Mike answered, "but I think we should all get some rest."

. . .

Jagger and Whip made their clothing selections. Boyle didn't haggle much over the price, which was a welcome relief. He gave them a ride back to the trailer, albeit via the Pleasant Corner, where their help unloading twenty cases of grog knocked a few dollars off the garment invoice.

"See, this job ain't so bad," Boyle said as they piled into his pickup for the final leg to the trailer. "Two of you and the other one could fill in a couple days a week. Make some honest money."

"How much?" Whip inquired.

"Not enough," Jagger said.

"Damn short-sighted, if you ask me," Jerry muttered.

After he dropped them at the end of their drive, Whip took up the subject.

"What's wrong with working for him?"

"Want to spend the rest of your life humping grog and pig feed, be my guest."

"Could save the money until your master plan comes together," suggested Whip.

"My master plan is now complete and will be the topic of discussion around the supper table," insisted Jagger, who paused when she saw Crush's jeans, shirt, and underwear hanging on the line outside the trailer. The couch cushions were also there.

Whip said, "Runt must have done some laundry."

Jagger took her time up the stairs, opening the door, too. Dylan's death had yet to settle in, and she would never admit it, but the writing was on the wall for Crush. Still, she hadn't expected it this soon. Internal injuries took their time killing someone. Crush being tougher than most meant it might be a week before they dug another hole.

The living room was hot enough to bake potatoes. Jagger left the door open as she stepped inside. Wearing only an oversized T-shirt, Runt stood at the stove, which was covered with pots of steaming water.

"Hey, boss," Runt said, cheerfully. "What's up, Whip?"

"Where's Crush?" asked Jagger.

"Sleeping."

"You sure?"

"Been snoring the past two hours."

Jagger cocked an ear toward the hallway.

"She took a bath, and I washed all her clothes," continued Runt. "Water was icky so I'm heating more for me."

"You do that," Jagger said on her way to the larger of the two bedrooms.

Crush lay on her back in the middle of the bed. Her snoring almost shook the dingy curtains. Her color seemed normal. Jagger let loose the widest grin, then checked it with her usual scowl. Dylan had a good day before he gave up the ghost.

Back at the stove, Jagger asked Runt, "She eat today?"

"Nope."

While Runt washed, Jagger and Whip cooked supper on the already hot stove. Beans and rice with some canned corn was the main dish. A few dashes of hot sauce gave it a kick. Deer jerky kept them chewing more than talking, which was to Jagger's liking. When the table was cleared, she brought out a notebook, opened it wide, and drew a rough grid of Mount Carmel with the railroad tracks leading out of town. She added Route 61, marking where the bus was hidden.

Whip approached the table saying, "Crush is still sleeping."

"Good. You been asking about the plan. Well, take a seat and pay attention."

While Runt sat on the big chair in the living room, Jagger played kitchen-table general. She kept her voice quiet, salting it with a touch of gravitas to make an impression on her only capable soldier.

"Far as I know, John Carroll ain't got wheels, which means same as us, he's on foot. He comes out to our place with Claire to recover his paperwork. Then he shows up for the meeting that got Murray killed at the old Number Four. After that, he disappears. But he ain't no apparition, is he?"

Whip wasn't sure what the word meant. She nodded just the same.

"He's not. Nor does he smell as bad as a guy living in a cave somewhere. What's that indicate to the clever and perceptive?"

Whip shrugged.

"He's got a place to stay, somewhere to take a bath, and not boiling water on the stove like our little missy has to do, either. He eats, maybe not plenty, but regularly, without showing his face at a store where someone would spot him."

"Could be with any of his people in town."

"Can whittle that number down to one."

"Claire Whelan?"

It was Jagger's turn to nod.

"But her daughter is the compliance specialist we rolled. He couldn't hide out in the same house where she's staying."

"He could have, until not our friend but our possible benefactor, Ms. Whelan herself, arrived in town and kicked over the hornet's nest."

Whip started to understand.

"Yeah, he's shacking up on the run now. My guess is one of the abandoned houses somewhere in town."

"Wait. Why do we care about him anyway?" asked Whip.

"I can't fix the crack in my ass, but I can change my name," explained Jagger. "So can you, and Runt, and Crush. All we have to do is find him and that book of his. Zoe Whelan's the high bidder and has the clout to get us new identification to go with our new clothes, which we will proudly wear in another locale when we spend double Selman's reward, which is the amount agreed to by her."

"What about Bartok and Selman?"

"If we turn Preacher John over to Bartok, he wants to call it even for pulling off the bus job, with a bonus of the standard ten-grand reward."

"Cheap bastard."

"Worse. He'll double-cross us. We'd be lucky if he keeps the money and lets us loose, but I suspect if we deliver the man of God, we'll all disappear."

"What's to stop Philly Chick from screwing us?"

"Nothing but our wits. First, we find Preacher John and his scribbles. Then, we parlay it from there."

"No," Crush said from the end of the hallway, a blanket draped over her shoulders, and a prison guard's pistol at the ready. "We leave Preacher John alone."

• • •

What a difference a week made. Seven days ago, Candy was concerned for her unborn baby's health and Lenny Donovan finding out the kid wasn't his. Now? If Zoe Whelan didn't send her to prison, the whole town would hate her. She wasn't to blame, either. She'd done nothing but say her prayers, live a good life, do her job, and mind her own business. Technically, she was having an affair with Kyle while in the stupid unity pact with Lenny. She actually saw it the other way around because it was Kyle she loved, not Lenny. Besides, Lenny didn't want anything to do with her since she got pregnant, which was just as well.

Of course, Lenny didn't mind showing up for supper most nights. Given the food Denise brought home, no one could blame him. Tonight was no exception. There were steaks and huge potatoes, fresh green beans and cranberry sauce. None of it was left-over, pre-war canned crap. Amazingly, Denise rarely ate much of it herself. Candy knew her sister was a drug addict and did everything possible to help her, but it was a lost cause.

"Steaks again?" Lenny complained no sooner than he came through the door.

Candy ignored him as she turned the meat over in her grandmother's cast-iron pan. What he didn't eat, she would save for the trip with Kyle. Cold steak was still steak and would keep them full on the long journey.

"Walk your ass out to Jerry Boyle's and get me some pork chops for tomorrow."

"I'll take the car and go tonight," Candy offered.

"Shut up. You don't know how to drive."

She did know how to drive. Kyle taught her in his dad's pickup. It wasn't difficult. In fact, if Lenny went to the Pleasant Corner like every other night, she planned to help herself to his car while he was sipping grog. She and Kyle were skipping town, to a spot near Pottsville where the coal train slowed. There they would ditch the car and hop aboard. They'd hide in one of the cars until the train began the final leg to Philadelphia, thereby avoiding the checkpoint. Once in the city, they could disappear among the Surviving Few.

"That damn steak ready?"

"Almost," she said.

"Get out of the way," he said, shoving her to the side, "before the damn thing is shoe leather."

Lenny flipped the bloody steak onto a plate and took his seat at the table.

"I have a potato in the oven."

"Give it to the kid," he said, carving off a chunk almost too big for his mouth. "Bring me the ketchup."

She got the bottle from the fridge, then returned to the stove where she prepared herself another steak. By the time it was ready, Lenny had scarfed his.

"When's that baby coming out?" he asked as Candy sat down

to eat.

"About four months."

"Long time to go without marital relations."

A blessing, she thought.

"Lot of other things you could do for me."

"Made you supper."

If she had any reservations about leaving, his slap put them out of her mind.

"Ought to make you do something right now."

"I'm eating."

He slammed both fists on the table. "Feed your face, you fat cow!"

She expected another slap. Instead, he grabbed his jacket and stormed out the back door.

Candy took a moment to relax before chewing the next bite. Before she got to the second one, she heard two quick taps on the side window. Seconds later, Kyle slipped in the same way Lenny had just left.

"He hit you?" Kyle asked.

"The last time," Candy confirmed. "Let's eat and get out of here."

"He took the car."

"I know where it'll be parked, and where he hides the spare key."

• • •

They were outside, away from the others, Crush seated on the chopping stump. Jagger paced back and forth.

"Fell flat on my face. Piss and blood running out of me. My ears ringing with the hell's bells. It got real dark then. I knew I was going to die."

"You weren't going to die."

"Hell, yeah, I was. But then I felt this cool water on my forehead. Little by little the pain went away. Don't know how long it was but I opened my eyes, and there he was, Preacher John, himself." Crush shook her head. "He healed me."

"Bullshit!" Jagger countered. "You healed yourself."

"I was dead."

"If you were dead, we'd be digging a hole for you over there next to Dylan. The troopers know just how and where to hit that it hurts without doing permanent damage."

"Trust me, I was permanently damaged. Not anymore. Nothing hurts. Not even the bruises."

"I don't believe it."

"Then don't," Crush said.

"That phony didn't do nothing for Dylan, and I'll bet he didn't do nothing for you but what Runt was already doing. You're sentimental because he showed up for the last minute in your hour of need."

Although no longer in pain, Crush lacked the energy to argue.

"John Carroll's our ticket out of here and on to better things."

"Don't care. I ain't helping snare him."

Jagger put out her hand. "Give me the gun."

"What I did with this going to haunt me the rest of my life."

"Preacher John didn't wash away all your sin?"

"Nah," Crush replied, tapping the side of her head with the barrel. "Got it all up here."

"Sounds to me like a case of the guilts for giving back a little what they done to us a whole lot."

"Calling it even is all I'm saying."

Jagger spit to the side, then said, "Ain't never even with them. They take until there ain't nothing left."

Her arms open wide, Crush agreed. "They already took it all. Look at us. Wearing rags. Living in a dump. No running water. Stealing to eat. We're finished."

"You're finished. I'm just getting started."

"At what?" Crush huffed, "Winning the race to a dead end?"

Jagger let her go inside, wondering if her cousin's departure was for the best. She wasn't going to beg or bully. If she had to, she would catch John Carroll on her own. Leave Whip to look after Runt and stay light on her feet. Sure, it would be nice to have another pair of eyes scouring the streets. On the other hand, if her hunch was accurate, there might not be much real estate to scope, because Preacher John was probably hiding close to Claire Whelan. As for sharing the loot, well, too bad for those not participating, because they were entitled to zilch.

· · ·

"One sec," Candy said to Kyle, who stood with his hand on the doorknob.

She ran up to her bedroom, where she slipped on the fine gold necklace that had been her mother's, the one with the cross on it. She took a last look in the mirror, then returned to the kitchen.

"All set?" Kyle asked.

She kissed him hard. They were outside a moment later.

Candy's bag was heavy. She had dithered about what to take. Clothing? Keepsakes? Snacks? Some of each? Nothing? She couldn't decide. In the end, she frantically settled on two changes of clothes, an extra pair of shoes from Denise's closet, two hats, and some gloves. Several bottles of water, crackers, cookies, and four hastily made steak sandwiches and the bag was stuffed.

"You remembered the car keys?" Kyle asked.

"Got 'em."

They were the first thing she put in her pocket. Lenny hid them in the toe of his old work boots. She saw him fish them out one day when his regular boots got wet. It wasn't his only habit. He always parked in the same place near the Pleasant Corner, two spots away from the door. Not that there was any competition for parking spaces, because all but a few of the clientele arrived on foot. However, when Candy and Kyle peeked out from Cedar Alley, the car wasn't there.

"Damn," Kyle groused. "If we don't find the car soon, we'll miss the train."

"Maybe he's worried about the miners slashing his tires," Candy suggested, "and parked somewhere else."

"Okay, but where?"

Candy thought for a second. "He's lazy, so it can't be far."

They jogged past the Pleasant Corner, going two blocks north before turning into the next alley. A hundred feet on, they found the car tucked between two sheds. They hugged to celebrate then agreed Candy should steer as Kyle pushed the car into the street. From there, they would coast down the block before starting the engine.

It went exactly to plan. Kyle hopped in at the last second, as Candy turned the key. The car was still warm and started easily. She dropped the lever from neutral to drive and they were off.

Not worried about wasting gas, Candy floored it as soon as they were out of town. Neither of them had driven in so long that it was like a childhood thrill. The old sedan chugged up to seventy miles an hour on Route 901. Kyle lowered the window, stuck his head out, and hollered at the sky.

It only took twenty minutes to drive to the hamlet of Buck Run, which had been uninhabited for a decade. The state trooper checkpoint was a mile down the road. They dispatched patrols to scour the vacant streets for squatters. On the south side of the little town, the railroad made a hard bend on old tracks. The coal train slowed to five miles per hour through the turn. Still, it would be a tricky jump, especially with their bags and the possibility of being caught.

Candy drove over dead weeds poking up from the streets. A tree grew through the collapsed roof of one house. Other homes had burned or collapsed from neglect. Anything metal had been taken away. Clusters of bullet holes, probably from drunk troopers having fun, pocked random walls.

"Look!" Kyle gasped as a herd of deer scampered at the edge

of their headlights.

"Wow," Candy said, hitting the brake. "Must be thirty."

"Or more. If the government let us hunt, we'd have a lot more to eat."

They left the car in the driveway of a corner house, one they might have owned had things been different. The big backyard would have been an ideal playground for their little girl. Candy saw herself sitting on the porch, watching her future child chase friends in a game of tag. If she wasn't furious about the terrible turn her life had taken, she would have cried over what should have been. Instead, she steeled herself for the leap aboard the train and followed Kyle the last hundred yards.

Suddenly, Kyle stopped and said, "Listen."

The low rumble of the locomotives carried down the tracks.

"It's early," he said. "Come on. We have to go."

They picked their way over the rails, ducking behind a tall pine on the other side when the lead engine swung into view, its headlamp poking through the darkness.

For all the rush to get this far, time slowed down as the train crawled along the line. The engine noise grew louder, punctuated by wheel flange squeals as each car swung into the tighter radius of the curve.

Candy covered her ears when the locomotives passed. Glancing right, she saw a gun in Kyle's hand. It was Lenny's service revolver. He must have taken it from Lenny's duty belt which hung on the coat rack at the back door.

"Oh, my God," she mouthed.

He replied with a smile, nod, and, "No worries."

Once the engines and several cars wound by, they broke cover. Keeping pace with the lumbering coal cars was easier than expected. Kyle heaved his rucksack onto the platform at the front of a laden car then did the same with Candy's smaller bag.

"Grab the ladder and keep climbing," he said.

Candy reached up, caught a low rung, then struggled to hang

on and simultaneously run. She stumbled and almost fell, but Kyle gave her a last-second boost. Up she went, followed by the man she loved. They swung onto the platform, panting, surprised they actually made it.

"We'll hide out between the cars if the train stops in Pottsville," Kyle said. "But we're going all the way to Philadelphia." He planted a big kiss on Candy's lips to prove he meant it. After a few minutes watching the trees go by, he tucked the unneeded gun into his rucksack.

CHAPTER 25.

After meeting with Colonel Stewart, Selman lingered in Pottsville. He sought his usual indulgence, for which there should have been at least two locations for a town that size. He was disappointed to find only one. It featured women, not his first choice. Worse, all of them were twice the age he preferred. He decided to forgo the entertainment for an excessive meal at the exclusive Black Diamond Club. Naturally, it cost him nothing, another benefit afforded ranking Common Faith officials.

Lacking anyone worthy of decent conversation, he got mildly drunk through the meal on a bottle of red wine. At the bar afterwards, he sipped several glasses of port, reminiscing with himself about the days when he aspired to take over the megachurch from its founding country preacher, who had evolved it into a slick money machine. Incredibly, the man never lived a lavish lifestyle. He fostered a list of causes that depleted the coffers as fast as they were refilled. Fair enough, that's what he promised to do. Still, he never took a vow of poverty. More important, nor did Selman. He worked for a paycheck. Sometimes it was late. That was no way to live.

Thankfully, chaos came. As with every upheaval, temporary sacrifices resulted in more rewarding opportunities for those capable of and willing to exploit them. His current trouble with Zoe Whelan aside, Selman was living proof of how far an ambitious man could go. He had transformed the nature of religion in the modern era. Not bad for a back-bench pastor. He raised a glass to himself.

As for the country preacher who hit the big-time, that poor soul suffered a horrible end. He mediated a peace parlay between two factions warring over which one controlled Baltimore. Everyone died when a third group swooped in with a remote-controlled car bomb. Leveled a city block. Six months later, the bombers also perished when federal soldiers retook the entire city. Selman knew better than to get between the irrational and the delusional.

In honor of what the man taught him, Selman raised another glass. As he swallowed the mouthful of port, he was astonished to see Randy Bartok appear.

"I hope you didn't walk all this way," Selman greeted his underling.

"Took the coal train."

"Sounds frightful. What prompted the journey?"

"A tip from our friend."

"To do with our fallen priest and his testament?"

"Not directly, but a surprise for the compliance specialist from Philadelphia."

Selman reveled in Bartok's surprises, especially those announced with a grin. On unsteady feet, he left the bar for the street outside where several trooper personnel carriers were parked.

"No need for a parade," Selman remarked.

Bartok led him to the last one in the line. A trooper opened the rear door, revealing a covered body. Another pulled back the sheet to reveal Kyle Smith's bloody face.

"Oh, dear," Selman said. "Don't tell me you shot this poor young man."

"The troopers got him," Bartok replied, holding up a clear bag with a prison guard's service revolver in it. "This pins him to the bus hijacking."

"Ahem, well, too bad he had to lose his life."

"There's a survivor," Bartok said. "Follow me."

They walked to the lead personnel carrier where Colonel Stewart stood facing Candy Walsh, who sat in the back, her hands cuffed.

"Figured you want to take this one back for trial," Stewart said.

"Oh, not me," Selman told the senior trooper, "but I'm sure Compliance Specialist Whelan will."

• • •

There was no reasoning with Zoe. Claire settled on appeasement. It didn't mean she was surrendering. In fact, Zoe's demand that she move to Philadelphia solved Claire's biggest problem: getting Father Carroll's testament out of Mount Carmel. What could be safer than riding with a compliance specialist? The troopers would see her ID and wave them through any checkpoint. They wouldn't dare question her.

"I'll drive you myself," Zoe promised.

"I can take the bus," Claire suggested, pretending to be worn out.

"Not a chance."

Taking orders from her daughter wasn't the least bit pleasant, but Claire did as she was told. She agreed not to tell Mike until they were about to depart. Zoe refused to give a time or date, only a request for readiness. To that end, Claire cared more about how to disguise the testament versus what to put in her suitcase. She considered repeating the cookbook ruse. The troopers hadn't given them a second look. However, it was unlikely she would be taking cookbooks to Philadelphia.

With Zoe in the house, Claire made a point of staying away from the basement. Upstairs in her bedroom, she took out her old luggage. None of it had been used since she and Patrick went to New York City for a weekend getaway. They saw three plays in as many days, spent too much money on dinners, and swore to come back again. They never did.

Running her hands over the inside of the musty suitcase, she recalled spy movies in which agents hid documents under the lining. It wasn't the worst idea. A search was unlikely. On second thought, if something did go wrong, she'd have to hide her entire suitcase as opposed to something much smaller.

Suddenly, Claire felt truly persecuted. To this point, being a Christian in Mount Carmel was more like membership in a quaint, secret society. Selman was little more than a nuisance. He sent Randy Bartok knocking on doors, asking inconvenient questions that could be answered with money or a gift. It was more a payoff scheme than an act of enforcement. Claire, herself, handed over some clothes to him, things she knew would fit Joannie T. As a result, she and the others went about the rites of their faith with little interruption. They met in basements mostly. Christmas and Easter, Father Carroll held services at the breaker turned cathedral. Claire prayed in her chapel more out of personal devotion than clandestine necessity.

Then Selman found out about Father Carroll's writing. Lenny Donovan happened to be driving to the Pleasant Corner and spotted the former priest on his way to give the last rites. Bad luck? Maybe. An informer? More likely. But who?

Claire spent hours thinking about the people in her group. Joe Grant could be an officious jerk. Had he made a deal for a position in the Common Faith in exchange for turning over Father Carroll? From a family that once owned several gas stations, Pam Reed liked nice things. Had she grown tired of the impoverished life and gone looking for another source of income? And then there was Bill Myer, who never said much about anything until he muttered his dissent. He might have been passing information along for years. Nothing warranted serious attention until Father Carroll mentioned his revelation. Upon learning about it, Selman began his pursuit. But who told him in the first place?

Perhaps it was none of them. Since beginning his testament, Father Carroll lived like a hermit. Claire provided food, kerosene for his lamp, and let him use the shower, but otherwise rarely saw him. His seclusion insulated her and the others from direct association. He checked the old mailbox outside the Post Office every few nights to see if anyone was in need and responded accordingly.

The air of distrust depressed Claire. She believed that people were basically good, especially those she'd known for years. Did that extend to her daughter? Yes, it did. Claire accepted Zoe's course to God's grace was not the most direct. History was full of those who'd done worse and took longer. She was confident Zoe's moment would come. Father Carroll had told her as much.

Just as that thought passed through her mind, Claire had the strange feeling of being watched. She turned toward the open door, to see Zoe there.

"Glad to see you're packing."

Claire gave her a reassuring nod.

"Listen, I have to go to Pottsville."

"At this hour?"

"Not sure when I'll be back."

• • •

Zoe requested a private space to question Candy other than the standard interview room where suspects were interrogated. Colonel Stewart volunteered his office, which was completely inappropriate. She settled on the dispatcher's break room, to which two troopers brought Candy, her hands and feet manacled as if she was a terrorist as opposed to a pregnant schoolteacher.

Zoe gave her a moment to settle into the chair, then asked, "What were you doing with Kyle Smith?"

"Going to Philadelphia," Candy answered.

"If you'd listened to me, the ride would have been a lot more comfortable."

"Thanks for caring."

"The report says he pulled a gun on the troopers."

"It was in his bag! He put his hands up, and they shot him!"

Zoe let Candy's exclamation fade, then said, "Witnesses say it was in his hand."

Candy just shook her head. "By witnesses, you mean the troopers who shot him in cold blood?"

"You can still make this right," Zoe continued. "It's not too late."

"It is for Kyle," Candy sniffed.

"He was the father of your child?"

"What if he was?"

"I'm looking for an excuse," Zoe explained. "A reason you'd risk your life hopping on a coal train in the middle of the night."

"To get away from you," Candy sneered.

"Why? I was the only one trying to help."

"I guess you arrested everyone on the list. Except your mom, eh?"

Zoe held her face in an impassive stare.

"Your mom's one of us. Good old God-fearing Christian, she is. She's closer to John Carroll than anyone else is," Candy rambled. "Makes sense, considering he baptized all of you."

"Be quiet."

"A little too close to home for the wicked compliance specialist from Philadelphia?" Candy dared to ask.

"Careful, Candy."

"About what? Not telling Selman your mom's a Christian? That baby Zoe tasted a few drops of holy water?"

Zoe laughed. "Wait. You think anyone's going to believe accusations made by someone they just arrested?"

Candy did chuckle. "Oh my, Zoe. And to think, you were always the smartest girl in class. Let's play this out. What would you do? Huh? A prisoner gives you a list of names. Throw it in the trash? Heck, no!"

"You gave that list to me."

"Maybe I gave it to Selman ten minutes ago."

"You're a lousy bluffer."

After an exaggerated shrug Candy said, "Got me!" Then added

in her third-grade-teacher's voice, "But what if I left a copy with a friend who's going to drop it on Selman's desk when I don't check in from Philly?"

"A dead-letter drop? Really, Candy?"

"Believe me or don't. Just remember, I have nothing left to lose. You, on the other hand, well, there's the career and all the perks that come with it. Not to mention your mom spending five to ten in prison followed by time in a coal mine, if she lives long enough."

Zoe leapt to her feet, shouting, "Don't you dare blackmail me!"

"Go ahead. Slap me silly. The troopers did. I can take it."

"Shut your mouth."

"You owe me, and you're going to pay," Candy sneered. "I want a free ride to Philly. And that job at a fancy school. The nice apartment, too."

Zoe fumed at Candy's sudden cleverness. Yet, she wasn't going to lose her temper again. "Anything else?"

"I'll think about it."

"Please, do. I wouldn't want you to be disappointed." Zoe went to the door, opened it, and told the troopers outside, "Gag the prisoner for transport."

They happily obliged.

●   ●   ●

Visitors after dark were a rare thing for anyone in Mount Carmel. Normally, Claire would not open the door, especially when home alone. But she recognized the knock, and rushed downstairs to the kitchen.

"What happened?" she asked Joe Grant, who waited under the awning.

"You don't know?" he answered with a combination of anger and bitterness.

"No. Please, come in."

Grant looked at his feet, then raised his face to glare. "Everyone thinks you're a traitor."

"Then why come to see me?"

"My conscience wouldn't let me run away without at least giving you the benefit of the doubt."

"Then come in. Tell me what happened."

"I don't have time. Maybe you don't either," he said.

"Did they catch Father Carroll?"

"No. The troopers got Kyle and Candy."

"For what?"

"They tried to ride the coal train to Philly. Kyle's dead. Zoe's on her way back here with Candy."

"How did you find out?"

"My cousin lives near the trooper barracks. He called after Zoe left with Candy."

"Bad news travels fast."

"Listen. I have a car. We can get out of town quick. Myer knows a path through the woods around the checkpoint near Hazleton. Bring Father Carroll's testament."

"I don't have it here," Claire lied.

"Can we pick it up along the way?"

"Not a good idea if Bartok and the troopers are looking for us."

"You don't trust me, do you?"

"I can't afford to," answered Claire.

Frustrated, Grant said, "Whatever you're up to, I suggest you find a place to hide."

With that warning, he turned for the sidewalk, where a car waited. When he got in back, the dome light came on, revealing Pam Reed staring back at Claire. They drove down the block, made the first left, and disappeared.

Claire assumed Zoe was already on her way back from Pottsville with Candy. Would Zoe confer with Selman? Would she make calls to Philadelphia for orders? Claire figured the relocation to the city was on hold, which meant she had to get Father Carroll's testament out of the house. Sooner or later, someone with a badge would come for her and then rip the house apart for incriminating evidence. Reports on television showed how compliance specialists like Zoe tore houses down to the studs in search of religious contraband.

Claire ran to the basement, where she was shocked to find the mess Zoe left after searching for the hatchet. She panicked at the possibility her daughter had already found the testament. She gathered the heavy winter clothes from atop the spilled boxes and placed them to the side. She immediately spotted the scattered cookbooks. Her hands sorted them until she located the one she carried back and forth to the mine office. Opening the cover, she saw Father Carroll's writing remained undisturbed.

Relieved but still fearful, she thought about where to hide the stack of handwritten pages. Her first idea was to put it somewhere in the Cathedral. The old coal breaker had hundreds of suitable places inside. But eventually the authorities would search there, as they would the homes and any other meeting locations Candy might reveal while in custody. She didn't want to put it in some random place, either, where it might be discovered by accident.

She settled on a spot near her chapel. In the copse of trees to the west there were several large rocks. Under one of them was as safe a place as any. It was also not in the building, which meant if they ripped her private space apart, they'd find nothing. For an extra measure of protection, she wrapped it in an old raincoat, secured with a length of twine.

Winding through town, Claire recalled the people who once lived in the abandoned houses. They were friends of the family or recognizable strangers. Most of them died in the war. The rest moved away. A collection of widows remained in one of the larger homes until the last one, Mrs. Czerny, committed suicide. Claire had offered Zoe's former room to her, but she'd had enough. Her husband taken by the war, hiding her Christianity, losing the others to the Flu of '52 but surviving herself, it was all too much.

Claire understood the desire to be free of worldly burdens, especially the torture of survivor's guilt. Over the years, people all around her died, beginning with Patrick and continuing to Murray Smith less than a week ago, and now Kyle. Yet, she went on as if protected by the hand of God. And maybe she was. Most recently it felt that way. She'd avoided any number of life-threatening hazards, from Randy Bartok's shotgun, to the troopers, to her own daughter's quest to prosecute Father Carroll. The unfairness of the situation haunted her. However, she believed God would call her name when her purpose was fulfilled.

To that end, she entered the cluster of trees near her chapel. She felt her way among the rocks, searching for the largest one. Her fingers grasped the edge of a slab that was perfect, but too heavy for her to move. She fell back on her rump, laughing at her ambition. Back at work, she found another chunky boulder. This one she rolled to the side. Into the depression she placed Father Carroll's testament. Returning the stone to its original position, she told herself she wasn't abandoning the message but securing it for the future. She knelt to pray in the moonlight, asking God's protection for the document and that she might someday hear it read aloud.

Her mission complete, Claire walked away with a powerful sense of fulfillment. Not intentionally or out of pride, but due to necessity, she had created a Holy Site. She imagined that someday people would come to her little shrine and learn the story of Father Carroll, of all of them in this little town.

• • •

Claire was about fifty yards away when Jagger rose from the tall weeds beside the trail. The leader of the Mollies wished her comrades had been along for the ride. It went without a hitch. From the time she staked out Claire Whelan's house, through the tense moments when Joe Grant rolled up, all the way through town and to the spring house, Jagger stalked the poor woman like a lioness hunting gazelle. And Jagger knew exactly how the African hunt went because she watched it on the stolen DVD player in between the war movie. Of course, not wanting to upset Runt, she switched it off just before the kill. Anyway, Jagger mimicked the moves of the lead lion, staying low, keeping her eye on the prey, sometimes getting ahead, sometimes trailing behind. Always, always, checking her back in case someone is hunting the hunter, which is exactly what Whip and Crush had done to Zoe last week.

The thrill of a successful mission aside, Jagger was ecstatic at having anticipated Claire Whelan would have John Carroll's scribblings. Well, not exactly. She actually thought she might catch the man himself stopping in for food or a shower. Instead, as soon as she saw Claire exit the house clutching a folded jacket, she knew the pages were in there. Why else would she split after a frantic exchange with Joe Grant? Tedious as it was trailing the lady, Jagger was relieved to avoid detection and violence. Not that she would have held back had there been resistance.

Jagger slipped through the trees, pausing in a crouch for several minutes to be certain Claire did not return. Then she switched on her tiny flashlight, which cast a quarter-sized spot of light on the ground. Moving it to and fro, she saw rocks, weeds, and tree roots. One by one, Jagger shifted the rocks.

Number eight was the charm. Beneath the rock was a raincoat bundled around something dense. Jagger took it in hand, curious to read what all the fuss was about, but decided to do that where the light was better back in the trailer. Then she'd give it to Runt for installation of a cover before presenting it to the Philly Chick, with John Carroll, when she found him, and collecting her payday.

CHAPTER 26.

In the interest of protecting her case and doing a high school classmate a favor, Zoe took Candy to Mount Carmel's jail. Not that the ride was pleasant. The chains were dramatic, the gag humiliating. That was the point: to cow the prisoner. Force her to see her hopeless position. Surprisingly, Candy endured the restraints with stoic acceptance. Zoe expected some tears, perhaps some screaming or kicking. None punctuated the ride over the mountain.

More startling was the scene at Mount Carmel's disused police station. The holding cells were more kennel than lockup. Three pens fitted into the back of the first floor served the purpose. Each one contained a cot and a five-gallon bucket latrine. Bad as that was, there were no regular officers on duty. None other than Lenny Donovan greeted Zoe at the door.

"Director Selman called," Donovan explained. "Said I'm supposed to keep an eye on her until the troopers send a few auxiliaries."

"Unacceptable," Zoe retorted. "You're her significant other."

"Yeah, but just for the benefits. Ain't like we sleep in the same bed or anything."

"Call your backup."

"I got no backup. It's only Randy Bartok with me filling in when I'm not at the prison in Pottsville."

Through this exchange, Candy stood by as if the conversation was about someone else. Her feet were killing her. She also felt nauseous. Leaning against the wall, she waited for a resolution.

"There's not another qualified police person in town?" Zoe asked.

"No," answered Lenny.

Zoe noticed he wore his duty belt with cuffs but no holster. "Where's your weapon?"

"Don't need a gun to keep an eye on her. She's five months pregnant."

Candy grinned around the gag. Wait until they find out Kyle took Lenny's gun, she thought. That'll be a problem for everyone.

Zoe found it less amusing. "What if other Christians come to make a scene?"

Lenny waved off the idea. "Bunch of sheep," he said. "I'll bark; they'll run away."

The moron wore Zoe out. After he unshackled Candy, took off her gag, and secured her in one of the pens, Zoe sent him to get the mother-to-be something to eat.

From outside the cage, Zoe said, "Let's talk about your future."

Candy sat on the cot, wiggled her feet, and replied, "Rather we talk about yours."

"If you want to make a deal, time's running out."

"For both of us," Candy said, stretching out, rubbing a hand over the bulge in her belly. "I don't know how long it takes to drive to Philly, but if we leave now, we can probably get there in time for me to stop Selman from finding out your mom's the closest Christian to John Carroll."

"That ploy's worn out. Give it up, okay?"

"Okay," Candy sighed. "When Selman's done with me, he'll get you."

"Hah!" Zoe spat.

Suddenly, Candy sat upright then lunged for the bucket. She vomited a stream that splattered onto her face and hair.

"Now what's the matter?"

"I was beat up by a bunch of troopers then gagged for an hour! I should see a doctor."

"You're fine," Zoe remarked.

Candy heaved again and again. The sound was awful. Less came out until there was nothing but spit. Zoe passed a rag through the bars.

"You could be home. Taking a shower. Relaxing in your own bed."

"Oh, well," Candy shrugged, using the rag to wipe bile dripping from her hair. "Only four months and my baby will be born. Your mom's going to spend years in jail. Maybe the rest of her life."

"It's too bad you got caught up in a game played by evil people willing to use others like yourself to get what they want."

"Last call for Philadelphia," Candy said. "Can still make it if we leave now. Excuse the smell of puke."

"I'll be back in the morning with formal charges."

• • •

Recent unannounced visits from Bartok and the troopers caused Jagger to approach the trailer indirectly and cautiously. She didn't want to lose half the prize en route to the whole enchilada. She went the long way around, out through the woods, off the trail, careful not to stumble and thereby make detectable noise or twist an ankle. The detour took an extra hour. Totally worth it, too, because just before she exited the tree line, a pair of headlights poked up the driveway.

Turned out they belonged to Jerry Boyle's pickup. The man himself barely got to the door when, bags of belongings in both hands, Crush exited. Then Runt ran out, making a fuss until Whip joined them. Some back and forth between Whip and Crush came next.

Jagger interpreted from afar. Crush begged Whip to go with her. Whip turned her down. Her reasons? Not entirely clear. It ended with Runt on the ground bawling her eyes out. That was hard to watch, but a good lesson for the little one. Life dealt some shit cards. Learn to play them better than the next guy or get used to losing. Or so Jagger believed.

Crush hefted Runt off the dirt for a final hug, which surely came with a promise to see her often or soon or something like that. Runt accepted it as goodbye, then clung to Whip as the pickup backed into the wood-chopping area to turn around before rolling down the driveway. Whip waited until the taillights were gone, then ushered Runt inside.

Jagger gave everyone time to settle down, including herself. As much as she boasted internally that she was content to cash the reward check alone, she truly wanted to share it with her gang. They'd been a team, a family. Flaws and all, together they survived. To some extent, they prospered. Losing Crush hurt. Bad. Yet Jagger understood her cousin's reasoning. She'd gone hungry now and then, cold quite often, and been beaten to a pulp. Shacking up with Jerry was definitely greener grass.

"No hard feelings," Jagger said aloud. If things worked out, she'd hand Crush a wad of cash for old times' sake. Not the cut of a full member, but a nice chunk as a reminder that their history was appreciated.

When Jagger entered the living room, Whip greeted her from the couch.

"Crush left to live with Jerry Boyle."

"No surprise to me," remarked Jagger.

"Not like as a girlfriend."

"Her choice to do as she pleases. Maybe you want to go, too."

Whip held her gaze. "Thinking about it. What about Runt?"

"What about her?"

"She can't stay here with you."

"Took you and Crush in after your parents died. Nobody starved or froze to death under my roof, did they?"

"I meant—"

"What? I'm not the best mother? Okay, that's an irrefutable fact. Doesn't mean I don't care. Figure out what you want for yourself and what's best for Runt. Let me know."

Jagger went to the smaller of the two bedrooms where Runt lay face down sobbing.

"I found something you lost," she said from the doorway.

Runt peeked out from under her forearm.

"Want it now or for your birthday?"

After a swipe of sleeve across her nose, Runt averted her eyes.

Jagger sat on the bed, placing Father Carroll's manuscript to the side. "You didn't lose a friend today," she began.

"I did! Crush is gone!" Runt whined, burying her face in a pillow.

"She's not gone. She just lives somewhere else."

"Why can't she live here?"

"People have to do what they have to do."

"That's stupid!"

"It's called growing up," continued Jagger. "Another part of growing up is getting your work done."

"I already washed the dishes."

"Very good. But this is a special job, one you promised to do. Remember?"

"No."

"You said you were going to make a cover for all those pages you found. Turn it into a real book."

Runt rolled over.

Jagger held up the manuscript. "They're all here."

The kid stared at the pages in disbelief.

"Make a fancy cover, okay?"

"Why fancy?"

"Because we'll get more money when we sell it."

Runt took the bundle of pages into her hands. "Did you read it?" she asked.

"After you make the cover, we'll read it together. Deal?"

• • •

When it came to eating, Lenny Donovan was used to people preparing his meals. Candy did most of the cooking at home. Once in a while Denise gave it a try, but usually burned the meat and boiled the vegetables to mush. He snacked at the Pleasant Corner when Steve Regan put out a spread. At the prison, he ate in the employee commissary. Therefore, taking food to Candy in prison challenged his domestic skills.

He rummaged around the cupboards but couldn't decide what to take. How much he was supposed to provide was another problem. A single meal? Enough for a day? Two days? Zoe hadn't been specific. And why hadn't she taken Candy to the Pottsville prison anyway? They had a women's facility, complete with separate cafeteria. It was stupid to drag her to Mount Carmel.

He settled on peanut butter and jelly, a jar of each stuffed in a bag with a loaf of bread and a jug of iced tea. Yeah, Candy scarfed more since she got pregnant, but it was plenty to hold her over for a night. At this hour, she would probably just go to sleep, rendering his jog back and forth a waste of time. If that turned out to be the case, he'd have a sandwich himself.

At the police station, Lenny presented his solution to Zoe, who now sat in the front office with her feet on the desk.

"Good job," she said. "By the way, Candy's not here because of what happened on the train. Understand?"

"Ummm, okay."

"She's here in protective custody. That means no visitors. No friends. No family. No one."

"Yes, ma'am."

"Can you stay awake all night?"

"Do it all the time," Lenny bragged. "Pull a double shift at Pottsville twice a month." He didn't add that during most of the overnight hours he slept in an empty cell.

"Great. Here's my direct cell number. Anything happens, call me immediately."

"Some crazy Christians aren't going to bust her out."

"For your sake, I hope not."

Always with the drama, Lenny thought, as Zoe left the building. With her out of the way, he could settle in for the night.

"Got your food," he announced as he entered the holding area.

"Wow, thanks," Candy replied, taking the items one at a time through the bars. "I made you a steak dinner. You bring me PBJ."

"Wasn't me ran off with someone else," Lenny grumbled. "Mind telling me where I might find my car?"

"Left it safe in Buck Run, but I'll bet you Randy Bartok got it by now."

"Figures."

"I'm supposed to spread this with my fingers?" Candy asked, holding up the jars of peanut butter and jelly.

"Yeah."

Her stomach had settled, leaving her quite hungry. Like a child, Candy made herself a sandwich, licking her fingers clean at the end. It wasn't pretty, but it tasted wonderful. As she ate, Lenny removed the cot from the next pen, taking it to one of the empty offices out front.

"You're not going to sleep in here?" asked Candy.

"And listen to you snore? No way."

"Can I at least use the real bathroom?"

"The compliance specialist," Lenny answered sarcastically, "gave strict orders."

"What's it like having her as your boss?"

"She ain't my boss."

"Just told me she gave you orders."

"Shut up with that!"

"Come on, Lenny. After tonight, they'll take me to Graterford, and you'll never have to deal with me again. Can I please use the bathroom?"

He stood outside the ladies' room while she did her best to clean up from what happened on the train. She rinsed away bits of Kyle's dried blood still on her hands from when she stooped to his body after the troopers shot him. Next, she tended the cuts and scrapes on her arms and legs. A trooper shoved her away from Kyle. She landed hard on the ballast rock. Two others smacked her several times until she finally gave them her name. Finally, she washed her hair in the sink, getting rid of the puke, sweat, and dirt.

Miserable as she was for all the horror that befell her, not to mention the terrible days ahead in prison, Candy returned to her cell in a better frame of mind. Revenge was a sin, but she was human and therefore born a sinner. So be it. She wasn't bluffing. There was a letter, the kind of well-written explanation Selman could use to ruin Zoe's career. In her heart, Candy believed Claire would escape. She had given her fair warning, which was a way of mitigating the consequences. Claire was smart. She was probably long gone with the others on the list. Without mentioning why, Kyle told Joe Grant that Selman might be looking for them, too. Thus, everyone had a chance to get away.

"I'm going to watch some TV out front," Lenny said, switching off most of the overhead lights.

"Enjoy."

Candy settled onto the cot, taking a moment to gloat over Zoe's demise. Compliance specialist? Not for long. That swanky apartment in the sky? Gone. The personal car? Taken away. Next stop? A stint in Tolerance Training Camp, followed by a supervised job involving hours of repetitive manual labor.

As you sow, so shall you reap, Candy recalled from the Bible. The proverb couldn't be more applicable to Zoe's life.

She let the thrill fade away. It was wrong to wish ill toward anyone. She prayed for forgiveness. She asked God to welcome Kyle to heaven, and that He guide Zoe through the trouble ahead and protect Claire. She also asked for strength to get through her own difficulties. The prayer wasn't a sudden conversion intended to reverse damage done. She vowed to do her part in the future, bringing God's love to other women in prison. After all, that's who she really was; a teacher.

Still heartbroken, but content that she was righting wrongs, Candy pulled the blanket over her shoulders. Her final thought before falling asleep was about the simple pleasure of eating a peanut butter and jelly sandwich.

Much later, in the weirdest dream she ever had, she heard her own voice softly call, "Lenny."

And again, "Lenny."

Why would she ask for him instead of Kyle? It didn't make sense, but dreams never did.

One more time, "Lenny."

She felt chilly then and pulled the blanket tighter.

CHAPTER 27.

Colonel Stewart knew how to throw a party. What better indicator of how good it had been than Selman's hangover and soreness from events and specific personal acts between the time Zoe Whelan took Candy Walsh away and sunrise? Forget quality alcohol. There were drugs: cocaine, marijuana, and pharmaceutical-grade amphetamines. Initially, it was difficult to decide. Later it was more difficult to stop. Then came pleasures of the flesh, women and men to choose from, including his personal delicacy, of which he sampled two. The second reminded him of Ian Walsh. It felt like cheating.

To think it cost him nothing. As a thank you for the tip that led to live target practice on Kyle Smith, the troopers had taken him to the top floor of the former Crown Hotel, where they maintained a private club for their exclusive use. Where more than a century ago coal, steel, and railroad magnates entertained themselves in high style, Selman indulged in glorious vice among serious connoisseurs.

Unfortunately, Randy Bartok was not invited due to his quelling of the riot. It was just as well. Selman knew Bartok's regular girlfriend, Joannie Telford, satisfied his limited taste. More important was his work in Mount Carmel, furthering the plan to create a Common Faith martyr in the person of Zoe Whelan. After a meandering and fretful start, it was now accelerating toward a satisfactory conclusion. In a couple of days, he would be driving to Philadelphia to accept his Meritorious Service Medal.

During a break between his first and second private sessions of the evening, Selman spoke with Colonel Stewart. They sat in a corner booth, watching the crowd cavorting on the dance floor and drinking at the bar.

"Was thinking about stationing a platoon in Mount Carmel. Reopen the police station," the colonel said. "Keep those miners under control."

"Not a bad idea," Selman concurred. "First, let's talk about bigger things. Like Philadelphia."

"Out of my jurisdiction."

"Soon it will be in mine," Selman informed the trooper. "I'm going to propose a reorganization of Common Faith's Compliance Division. That means a new commander."

"I've read dozens of proposals. None have been implemented."

"This one will take time, but the pieces are in place—that is, if you're interested."

Looking at the merriment around him, Stewart remained circumspect. "It would have to be worth it."

"A bigger pie means bigger slices for those at the table," Selman told him, then shifted his focus to a blond prepubescent sitting in the corner by his lonesome self.

"And the long line of officers ahead of me?"

"There are plenty of good men for the job," answered Selman. "None of them are my friend." Having planted the seed of ambition, he left the table.

After that, the night was a blur until he finally collapsed. Thankfully, his last companion had the courtesy to leave on his own. He despised the ones who remained until morning, lingering in pursuit of a tip or a favor. Their greed appalled him.

Four cups of coffee and as many aspirin energized Selman as he prepared for a busy day. He remained in his hotel suite. It was critically important he not be in Mount Carmel until after the crisis boiled over. Having put all the pieces in place, he had no doubt that it would. Nonetheless, waiting for matters to unfold was no easy task for a man who enjoyed being the guiding hand.

Next time he would save a few joints to calm his nerves.

He made a game of guessing who would call first. He placed odds based on the person and the role they played. It was a silly exercise, but there was nothing else to do. Bartok was even money, given his skills, attitude, and record. Lenny Donovan paid three to one due to loyalty divided by underlying stupidity. Compliance Specialist Zoe Whelan returned twenty times the bet, not that he expected her to use the phone unless she was held at gunpoint. They were the top three options. There were others: Doctor Erbil, Hester Thompson, even bar-owner Steve Regan. He put them all at fifty to one. He would remain celibate for as many days as the odds returned. The horror he faced if the second tier called! After a night like the last one, it might be just the thing to restore sensitivity.

No sooner had he calculated the odds than his cell rang. He glanced at the clock. Twenty-two past nine. The handset chimed again. Who could it be? A third ring. A fourth. A fifth. This was someone desperate; a casual caller would have disconnected. On the sixth, he answered.

"Martin Selman speaking."

"It's Lenny Donovan. Holy shit, we got a problem!"

"Take a deep breath," Selman said.

"I tried calling Bartok, but he don't answer."

"Have you spoken to anyone else?"

"Hell, no! This is serious, Mr. Selman."

"Whatever it is, we'll get through it together. Tell me what happened."

"Zoe Whelan sent me to get some food for Candy," Lenny began. "I did that. Came back to the jail. Then Zoe gave me orders to stay here all night."

"And you did, correct?" Selman feared Lenny might have skipped out and the Mollies or one of the Christians, maybe Father Carroll, disrupted the operation.

"Was here the whole time. I swear."

"Very good. Go on."

"I slept out front, in the office, you know, just a few hours. Gave Candy privacy."

"Very courteous."

"Yeah, that. I came in a minute ago and—"

The line went quiet. Selman checked to be certain the connection had not been lost.

"Lenny? Are you there?"

"I seen some shit, but this is bad." Sobs came over the line, then, "There's a ton of blood."

• • •

"Where's your cellphone?" Zoe demanded.

"I don't have one," Claire answered.

"Damn it, Mom! We need to stay in touch!"

"Why are you shouting? What's wrong?"

Zoe holstered her gun, and tugged on her jacket, "The landline works here, right? The number's the same?"

"Yes."

"You're packed and ready to go?"

"I was ready last night."

As Zoe pounded toward the back door, she said, "Don't leave the house!"

Minutes later she stared at Candy Walsh's body on the floor of the holding pen. Doctor Erbil, Lenny Donovan, and Randy Bartok were there, too.

Smears of blood led from the cot to Candy, who lay face down on the concrete. More blood soaked the lower portion of the blanket that her dead fingers clutched as if trying to pull it tighter.

"Looks like she started hemorrhaging and bled out," Doctor Erbil put in. "No fetus, but no obvious signs of foul play aside of some bruises. Was she feeling okay when you left Pottsville?"

"Yes," Zoe answered. "She was fine. Maybe a little shaken up.

That's all."

"Did she ask for a doctor?"

"There wasn't time."

"There's an emergency room open all night in Pottsville," interrupted Lenny. "But you brought her straight over here."

"And you spent the night with her," Zoe returned.

"Wasn't me who broke the rules."

"You're relieved of duty."

"Why?" he protested.

"For not doing your job," she answered. "Starting with checking for a pulse."

"Don't try to pin this on me," he said.

"There's nothing to pin on anyone!" Zoe shouted. "Candy died from complications with her pregnancy."

"I'll be the one who determines that," Doctor Erbil reminded everyone.

"You will," affirmed Zoe, then pointed at Lenny and said, "Write a full report of everything that happened from the moment I left last night until now. Leave it on my desk with your ID and weapon."

"I'll do that and give a copy to Mr. Selman with all the facts."

"Get out!"

Lenny was happy to turn his back and leave.

"Document the scene," Zoe instructed Randy Bartok. "Then have the body secured at the clinic. I'll be at the Common Faith Center if anything else comes up."

Bartok acknowledged his orders with an unqualified, "Yes, ma'am."

Zoe's next stop was her office, formerly Selman's, at the Common Faith Center. Alone behind the desk, she assessed the situation. With Candy dead and John Carroll nowhere to be found, her case was unraveling by the minute. It was her own fault. She'd made too many rookie mistakes. From the moment she jumped on that truck to stop Jagger to last night when she left Lenny

Donovan alone with Candy at the police station, she never stopped to think.

Why?

She had the best conviction rate in the Compliance Division. So good was she at the game that the Surviving Few sent a bomber to blow her off the face of the earth. Therein was the answer. She assumed she was smarter and more capable than these hicks, which was true, but those qualities didn't guarantee a successful capture and conviction. Just as often, cunning and brute force did the job. However, it took time to figure out which technique to apply. She had ignored that reality, along with all her training and experience.

"I'm better than this," she said aloud.

Solutions came to mind. None of them were quick or easy. She needed more resources, and not a platoon of clumsy troopers kicking down doors or any of Selman's dolts. First, a proper command center with staff to manage eavesdropping, process interviews, and transport suspects to secure facilities. Next, a couple of her compliance specialist associates, unknown to anyone in Mount Carmel, to infiltrate the local scene. She wrote the names of her top choices on a blank sheet. All of them had spent years as undercover operatives. Finally, an Army Ranger team sweeping through the woods would prevent any holdouts from escaping.

All this for one man and his glorified diary?

Most definitely.

The nation was almost back on its feet. The Common Faith had taken hold. Not among everyone, but internal statistics showed attendance steadily increasing at local centers. Furthermore, the economy was improving. Workers earned real paychecks. The money bought a growing variety of consumer goods in formerly closed stores, and from online services in limited areas. Some travel restrictions had been lifted. Continued progress was only possible if the peace held. It was her job to prevent zealots like

John Carroll from ruining it for the good people who accepted defeat and moved on.

Any delay in contacting Secretary Thompson risked having Selman exaggerate the situation. There was no denying she made mistakes, but there was plenty of blame to go around. The Secretary was a reasonable woman who understood the path to success had its detours and dead ends. As she reached for the phone, Zoe decided to back up the facts with a solid plan for better practices going forward.

As she touched the keypad, the door swung open, banging against the wall. The fury that was Denise Walsh strutted up to the desk, an accusatory finger pointed at Zoe's face.

"You killed my little sister!"

• • •

In Runt's mind, she saw a silver cross on a purple background for the cover of Preacher John's book. She got the idea from the parts of it she'd read. The challenge was making the cover from materials and tools available. She rummaged through the trailer and among the various hiding places in the woods until she gathered what she needed, setting everything outside on the chopping stump so as not to wake Jagger, who slept in the far bedroom.

For the backing boards she salvaged the sides of an orange crate from a score last spring. Jerry Boyle had paid them handsomely for the oranges, but Runt got to taste one. She'd never forget the flavor. The crate's thin planks were slightly warped but the perfect width, if a bit too long. Whip cut them to length with a rusty saw.

Next, Runt covered the boards with fabric sliced from the front and back of an old T-shirt that had been Dylan's favorite. It seemed all the more appropriate given she met Preacher John because of Dylan. Having been hand-washed countless times, it wasn't the rich purple color she had in mind, but it was all she had. She stretched it over the thin wood, using thumb tacks to secure it in place.

Then came the cross on the front cover. Runt used some thin, shiny metal left over from when Crush patched the roof. Wearing heavy gloves to protect her fingers, Whip cut it into two strips for her. Not experienced metal workers, the edges were sharp and not exactly straight. Whip smoothed them with a coarse rock until they were no longer a hazard. Runt laid the metal over the fabric-covered boards to gauge their placement before Whip folded the ends with a pliers. She squeezed the metal tight, clamping it into the fabric and wood.

Runt held the covers up for inspection and was proud of what she saw.

"Darn nice," Whip pronounced, "but how're you going to get the pages to stay in between?"

"With this," answered Runt. She held up a length of thin nylon cord.

"Stitch it all together?"

"Yep. But first I have to put this piece of cloth on the top and bottom," continued Runt, holding up a rectangle of bedsheet.

"Why?"

"Keep the pages from getting scratched by the cover."

The kid was smart, Whip thought. She noticed the bent metal and folded tacks could damage the pages once the cover was attached.

Runt insisted on punching holes through the covers and pages herself. She used the ice pick, which Whip honed needle-sharp. One by one, she pierced six holes, first through the cover boards then into the many pages of Father Carroll's testament. There were two above the horizontal bar of the cross and four below.

No longer concerned with Runt hurting herself, Whip said, "I'm going to run into town."

"What for?" Runt wanted to know.

"Do some business." Pointing at their binding project, Whip

added, "Can't wait to see that when it's finished."

"Hurry. It won't be long."

Stitching the book together was a tricky job that took more than an hour. Runt spent the first fifteen minutes struggling to get the cord through the holes. Even with lengths of cord in each hole, the cover and pages were too loose. She realized she'd have to kneel on it to keep the leaves tight. The pages now compressed between the covers, she pulled each loop until the cord bit into her fingers, then tied a solid knot.

She stood back to admire her work. Worth at least a dozen oranges, she decided, wondering if Preacher John would pay that price.

Behind her the trailer door banged open. Bleary-eyed and barefoot, Jagger bolted down the stairs, bound for Runt. The reason for her panic: oversleeping while in possession of John Carroll's book. She had assigned Whip to keep an eye on Runt's cover-making endeavor, but that didn't mean they were safe from a prowling Randy Bartok or an interloper seeking profit and fame. No one said the troopers wouldn't be back for another one-sided boxing match, either. They needed to be on high alert until the check was cashed and life after Mount Carmel began.

"Hey, boss," Runt greeted her, holding up the book. "What do you think?"

Despite the cold and the sharp stones poking in her feet, Jagger paused at the primitive beauty of the kid's creation.

"That's really nice," Jagger said, impressed by the youngest Molly's ingenuity.

"Thanks. Whip helped, but all my ideas."

"For sure they were. Where is Whip?"

"Went to town," Runt replied. "Do some business."

This close to claiming the prize and Whip decides to make a run into the snake pit. Stupid and risky—the brother and sister of captured and punished—seemed to have taken over her brain. Then again, Jagger would have done the same for a good reason, which Whip must have had. Anyway, seeing the kid happy was one of their few joys, one that didn't take much to earn.

"Let's go inside, okay?"

"Yeah. You shouldn't be out here without a coat."

What a damn good girl, Jagger thought as they returned to the trailer. She vowed to get the hell out of Mount Carmel, all the way to that beach, wherever it was. Runt was going with her, Whip and Crush, too, the four of them laid out in the sun, sand in their ass cracks.

As they snacked on deer jerky, Runt tapped the corner of her newly bound book and said, "I read some of it."

"No shit?"

"A lot of it's about someone called the Savior. He's one of the big characters. Has a lot to say. There's a bunch of others."

"Like who?"

"Good people. Bad people."

"What're they doing?"

"That's a little confusing. It's written funny."

"Like make-you-laugh funny?"

"No. Like weird. I think some of it already happened and some of it is going to happen."

"Maybe when you get to the end it'll make sense," Jagger suggested, "but get there quick, because we have to sell it soon. Remember?"

"I remember. Think we'll get more with my cover?"

"Guaranteed."

A breathless Whip entered the trailer, startling Jagger, whose jangled nerves had just settled.

"You ain't gonna believe this," she gasped.

"No freaking lottery to win. How unbelievable can it be?" Jagger returned. "And why'd you stray off the patch in these times of tension?"

"Was going to peddle those pain pills Crush didn't use," Whip replied, "but couldn't because you'll never guess what happened!"

"Out with it."

"Philly Chick killed Candy Walsh," Whip said.

"No way!"

"Heard it straight from Nurse Porter, who was behind the old police station, puking her guts out. Said it was a bloodbath in one of the holding pens. Something she ain't seen since the war."

The beach might as well be on the moon for the chances of Jagger and the Mollies getting there now. Compliance Specialist or not, Zoe Whelan offed a dear daughter of Mount Carmel, the reaction to which would be serious anger quickly expressed in a physical nature requiring a return of the troopers to put down. More relevant to Jagger was losing the best deal ever. Before a bitter wave of depression cast her into a funk, she organized a hasty retreat.

"Pack bags. Keep it light but load out the essentials for an extended stay away," she said. "And dig out them clothes from the prison bus driver and guard. Remember where we hid them in the trees?"

"Yeah," Whip replied, then asked, "Where're we going?"

"Hang on," Runt requested. "There's something in the book about what's going on."

"Seriously?" Jagger said, watching the girl flip through several of the handwritten pages.

Runt's dirty index finger slid under the words as she read, *"The agents of tyranny will spill the blood of one too many innocents, provoking the righteous to action."*

Amazed at what they heard, Whip and Jagger exchanged a puzzled look.

"So bursts the dam," continued Runt, *"unleashing flood waters that shall cleanse the present in preparation for a future in the light of God's wisdom."*

"Amen, little sister," said Jagger. "Now get packing."

• • •

Lenny expected Denise to help him write the report, but as soon as he told her what happened to Candy, out the door she went. Truth be told, the paperwork was the least of his worries. The big problem was his gun. It was missing. Candy wouldn't have taken it; she was always afraid of guns. Denise wasn't afraid of anything as far as he knew, but she never showed any interest in the weapon. Ian? The little freak never put down his drawing pencil long enough to cause any trouble.

That left Kyle Smith, which didn't make sense because Christians like him were all about non-violence, or so Lenny had been told during the latest training session at Pottsville Prison. The few Christians locked up there were like a kindle of kittens. They made some noise praying and singing, but otherwise caused zero trouble. Maybe Kyle wasn't really a Christian, just a guy stealing another guy's wife. Correction, a guy stealing another guy's significant other as made official by the unity pact signed and sealed by Director Martin Selman.

Just as Lenny contemplated the consequences of losing his gun, Randy Bartok barged in the back door and dropped it on the kitchen table.

"Why'd you take my gun?" Lenny blurted.

"Because Kyle Smith was done with it," answered Bartok.

"Shit. The troopers are gonna have my ass."

"Thank me for making sure they don't know it was yours. I pinned the prison bus hijacking on him."

"They didn't want the gun for evidence?"

"Told them I wanted to match it to some slugs I found."

"Thanks, man. I owe you one."

"Which you're going to deliver as soon as the Pleasant Corner opens."

A perplexed Lenny squawked, "What?"

"First," Bartok said, putting a typed report beside the gun. "Read your report for the compliance specialist. Then read it again. Then sign it."

Lenny scanned the sheet.

"When you're done, hand it over to Ms. Whelan. Take any shit she gives you with a smile. Then get your ass to the Pleasant Corner."

• • •

Without a second's hesitation, Zoe pulled her gun. "I didn't kill anyone. Put your hands up! Face the wall!"

Denise laughed. "Scary bitch, look at me shaking."

Zoe was beginning to think everyone in Mount Carmel had gone crazy. If they weren't following an oddball former priest, they were laughing into the barrel of a loaded weapon in the hand of someone authorized to use it. To confirm insanity, Denise asked a completely incongruous question.

"Got any money?"

"What?"

"Let me put it another way. How much can you get?"

Zoe had no clue where Denise was going.

"And gas vouchers. Need at least thirty gallons worth, or you're on a slab next to Candy."

"Don't threaten me."

"Hey, I ought to gouge your eyes out, and I would if it brought Candy back from the dead. But that ain't happening. So let's make this a payday and call it even for my loss."

"On your knees. Hands behind your head."

Denise spit on the desk, raised her finger again, and shouted, "I'm your ticket out of here! Me and Lenny's jalopy soon as I find it. But I ain't giving you a ride without getting paid, and that piece of junk burns gas like it's free."

"I have nothing to be afraid of," Zoe said.

"Oh, yes, you do. People are talking, and the word is you killed my little sister."

"She died from a miscarriage."

"Who says? The clinic quack? He's a shitty drug dealer and a worse doctor."

"Last chance, Denise. Considering you lost a sister, I'm willing to forget you came in here threatening me. Get out before I place you under arrest."

Denise put both hands up. "Hey, I tried. Remember that when they come for you. 'Cause they're coming. Today. Tonight. Tomorrow at the latest."

"No one's coming for me," insisted Zoe.

"I'll be home the next couple hours if you change your mind. After that, good luck."

Denise strolled out of the office without closing the door.

Zoe holstered her gun then crossed the room for a look at the hallway. Denise's raving about pending violence seemed as phony as her ploy for money. They were the desperate claims of a drug addict looking to score. Zoe remembered Denise as a regular pot smoker in high school who dabbled in cocaine and whatever else could be had.

The empty hallway reassured Zoe that she was in no immediate danger. To be sure, she went to the end and entered what had been the sanctuary of the church the Common Faith Center now occupied. Stripped of any Christian adornment, the space appeared bland. The Circle and Line hung on the wall behind where the altar used to be. Other than that, it was whitewashed walls, plain windows, and rows of plastic chairs. "A Clean Slate," she recalled as the slogan from the early pamphlets about the Common Faith.

Suddenly, Zoe recognized the symptoms of a fading adrenaline buzz. She felt nauseous and sweaty, a little weak and slightly disoriented. She sat on one of the chairs, lowering her head for better blood flow. Several deep breaths helped.

On her feet again, she was heading toward the office when she caught a flash of movement to the left. She spun toward it, hand reaching for her gun. No one was there. She backtracked to the center aisle, scanning the walls on each side. Nothing. Then facing forward, she stopped. Behind the Circle and Line, or maybe in front of it, was the ghostly shape of a cross. Or so she thought, because an instant later it was gone.

A false memory, she decided, or possibly a real one from her childhood when she'd come to this place with her family. Whatever the case, she wasn't about to get paranoid. Denise could make all the accusations she wanted; the facts were on Zoe's side. If Candy's friends, family, or anyone else caused trouble, they'd be up against all the branches of law enforcement, from the state troopers to the Compliance Division.

She wasn't going to make the mistake she made with Jagger, jumping into the fray without backup. Therefore, she called Colonel Stewart's headquarters to put her plan in motion.

"Colonel Stewart is on maneuvers," his adjutant informed her.

"Transfer me to the officer in charge," requested Zoe.

"That's me, ma'am. How can I help?"

"I'm requesting a rapid response platoon to support an ongoing investigation in Mount Carmel."

"Deploying when?" he asked.

"Today."

"Sorry to say, Alpha and Bravo teams are with the colonel. Charlie is on leave. That's all we have."

"There's no one else?"

"I could send a buck sergeant and several senior academy recruits. Would make a good training op to cut their teeth on."

"This isn't a practice run," Zoe shot back.

"Well, check with Allentown or Harrisburg. They might have personnel available."

"I will."

"Glad to help. Good luck, ma'am. Thanks for calling."

Zoe spent ten minutes staring out the window, calming down. She didn't need troopers anyway. The streets outside were deserted. No cars or trucks. No pedestrians. Not even a stray cat. That left her next call; the more difficult one, to Hester Thompson.

The discussion was one to be had on a personal level. Thus, Zoe dialed the Secretary's private cell number as opposed to her office.

"Hello," Thompson's recorded voice came over the line. "I'm currently unavailable. Urgent matters can be handled through my assistant. Thank you, and remember to celebrate the Bounty of Faith every day."

Zoe hung up with an aggravated sigh. She couldn't decide if Thompson's absence was good or bad. On one hand, it gave her time to make progress. On the other, she was without the resources she needed to do the job. She was down to herself and one informant, namely Jagger, whose motives and reliability were suspect at best.

Nothing could be accomplished from behind a desk, she resolved, reaching for her jacket. She would get an update from Jagger, then pursue the other people on Candy's list. All the while, she'd be on the lookout for signs of restless citizens bent on revenge. If there were more than a few, she'd have to make a tactical withdrawal to Pottsville.

A second later, the largest window in the office shattered, spilling broken glass across the floor.

CHAPTER 28.

Lenny did exactly as he was told. Rather, he tried to. The report was an easy read. It was as accurate to what happened as if he wrote it himself. Cleaning the gun took a little longer than after a day at the range because he wiped every square millimeter to remove any trace of Kyle's fingerprints. The hardest part was showing his face at the Common Faith Center, but that turned out to be painless, because he didn't go. Denise talked him out of it.

She flew into the house, slammed the door hard enough to rattle dishes, and said, "Hey, Candy might have been cheating on you, but she was still your wife."

"Significant other," he corrected her.

"Whatever. With you at the Pleasant Corner every night, no wonder another guy slid in where you should have been. Still, your baby died with her. Whatever Candy was up to with Kyle, the unity pact gave you rights to that kid. Any of this sinking in?"

Although Lenny never wanted a kid, the sight of Candy, and the baby inside her, dead on the floor left him morose and angry. It was an odd mix of emotions for a simple man like him. Recent revelations regarding Kyle aside, he and Candy had good times. She wasn't the best cook and her endless chatter was annoying, but they enjoyed laughs at the bar and some serious pleasure in the bedroom, at least until she got pregnant. No matter what, she wasn't like the criminals he tended at Pottsville Prison. They were scum of every description, from hard-core gang members to political assassins. What was Candy's crime? She hopped the train, which was a federal violation, but why? To run off with her boyfriend. Since when did that warrant the death penalty? And why didn't Zoe leave Candy with the troopers? They partied hard sometimes and threw their weight around now and then. Otherwise, they were professionals. They followed procedure. He heard they gave Zoe's mom a ride back from Number Six the other day.

Not all Lenny's thoughts were his own. Some came from Randy Bartok. Denise reinforced them.

"The first thing Zoe did was blame it all on you, right?"

He nodded.

"That's why she wants the report. She shows it to the bigwigs, says 'See, Lenny Donovan admits he screwed up.' She doesn't say shit about her own mistakes, which I don't think were mistakes at all. Don't ask me why, but she had it in for Candy from day one."

Lenny nodded again.

"We can't let her get away with double murder," Denise grumbled. "Which is exactly what's going to happen if you walk in there with your tail between your legs and hand over that report and your gun."

"Double murder?"

"Candy and your kid inside her!"

He launched off the chair, tucking his pistol into his pants.

"Where're you going?"

"To get some help."

Denise didn't like the idea of starting at the Pleasant Corner. It was barely noon. Only the worst boozers would be inside and not many of them. Lenny stayed the course because if things went the way Bartok said they would, he might not have to turn in his gun or the report. However, if he skipped the bar for somewhere else, Bartok would do worse than beat him senseless.

An odd couple they made. Denise's scrawny frame nearly disappeared behind his pudgy bulges as they settled into spots at the bar. Steve Regan raised an eyebrow at their presence, especially Lenny not in his regular corner seat.

"Bourbon," Lenny ordered. "The stuff the troopers were drinking. One for me, one for Denise."

Dead wife or not, Regan gave away no top-shelf liquor, not even to a regular like Lenny. "How about two jars of grog?" he suggested.

"Give the grog to them," Lenny said, gesturing toward the other guys in the bar. He never bought other people drinks like a needy fool, but this wasn't his money. His pocket was stuffed with a Bartok-supplied wad of cash thick enough to keep the grog flowing all afternoon.

"Sorry to hear about—" Regan began, stopping short when a hundred-dollar bill landed on the bar. "Bourbon it is."

"And one for yourself," Lenny told him.

Regan banked the drink for closing time. In contrast, he immediately converted the hundred into grog and bourbon, appropriately distributed down the bar and across the room. What change there was he put down in small bills in front of Lenny atop another hundred that had appeared, from where he did not know.

"To my sister," Denise called out, raising her glass.

"My significant other," added Lenny.

Someone down the bar said, "Wife, Lenny. Your wife."

"Yeah, my wife. Gonna miss her."

"Ain't right what they did to Candy," said Denise, exhaling bourbon fumes.

Lenny gave her a hard look. "Let it rest a while," he quietly told her.

"If I knew we were doing that, I would have sipped my drink."

Lenny pushed a twenty out of the pile of bills, saying, "Then let's have another."

Bartok's instructions had been clear: Buy some drinks, bawl your eyes out, punch the wall if you feel like it, but don't tell anyone anything until they ask. When they do ask, and someone definitely will, act like you don't want to talk about it. Let them pry it out of you.

Denise got him off to a wobbly start, but Lenny was confident. The second bourbon occupied her as much as it sent him down memory lane. He and Candy never had a honeymoon, not like the kind his mom and dad talked about. They camped out by a lake, swam naked in the cold water, and slept close in the tent. Considering how messed up the country was, it felt like being on Mars.

He noticed the other drinkers had emptied their glasses. "One more for those guys," he said to Regan, who happily obliged.

"You gonna say something or just get drunk?" Denise whispered too close to his ear.

"When I'm ready," Lenny snarled, pissed off that he and Candy never camped again. After Bartok got him the job at the prison, he worked a lot of nights. Candy became Teacher of the Year, thereby earning the privilege of teaching challenged learners on weekends. And Kyle, that prick, janitor at the school, put Candy in his sights. She deserved better than him.

"I keep those animals in their cages," he said aloud.

"What?" Denise asked.

"Nothing."

Mick Haggerty shifted down the bar, a swallow left in the bottom of his glass. "So, uh, had some tragedy come your way, huh?"

"I look like I want to talk about it?" growled Lenny.

"Sorry, just trying to be sympathetic."

"Say thanks for the drink and leave me alone."

"Sure thing, Lenny. Sure thing."

All eyes followed Haggerty's retreat, including Regan's. The barkeep was grateful for the extra business in the middle of the day. He also saw the potential for more if Lenny remained.

"Got some sausages in the back," he said to the widower. "Have one on the house. Put a floor under that whiskey."

"Don't want no charity," Lenny grumbled.

"Bought me a drink. I'm returning the favor."

Soon the smell of bratwurst and spent dollars wafted through the bar. A member of the George Nash crew came in, guzzled one of Lenny's free drinks, then snuck out to tell his pals and co-workers.

"Candy Walsh died last night," he said. "Lenny's on a wild bender."

"What the hell happened?"

"Hell if I know, but as long as he's buying, I'm drinking."

Finally, Lenny unloaded in a speech that Bartok missed but heard about later. It was Haggerty who set him off.

"Be good to get it off your chest," the old boozer said.

"Alright, I'll tell you the truth and don't none of you assholes repeat nothing but what I tell you. Hear me?"

The crowd recognized a guy ready to pop off and granted their ascent.

"Last night, they threw my wife in one of the pens like a stray dog."

"Who, Lenny?"

"Yeah, who?"

"Compliance Specialist Zoe Whelan," he answered after slamming one more shot of bourbon. "Dragged Candy back here from Pottsville, she did."

"What was she doing in Pottsville?"

"Shut up and listen!" Lenny hollered. "Don't make no difference what she was doing in Pottsville or who the hell she was with over there. What matters is Zoe Whelan did not follow procedure. I know procedure. I work in the criminal justice system. What she did I wouldn't do to one of them savages on the other side of the bars who deserve it."

The crowd waited for him to catch his breath.

"Candy was pregnant. Five months pregnant. Little baby inside her, kicking away. But did Zoe Whelan give a damn about my wife or my kid not yet born? Hell, no! Whatever Candy did wrong is unclear as a shit creek to me, but not to Zoe Whelan, who gave the order for Candy to be thrown in the pen. No official charges. No doctor check-up. And the clinic only five blocks away!"

A groan spread around the room.

"Not even a snack. A pregnant woman denied food! If I didn't run home for something, Candy would have gone to sleep hungry. Turned out to be her last meal."

George Nash came in at this point, stationing himself behind and to the right of Lenny.

"If all that's not bad enough, the compliance specialist from Philadelphia orders me to guard my own wife. What was I supposed to do? Shoot her if she tried to escape?"

No one answered the question.

"Orders are orders. When they come from a senior officer, we obey or get busted down to toilet scrubbing. I stayed with Candy as long as I could but seeing her behind the fence broke my heart."

"Would have broken mine," someone said.

"I took a little nap, not long, and when I came back to check on her, there she was on the floor. So much blood, I slipped and fell trying to do what I could to save her. It was too late."

"Jesus H. Christ," Steve Regan said. "We've heard enough."

George Nash putting his arm around Lenny's shoulders, looked at the crowd, and said, "What're we going to do about it?"

· · ·

Jagger changed her mind. The deal with Philly Chick might not be lost. How did she know? She read about it in Preacher John's book. While Whip and Runt prepared for departure, she peeked at a few pages, including several lines above where the kid left off.

"Know this, fellow believers, because as other things have been revealed to me, I have also seen that my testament shall be brought by one who was your enemy, but now carries the Word of God. Trust her for she has embraced the Spirit."

Jagger almost gagged on the lump in her throat. Before making an interpretive conclusion of Preacher John's writing, she checked herself. Did a few vaguely worded sentences qualify as a vision of the future?

Looking for some context, she started at the beginning. In the first couple paragraphs, he pegged the present situation for exactly what it was, but anyone could have written something similar in the last year or so. She got to the part Runt read aloud. It gave her a chill. It also rang true. Candy Walsh was an innocent; Zoe Whelan was an agent of the Common Faith who laid down the heavy hand of the law. And Preacher John wrote about this when? Sometime before it happened, because Runt scooped up these pages when they broke him out of the dungeon.

Then came the twist in the form of, *"my testament shall be brought by one who was your enemy."* The one about whom he wrote was also female as indicated by the pronoun "her." Who was a worse enemy of the Christians, and a female, than Common Faith Compliance Specialist Zoe Whelan? She was the one who left Candy Walsh to die in jail. According to the passage, Philly Chick was going to change her ways and take this book somewhere. Really?

If Jagger was doubtful of Zoe Whelan's conversion, she was incredulous at the claim in the next paragraph.

"The deliverance of the once-despised Messenger shall be made possible by a cohort of the poor who first protected this, my testament, and were then tested by evil. Yet, they will have stood firm against the tyrant's wrath, escaped his prison, and outwitted his soldiers. Honor their suffering."

A cohort of the poor? Did he mean them? The Mollies? Impossible! Jagger was protecting Preacher John's writing in anticipation of trading it for cash and intangibles otherwise unobtainable. That put her on no side but her own. Her belief in the Big Man upstairs went down the drain when Dylan ended up six feet under instead of on two feet.

"Ready in a minute," Whip called from the bedroom.

With no time to read more, Jagger re-wrapped the book in the old raincoat as Claire Whelan had done. Whether it was soon to be fact or nothing but fiction, she couldn't decide. If what she read so far turned out to be real, she feared the consequences of misjudging Preacher John, almost killing him on the bridge, pulling the gun, plotting to sell him off to the highest bidder. Then again if it was true, it would also mean she was destined to spirit Zoe Whelan and the book away from harm. And what about that suffering? Was it in the past or yet to come?

"Where to?" Whip asked, carrying her rucksack into the living room.

"Give Jerry Boyle the news about Candy, if he doesn't have it already. Huddle with him and Crush. Tell no one, not even Crush and especially not Jerry, about that book Preacher John wrote. Squirrel it away in his labyrinth of junk," Jagger said, handing it over.

"What're you going to do?"

"Stay two steps ahead of Randy Bartok until I figure out how to sail through this shit storm."

On the way out, Whip showed Jagger the gun she almost used the other night at the Pleasant Corner, the one that belonged to the prison bus driver. "Take it," she said.

"I got the one Crush didn't want," Jagger replied.

"Hope you don't need it," Whip said, and left for Boyle's Long Foot Nation.

Walking through town alone, Jagger hoped she didn't need the gun, either, but she was glad to have it. People were on the move. Not throngs, but from every corner along Cedar Alley she saw ones and twos going in the same direction as she was. At Hickory Street, they peeled off; she went another block east, then doubled back to see where they were gathering.

Her prediction was correct. Candy Walsh's death stirred the pot, which at the moment was the Pleasant Corner. It must have been full inside because a knot of bodies huddled at the entrance, vying for a view inside. From a block away, Jagger heard crowd cheers spewing from the open front door. A participant in a divine prophecy or not, the clock was running out on her opportunity to stay in the game.

She bolted for the Common Faith Center, anxious about being in town when the sun shined. If Philly Chick wasn't there, she'd set off for the woods until nightfall. No doubt a posse was forming at Regan's place, and once unleashed, who knew what scores they might settle.

Selman's car, now a perk enjoyed by Zoe Whelan, was parked in the rear lot, a solid indication of her presence inside. Good news for Jagger, bad news for the compliance specialist, who must be oblivious to the mob fueling up the payback machine two blocks south. Given the choice between walking inside to make her case and doing something more dramatic, Jagger went with the latter. It was her style.

She found a fist-sized rock, wound up, and threw her best pitch at Selman's office window. A satisfying crash was the reward. Not lingering to gloat over an act of vandalism she had longed to commit, Jagger ran inside without so much as a locked door slowing her down. It was almost disappointing.

"Freeze!" Zoe shouted past her raised gun.

"I got that book you've been looking for," Jagger replied, hands up, hoping the finger on the trigger was more stable than the pair of eyes behind it. "And you ain't got enough bullets for the mob out there."

CHAPTER 29.

From his private office three stories above the dungeon, Randy Bartok watched the crowd swarming at the Pleasant Corner. Nothing stood between them and the Common Faith Center but a hundred yards of old asphalt. Zoe Whelan was probably inside. Too bad she lacked the good sense to skip town. In the event she did motor away, the troopers were parked on Route 61 at the top of the mountain to intercept. They were also awaiting the call to sweep the town clean, but no sense spoiling the party this early. He'd linger until he smelled smoke or more than three died, whichever came first.

He sat down to complete his assignment. Although confident Zoe Whelan would never see the report, he wrote it with meticulous detail. He used an ancient manual typewriter that featured hand-inked ribbons. His diagrams were neatly drawn and appropriately labeled. This professional document would be available for inspection or electronic reproduction. As if anyone cared.

With no smoke in sight, he made his own, lighting an Amish cigar. Now there were some clever people. Although Christians, the Amish kept it to themselves, not evangelizing nor taking a side in the Second Civil War. The Common Faith steamrolled their churches and schools but left the farms alone because they grew tobacco by the square mile. Tobacco, like coal, was sold in huge quantities to the Chinese to pay the war debt. The Amish never made so much money, not that they knew how to spend it. Ah, hell, it was for the best, because eventually a sharp guy like himself or Selman would screw them out of it.

Enjoying the cigar, Bartok spun his mental calendar back several days to the afternoon when the Graterford bus made the rounds, delivering two convicts to the Pads, after which, the driver and guard spent a couple hours drinking before heading for Pottsville. They never arrived. Contrary to what he led the troopers to believe, Kyle Smith didn't hijack the bus and murder the two men aboard. Kyle Smith, school janitor, Candy's handsome hunk, and most likely her impregnator, might have had the balls to steal the gun, but he didn't have the guts to use it.

"The stupid bastard jumps off the stopped train, falls flat on his face," the sergeant said. "We let him get up, turn around, and one of the boys meant to pop him in the leg, but had his weapon on full auto. Stitched him with eight rounds."

They found the prison-issue pistol in his bag before they found Candy, who was huddled on the platform between the cars. Smacked her around a few times when she accused them of murdering Kyle, and wouldn't give her name. They didn't believe she was pregnant, just fat. Oh well, the troopers weren't the most sensitive bunch. All this had happened by the time Bartok had walked the half mile from the caboose where he'd been playing cards with the conductor. Why was he back there in the first place? The same tipster who gave up John Carroll gave up Candy and Kyle. Said tipster saw things falling apart and wanted run-away money. Bartok promised two grand cash and no harm done to Candy or Kyle. The troopers inadvertently voided the second part.

Back to the point. Who killed the bus driver and guard? Must have been Jagger, but that didn't make sense. Checkpoints and travel restrictions penned her in like one of Boyle's sows. For a moment, he dismissed who and focused on why. Whoever pulled the job, what did they want with a prison bus? It held twenty people. It was relatively slow. It couldn't be disguised as anything else. Were John Carroll's people planning a truck-bomb attack?

"Not a chance," he said to the smoke rings drifting across the room.

If not who or why, then where? Where was the bus? He found no fresh tracks to follow. But it had rained late the night it disappeared, a pounding shower that probably beat down any new tread marks. Just the same, he dead-ended every old logging road he knew. He damn near got stuck on a double track into a test shaft before giving up and backing out. Had the killer thief made it in there before the rain when the road was in drivable condition? Soon as Zoe Whelan got hers, he'd give it a second look. Maybe sooner.

Clear progress was visible in the streets outside. From Bartok's vantage point, he saw the crowd had the Common Faith Center's exits covered. Windows were broken. Lots of people holding bats, pry bars, and steel pipes. Too bad he wouldn't be coming to the rescue. When the troopers descended it was going to be a shooting gallery.

He'd give them another hour. By then they'd be dragging Zoe Whelan out of wherever she was hiding, probably by the hair.

• • •

They argued a solid five minutes before Zoe heard the crowd approach. Then she heeded Jagger's warning and dashed to the car.

"Let me drive," Jagger said.

"Forget it."

"Listen, lady. I know where we're going, and you're better with the gun."

Zoe shoved Jagger away from the driver's side with, "Nobody's going to get shot."

"Don't hold your breath."

Moments later they were off.

"Take a right on Park then left on Chestnut," Jagger said.

Zoe followed the directions until they turned north on Locust. "We're going in a circle."

"Exactly, wide around the back so any reserves at the Pleasant

Corner don't spot us crossing Market."

"Okay, then what?"

"Snake Road out to the strippings. We cool it until dark. Or, you do, while I get Preacher John's book."

"The deal was for him and his book," Zoe said.

"Half a loaf is better than starving," Jagger replied.

Suddenly, Zoe slammed on the brakes. The car slewed sideways across the centerline, the rear bumper scraping a tarped car, before stopping facing the wrong way on Fifth Street.

"We have to go back," Zoe said.

"For what?"

"My mother."

She jammed the accelerator, whipped the wheel, and hurtled west.

"Stupid chance you're taking," protested Jagger.

"Only scum like you would leave your mother behind."

"She'll be okay. I guarantee it."

"Hah!"

"Seriously, I read it in Preacher John's book," Jagger said, stretching the truth. She read nothing bad about anyone's mother. Of course, she read nothing good, either.

Zoe laughed at the lie.

"You're in there, too," Jagger continued. "It says the one who was the enemy of the Christians will become the Messenger."

"Please, it's a tactic religious groups use to convert people to their cause. Make you feel more important. Plant seeds of doubt about your life up to a certain point when you're supposed to join them."

"It also said I'd help you escape."

"You?"

"Cohort of the poor is what it says. See for yourself, this passenger ain't dressed for a first-class seat."

"Sounds like John Carroll has converted you."

Jagger dodged the question. "Don't make a dime's worth of

difference. You want the book, I got it, and if we screw around town, we'll both be on a slab next to Candy."

"Spare me the drama, okay?"

Zoe swung down Poplar Street. Her mother's house was eight blocks away.

Jagger rode the last minute in silence. Maybe Preacher John's book was bogus. At present, she didn't see Philly Chick finding her way to his line of thinking. Besides, if the mob caught up to her it was doomsday today, not kingdom come when God said so. That left her dealing with Selman via Bartok, a squeeze play that had her squirming on the seat.

"Let me ask you a question," Jagger said as Zoe stopped in front of her mother's house.

"Make it quick."

"Were you going to give me the reward and ID like you promised?"

"Yes."

"We really could have started a new life? Me and the Mollies, that is."

"Still can."

"Nah," Jagger concluded. "It's gotta be us getting out of here together or we're both dead."

"How do you know?"

"Because Selman always wins." Jagger popped the door, stepped out of the car, and leaned back in to say, "Good luck, Philly Chick. You're on your own."

• • •

Selman never liked Christmas, not even as a child. What a terrible disguise for commercialism that strayed far from the concept of Christ as God's gift to the world. Waiting for gifts hidden by colored wrapping paper was a waste of time. Then came the judgment of family and friends if sufficient surprise and gratitude were not displayed afterward. Oh, the phony smiles, thanks, and hugs for receipt of silly baubles.

Mulling over this and other shortcomings of previously dominant religions occupied Selman until mid-afternoon. Then he ran out of patience. He wasn't worried or even anxious about his plan going awry. He was terribly curious. He had more fun in the mix of things than watching from afar.

Because Bartok returned to Mount Carmel in his jeep, Selman was left in Pottsville without personal transportation. His least expensive solution was to have a trooper take him, but that would ruin the mystique of a sudden appearance. Thus, he bribed a waiter at the Black Diamond Club, a young man with access to a car. The goofy lad asked for a five-gallon gasoline voucher.

"Next time don't be so cheap," Selman cautioned him upon arrival at the Common Faith Center. "Ask for ten."

The sight of his office was awe-inspiring. An angry horde had passed through like a tornado. Very angry, indeed. All the windows were broken, also the furniture. Someone had chopped holes in his desk with an axe. They hit the walls with hammers big and small. He noted the smell of urine, but that could have been from Ian. No, it was fresh, confirmed by a heap of stained papers in a corner.

Most important, the fury had not been directed at him. If he, or the Common Faith in general, had been the target, they would have trashed the main hall. It remained untouched. They concentrated on the office because that's where Compliance Specialist Zoe Whelan had been. Where was she now? He delighted in the possibilities. Held in a dark room? Tied to a chair? Or hanging by her wrists? Oh, to think of her in such dire circumstances stirred his deepest passions.

While each an exciting option, he knew they were all unlikely. Every movement had its more reasonable side. In the beginning, the more rational went along for the ride with the irrational. They smashed things, bruised knuckles, and threw easy punches to establish their credibility. However, when the severe violence appeared imminent, these somewhat wiser types advocated restraint. They had something to lose when the intensity faded and the more organized forces of the existing power structure put them in their place. Deep down they knew their cause was destined to fail, but like lemmings rushing for the cliff, they got caught up in the romance of collective danger. They came to their senses around the moment it becomes too late, as if suddenly reminded of the consequences. At least, that was Selman's theory. The current situation gave him the perfect opportunity to test it.

He had taken out his cellphone to call Bartok when the sound of feet crunching broken glass caught his attention.

"About time you showed up," Denise Walsh said, holding out an envelope she'd found in her stash of pills.

Selman almost reached for it before remembering Denise never gave anything without first getting something.

"What's a bunch of Christians worth?"

"Depends who they are, what they did, how many," Selman answered, pleased that again his instincts were correct.

"Friends of John Carroll, the inner-circle kind, five of them."

"Perhaps two or three thousand dollars in total. More if they confess and lead to the capture of others."

"Deal," she said. "I just found a letter my sister left for you."

Selman took the envelope, which had been torn at the seam. "You opened it?" he asked.

"Shit, yeah. Read the whole thing, so don't try to rip me off the way you did Lenny."

After a throat-clearing cough of displeasure, Selman unfolded the sheet from within. Candy Walsh wrote well; it was a clear chronicle of her last week. There were five names among the paragraphs, one of which was all he needed to relieve Compliance Specialist Zoe Whelan of duty as acting director.

"Good stuff, eh?"

"Perhaps."

His cellphone chirped. The screen displayed Bartok's number. "How are things, my friend?"

"There's a wrinkle we need to iron out."

• • •

Zoe never showed fear, not when she had faced suicide bomber Andrew at Common Faith Headquarters, nor when Jagger had pointed the gun at her in the alley. It didn't mean she wasn't frightened. Fear was a healthy emotion, a signal to get help or get out, and it was time to get out because there was no one to call for help. She had the means—Selman's car with plenty of gas and a gun to fend off those who might stop her. What she didn't have was much of a plan beyond driving away from Mount Carmel.

From the car to her mother's door took ten seconds, during which Zoe reflected on a lousy week and a crumbling career. Her intentions had been well-meaning. She'd been rough on Candy, but as with Jagger, she was sincere about rewarding cooperation. She had taken Candy away from the troopers to give her another chance. Impressing Candy with the seriousness of that responsibility required a stint in jail. As for the town's reaction to Candy's deadly miscarriage, she would attribute that to carry-over from the previous riot, which was Selman's failure. He had allowed tensions to fester. Furthermore, the local director and his personnel, namely Randy Bartok, disappeared at a time of crisis. That was dereliction of duty. As a result, significant property damage occurred, and the life of an official had been threatened.

Would Secretary Thompson accept her account as presented? Maybe. There would be an inquiry guided by another senior compliance specialist. They were all her friends from the academy, the ones eligible for inquiry-level assignments, anyway. She wasn't expecting a free pass. Three months of retraining and a five percent pay cut were reasonable sanctions. If the Secretary was unwilling to give her a second try in Mount Carmel, she'd go back to rooting out Surviving Few members in Philadelphia.

"Mom!" Zoe called upon entering the house. "We're leaving!"

The patch on the dining room wall caught her eye. It was smooth and even, needing only fresh paint to complete what she assumed was her brother's repair. When had he completed it? The area held her attention a long moment, during which a halo seemed to form around the edges. She took a step closer when the outline of the cross appeared. But that couldn't be; she had chopped it out herself. She backed up and moved sideways. The cross disappeared.

"Oh, I get it," Zoe said to the empty room. It was a trick, probably the work of Sara Darcy, who used something in the plaster to make a cross visible from certain angles. Well, before she left town, the least she could do was remind that interloper not to brandish her illegal beliefs.

Obsessed with making a final statement, she retrieved the same hatchet she used previously to clear the wall of that symbol. Whack, whack, whack, and down it came. Another pile of plaster awaited Ms. Darcy, who would be mentioned in the report as a recalcitrant offender in need of a tolerance refresher course.

"Mom!" she shouted at the ceiling, suddenly aware she had wasted valuable minutes ruining the wall.

She took the stairs two at a time, to discover a suitcase at the top. Running room to room, she did not find her mother. She cursed the circumstances: no cellphone and her mother's continued belief in an archaic religion.

The sound of the back door opening and closing got her attention. She grabbed the suitcase and bounded down to the first floor, but no one was there.

"Mom?"

The moment Zoe turned for the kitchen, she saw two men. For the first time in her career, she froze. They crashed into her like linebackers, driving her against the wall. Massive hands locked onto her wrists, holding them fast.

A third man stepped into view, older, not quite as big as the others. "Haven't seen you in maybe twenty years," he said. "Your high school graduation, I think it was."

"Sorry, I don't remember you," Zoe replied. She held still as he took his time removing her gun from its holster.

"I worked with your father. George Nash is my name."

CHAPTER 30.

A record day, and it wasn't over. It had been years since Mike and his gang cut this much coal in a single shift. Everything went right, and as the hours passed without a hitch, the crew noticed. One shift didn't make a bonus but did put a dent in lost production due to the collapse. They relaxed as much as workers five hundred feet below the surface can, thinking life was back to normal. No one wanted to stop for lunch, but they agreed to pause while Rat walked through the nearby maze of tunnels and side cuts, listening for trouble.

Mike leaned against the track of the continuous mining machine, munching a sandwich, while Sara did the same several feet away. Having spent only a few days underground, she found the work strangely satisfying. She never had a job where progress was visible by the minute. The rotating head of the continuous miner chewed coal from the seam at an astounding pace. Foot by foot, it went from ceiling to floor then advanced without stopping. The tunnel grew longer every time she returned to the face.

As much work as the machines did, the people labored just as hard keeping them going. The noise made it impractical to have a conversation, which was just as well. It wasn't like moving between desks in an office, where most everyone wasted time with trivial prattle. She chased power cables, greased bearings, cleared muck from tracks and rollers, ran to the storage cage for lube oil, and passed messages between the crew and Mike.

She didn't mind getting dirty. Prison chores cured anyone of that affliction. The grit was annoying, however. Bits of coal and rock stuck to exposed skin, leaving her itchy. Still, life in Number Six, even without the possibility of sunshine, was better than Graterford. A lot better.

Rat returned with good news. "All quiet to the east," he said.

The gang cheered his assessment.

"Some water to the north," Rat added. "A little more than usual, but we should be okay."

During the last hour of the shift, Mike's gang mined so much coal that they overloaded the discharge conveyor. Sara passed the message around, bringing the operation to a halt.

"When was the last time we did that?" Sheldon Hunter asked.

"Never," someone answered.

"We're going to do it again tomorrow," Mike said. "Let's call it a day."

There were high-fives all around as they gathered at the lift for the ride to the surface.

"I can taste that grog already," Rat said.

"I'm going to bed," Hunter moaned.

"Awww, come on, let's celebrate. What about you, Mike? Sara?"

"Might join you for one or two."

When the lift didn't appear as scheduled, Mike grabbed the handset and rang the operator. Planning on visiting the bar or not, the gang was anxious to go above.

"What'd he say?"

"Couple minutes," Mike said, which wasn't the truth. The line was dead.

"Probably one of the Nash crew late again."

"As if they don't hassle us for that."

"Who's ever late?"

"Just saying."

"Keep it to yourself."

"Take it easy, guys," Mike said. "Don't ruin the ride home."

Sara agreed wholeheartedly. She was dead on her feet from walking what had to be umpteen miles, wearing heavy boots and coveralls, carrying tools and supplies. Happy about the success-ful, injury-free day, she didn't want to hear an argument over nothing. To her relief, banging and creaking from the lift prevent-ed any further bickering.

The cage descended into view with no faces showing through the steel mesh.

"Where's George?"

"And the rest of them?"

"This is bullshit."

"Relax, guys," Mike said. "We're all going home. Maybe some-thing happened up top."

Pulling open the door, he was astonished to see his sister, Zoe, lying on the floor beside a stack of BoF boxes and jugs of water. She was bound and gagged. A note was pinned to her.

"What the hell?" Rat gasped.

• • •

Jagger had been angry before. Even furious. Disappointed, too. Frustrated more times than anything. But flat-out sad? Not very often. Nonetheless, after leaving Philly Chick to her own demise, she collapsed with grief. Not immediately. She walked past the edge of town, jogged along the trail, and made it to within a hun-dred yards of the trailer when she was overcome. Then it came on like a boulder rolling downhill. Her eyes burned with tears that she blinked away until there were too many to stop. She started stumbling. Then her left calf cramped. She spun to the right and tumbled into a gangly ball of worn-out clothes. On the ground she stayed.

The last official bout of sadness had come the day she real-ized her father had lied about coming home. She cried for hours and walked around in a daze for a week. Her mother's death was easier to take. She was in such bad shape, her passing was a re-lief. Dylan? Yeah, she knew he was a goner as soon as he puked that red splotch all over his last clean T-shirt. She tried Preacher John's mumbo jumbo out of desperation and the odd chance that, if there was something to it, they could celebrate. Thus, another expected outcome to be taken with dignity.

Crusty leaves stuck to Jagger's face and hair as waves of body-racking sobs shook her like the last wave of '52 Flu. Her hands clawed into the damp earth. Legs cramping and gut twisted, she released howls of pain that carried through the forest. Her hand was drawn to the weight of the gun in her jacket. She gripped the handle, slipped her finger past the trigger guard, and rolled onto her back. Staring at the sky, she coughed hard to drive away the crying.

Her short life had been an adventure, full of misery and minor triumphs. She thought it always would be, until Philly Chick punched her silly in the cab of the BoF truck. Something happened that day. Maybe she saw what she could have been, someone with official status, who belonged to the winning team instead of the ever-losing dead-enders. Whatever, she was overcome with ambition, which was remarkable because few of her days had been idle. No more tearing up floorboards in abandoned houses looking for left-behind valuables or treks to distant towns for five-finger discounts at closed warehouses. She went after the big game, taking the prison bus, bargaining with Bartok for John Carroll, snatching his book from Claire. Why? To get so close to the ultimate prize that she could taste it but then go hungry one more time? Did she really believe Philly Chick would pay up upon delivery? She was as likely a double-crosser as Selman. And so she turned out to be, refusing to get out while the getting out was good.

The pointlessness crushed her outlook. Nothing was worth anything. Everything was nothing.

She recalled the night Crush was in the clinic. She wanted revenge as much as Whip but knew it was a suicide run. At the time, she secretly admired Whip's willingness to fight back. And here she was lying on the ground, ready to end it all, without even taking a shot at the people who made her life a first-rate shit show. It was embarrassing. She threw an arm over her eyes to soak up another round of self-hating tears.

"Ashley."

Jagger reflexively answered, "Yeah?"

"It's time to go."

"Nah. I'm staying here."

When another coughing fit ended, she again heard her name. "Ashley."

Jagger pulled her arm away to reveal Preacher John standing over her.

"I've been looking for you," he said.

Her aching legs wouldn't move, and the gun was too heavy to lift.

"Give me your hand. I'll help you up."

Suddenly, she felt like she was out of her own body, watching from the side as her free hand rose to meet his. He gently pulled, taking her weight off the ground until she stood on her own feet. An instant later, her perspective returned to normal. She nearly fell over from the strangeness of regaining control of her legs. She steadied herself then smoothed her hair with all ten fingers.

"Feeling better?" Preacher John asked.

"Feeling weird."

"I'm glad I found you."

"Not for nothing, Preacher, but you're worth a ton of money to me."

"You'll receive much more than that. Hundreds of times more. Eventually."

Jagger was dumbstruck by his reply. She stepped back, eyes darting to the trees, bushes, and rocks behind him in case he wasn't alone.

"Did you read my testament?" he asked.

"Some. How'd you know I have it?"

"Weeks ago, I wrote about you protecting it."

"It's a package deal they offered me," Jagger said. "You and your book for the money and tickets out of here."

"You won't need the reward or the tickets, but you will have to help me surrender."

Her eyes locked on his. "You're giving up?"

"Fulfilling my destiny as you must fulfill yours."

"Not for nothing, but this sounds like you're walking me into a trap."

"Then you didn't read my testament."

"I said only some of it," Jagger confessed.

"Ah, well, that's probably better," Father Carroll said. "It won't be easy, but I promise you God rewards those who serve Him."

· · ·

With the windows boarded up, Selman's office was more storm shelter than administrative center and nearly as dark. The damaged furniture had been removed, replaced by a table and plastic chairs from storage. To make it official, he placed the Common Faith flag in its stand against the wall.

"Quite suitable for this humble servant of the Universal Creator," Selman remarked, signing his name on the bottom of an arrest warrant for Claire Whelan. "Don't you think?"

Randy Bartok shrugged his reply.

"Sit. Relax. All is well."

He wasn't sitting on one of those Commoner chairs if his boss ordered him at gunpoint.

"Once again," continued Selman, "you're worried about nothing. Nash has done us a favor."

"He has control of the mine, which he can have. It's the explosives that we need to consider."

"Oh, dear, maybe he'll use them."

In the right hands, and George Nash's two were just right,

industrial explosives were as effective as anything the military deployed. If the miners blew up Zoe Whelan or Filner or themselves in a suicide pact, Bartok could not care less. He didn't want to be collateral damage. More than a few of the miners were probably crafting potent handheld bombs to toss his way in reprisal for past beatings and unofficial tax collection. He couldn't blame them. He'd do the same thing, given the opportunity. In fact, when the siege was over, he'd help himself to whatever he could find.

"Nash's working for you?" Bartok queried.

"He thinks he is," answered Selman. "I took his call, listened to his plea, gave him permission to proceed. He agreed to put Ms. Whelan in seemingly mortal danger in exchange for something he'll never get."

"The troopers are going to take him out?"

"They will, but we have to wait until midnight. Perhaps a bit longer."

"A lot could go wrong between now and then."

"Much more will go right."

Because his copy machine had been smashed, Selman filled out a duplicate of the arrest warrant by hand. He enjoyed writing with an actual pen. It was quiet; no keyboard clatter or whirring of the printer. Finished, he placed the document to the side.

"Leave the miners to me," Selman said. "I'll pretend to negotiate with Mr. Nash then let the troopers take revenge. Done."

Bartok didn't bother asking who was going to mine the coal after the workers were dead. Apparently, details like that didn't interest a man of big ideas.

"John Carroll," continued Selman. "It would be nice to present him and his book as a gift to our friend Secretary Thompson."

"I'm looking."

"Look harder."

Bartok dismissed himself with, "On it."

Selman took out his cell and dialed Common Faith Headquarters in Philadelphia. He deliberately used the main number, ensuring the call would be logged through the system, thereby preventing the Secretary from denying his initiation of contact.

At some point over the past week, his goals and hers had diverged, which was emotionally painful. They'd always been on the same page, from the day they met. For years they worked hand in hand, accomplishing a tremendous amount of good for the country and themselves. He couldn't imagine what he'd done to offend her. If not for the distractions of the Pottsville entertainment, he might have been more upset.

"Yes, I'll hold."

Furthermore, he was surprised by the impatience of his old friend the Secretary. While he might have overpromised a bit, her lack of confidence in his ability to recover from a setback was stunning. After all the ups and downs they'd been through!

"I'm sorry. The Secretary is not available at this time."

"Very well, I'll call back another time."

He took the rejection as carte blanche to implement his own solutions. If they succeeded, Secretary Thompson would sing his praises. If not, she'd send him to New Mexico.

• • •

With the help of Rat and Sara, Zoe got to her feet. They guided her out of the cage. No one rushed to remove the gag from her mouth or cut loose her hands. Bright eyes sunk into dirty faces gave the miners a troll-like appearance. For capable people, they seemed terribly confused about what to do. She wondered if they'd obey George Nash. He was the one who had trapped her at the house. His henchmen drove her to the mine, where they had already taken control. From what she heard on the way, their grievances had less to do with Candy Walsh's death than conditions underground and how much they were paid.

"What's the note say?"

Her brother Mike read, "Everyone is welcome to come up but her. You have five minutes. There's plenty of water and BoF boxes to keep her belly full."

They stood fast, glancing at each other, scratching their chins, folding and unfolding their arms. Would they leave her down the hole like a dog by the side of the highway? She was about to find out. A burst of declarations and questions broke the silence.

"Whatever happened up there got nothing to do with us."

"It does now."

"Says who?"

"Says whoever tied her the hell up."

"Let her talk."

"Cut her loose."

"Who's got a knife?"

A scrawny guy snapped open a pocketknife.

"Just the gag, Rat; maybe she's some kind of wacko."

"It's Mike's sister," the one called Rat said. "What's she gonna do?"

"Get to it, the clock's ticking."

Rat sliced the rag tied through Zoe's mouth. She spit fiber strands and wiped her mouth on her shoulder.

"You okay?" Mike asked.

Zoe nodded.

"Tell us what's going on."

Accident or not, she had no idea how these men might take Candy Walsh's death.

"George Nash called a wildcat strike," Zoe began, deciding to mete out pieces of the truth. "He's holding me hostage as a bargaining chip."

"Get the hell out of here!"

"Shut up! We got two minutes."

"Nash said if I come up before his demands are met, he'll shoot me dead. If any of you try to protect me, he'll shoot you, too."

"Nice try, sweetheart."

"It's what he said," Zoe confirmed. "Do what you want."

The lights in the cage flicked on and off three times.

"I'm going up."

"Yeah, this isn't my problem."

The first two men entered the cage, hurriedly stacking BoF boxes and water jugs just outside the entrance.

"I'll stay with her," volunteered Mike. "Everyone else in the cage. Move it!"

With permission to go, the others stepped quickly into position, except for Rat.

"Might need a hand down here," Rat said to Mike.

"We'll be fine," Mike told him. "Tell Nash to call it quits before someone dies."

"Okay," Rat said, handing over his helmet with a nod toward Zoe. "Safety first." Then he backed in with the other men.

Sara remained outside.

"I spent six years in prison," she said, moving away from the lift. "What's a few days down here?"

Mike signaled with his right hand, and Rat shuttered the miners in a moment before the lift started.

Zoe watched it rise out of sight, then focused on her brother. He untied her hands and placed Rat's helmet on her head.

"Welcome to the underworld," he said. "Now tell me the rest of the story?"

"Not in front of her," Zoe replied.

"Get over it," Mike urged. "We're all friends down here."

Zoe glared at Sara. "You're screwing with me, aren't you? Painted a cross into the plaster on the wall knowing I would see it."

Sara shook her head.

"I saw it! Right before Nash's men grabbed me. It was there. Not anymore. Chopped it out again."

"Calm down," Mike told her, holding out his water bottle. "Take a drink."

Furious at being sucked into a plot by a third-rate labor leader, she waved it away.

"What did Nash say exactly?"

"He's using me. I guess to make himself look like a big man in front of his people, or maybe this is his audition to become a union president."

She was stunned silent by a stream of water striking her face.

"There's more where that came from," her brother said, growing restless. "George Nash didn't pick you out of the crowd for no reason. Let's hear it."

Because he would find out sooner or later, Zoe told him everything, from the time Candy and Kyle were caught on the train to the point where Jagger warned her of the mob coming to get her.

"What about Mom?" he asked.

"She was gone when I got to the house."

"She has friends around town. She'll be okay."

"Not if Selman catches her."

"For what?"

"Being a Christian," Sara put in.

"Not much of a secret," Mike added. "Why would he be after her now?"

"You want to tell him?" Zoe asked Sara.

"Because a compliance specialist like your sister is doomed if a blood relative is an active Christian, but Selman's not going to trash your career. He could have done that years ago."

Zoe cast a sardonic smile at Sara. "Tell me, oh prophet, what is my future?"

"Selman's going to let you die and blame it on the Christians. Probably me."

• • •

The Mollies had bugged out. How did Bartok know? There was some canned food in the cupboards, sheets on the beds, clothes in the closets, all the indications of habitation. But the stove was cold, the trash can empty. No self-respecting, dirt-poor clan like them let the stove go cold in late October, and that same self-respect dictated a clean hovel, as in removal of all trash to prevent rot stink. Furthermore, there were gaps in the cupboards and drawers. He estimated they took as much as they could carry, which would last them several days.

Bartok left no trace of his search. He reset the door lock, pathetic as it was, and scuffed his boot tracks with a tree branch. Unless they were watching him from the woods, which he doubted they were, they would never know he'd been inside.

He walked out to his jeep, took a seat behind the wheel, and fired up another Amish cigar. Unlike dipshits Candy Walsh and Kyle Smith, the Mollies probably knew better than to jump the train. It didn't make sense that they would, anyway. For whatever reason they split, it wasn't a big enough score to be gone forever or they would have taken everything short of the nails holding the place together.

Were they spooked by Candy's death and the townspeople's rampage? Had they spotted John Carroll and were circling for the kill? Were they prepping the stolen prison bus for something? When he stubbed out the cigar, he hadn't settled on any of those theories, nor did he conjure another one worth considering. His only conclusion: they were nearby and somewhat comfortable.

Unless he had it all wrong.

Just as that possibility passed through his mind, he heard the solid click of a revolver hammer cocked to the firing position. It was directly behind him, but too far for a quick grab.

"That's no way to greet an old friend," he said without turning.

"Friends use ashtrays," Jagger replied.

"Please accept my apologies. Where's the sisters-in-crime?"

"Vacation."

"Spending that reward money before you collect it?" asked Bartok.

"Ready to cash out soon, and Selman ain't the only one making offers."

"Well, my hat's off to you, madam entrepreneur," Bartok said, "taking bids on something you don't have."

"I got more than anyone else and pictures to prove it. First one with hard money and the right paperwork gets the prize. Ask Selman if he wants to step up or let it go."

"What's the number?"

"Twenty-five large, brand-new ID, and travel passes to a sandy spot near the sea."

"No one's giving you all that," scoffed Bartok. "No one can."

"Problem with being a big fish in a small pond is you think the world's all about being a fish, never realizing that dark spot above ain't no cloud in the sky. It's people in a boat come to catch your ass and piss in the water when they're done. See how that works?"

This was exactly the kind of issue Bartok warned Selman about a few hours ago. If Jagger wasn't bluffing, if she managed to get someone further up the food chain to believe her bovine feces, then the play with the miners could quickly unravel. Secretary Thompson might send a SWAT team to relieve the troopers and a new director to replace Selman. Game over.

"Am I talking to myself here?" asked Jagger.

"Doing business with strangers can be dicey," cautioned Bartok.

"Then make us both happy. Get the money and the paperwork sorted before the clock strikes midnight. Otherwise, I'm on the road to greener pastures. Got it?"

"Assuming I perform as requested, where do I make delivery?"

"Be where you are. Soon enough I'll be there, too."

• • •

Out of her element, Zoe listened carefully to Mike and Sara discuss the situation. She was less certain than they were that

Selman had a diabolical plan. She saw the local Common Faith director as incompetent rather than malicious.

"We have three hours of battery power for the lights, maybe a little longer," Mike explained as he moved over to the tool locker near the lift. "We can triple it if we switch two off."

Sara immediately turned off her helmet lamp.

"We'll need a pry bar, a hacksaw, rescue breathers, some food and water. We probably can't carry more than that."

"For what?" Zoe queried.

"We're going to walk out to the ventilation shaft," answered Mike, gathering the tools from the shelves.

"How far is it?" asked Sara, hooking a pry bar on her belt.

"Three miles and five hundred feet up. More or less."

"There's nothing blocking the entrance?"

"A metal grate covers the intake. Hopefully the hacksaw will cut through the bars."

Already Zoe was cold. Her feet would be shreds if she walked any distance over rough terrain in her old sneakers. And how were they going to climb that high? Common Faith Headquarters was that tall. It would be a serious workout to walk up the fire escape stairs to the top in dry shoes.

"We can't climb that high," she protested, preferring to take her chances with the miners and Selman.

"We don't have to," Mike went on. "This mine's like a layer cake. Seams of coal under beds of rock. As we went deeper, we cut a slope, like a ramp, from the upper levels down to lower ones to bring the machinery to the work area. We'll go up those ramps to the highest level where the ventilation shaft is. Then break out through the grate at the end."

"Okay. Assuming we find our way out, then what?" Zoe wanted to know.

It was a good question, one to which neither he nor Sara nor Zoe herself had an answer.

"Anybody have any ideas?"

"What's the alternative?" Sara asked.

"In any hostage situation, there's always a negotiation. One side makes demands, the other counters. Eventually it resolves."

"The last one didn't go so well for you," Mike said.

"Thanks to people like her."

"None of us sent you down here," Sara reminded Zoe.

"Us?" Zoe questioned. "I knew you were still a Christian."

"Always will be."

"In spite of a civil war that killed tens of millions and destroyed parts of every major city, you won't give it up."

"War wasn't the answer," agreed Sara, "but the Common Faith won't hold the peace."

"So far so good," Zoe retorted.

"Stop arguing," Mike demanded, handing Sara a hacksaw. "The sooner we get moving, the sooner we're on the surface."

"Before we go for this underground trek," Zoe said, "aren't you assuming they won't guess we'll try to escape?"

"Maybe they will," admitted Mike. "Here's the thing. If Selman or George Nash wants to kill you, all they have to do is turn off the power. Forget the dark, that's not the problem. Once fresh air stops circulating, the carbon dioxide and methane build up until we either suffocate or die in an explosion."

"No one's trying to kill me!" Zoe shouted.

"Gamble with your own life," said Mike, "not ours." He gestured for Sara to pick up some rations while he took a jug of water and leaned a pry bar over his shoulder. They started down the tunnel, boots splashing through the puddles.

Zoe leapt to her feet and called, "Mike!"

He continued without slowing, his headlamp pointing straight ahead.

"Mike!"

It was reckless to leave the relative safety and comfort of where they were. The steel frame through which the lift traveled appeared solid. The lights glowed bright. Any minute, the troopers or a SWAT team might come down to tell her the strike was over.

Might.

Zoe grabbed a jug of water and charged after Mike. Two steps later, her feet were soaked. She plowed on, swearing under her breath, promising herself that when this was over, she'd spend a week in the California sunshine to thaw the damp out of her bones.

When she caught up to them, Mike switched off her headlamp. To his credit, he didn't chide her about joining late.

"Here we go," he said, like they were taking a stroll in the park.

Together, the three of them walked past the last hanging bulb and into the gaping darkness.

CHAPTER 31.

Claire had second thoughts about leaving Father Carroll's testament behind. She had left the house, bound for her chapel, when she encountered the crowd roaming town. She turned around, figuring Zoe would be headed home to pick her up. She arrived just in time to see them take her daughter.

She was a block away when the two big miners lifted Zoe, blindfolded, bound, and gagged, into the back of Nash's pickup. She didn't know them, but she recognized Joe Grant, who saw her running toward the house. He reached her just as she stopped to catch her breath, tears streaming down her face.

"You're not taking my daughter!" she hollered.

"I'm trying to save her," Grant replied, blocking Claire from a dash to the pickup.

"Hah! I saw the mob in town. They blame her for Candy's death."

"The miners want to be taken seriously. With Zoe among them, the troopers won't attack. The government will have to bargain."

The driver of the pickup blasted the horn.

"How long have you been informing on us?" Claire asked.

"I was keeping us safe!" Grant barked. "The worst Selman did was take some money. In the words of our Savior, 'Render unto Caesar... ' And that's what we did."

"What you did, Joe," argued Claire.

"Yes, I did it. And I warned Candy and Kyle to stay off the train, too. They didn't listen. Now you're not listening."

"Selman, the miners, they're using you, using Zoe, to get what they want."

"Zoe brought this on herself," Grant said. "Same for Father Carroll."

The driver hit the horn again.

"They're going to kill my daughter."

"Not if she cooperates," insisted Grant. "And—

A long blast of the horn preempted Grant's final word. He bolted for the truck.

"They'll kill you, too!" Claire shouted at his back.

Grant squeezed in the passenger side, and the pickup sped away.

As much as she feared for Zoe, Claire raged inside because she had not acted on her suspicions. Furthermore, no one had warned her about the mob. None of her friends had called or knocked on the door, not even one of the gossip mavens who reveled in bad news. They had kept her in the dark on purpose. She found out about Candy's death and the mob by accident, passing Nurse Porter on the street.

"Your daughter's a fiend!" Porter shouted, without further explanation.

People had said worse, but then Claire saw the crowd swarm the Common Faith Center. What they did to the building was a disgrace. Finally, as she rushed toward home, Steve Regan told her from the back door to his tavern, "The story is your kid killed Candy Walsh. Or let her die. No one cares which. They want justice." Preposterous as that was, Claire knew better than to attempt to reason with a cynical barkeep or a ginned-up crowd.

Now she was home, her mind racing with terrible possibilities. What would they do to Zoe? What was her own fate? Would Selman have her arrested? She had no one to call for help, not even Mike who was working deep in Number Six. What would happen to him? She couldn't flee. She was trapped with no vehicle, nor friends with one, nor another means to get out of Mount Carmel.

And Joe Grant had betrayed them all.

In the dining room, she found the pile of plaster on the floor. Why anyone did that was beyond Claire's understanding. Any semblance of a cross had been removed when Mike repaired the wall. She cleaned up the mess for a second time. The mindless work actually allayed her fears for a few minutes.

Putting away the dustpan and brush, she paused at the sound of a knock on the front door. After witnessing Zoe's kidnapping, she was loath to answer it. Whoever it was persisted. She retreated to the kitchen where she waited until hearing the door open.

"Hello? Mrs. Whelan? Hello?"

Recognizing the voice, Claire walked to the parlor.

"There you are, Mrs. Whelan," Selman greeted her. "Sorry to barge in. I wanted to check on your well-being."

The sincerity of the bald-faced lie gave Claire a smile. "Thank you. I'm fine," she said. She assumed he had the list Candy made for Zoe and was here to make a personal arrest. She decided to delay the inevitable by pretending not to know and telling him, "A mob kidnapped my daughter. I saw them take her away. What are you going to do about it?"

"On my way to make an appeal to the miners. They've called a strike over working conditions and whatnot, which is their right. However, it seems Zoe complicated things by neglecting procedure with regards to Candy Walsh."

"So it's mob justice?"

"Not at all," Selman assured her. "Still, we must take precautions for everyone's safety, which is why I've come to invite you to make the short trip to Pottsville."

Suddenly Claire recalled her thoughts as she was hiding Father Carroll's testament, how God had a mission for her. She realized her work was finished. She'd secured it under the rock near her chapel, where it could be recovered by the right person at the right time. Her only regret was not reading it.

"Really, Mrs. Whelan, I believe you may be in danger if I'm unable to reason with the miners. Lenny is waiting outside with a car to take you to Pottsville."

"I'd like to leave a note for my son," Claire said.

"Allow me the favor of personally telling him where to find you."

• • •

When walking half an hour on the streets of Philadelphia, Zoe had covered more than a mile. In the tunnels of Number Six, she estimated they traveled a third that distance in the same amount of time. With only Mike's headlamp lighting the way, the going was tricky. They went single file, him in the lead, her second, and Sara last. There was no point to avoiding the puddles; it only slowed them down. They were a noisy bunch, too, gear rattling and clanging, the sound echoing around them.

At each turn, Mike used a hammer to mark the side of the wall with a vertical line. Bang, bang, bang, bang, bang. Sara did the same crosswise, which infuriated Zoe, but she kept it to herself. However, she did want to know why he did this.

"A trail of breadcrumbs," he explained. "In case we're separated, and anyone has to come back. Just look for the mark."

"Why are the walls white?" asked Zoe.

"Sprayed with limestone. Keeps the coal dust down. Otherwise all us miners would get black lung and die before making the quota."

Minutes later they came to the first ramp.

"Put your hand out," Mike said, holding his up as if hailing a taxi. "Feel the breeze?"

"I guess," answered Zoe.

"The flow goes toward the fans as air is sucked out of the mine."

"Sucked out? Where does it come in?"

"Down the shafts by the lift that brought you to the work area."

"And it's pulled three miles?" she said, incredulous at the power required.

"Like one big vacuum cleaner."

"Wow."

The ramp took them up to the next level where coal had already been removed. Zoe got the sense they were spelunking through vast caverns, not so tall as they were wide and deep, infinitely deep. At some points, Mike's light didn't reach the edges. Like a giant honeycomb, the space once held millions of tons of fossil fuel. It was amazing. It was also frightening to imagine being lost inside.

On a dry area at the top of the ramp, they sat for a rest and a snack. Sara passed a BoF box to Zoe, who took out the cookies, then handed it to Mike. The cookies tasted like sugared sawdust. Dry and gritty, they made her cough. She missed her favorite bakery in Philadelphia where she grabbed a couple of muffins every morning on the way to Headquarters.

From his shirt pocket, Mike took out a notebook. He drew a crude line diagram of the tunnels from the lift to the ramp. Next, he traced a line on the second level back toward the lift with several right angle turns until it stopped at the next ramp.

"Two rights and a left," he said tapping the page. "Then we go up again."

Zoe drank from a jug of water then got to her feet. In the beam of Mike's headlamp, she noticed particles of dust falling. No, it was bigger than dust, almost pebble sized. Several hit her helmet. Then she heard a series of pops, like a jazz drummer's syncopated rimshots.

"Is that normal?" she asked.

"The earth is always moving," Mike said. "Let's go."

She didn't believe him. "Maybe we should go back where it was safe."

Mike and Sara ignored her suggestion, plodding forward. Once again, Zoe caught up.

"This is stupid, we should reconsider," she pleaded.

"Worry about what you're going to do after we get out of here,"

Mike said without looking at her.

She couldn't remember much about their father, who died when she was in third grade, but she imagined he used the same tone when scolding them. To her brother's point, she occupied her mind with the future. What was she going to do if, when, she was above ground? A hot shower, clean clothes, and dry shoes were all on the list, but she put them far below the first possible phone call to Secretary Thompson. Where would she find a phone? Cell or landline?

Over the next hour, more small rocks plunked into puddles and onto her helmet. It was like kids taunting her. It was also an unnerving reminder of the incalculable mass hanging above them. Water was everywhere, too, dripping from above, flowing across the ground in tiny streams. She couldn't fathom working in a mine on a day-to-day basis. The job would drive her insane.

At the next crosscut, Mike put his hand up for them to stop. "Hang on," he said.

Zoe propped herself against the tunnel wall, instantly regretting it as damp soaked through her shirt.

Mike checked his notes, started one way, then doubled back. "Wait here," he said, "I want to check the next intersection."

"Oh, no," Zoe replied, "we're staying together."

"It's only a hundred feet away. Switch on your light and take a rest. Have another snack if you can eat."

A rest sounded great, being alone less so, and she wasn't about to linger with Sara. She turned on her light, its beam giving a modicum of security.

"Okay," she said, "you two go ahead. Yell if you want me to meet you over there."

Mike and Sara went to check the way ahead while Zoe fished through the box for another snack. Between walking and the cold, she craved calories. The soy powder was good for nothing. Canned cheese and crackers? Worth a try. She pulled off the lid. The rubbery substance stuck to her finger. It smelled like musty wax and had virtually no taste. The crackers disintegrated to crumbs as she tore the plastic wrapper. Washed down with several gulps of water, they filled her stomach.

She felt the ground shift, or so she thought. A couple of deep breaths calmed her nerves.

"Zoe!"

She immediately turned toward her brother's call. His helmet light flickered in the distance.

"Zoe! This way! Run!"

"I'm coming!"

She took a step toward him then froze at the sound of thunder. Next came the roar of falling rock rushing toward her behind a rolling cloud of dust that erased Mike's light. She stumbled backward, twisted, and fell face down. A boulder landed inches away, dousing her with a wave of filthy water. She managed to turn away just in time, but then another rock struck her helmet. Silence followed.

• • •

Jerry Boyle wasn't deaf. He heard Bartok roll into the compound, slam the jeep door, and shout. Heard the first gunshot, too. It was the second report that brought him out of hiding. That and the sound of the pigs squealing. He couldn't bear the loss of the animals. No one got away with killing them, not even Mount Carmel's chief enforcer and sometimes customer.

Shotgun leading the way, Boyle approached the pig enclosure. The gun held double-aught buckshot alternated with slugs for a total of six rounds. As for which he'd send Bartok's way, he settled on one of each if there wasn't a damn good reason and compensation for any loss.

On the off chance that Bartok might get the jump on him, Boyle took precautions in the form of letting one of the Mollies serve as backup. The bigger one, Crush, said she couldn't do it.

The skinny one, Whip, held the pistol confidently, offering to go out on her own to see what he wanted. Didn't that young lady have the gunslinger look in her eye! He only wished he had brought them into the fold sooner. The money he could have made; the fun they all could have had. Anyway, he told her to circle around on the quiet and not to shoot until someone else shot first. After all, Bartok's dealings were never straightforward.

"Come on out, Jerry!"

Boyle stomped into the open, shotgun leveled, finger on the trigger. "Why're you firing on my pigs?" he demanded.

"You broke the contract," Bartok replied, his own pistol casually hung at his side. "Harboring fugitives without permission."

"No fugitives around here, and two dead porkers going to cost you a thousand green, maybe more if I can't salvage the meat."

Bartok nodded. "Keeping the Mollies under your wing means I'm canceling your license to operate."

"They ain't here!"

Without looking, Bartok pointed his gun at the pen and fired. The last pig squealed and fell dead against the fence slats.

Boyle shouldered his weapon, right eye sighted past the bead at Bartok's chest.

"Give 'em up. I'll get you a reward," Bartok said. "A couple of cows to replace the pigs."

"Can't collect what ain't due," Boyle replied.

"The troopers are coming back to town," continued Bartok. "A whole company this time, more than a hundred men. They can burn this place on the way to Number Six, or you and I make a deal."

No idle threat, the economic reality of this fact struck hard. Boyle had no friends among the troopers. They were an ugly bunch who lacked entrepreneurial flair in the sense that they used brawn to collect tolls instead of brains to inspire new ways to earn. He paid them off when necessary, but it was strictly business.

"Call them out before my patience expires," said Bartok.

At the risk of losing his business, Boyle decided against turning over the Mollies. Bartok and his history aside, most of which had been pleasant, if the troopers were coming in force, he was doomed. What would his old pal Bartok do then? Certainly not lend a hand or a kind word to stop the inevitable, because hundred to one against can't be called cowardice. Running from those odds was called survival. Furthermore, he liked the Mollies. Always did. The little one especially. She was smart. And that Jagger, a two-legged mountain lion though she may be, was marrying material. For her he'd shave his beard, and his chin hadn't felt a razor in a decade.

"Told you before and I'm telling you again," he said. "They ain't on the patch. The troopers torch my place, I'll torch yours."

"Was hoping we could keep things friendly."

"We can, starting with an apology and payment for the livestock."

"Alright," Bartok said, holstering his weapon. "I'm sorry for shooting your animals."

"The hell you are."

"Really, I am. Who loves bacon and pork chops more than me?"

They shared a chuckle over that true statement, relieving some of the tension.

"What do you want with the Mollies, anyway?"

"They have a book I want."

"You came out here and shot my pigs over a book?" Boyle said. "I got hundreds of books. Take any you like. Take ten. Ain't like no one reads anymore."

"What I'm looking for is a limited edition of one, handwritten by John Carroll mostly when he was Selman's basement guest," explained Bartok. "I figure the Mollies got it when they sprung him last week, then somehow lost it to Carroll's flock, but got it back again. Otherwise, Jagger wouldn't be strutting around asking for top dollar."

"What's so special about what Father Carroll wrote?"

"Said to be a revelation from God that's going to kick up one hell of a storm. Maybe another civil war."

Boyle feigned amazement. "Four girls with a revelation from God? Holy shit! If you told me that up front, we could've drank a bottle of whiskey and laughed the night away."

"Nothing funny coming our way, so consider yourself officially notified. When the troopers sweep through here, everything's going up in flames. Probably you, too. The Mollies, if they aren't here, well, good for them. If they are? They'll do a turn at the Crown Hotel before Colonel Stewart sells them off to a Chinese coal inspector or trades them to another officer down the line. Who knows? Selman might keep the little one for himself."

Boyle asked, "None of that bothers you?"

"It does," answered Bartok, "but not at the moment."

John Carroll's book under her arm, Runt marched out from behind the nearest container. She strode past Boyle, pushing his gun barrel down with her free hand on the way.

"Here it is," she said, presenting the book to Bartok.

"This the real thing?" he asked.

"Calling me a liar?"

"Asking for certification is all."

"You can go now," Runt told him.

Bartok took it and said, "Thanks for your cooperation, young lady."

When the jeep rolled out of sight, Boyle asked Runt, "Why'd you give it to him?"

"Because he'll never read it."

CHAPTER 32.

Shocked as she'd been at the sight of rock falling all around her, Zoe was horrified to awake in silent darkness. At first, she thought she'd died. Then it occurred to her that if she was thinking about being dead, she couldn't be dead. Furthermore, the pain in her body was undeniable. She'd been in some fights in her life, all with suspects taller and heavier than her. A combination of mixed martial arts training and handy weapons assured her victories. Not this time. She was beaten into the muck on the tunnel floor.

She suddenly felt seasick, as if trapped in the bilge of a ship in a storm. She wretched twice then spewed the contents of her stomach. A coughing fit followed, brought on by the stench of bile.

Lifting herself to a seated position, rocks slid off her back and arms, the sharp edges clawing at exposed skin. A few landed on her legs, bruising already damaged flesh. She cried out but was struck quiet by the subdued sound of her own voice. There was no echo. It was like yelling into a coffin. She got the sense that she was in an incredibly small space as opposed to the vacuous tunnels of the mine.

She realized her helmet was no longer atop her head. Her sore hands searched among the debris, delving into her own warm vomit. She settled into a logical search pattern until she touched the plastic. With extreme care, she placed it on her wet hair, then found the switch for the lamp.

The instant burst of light revealed her position among several massive boulders and piles of smaller rocks. At first glance, she was trapped. While the largest stones held up the roof, they also blocked any way out. Movement in every direction was limited to a few feet. Of all the training she had, nothing prepared her for being entombed like an ancient Egyptian.

She leaned back, breathing heavy, mind spiraling through worst case scenarios she had survived. Andrew hadn't blown her to bits, had he? He wasn't the first one to try to murder her. She'd been shot at, attacked by a trio of thugs in an abandoned church, and nearly run over by a speeding van on Oregon Avenue.

"Do not panic," she said. "Do not panic."

Then she thought of her brother. He was somewhere on the other side of the debris blocking the tunnel. Or under it.

"Mike!" she hollered. "Are you over there?"

No reply didn't mean he was crushed. He'd walked out of the last collapse. He and Sara both did.

"And I'm getting out of here, too," Zoe said.

She directed her helmet lamp around the area. Ahead and to her left were solid stone faces. Behind and to the right, the material was large but possibly movable. Better still, a small opening at the top of the pile hinted at a route out. She clambered up, squeezed her head into the slot, and peered into a sort of rough-hewn shaft the size of a drainage pipe. Where it ended, she couldn't see.

She slid down and took a few moments to contemplate the next move. What if it was a dead end? What if there was another collapse? The small chamber where she was seemed stable and well-supported, the slot much less so.

The lack of options pushed her to take the risk. She dragged some rocks away from the opening, then in she went. Slithering over the rough surface, pushing stones out of the way, she made slow progress. For every yard, her body took more punishment, but she pushed forward. Claustrophobia crept up on her as the gap became so narrow she had to exhale to slip through, only to have her belt buckle catch on an edge. She kicked hard, shoving herself past the hitch, earning a nasty scrape on her stomach for the effort.

On the other side, the going was easier. The niche wound snake-like, but it gaped wide enough for her to crawl. Minutes later, however, she found herself up against another slab of immovable rock.

"This can't be the end," Zoe said. "Can't be."

She lay flat a long while, listening to her own breathing, thinking of her brother and how he would persevere through the situation. Her lamp seemed to dim. She gave it a tap and it glowed bright again.

Not wanting to die in the dark, she reached for the first stone small enough to move. She wiggled it back and forth, then shoved it to the side. She tried another that was too heavy. A third broke free, then a fourth. She had no idea if she was inviting disaster or digging into oblivion, but she didn't stop. With nowhere else to put the rocks, she used her feet to push them back into the shaft.

Another heavy one resisted her efforts. She swung around, braced herself, and pushed with both feet. It angled back a little, then a bit more, and to her surprise, finally fell away out of sight. A second later, she followed it atop a cascade of stone that spilled into one of the mine's regular tunnels. A deep puddle broke her fall.

An adrenaline rush and the thrill of breaking free of confinement had Zoe on her feet. What had Mike said? Follow the direction of the breeze. As he had done, she put out her hand but felt no air moving. Had the collapse blocked the flow? If so, how long before the toxic gases built up and suffocated her?

She recalled the marks Mike made at every turn. They were on the right side for a right turn, the left for a left. In between, go straight. All she had to do was follow them back to the lift. With no alternative, she set off in search of her brother's trail.

Walking through the tunnel with only the dim beam of her fading light, she almost missed the first cross. She was entranced by the sound of her own feet taking step after step through the envelope of grey. She recognized the hypnotic feeling as a symptom of exhaustion when she passed an intersection of tunnels without checking for the mark. Or did she? She went back, checked the walls, and there was the cross.

"Rest," she said, "then a right turn."

Finding the next cross assured her she was on the correct path. Fearing her light might run out of battery power, she went as fast as she could, humming popular tunes to ward off mental fatigue. A third cross boosted her spirits further. She refused to temper them with thoughts of what awaited her on the surface. She was still a ranking compliance specialist with a spotless record. She would have her day in court.

At the next cross, she turned right again and found herself at a ramp. However, instead of going down, it went up. How could that be? The ramp should be going down, retracing the route to the lift. She double-checked the cross. Yes, right turn, up the ramp.

Fearing her mind was playing tricks on her, like someone lost in the desert seeing a mirage, she knelt and rubbed her eyes. Again, she examined the cross. Right turn indicated. But how could she go up a ramp?

The answer gave her a reason to smile.

Mike survived the collapse! Not just him, but also Sara. She was the one who added the horizontal bar to her brother's vertical line of hammer strikes. Because the mine was a maze of tunnels and crosscuts, ramps and shafts, they must have found a way around the blockage and were marking a detour for her to follow.

"Mike!" she yelled up the ramp. "I'm right behind you!"

• • •

So much formality. To Selman's way of thinking, his trip to Number Six was like a state visit, albeit between two tiny nations. When the Chinese premier met the U.S. president in Washington, D.C., to finalize the war debt arrangement, Selman had been there. It was a grand affair to remember. He had nothing but admiration for the premier, who held on to power for thirty-five years and counting. No pesky elections for him every four years. At any rate, two miners with kerosene lamps escorted him from the gate to the office. The road was flanked by coverall-wearing others, some holding small arms or with primitive weapons, baseball bats and the like. More men stood at attention at the top and bottom of the stairs. Selman sensed their contempt even as he silently admired their dignity. In their minds, he supposed, they were honoring their great-great-grandfathers who stood up to the coal barons and Pinkertons. It was a shame, because unlike the cause those hardy souls of yesteryear fought for, the current one was for naught. But he would go through the motions to give them the illusion of distinguishing themselves.

Superintendent Filner sat in his office, but not behind the desk, which was helmed by George Nash. More kerosene lamps cast shadows from the corners.

"Wait outside and close the door," Nash told the two workers.

Filner did the honors, pouring each of them two thumbs of whiskey. He raised his glass for a toast. "To settling this thing," he said.

The whole measure down the hatch, Nash responded, "In everyone's favor."

"The motion is passed," Selman agreed.

Nash pointed to his glass for a refill as he said, "I did my part, sent the Whelan girl to the bottom of the pit."

"George has always been a team player," Filner put in.

"I'm very grateful."

Behind his slack smile, Selman congratulated himself on having the wisdom to be patient. The Bounty of Faith indeed! Faith in himself, that was. He might have forced the issue with Zoe Whelan sooner using crude means, something Bartok could have arranged. Of course, the results would have been accepted by Secretary Thompson and the public. But what fun was that? Furthermore, using the miners diversified his influence. While he knew no one on the Labor Relations Board, solving the strike would give him a reason to interface with them. Rooting out dangerous Christians among the miners (and the labor ranks in general) meant the board would owe him a favor. He would dare to suggest he take a seat with them to represent the Common Faith's interests.

"Her brother, Mike, and the convict Sara Darcy stayed down there with her," continued Nash.

"Predictable."

Upon devising his plan to end the strike, convert Zoe Whelan into a Common Faith martyr, and capture John Carroll, Selman figured Mike Whelan would remain with his sister. What self-respecting man wouldn't? That Sara Darcy was down there sweetened the pot. She'd been convicted of intolerance-related crimes, i.e., being a member of the Surviving Few. Her presence enhanced his narrative with an essential fact. If she hadn't appeared, he would have been forced to find another patsy.

"The mine is without power," Nash said next.

"Is that bad?" Selman asked, knowing full well the consequences. Years ago, a dozen men drowned when a transformer failed and a section of Number Six flooded for lack of water pumps. Then there was the issue of proper ventilation. He also knew the power was off before Nash mentioned it. He had the troopers disconnect a critical junction exactly one hour ago.

"It could be bad," Nash answered. "Or, it could be good."

Selman expected this from Nash, although not so soon. He remained silent, waiting for the attempt of an ambitious incompetent to climb above his station.

"We need to thin the ranks around here," said Nash.

"I'm not an economist," Selman replied, "but I'm sure we need every qualified miner available. Meeting the quota is essential to the financial health of this region and the nation. We must meet our obligations to the Chinese."

"First, screw the Chinese," Nash spat. "Second, I know the troopers are parked at the top of the hill, guns loaded, waiting for you to give the word. Third, in anticipation of the raid, I've rigged this whole building to blow when the troopers make their move. Yeah, I'll die, but so will a boatload of them. Fourth, I sent a crew with more bombs to avenge my death should we not arrive at a mutually beneficial arrangement. Who they target is up to them. Could be you, Bartok, Colonel Stewart. One or all. I don't give a damn."

"An unnecessary precaution," Selman said. "Perhaps you can be more specific about what you want."

"I'm taking over as superintendent with two other ghost salaries. One for Joe Grant, the other to be named later."

This caught Filner off guard. Thankfully, he sat quietly, listening with his full attention.

"The troopers take out Mike Whelan's men. They're locked in the storeroom. Plant guns on them after so it'll look right for Bartok's report and the news cameras."

It was Selman's turn to finish his drink. Whether Nash had made all the preparations he listed was of no consequence. His demands, while realistic, were impossible to meet. If Selman acquiesced to them, then he had a new partner, who would ask for more in the future. Unacceptable. Similarly, the mine did require skilled workers. Mike Whelan's gang were the best. None of them would be killed.

"I suppose I don't have much choice," Selman said, rising to leave.

Filner finally found his voice. "You're agreeing to this?"

"It's okay, Alvin. If you can't find another position in coal mining, the Common Faith will make a home for you."

"Alright then," Nash concluded, pouring himself and Selman what remained of the whiskey.

Selman raised his glass, toasting, "To the Bounty of Faith."

. . .

Up was out, Zoe reminded herself whenever fatigue sapped her strength. At every cross, she sat down for a break. Because her watch was broken, she counted to sixty before setting off again. She paced her walking, carefully choosing her footfalls to avoid twisting an ankle. She'd been up four ramps, three of them rather long and steep, which had to mean she was getting close to the ventilation tunnel.

"Mike!" she shouted as she departed from a cross that indicated a left turn.

As relieved as Zoe was to be approaching freedom, she was worried about not meeting Mike and Sara. The closer she got to the exit, the nearer to them she should be. Then again, she had no idea how long she'd been unconscious. A few minutes? An hour?

"Mike! Sara!"

No reply.

She continued for what seemed like too long between crosses. Keep moving forward? Go back to the last cross? She couldn't decide. Or, was she suffering from carbon dioxide poisoning? Confusion was one of the symptoms.

"Mike!" she hollered again.

Her light was fading, which was another source of worry. She recalled Mike saying their lights had two hours of battery life, maybe three. The terror of returning to complete darkness drove her onward. Soon she was jogging. The pool of light ahead swung to and fro over the ground. She increased speed to a full run. Several times she stumbled but didn't fall.

How far she ran, Zoe didn't know, but she almost missed the mark on the wall. She caught it in the corner of her eye, something brighter than the dull grey. She pulled up short and walked back several yards. There was a cross, but not one made by hammer marks. This one was perfectly shaped. Or was it? Just as she reached out, it disappeared. If it had ever been there.

"What the… "

I'm going crazy, Zoe thought. The toxic air is getting to me. But how? She had been running and wasn't exactly gasping for oxygen.

She bolted down the tunnel, her eyes focused ahead. There were no more side cuts, no other place for her brother to strike the wall. Then she saw a faint light ahead. It had to be Mike.

"Mike! I'm here!"

The spot grew larger and brighter, too big for a helmet lamp, and too close to the ground. Cautious, Zoe lessened her pace, her fingertips skimming the wall for balance. She peered at the brightness ahead. It took the form of a tall rectangle. An illusion? She wasn't sure. She continued step by step, soon smelling fresh air. It was real.

Finally, she arrived at a metal grate, behind which sat a glowing camp lantern. The grate was like a set of prison bars. It spanned the width and height of the tunnel. Huge bolts sunk into the rock held it in place. She gripped the iron with both hands, pushing and pulling as if the last of her strength might knock it away.

And then she realized her brother and Sara hadn't been ahead of her, marking the way, like she assumed. They were somewhere deep below, probably buried in the collapse that almost killed her, too. She slid to her knees. Too ashamed to weep for those she had doubted, she leaned her head against the bars, recalling the horrible steps taken to this point. It was her own choices that put her in this prison, that left her vulnerable to the deceit of others.

She rose from the ground, pulling herself up on bars of the grate, forcing herself away from panic. She couldn't go back through the mine nor call for help. No one was on the way to rescue her.

It's the price I have to pay, Zoe thought. Survive the hazards of the mine to get safely to the end and still be trapped. The final insult had been delivered.

The voice in her head asked, How did you get here?

"Honestly?" Zoe replied aloud, thinking the question was about her journey through the mine. "I followed the cross."

Suddenly, she recalled being in church as a little girl. Her mother always sat on the right side, about five pews back from the front. Other miners' widows sat in the same area with their children. Zoe couldn't remember their names nor the one of the boy who knew the words to the hymns without looking. He sang in a clear voice with perfect pitch. She wondered what happened to him.

She next thought of the service and how it proceeded. There was a processional when Father Carroll entered. There were readings from the Bible. Music. Singing. A sermon. Communion. And prayer. Her mother knelt to pray. So did Zoe. How did that go? She should know, but not because she attended church. She'd been too young to have committed all the rites to memory. She should know because she studied Christianity as part of her coursework to become a compliance specialist, a specialist in Christian practices.

"Know them," her instructor said. "Know what they do and how they do it."

She mastered the subject. Had to, in order to pass the exams. Yet at the moment, none of that information came to mind. All she could hear was the little boy next to her. He was singing. The words were from the page Andrew had given her, the one she took from that member of the Surviving Few she caught.

"A mighty fortress... "

She gripped the bars tighter in her hands. She pulled with all her weight, leaning back against the immovable barrier. It didn't budge.

She pushed forward, wedging her shoulder into the verticals, grunting at the strain. An instant later, she heard a deafening crack. To the left and right, the metal bars snapped. She almost lost her balance, and would have, if she hadn't reacted in the split second before an entire section fell away. The grate landed with a glorious clang that echoed down the tunnel.

CHAPTER 33.

The sign on the door read VENTILATION MOTOR ROOM. That much Zoe could have deduced on her own by the equipment inside the concrete-block building into which she emerged from the tunnel. A peek outside revealed a gravel road leading down through the woods. She assumed it led back to the mine entrance and office, a distance of a few miles at most. However, it was dark and getting colder by the minute, and her shoes were ruined. Besides, did she really want to go there? Probably not. Then where?

She sat on the cold floor, back against the wall, head tilted to the ceiling. The lantern cast a pool of yellow light, its oily flame gently waving. Beside her lay the miner's helmet, its lamp now dark. A week ago, she was working informants in preparation for a roundup of the Surviving Few. Now? She wondered if she was one of them, which was the farthest thing from possible she could have imagined.

Mere words didn't cut steel. Yet the grate broke away like it was made of twigs. She stood there, mouth agape, unable to fathom how something seemingly solid could suddenly be rendered fragile enough to collapse. She inspected the edges. They were hot to the touch, but as rigid as any piece of steel should be. And who put the kerosene lamp there?

She couldn't deny some unknown force set her free. God? Couldn't be. She wasn't a believer. She'd heard that little boy singing a hymn, but it was nothing but a childhood memory. Had God planted it in her mind as a signal? If so, why not simply talk to her?

She'd never been so confused. In fact, she'd always been clear-headed about religious matters. Her early exposure to her parents' church aside, she embraced the Common Faith and its message of inclusion and tolerance. She was all for it. She saw it in action, bringing people together, providing benefits and guidance. How could it be wrong?

Throughout her education and training, she'd been taught the dangers of Christianity. It was the religion of revolution from its founding, a disaffected group of Jews, then heretics among the pagan Romans. Jesus was a troublemaker, always had been. Instructors spoke of the worst adherents to make their points, and well-made they were. She couldn't wait to hunt some of the people responsible for nearly destroying the country. And that's exactly what she did.

She thought of the people she sent to jail, among them Sara Darcy. What had been her crime? She was a member of the Surviving Few. Okay. Did she attack anyone? No. Did she have plans to attack anyone? Not according to the person who informed on her activities. What were those activities? Distribution of Bibles, adherence to Christian practices, and the recruitment of others to do the same. Not exactly the stuff of violent insurrection.

"They're like weeds," her instructors said. "They grow quickly, choking off the good plants. That's why we root them out."

The analogy made sense, but in her experience, was it true? There might have been revolutionary Christians during the Second Civil War. Maybe there still were. Some of her arrests had been for weapons charges or having an explosives lab or any of the other myriad offenses that warranted serious inquiry, but these were a rarity. Many more were for innocuous offenses like copying Bibles or distributing Christian pamphlets.

What about Andrew, the man who nearly blew her to pieces at Common Faith Headquarters? "Your journey begins here," he said. He was correct. If he wanted to murder her, she wouldn't have survived the blast. She recalled those last few moments with him. He struggled to detonate the vest, desperately pushing the button as the sniper bullets struck him. Then came the flash. Just before she lost consciousness, she saw a puff of smoke rise from his body and transform into a bird. A false memory? Or, the first clue to her future?

There were more clues, all of which she denied. Father Carroll prayed at her bedside in the clinic. She saw the cross on her mother's dining room wall. She saw it again after the wall had been repaired and in the Common Faith Center. She saw a series of them in the mine, some made by Mike and Sara. The others? Were they the work of humans or the divine? She wasn't sure, but they led her to safety. And finally, the steel grate and the lantern.

If they were all signs from God, then what was she supposed to do?

"Anyone in there?"

Zoe's head snapped up at the sound of a woman's voice, and not the one she expected God to use. A powerful flashlight beam poked in from the doorway.

"Philly Chick! Can you hear me?"

"Loud and clear," Zoe said, struggling to stand.

"Don't want to be rude, but you're one sorry wrung-out rag," Jagger said.

"Thanks. How'd you know I was here?"

"He told me you'd make it," Jagger said.

"My brother, Mike?"

"No. Preacher John. It's in his book, or so he says. I didn't get to that part, but a bunch of other stuff worked out just like he said it would."

"You're one of his followers?" questioned Zoe.

"I'm me, but I ain't telling lies about what I've seen."

Zoe felt the same way.

Jagger dropped a satchel on the floor. From it she removed Zoe's boots, the ones taken on the first day they met. She swapped them out for another pair of shoes given to her by Preacher John.

"Going to miss those," she said, "but you need some good tread if we're going to get out of here in a way don't involve a cold box at the clinic."

Zoe accepted a towel with which she dried her feet. Then she changed into fresh clothes before tugging on clean socks and her boots. Finally, Jagger gave her a warm coat and gloves.

"Got a can of soup," Jagger said. "Ain't bad cold when your gut's been empty."

"Sounds delicious, but where're we going?"

"Catch a ride down the line to a spot where we can change vehicles or hop the train."

"Not the train," countered Zoe.

"Might have to be. It's clear south of Pottsville. So I'm told."

"Where's Father Carroll?"

"Uh, tried to talk him out of it," Jagger stammered. "But the man had his mind made up about destiny or some shit, which if you ask me is more of our own making, especially if you're going to take a stroll into the lion's den on your own, as opposed to at the point of a gun as yours truly has had the honor of doing, and surviving, as current circumstances prove."

Bewildered, Zoe asked, "What does that mean?"

"Said he was going to turn himself in at the mine."

Unless he had divine protection, it was a death sentence. "When?"

"Post haste, and the two of us parted company."

"Please, just answer my question," Zoe pleaded.

"Less than an hour ago."

"We have to stop him."

Jagger shook her head. "Not part of the plan, lady."

• • •

"Come on, Randy, join the fun," Colonel Stewart said.

Bartok wasn't about to participate in the assault on Number Six.

The troopers had never been his friends. Plus, he had aggravated them by interrupting the brawl outside the Pleasant Corner. While he saved at least several of their lives, the miners won a victory. The troopers looked weak and stupid. The score had to be settled. Giving them Kyle Smith for unintentional target practice was a step in the right direction but not enough. All good humor and common interests aside, he was on the wrong end of the equation. Thus, the invitation to a convenient death by the colonel himself, who no doubt had an underling ready to assume Bartok's spot in Mount Carmel. Bartok declined with a believable truth.

"Selman has me on other things," Bartok replied, as he slid behind the wheel of the jeep.

"Lenny Donovan brought us Compliance Specialist Whelan's mother. What else could you be doing?"

"Boring details but my sworn obligation."

"If you say so. Next time, eh?"

"Sure enough."

The lies of this conversation not withstanding, he wasn't going to miss the show, because he had a front-row seat waiting. He drove toward Number Six, cutting off Route 61 on a gravel double track that climbed the hill opposite the mine's entrance. It turned east to a spot near the dilapidated fence then ran parallel deep into the woods. He parked and hiked the rest of the way.

About ten minutes later, he climbed a familiar tree, one less than a hundred yards from the office at Number Six. Years ago, he installed a deer stand high above the ground. From here he claimed dozens of kills, most of which went to Joannie T. She prepared venison better than anyone, including his late mother. Framed with heavy planks, the stand offered marginal cover in terms of camouflage or bullet-stopping capacity. It did have a comfortable seat and a prop to rest his shotgun. Bartok wasn't worried about getting hit. Trooper weapons would be pointed at the office as they attacked from the east. Any return fire from the miners would be aimed much lower than the stand's altitude.

Waiting for the first shot, he contemplated his Mount Carmel exit strategy, because the party was over. Selman's plan to whack Zoe Whelan was all but complete, which gave the man a stepping-stone to the senior Common Faith ranks. Bartok had no interest in working for the next guy, or being Selman's eyes, ears, and payroll clerk. Besides, sticking around town meant nonstop looking over a shoulder for a trooper with a silencer and a grudge. That left him with the unpleasant choice of going freelance for a smuggling gang or early retirement. The smuggler future was limited, given the continued progress toward a normal economy and sanctioned graft committed by law enforcement agencies. As for the end of official work, his savings were mostly tangible: cash, gold, silver, and untraceable firearms. He also held a few secrets, which were simultaneously assets and liabilities. Evidence he possessed of Selman's and Colonel Stewart's extracurricular activities could be traded or get him a bullet in the ear.

While the money wasn't as much as he'd like, he settled on departing at the earliest opportunity for Florida and a slack life shooting gators. He had two sets of identification, both from Red Death victims he found rotting in their homes, men more or less his age. He kept them current for just such an occasion as the one he now faced. He'd use the oldest to get south, the other to settle in somewhere. Of course, he'd have to leave the jeep behind and take a sedan he kept in storage. That was a shame. He loved the old jeep.

He raised his field glasses, an excellent pair made by Nikon, for a look at the office. Not a single miner was visible. They knew enough to take cover. He scanned down the road toward the gate. No troopers there yet. Returning to the office, he spotted movement.

"Oh, for Christ's sake," he muttered upon seeing John Carroll walk across the empty parking lot and enter the front door.

• • •

"Bring him here!"

As they had done earlier for Selman, the miners escorted Father Carroll up the stairs. Several of them were old enough to remember him as a priest. The rest knew who he was only from rumors and stories told by their parents. In any case, he carried himself like someone important, giving them all a reason to keep quiet and stand straight.

Joe Grant met him at the top of the stairs. "It was you who started all this," he said. "I only dealt with Selman to keep the group safe."

"The wrong thing for the right reason doesn't make it right," Carroll replied.

"I won't be condemned for listening to my conscience."

One of the miners shoved Grant to the side. "Confession hours are over."

They led Father Carroll to the office where now only a lone kerosene lamp lit the room. They'd recently finished painting the windowpanes black. Trooper snipers would have no silhouettes to target.

"Take a seat," George Nash said, waving to a chair.

"I won't be here long," Carroll replied, remaining on his feet.

"Is this the part where you tell me it's all part of God's plan?"

"Yes."

Nash chuckled. "I actually expected you to say something different."

"The troopers will attack soon."

"Doesn't take a prophet to figure that out," scoffed Nash. "We're ready. They'll get a bloody nose and run home to their mommies."

"They're not going to kill all the men," Father Carroll said. "Only yourself and a few others."

"But you've come to save us, right?"

"I can help."

"By all means! Let's hear it."

"Take me to Selman."

Putting his feet on the desk, Nash pointed, and said, "If you're the most wanted man in town, I'm the second. So, forgive me for not giving the troopers a two-for-one special."

"If we leave now, you'll survive."

"Is that what God told you?"

"He didn't have to."

"That sounds a little shaky, Father. Ah, no worries. I sent a few men to remind Selman what's going to happen if he doesn't honor the deal we just made."

"The troopers caught Chris Warren and Jeff Thomlinson. They're dead," Father Carroll said.

"Forgive me for not believing in that part of your prophecies," Nash replied without reacting to the claim of their demise. "Those two are better than any company of troopers."

"Not true, and you're almost out of time."

"To give up? No thanks."

"If not for yourself, for the sake of your men, I'm asking you to take me to Selman. He'll see you in a different light, as someone worth protecting."

"And what's Selman going to do with you?"

"Fulfill his destiny."

"My, oh my, the way you people talk. It's always the end of the world, or hellfire and brimstone, or some other magic tale that works on the minds of fools. Too bad you came to the wrong place tonight, Father. I'm not buying."

Before Nash could call his men to remove Father Carroll from the office, one of them poked his head in the door.

"Sorry, Chief, but Rick Barr spotted Zoe Whelan running this way. Want him to stop her?"

"Definitely, you idiot!"

As Nash leapt to his feet, Father Carroll charged out of the office, knocking the miner down on the way. He took the stairs in three quick bounds, ignoring the shouts and racking gun-bolts from above. On the ground floor, he headed toward the rear of the building. A shot boomed from behind; the bullet smacked the wall to his right.

Outside, Carroll stayed in the shadows, immediately rounding the corner and doubling back along the building to the front. He heard men running out the back door, their heavy footfalls fading. If Zoe was headed this way, she would be coming from the north, which was to his right. Glancing at the lot, he saw no one.

Hoping Nash's men were looking for him in the other direction, he ran for the tree line when he spotted Zoe. Turning sharply toward her, his feet slipped in the gravel, and he fell. With the taste of dust in his mouth, he rose to a crouch, locked his eyes on her, and launched himself.

The dash reminded him of high school football. He'd been a wide receiver, and while he was more than forty years older, the thrill of angling around linesmen, dodging tackles, and leaping for the end zone was in his heart. He pushed off his toes, accelerating with every stride. He felt air rushing past his face as he pumped his arms the way the coach taught him.

Then he saw Zoe slow and stop. He waved for her to go the other way, toward the trees. She hesitated, unsure if he was friend or foe.

"Run!" he shouted.

She stayed put until he was close enough to be recognized.

"Run!"

At last she started moving but while still facing him. Seconds later, he was at her side.

"I was in the mine," she said, "and—"

"You followed the crosses," he added, hauling her toward the forest.

"I did, and the metal bars—"

"I know, it's been foretold. Take my testament to the Time of Gathering."

"Where?"

"Read it. You'll know what to do. Now go!"

She turned toward him. "Come with me!"

Suddenly there was a loud pop and the entire area was bathed in harsh light from above. Then the firing started.

Zoe watched a line of bullets pock the ground, ending just behind Father Carroll. A few others whizzed past her before one, then a second, struck the man who had baptized her and who told her only a week ago that she was here for a higher purpose. He dropped to his knees, face impassive, eyes remaining open. A third and fourth bullet punched his chest, knocking him backward. She almost stooped to help him, but another line of fire splattered her with rock splinters as it struck the ground a few feet away.

The light above faded, and Zoe bolted for the trees. A stream of bullets sung close to her ears. One snagged her sleeve but didn't touch flesh. She cut right, then left, then farther left, before swinging hard right again. The first tree went by, then another. Bullets hit them in a series of syncopated thunks.

A few seconds into the forest, she slowed not for a look back but because she could hardly see the way forward. Then there was a series of pops and more bright light overhead. The next instant she looked to the side, and there stood Randy Bartok.

"What are you doing—"

She would have finished the sentence had there not been a tremendous explosion that knocked them both to the ground.

• • •

Selman spent less than an hour with Ian before returning downstairs where Denise sat in front of the television. "A glass of wine would be nice," he said.

"I didn't forget about that reward money," she replied, getting off the couch.

"Neither have I."

He looked forward to re-establishing himself within the Common Faith's highest ranks where he wouldn't have to deal with petty matters like reward money. He didn't expect to become a member of the Sacred Council immediately. Six months was a reasonable period for the hierarchy to digest events and recognize his contributions both past and present. To prod them along, he'd direct a documentary produced by a friend at National Television. Naturally, he'd keep his name out of the credits. The film would show the strife John Carroll fomented among the miners, how his followers caused the death of Compliance Specialist Zoe Whelan among others, and most important, how Martin Selman stopped the bloodshed. The audience would see children. Lots of them. In the middle, there'd be a long segment about Candace Walsh's third-grade class. They missed their favorite teacher! Also, interviews with parents, distraught and worried about the younger generation. He would volunteer to take Ms. Walsh's place until a new instructor could be relocated. He would tend to grieving-sister Denise and her dear son, Ian, in their home. Teasing clips would run during the evening news.

The second documentary would be all about the Original Doctrine. INSPIRED was the title. John Carroll was a mere false prophet. He, Martin Selman, had been THE prophet, chosen by the Universal Creator to forge all belief systems into one. It was time the world knew his name.

Denise entered with a full glass and the bottle. "This is the last of the red," she informed him.

"More on the way," he assured her, taking a seat on the empty recliner. He sipped the wine, which was an ancient California cabernet. Delicious but near the end of its drinkability, he thought, before his mind drifted back to career planning.

Exciting as it was to be on the path to Philadelphia, Selman had no intention of relinquishing control in Mount Carmel. He would need a place of respite, where he could relieve the stress of managing the nation's religious affairs. Mount Carmel was far enough away from inquisitive eyes, yet only several hours' drive from Headquarters, or a quick hop in a helicopter. It was the ideal location to indulge his desires under the guise of staying in touch with the people. He'd hand-pick his replacement, a person capable but with limited aspirations. To keep Bartok or throw him to the troopers was an unanswered question to be decided later.

He finished the glass and was pouring himself another when suddenly the house shook. Dishes rattled in the kitchen, and the TV blinked off. Bits of dust sprinkled down from the ceiling.

"What the hell was that?" Denise said.

"The answer to my prayers," replied Selman.

CHAPTER 34.

A trooper squad caught Jagger but not until long after the shooting stopped. She dithered at the ventilation shaft, debating whether to chase Philly Chick or head back to Jerry Boyle's and lay low with the Mollies. Her consternation's cause was the walk and talk with Preacher John after he found her in the woods crying like a sissy. It would have been embarrassing, but he started talking about her importance.

"You and your friends will help Zoe get to Philadelphia," he told her.

She should have asked him to be more specific in regard to the timing and method of transportation.

"First, you'll meet her at the mine. I've brought clothes and some food." He slung a satchel off his shoulder and set it at Jagger's feet.

"Whoa," she said. "The mine's enemy territory."

"She'll be waiting for you at the entrance to the ventilation shaft."

"Where's that exactly?"

As she had done the night the Mollies broke him out of Bartok's dungeon, he used a stick to draw in the dirt, explaining, "I've been living there for a while now."

"I can find it," Jagger assured him.

"You'll do great things," he said. "People will never forget you or your cousins."

The embrace that followed was a sign of affection and respect Jagger had never experienced before. She accepted it more than returned it, her arms hanging awkwardly slack, like a pair of old ropes.

"Go," he said with a gentle push. "Don't forget the clothes."

She took up the satchel and asked, "What about you?"

"I'm turning myself in at the mine."

Jagger argued, but he insisted it would all work out. And it did. Sort of. Philly Chick was in the ventilation building. She seemed to know she had a mission for Preacher John, but like him, she didn't listen to reason. Off she went to intercept the man when it was too late for damn sure.

Or was it?

Jagger wished she'd read every page of his book, but she'd only read a few. Therefore, she didn't understand exactly who was to do what and when. Was she supposed to stop Philly Chick from rushing down to the mine office, or go with her? Either way, when they did hook up again, then what?

After a long sit and think, she decided to run down to the mine. She got there just as the troopers launched the first flare. She'd seen flares in that war movie Whip watched, otherwise she might have mistaken them for who knew what, maybe even one of Preacher John's messages from God. Anyway, they lit the office and surrounding area like a triple full moon. Philly Chick and Preacher John were making a break for it when he was clipped by the troopers. Jagger was sure it was trooper fire that got him. Damn shame that was because, while they hadn't started off on the best of terms, he'd made a strong impression on her since. Then Zoe disappeared into the trees.

At least a dozen troopers stormed the office. One fired a handheld cannon that blew the door clean off its hinges. The others ran in, unleashing short bursts that started out as sharp cracks then became duller as the team penetrated the structure. Not long after came the kaboom that took down the entire building. The blast tossed her back a few yards. Rang her bell loud. Chunks of concrete block, glass, and metal showered the area. If not for the trees, Jagger would have been fragged by shrapnel.

Her ears were still ringing as she crawled into a thicket. There she remained, flat on the ground, unable to hear, blind to what was going on beyond a few yards in any direction. Her senses diminished, she settled in to recover.

She must have passed out, because when next her eyes opened it was early morning. She knew by the color of the sky and sounds of the birds. Awake and alert, she peeked down at the smoldering ruins of the office. Several armored personnel carriers were parked in the lot. Troopers picked through the debris. One spoke into a radio. Bodies were lined up on the gravel.

Jagger checked herself for wounds and injuries, finding none that were obvious. She took care not to rise to her full height. In a crouch, she scurried deeper into the woods, avoiding leaves and other noisy patches. She covered maybe a hundred yards when the trooper squad spotted her.

"Halt!"

She stopped, put her hands in the air, and hoped Preacher John had told the truth, that she was going to get a big score and make it to Philadelphia.

Moments later, she was surrounded by several troopers. They frisked her, took the pistol, but asked no questions. The sergeant walked out of earshot to radio whoever was in command. He returned with orders.

"We take her to the colonel," he said.

• • •

Soon after dawn, Bartok got up, made breakfast on the hot-plate in his office, and wrote himself an insurance policy. True to form, he typed a report detailing all his actions from recovering John Carroll's book at Jerry Boyle's camp to capturing Zoe Whelan before the mine office exploded. He altered the facts to make it seem he was in the process of taking the Whelan woman to jail as opposed to enjoying the sport of a live military assault. How did he know she was there? A tip from the Mollies. He threw Jagger and her gang another bone by making it sound like they called him to collect the reward for Carroll's book, which wasn't true at all, but Runt did hand it over.

The look on that girl's face wasn't the one of the scared brat he tossed across the room. Whether witnessing her chunky comrade take a trooper beating or another experience, Bartok didn't know, but something put the vinegar in her soup. Her eyes were hard set, like a serious poker player going all in: no anger, no fear, pure grit. He knew the look. He'd seen it in the mirror.

He cast a wary eye toward the corner of his desk where the book sat with its handmade cover.

Revelation from God? Bartok doubted it. He wasn't interested in what John Carroll wrote. He would prefer to be free of the thing and Zoe Whelan, who was currently chained to the basement wall. First, he needed some protection, i.e., the report. When complete, he would snap a few photos of the book and Whelan as proof of life. Finally, he'd call Selman with good news.

Why such thoroughness, other than his own good habit? Because he wasn't about to be accused of killing a compliance specialist, no matter how easily justified. The report and photo would show he delivered her alive and well to jail. What happened to her after that would be decided by Selman. If ever the local director or the troopers attempted a double cross by claiming she died at his hand, he had irrefutable evidence to the contrary.

The report finished, he grabbed his digital camera and John Carroll's book and descended to the basement, where Zoe sat on the floor. The length of chain between her ankle and the wall was just long enough for her to avail herself of the sink, which explained how the coal dirt was now gone from her face. She did have a shiner around her right eye where he landed the blow that rendered her compliant with his order that she was under arrest last night. After that punch knocked her silly, he cuffed her. Then they walked out to the jeep by the light of the burning office. The troopers were too busy shooting at nothing to consider there might be someone else afoot.

"Stand up," he ordered.

To her credit, she obeyed without a fuss, asking, "I want to speak with Secretary Thompson."

"Soon," he said. "Hold this."

For the first time, Zoe saw the book that contained Father Carroll's testament, the message she was supposed to deliver to the Time of Gathering, a task she now doubted she would fulfill. She accepted it from Bartok and immediately guessed who made the cover. The metal cross of pounded sheet metal was the kind of project she'd seen when visiting middle schools to lecture about the benefits of the Common Faith. However, this generation of students made copies of the Circle and Line, not crosses.

"Look here," Bartok said.

Zoe raised her eyes to find a camera pointed in her direction.

"Okay. Give it back."

She returned the book to Bartok. "I'm a ranking compliance specialist. I want to talk to my superior."

"Relax, sweetheart," Bartok replied and left the room.

In his office, he plugged the camera into a color printer, sipping coffee while the unit warmed up. After the beep, he pressed two buttons. Out came the photo. It looked good except for the book in Whelan's hands. Only the edges of the cover were visible. The center was a white spot. Probably a refection off the metal cross, he thought, and disconnected the camera to take another picture.

Glancing out the window, he saw an armored personnel carrier roll to a stop. It was Colonel Stewart's flagship. He left the camera and hustled out to meet the lead trooper.

By way of a greeting, Stewart said, "Too bad you missed the game last night."

"I heard it."

"Lost a dozen men in that explosion, several more injured."

"Too bad."

"Hazard of the job," acknowledged Stewart. "Once in a while there's a consolation prize." He banged his hand on the side of the APC. The rear door opened, and two troopers dragged out Jagger, who looked remarkably well.

"She's one of yours, right?"

"Been helpful now and then," answered Bartok.

"Caught her this morning at the mine."

"Scavenging or what?"

"Didn't bother to ask." Stewart took a pistol from his belt and handed it to Bartok. "She had this."

Bartok recognized the gun as the make and model used by prison guards like Lenny Donovan, like the ones who drove and guarded the transfer buses. His suspicions were confirmed. Jagger was stupid enough to keep the gun, which tied her directly to the crime, as well as exposed a flaw in his story that Kyle Smith did the job.

"I haven't asked her where the bus is, or if she shot the driver and guard," continued Stewart. "Thought you might get the answers quicker."

"I can do that," Bartok said.

"Corporal Kedron will be here around eight tonight to mop up the evidence. This time let him finish. Then write me one of those excellent reports of yours about that couple from the train. Include this one if it fits the narrative."

"Got it."

"By the way, did Selman have an interest in her?"

"No."

"Too old, eh?"

"Not his flavor."

"Shame to waste what she has, but this calls for a different kind of satisfaction. See you around, Randy." The colonel touched his hat as a reminder of who was in charge, then departed with his men.

"Sorry," Jagger said as they entered the building.

"Not as sorry as me," Bartok told her. Look out Florida, here I come, he thought. Gator hunting it is.

• • •

What a hectic day it was for District 17 Common Faith Director Martin Selman.

His first act was to tour the destruction at Number Six. Filner played tour guide, leading him through the wreckage of the office then to the mine entrance where there was surprisingly little damage. Troopers stood guard at various points, their automatic rifles slung casually over their shoulders, a sure indication they expected no more trouble from the miners.

"John Carroll died right there," Filner said, pointing to a wide stain on the gravel.

"History left him behind," sighed Selman.

"His body's at the clinic."

"Understandable."

"Nash and six men died in the explosion. Joe Grant's body was found with them," continued Filner. "Colonel Stewart lost an entire platoon, plus a few severely wounded by flying debris."

"A terrible tragedy," replied Selman, disappointed by the death of a good informant. Grant was a reasonable man. He understood the way things had to be.

"The troopers shot Chris Warren and Jeff Thomlinson in town. Said they were on the way to get you and Bartok. Had some nasty grenade-like bombs on them."

"A sad end for misguided men. What about the hostages below?"

"We restored the electricity and Rat Durkin and Sheldon Hunter went down to inspect conditions. Without the ventilation system working, I'd say it's a long shot anyone's alive."

"Let's not give up hope," Selman said. "I'm organizing a vigil this evening. Inform everyone an extra measure of the Bounty of Faith will be distributed."

"We're going to need more than that to get this place up to full capacity."

"The Bounty of Faith shall multiply," Selman said with a pat on the shoulder. "Keep me posted."

His duty done at the mine, the director spent the remaining morning hours calling various agencies in Philadelphia and Washington. He pleaded for resources. The Department of Energy didn't recognize his authority, but he transferred around the minions to the people who mattered, reminding them of the obligation to meet the Chinese quota. They agreed to send a team to train new workers and rebuild the facilities. Next, he touched base with Common Faith Headquarters in Philadelphia, purposely avoiding Secretary Thompson's area. Instead, he talked to the Education Secretary, requesting a replacement for Candace Walsh. From the Community Engagement Division, he was promised grief counseling and a truckload of BoF boxes for the evening's vigil. The Department of Faith Infrastructure agreed to have a crew in Mount Carmel the following week to repair his office.

Finally, Selman called the clinic, ordering Doctor Erbil to cremate John Carroll's body immediately. Christian history was replete with gruesome examples of followers taking hair, blood, and bone to use as objects of devotion. It was his obligation to prevent such nonsense. That destroying the body was an insult to Carroll's beliefs was a small bonus.

"The ashes go down the drain," he finished, ensuring there would be no trophies.

The only call unanswered was the one to Randy Bartok. Under normal circumstances, no news was good news. While he had full confidence in his enforcer's ability to accomplish the task at hand, he hoped for a successful conclusion before Secretary Thompson's curiosity was piqued and she called, or worse, appeared unannounced. Of course, she was aware of last night's events. She had to be, given all the communication channels that were full of authorized information and not. Most relevant was Colonel Stewart's report to trooper headquarters in Harrisburg, which passed the information to Philadelphia, where a Common Faith liaison observed all traffic. He wouldn't doubt it if Thompson knew more than he did.

Selman ate lunch alone at Denise Walsh's table. Afterward, he stretched out on the couch for a nap. Again, he harkened back to the early days of creating the Common Faith. He slept on couches then. Floors sometimes. There was still shooting in the street. Molotov cocktails hurled at cars. He came very close to death, and closer yet to an affair with Hester Thompson. Exciting times they were. He missed them. He also felt they were about to come again.

He awoke two hours later to the sound of his phone ringing.

"It's been too long, Randy. You must have very good or very bad news."

Bartok said, "I'm wrapping the package for delivery."

"How delightful! My office, when?"

"Going to be a while. Trouble with the jeep."

"Before the vigil begins?"

"If not, I'll leave it on your desk," offered Bartok.

"Yes, please do that. It'll be like Easter in the old days. A basket full of goodies."

• • •

In fact, Bartok's day was as busy as his boss's. After chaining Jagger in the dungeon, he retrieved his savings from various locations around town, a few of which he had trouble finding. Eventually he got it all, including the two sets of identification. What he didn't have was gasoline. The jeep was nearly empty, and the Chevy sedan he planned to drive to Florida was below half a tank. The only station in town was closed because the troopers took the last of what was there.

"Filled every jerry can they had and didn't pay a dime or present a voucher," the attendant said. "Taking it for their personal vehicles. Not that I can prove it, but you know it's true. Anyway, we're scheduled to get a delivery tomorrow. Two hundred gallons. If it shows up."

He risked the ride over the mountain to Pottsville where he traded vouchers and cash for a full tank in the Chevy. No one was supposed to get more than five gallons at any one time. He regretted it for the attention-drawing factor, but a fifty-dollar bribe solved the problem.

Back in his office, he packed his lighter clothes. He cleaned his favorite hunting rifle, a .308 Winchester with a crystal-clear scope. He stacked boxes of ammunition next to it, wondering how many shots it took to kill a gator. He'd find out soon enough. The other guns, the untraceable and therefore most valuable ones, he wrapped in towels and blankets then secured the bundles with rope.

Departure preparations complete, he skipped over to Joannie T for a last fling. Damn it if she wasn't home. Oh well, saved him another lie. When darkness fell, he loaded the trunk of the Chevy with luggage, saving the sack of cash, precious metals, and guns for later. Back in the office, he ate a sandwich and studied topographical maps of Florida.

Just what did gator taste like?

Around seven thirty, people started congregating near the Common Faith Center. Dead friends and a strike put down by force or not, they were collecting the Bounty of Faith, however meager it might be. They were also showing contrition. In other words, it wasn't us making trouble for the troopers. The BoF truck was parked out front, guarded by serious troopers, which probably led the poor bastards to believe they were in for something great instead of the usual soy powder and sawdust cookies.

Banging on the door interrupted his rumination. Spot on time, Corporal Kedron had arrived. Bartok recognized him as the one who pummeled Crush and who had taken his own beating at the Pleasant Corner.

"You have a visitor," Bartok announced on the way down the stairs.

Jagger and Zoe sat on the floor about five feet apart, which was as close together as their chains would allow.

Bartok pointed at Zoe, saying, "That one is off limits."

"Unless the other one goes quick," Kedron remarked.

"Then don't rush it. I have some business at the Common Faith Center. Be back in an hour or so."

Climbing the stairs to leave, Bartok felt a rare tinge of guilt. He held no grudge against Jagger, not even for the bus job. He'd done business with her and would have continued had circumstances not overcome her situation. The Mollies would lose their leader and probably end up in a trooper kitchen or brothel when Jerry Boyle took a heart attack. Unless Jagger managed to survive the encounter with Kedron. Then it was gladiator rules: the last one standing lives to fight another day.

At the top of the stairs, Bartok heard Jagger tell Zoe, "I think it's time to pray."

CHAPTER 35.

"All rise in honor of the Universal Creator," Selman announced in a voice too joyful for the occasion.

The sniffling and coughing people before him rose off the plastic chairs. They had nothing to celebrate, unless they were among the lucky few who'd get a gas voucher in their BoF box. On the other hand, he had a multitude of reasons, the most important of which was Bartok's presence at the back of the hall. Actually, it was the brown-paper-wrapped package in Bartok's hands that was the best reason.

"We gather to... to... recognize our common belief," he rambled, distracted by the prospect of reading John Carroll's book.

Then, late as always, Denise and Ian entered, bumping Bartok with the swinging door. Oh, very nice. He would read to the lad. Afterward, a call to Hester Thompson's private number. Or, better yet, a drive to Philadelphia with the evidence. Yes, a calming drive through the night, then a surprise visit to the Secretary's private residence. Imagine her face when he banged on the door!

"Excuse me. I was overcome with grief," he said upon realizing he'd been standing in silence long enough for the people to murmur among themselves and point. "Please, be seated."

They settled, giving Bartok a chance to slip out unnoticed except by Denise.

Selman was grateful this group was less demanding than his megachurch congregation in terms of a coherent, uplifting message. They were here for the handout. Most of them. The sooner the service ended, the sooner they collected their prize and went home. He accepted the reality, recognizing how different it was from his previous flock. Those people had actually come to give. Some of them gave generously to the point of stupidity. Others who couldn't afford to give still put something in the basket.

"The Universal Creator lays a winding path," he continued, "full of twists and turns and unexpected surprises. Are we to judge the path as good or bad? Are we to question the wisdom of the most high? Or, are we to accept the route ahead?"

Of course, he wasn't expecting an answer. Rhetoric was lost on them.

"Like fish in the ocean must accept the water, we must accept our lives are made possible by forces beyond our control. And those forces are equal for everyone, rich or poor, city dweller or country farmer; we're all one in the Common Faith."

Selman had planned on cutting it short, but now that he was on a roll, he droned on until several old-timers fell asleep.

• • •

One, two. Three.

One, two. Three.

Zoe watched Kedron toy with Jagger like a boxer sparring in the mirror. He threw a few slow jabs the Molly leader ducked, then tossed a fast one she slapped away. He repeated the sequence several times, walking back and forth the length of the chain to Jagger's ankle. The worst part was, Zoe couldn't do anything to help. The chain to her own ankle limited her range.

One, two. Three.

One, two. Crack!

Kedron anticipated Jagger's dodge left and slapped her face hard enough to send her reeling into the wall.

"Oh, good one," Jagger mocked him.

"Yeah? You like that?"

"Turns me on, baby."

"Then I better get comfortable," Kedron said, unbuttoning his shirt.

"Not for nothing, soldier, but we didn't pay for a show."

"This one's on the house," Kedron replied. "How's your fat friend doing? Still pissing blood?"

"Nah. She's out dancing tonight. Mugging it up with a miner at the Pleasant Corner."

Zoe watched him drape his shirt on the stairs then stretch both triceps.

"If we're going to party," Jagger suggested in a polite tone, "might as well unchain me. Eh?"

"Going to hang you from the ceiling by that chain," he replied.

"Whoa. Didn't know you were into the kinky stuff. I would have dressed different."

That remark earned her another slap. She bounced off the wall and dropped to the floor. Zoe didn't think the blow was that hard, but maybe she hit her head and was stunned.

"Get up," Kedron ordered.

"Give me a sec," groaned Jagger, who rose to one knee. Blood dripped from her mouth.

Kedron strode close, spun right, and landed a kick, the sound of which made Zoe nauseous.

Jagger rolled across the floor until the chain came tight and she jerked to a halt. Kedron squatted over her. Knuckles first, he punched her between the shoulder blades.

"Dirty bitch," Kedron scowled, backing away.

Jagger coughed then said, "No need for insults to the injuries."

"Get up."

Zoe said, "Give her a break."

Kedron marched over, forcing Zoe to quickly backpedal before tripping over her chain. He broke out laughing when she landed on the ground.

"Oh, this is getting to be fun!"

"Be careful, soldier boy," Jagger warned. "Don't touch her.

Bartok's orders."

"He doesn't give me orders." To make the point, he stomped his boot on Zoe's thigh.

"Hey!" Jagger called. "Over here."

Kedron heeded the call. He threw several lazy combinations, daring Jagger to dodge into the real swing. She ducked under his first one but was too late on the second. He hit her just above the eye, opening a nasty gash that bled down her cheek.

"Now we're talking," Kedron said, wiping his fist on his bare chest.

"Strange kind of foreplay," Jagger said, her voice weak. She staggered toward him, arms out for a hug. "Come on, soldier boy. Let's play nice while I still can."

He charged in, dipped his shoulder, and struck her in the solar plexus.

Zoe thought she heard ribs crack as Jagger flew back, hit the wall, and crumpled to the floor. The gasping breaths meant she had the wind knocked out of her. Kedron sauntered over and pulled her up by the belt, which seemed to help her recover. However, seconds later, he used his free hand to slap her several times in a slow, methodical beat.

One. Two. Three. Four.

All this pain, Zoe thought, is because of me. If I'd not chased after Father Carroll, we wouldn't have been caught. Now, she would never read his testament or deliver it to the Surviving Few. But how could this be happening? If God was all powerful, how could He let Jagger suffer and herself fail?

Jagger coughed hard, spittle and blood flying from her mouth. She sat with her back to the wall, one eye swollen almost shut.

"Get up!" Kedron shouted.

To Zoe's horror, Jagger struggled to her feet, swaying, reaching for the wall to brace herself.

"Going to work on your face a while," he said. "Close that other eye so I don't have to put up with you looking at me."

Jagger raised her hands in surrender. "You win, soldier boy."

"Stop calling me that!"

"Sorry, soldier boy."

He rushed forward but stopped as Jagger cowered, sliding sideways against the wall, the chain gathering at her feet.

"Just kill me," she pleaded. "Please, just kill me quick and be done with it."

After a satisfying cackle, Kedron said, "I'll kill you when I'm good and ready."

"Do it before Bartok gets back," Jagger reminded him.

"When I'm good and ready!"

Resigned to her fate, she faced him, dropped her arms to her side, and grinned.

Kedron grabbed her shirt, cocked his fist, and aimed. He hesitated, perhaps contemplating if he'd gone too far too soon.

"I love you, soldier boy," she said, puckering her lips.

Triggered, he smiled and hurled the blow.

Jagger's remaining good eye caught the flash in both of his, the signal to become dead weight, which is exactly what she did. Every muscle in her legs released, dropping her torso straight down. Still holding her shirt, Kedron was pulled off balance, unable to stop the momentum of his flying fist, which was no longer headed for her nose. It struck the stone wall with full force. The crunch of finger and wrist bones followed.

Kedron released Jagger's shirt to clutch his shattered hand, leaving her free to attack. She grabbed his legs and pushed off the wall with her feet, felling him like a sawed log. He attempted a wild swing with his good arm, but she blocked it and landed a flurry of blows to his stomach. Next, he made the mistake of trying to deflect with his damaged hand. Jagger caught it, twisted, and jammed it to the floor. Wailing in agony, he turned to that side, which left him more vulnerable than he would ever know.

Jagger snatched the chain at her ankle, pulling the slack until she had several feet between both hands. She crawled the length of Kedron's body, dragged the loop under his face, then pulled it snug against his throat. He tried to rise off the floor, which only gave her room to double the chain around his neck. As she yanked it tight, he rolled over, the bulk of him pressing heavy on her. She kept them turning until she was again on top. She jammed her knee into his spine and pulled the chain until the links dug into her fingers. Kedron's good hand flailed for a strike at Jagger, but he couldn't reach her. He snatched at the chain to no avail because his wounded hand couldn't hold his weight. Each time he clawed for it, she pulled the opposite way, ratcheting it tighter, pressuring his weak side.

Jagger felt Kedron's strength fade. She leaned all her weight against the chain, watching his head tilt at a sickening angle. Whether she choked him to death or broke his neck, she didn't care. At some point, his body went slack. He voided himself then, the stench of feces the last sign that the fight was over.

Panting from the strain, Jagger slipped the chain free and moved toward Zoe's side of the room.

"I'd appreciate it if you'd fight the next one," she said.

"We have to get out of here," Zoe replied.

"Trust me, lady. I tried every trick I know when I was here the last time."

Zoe examined the end of her chain where the bolt was fastened into the wall. She tugged it at various angles with no result. If God wanted her to be the Messenger and deliver Father Carroll's testament then how could He help her through the bars at the mine but leave her chained in a dungeon? She sat on the floor, wondering if she'd fallen for all the lies academy instructors warned her about.

A moment later, the door to the boiler room opened, revealing Runt, who held the bolt cutters they'd used to break out Preacher John.

· · ·

Tonight, Ian was nothing but smiles, tugging Selman's hand as they traipsed down the hall.

"You're too young to know about Easter," Selman said, more to himself because he knew the boy could neither hear nor speak. "It was the custom to make a basket of treats for children and search for hidden eggs that contained little prizes."

He parked Ian in the corner then gasped at the package on his desk. Bartok had done a neat job of wrapping it, the brown paper creased and folded, held in place with sturdy cord. He took out a knife but then set it down. Why hurry? To build anticipation, he fiddled with the knot instead of cutting it. With it open, he coiled the cord to the side. Gently, he slipped the flap of paper from the fold.

His first glimpse revealed what took him a few seconds to place. Opening the paper wide to reveal the entire object, he saw the cross was made of poorly cut sheet metal. He studied it carefully. The ends of each bar folded over the cover board, gripping it tightly and holding the purple fabric taut.

Was this really the Testament of John Carroll, now deceased, his body melting away in the flames of the clinic's crematorium? He wondered if Bartok was playing a joke. But Bartok was the least humorous man he knew.

Ian laughing distracted Selman, prompting him to think if it wasn't Bartok's prank then maybe Colonel Stewart was responsible.

"Quiet over there," he said.

Ian put a hand over his mouth.

Tilting the cover open, he found another sheet of fabric, this one white. He slipped his finger under the edge and peeled back a corner. He immediately recognized John Carroll's handwriting.

Ian released a roar of laughter.

"Quiet!" Selman barked. "I'm about to read the Word of God."

Again, Ian settled.

I must share this with someone, Selman thought. The idea of delaying contact with Secretary Thompson any longer seemed foolish. He'd won! He deserved to celebrate and in the company of the Senior Secretary. He dialed her number.

To his surprise, she answered on the first ring. "It's quite late for you to call," she said.

"If you'll indulge me, Madam Secretary, I'd like to read what has been purported by others to be the Word of God."

"You've recovered John Carroll's book?"

"I have," he answered. "Sadly, he died in a shootout at the mine. It seems some Christian insurgents had infiltrated the miners' union."

"This I already know."

"As you should."

"You've verified the authenticity of Mr. Carroll's tome?"

"I recognize his handwriting. Whether it is the Word of God, how will we ever know?"

For the third time, Ian began laughing.

"Shut up!" Selman hollered.

"Is something wrong?" Thompson asked.

"Sorry, just some noise from the hallway."

"Then read to me, Martin. I'm all ears."

He cleared his throat and began. *"The chains of this world are of this world and have no power to bind us."*

"Sounds rather biblical," interjected Thompson. "Go on."

"And so, as the Israelites were delivered from Egypt… " Selman paused, his eyes straining to focus on the text.

"I'm listening," prompted Thompson.

"And so as the Israelites were delivered from Egypt, as the love of Christ conquered the Roman Empire, the time has come… "

The paper seemed to grow brighter, blurring the words.

"Martin," Hester Thompson said, "take a drink or whatever you need and get on with it."

"Yes, Madam Secretary, I'm trying." He found his place and read, *"… as the love of Christ conquered the Roman Empire, so the time has come for us to be free."*

The page bloomed brighter and brighter, swelling past the edges of the book. The light glowed warm on his face. Selman held a hand over the page to shield his eyes, to no effect. Finally, he slammed the cover shut.

"Are you there, Martin?"

"I'll call back soon," he answered, white spots swirling through his vision.

• • •

Wearing the prison bus driver's uniform, Crush did the honors, cutting Jagger's chain first, then Zoe's.

"Thank you," Zoe said.

"Runt tells me you're worth it," Crush replied.

Zoe glanced across the room at the girl she'd first seen in the alley when the Mollies jumped her. Patched clothes and unkempt hair gave the kid an urchin's charm. But her stance, hand on a cocked hip, one knee slightly bent, suggested boldness. Had she learned it from Jagger or was it her own character developing?

"We need some help up here!" Whip called from the top of the stairs.

"Coming!" Runt replied.

"As if I haven't done enough already," Jagger huffed.

The gang entered Bartok's office to find Jerry Boyle pointing his shotgun at the enforcer, who stood with his back against the far wall. Piles of jewelry, bundles of cash, and stacks of gold and silver coins covered his desk.

"Load your pockets, ladies," Boyle said. "And take a couple of guns and ammo."

"Hallelujah!" Jagger beamed. "Preacher John said I'd get more than that measly reward."

"What the hell happened to you?" Boyle asked the Mollies' leader.

"Tripped on the dance floor."

Bartok watched the Mollies grab money and shiny metal, stuffing it in their jackets. Zoe took a rifle and opened the breach. Seeing it wasn't loaded, she reached for a box of shells.

"Not my favorite gator gun," Bartok said, getting only a smile in return. To Jagger he added, "You and Kedron party alone, or was it a group effort?"

"They got here after the music stopped," Jagger replied.

"Anyone else told me that, I'd shoot them in the foot for lying to me. But you're the luckiest damn savage to walk the jungle since Tarzan."

"Should've known better is what you're admitting," Jagger said.

"Yeah," Bartok sighed. "Got a plan to get out of here when the shooting's done?"

"We do," Whip put in.

"Leave my stuff, and I'd be inclined to ignore your many transgressions."

Zoe leveled the gator gun at his chest. Nodding at Jagger, she said, "You left her to die. Why should we let you off the hook?"

"Rules of the game," Bartok answered.

"Made up as you go along."

"No denying it. Let's deal and everyone gets what they want."

"We got the guns," Whip said, "not you."

"Seeing two of you dressed in those prison uniforms, I figure you're going to drive the bus down 901 to Cressona, hoping any troopers along the way won't pay attention. Assuming that works, it's the coal train south."

"The guards get off at Pottsville," Jagger said. "It's clear from there to Philly."

"Not anymore," Bartok informed her. "Since Kyle and Candy got it, they ride the entire route."

"He's lying to save his ass," Crush said.

"Wish I was. Before we waste enough time for the troopers to roll in and find one of theirs cold, let me suggest a viable alternative. Jerry and Crush take Jagger and Zoe like prisoners in the bus. Whip and the little one ride with me. I play dad with daughter and sick kid if they get curious."

"Pffft!" snorted Crush.

"Let the man talk," insisted Jagger.

"We go east on Route 61 then 54 to the checkpoint at Interstate 81. Tell the troopers there you're bound for Graterford."

"That's the long way to Graterford," Boyle said.

"True," agreed Bartok, adding, "it's also the only way with one checkpoint. Any other route has at least two and they lead to nowhere but backcountry. I'm not rolling the dice on a dead end."

"Assuming I let you out of here alive," said Jagger.

"Make it worth your while, same as I always did. We run 54 all the way east until it ends at 209. Ditch the bus somewhere, pile in my ride and head for the PA Turnpike. Gone."

"You worked this out a long time ago," said Zoe.

"Glad I did, too."

Jagger asked, "What happens if the troopers give us trouble?"

"Anyone with surrender in mind doesn't get a seat," answered Bartok. "Keep half my loot and let's roll."

"We're going to trust him?" asked Zoe.

"I am," Runt said, drawing everyone's attention.

"Why?" Jagger wanted to know.

"In Preacher John's book, I read, *'They recognized those who aided their quest; some, former enemies who see the cause as just and worthy; others, kind strangers willing to hear the message.'*"

"Good enough for me," Jagger said, helping herself to a stack of one-ounce gold bars. "Keeping what we got and a bit more for injuries recently sustained."

"I'm not leaving without my mother," Zoe said, bound for the door.

Bartok stopped her with, "Lenny took her to Pottsville where the troopers got her. And your brother's crew went down the hole to find him and Sara Darcy. Last I heard, they were still below."

Zoe froze. The gun in her hand, the people around her, even

the money on the desk, all together it could do nothing to free her mother or rescue her brother.

"They'll use them against me," she said.

"How do you know?" Jagger asked.

Bartok answered, "Because it's what she would do."

Zoe nodded that he was right. She'd arrested parents and siblings, husbands and wives, used them as currency to buy informants like Candy. A few she traded to other compliance specialists in return for favors on a difficult case. She always thought of her actions as doing the right thing for the right reasons. And to what end? After all that happened to her in the past week, she understood the Common Faith was a system of lies created by people like Selman and enforced by people like her.

Runt took the rifle from Zoe, passing it to Jagger. "Come on, Philly Chick," she said. "We have to get Preacher John's book."

Zoe thought she couldn't be the one to take Father Carroll's testament to the Surviving Few. She put too many of them in jail, including Sara Darcy. They would never trust her.

"*Some, former enemies who see the cause as just and worthy,*" Runt repeated.

Was this God's last call? The voice of an impoverished girl?

"*... others, kind strangers willing to hear the message.*"

Zoe stared down at Runt, trying to make sense of where she had been and where she might be going. "I don't know where it is," she said.

"Selman has it in his office," Bartok answered.

"Go get it!" Jagger said. "We'll pick you up at Fifth and Walnut in five minutes. You ain't there, we ain't waiting."

• • •

"They're coming," Ian said.

Selman almost asked who was coming when it struck him that those were the first words he'd ever heard Ian say. How could that be? The boy was diagnosed as physically unable to hear or speak.

"Say that again."

"They're coming."

Curious, Selman asked, "Who?"

"The ones who can read the book," answered Ian, stepping away from the corner toward the man who had tormented him the past three years.

"I can read the book."

The boy laughed. "No, you can't."

Restraining his anger, Selman said, "Perhaps you can read it." He rotated John Carroll's testament and pushed it to the far side of the table.

With pride showing on his face, Ian accepted the challenge. He opened the cover, peeled back the fabric liner, and began. *"Are we not called by our Lord? Our faith proves we are."*

"Not very original," interrupted Selman.

Ignoring him, Ian continued, *"Thus, let us cast off the tyranny that oppresses us, guided by the Savior, who died that we may live."*

"Oh, dear," Selman scoffed. "Another rebel screed. To think I was worried it might actually be a true revelation."

Ian started again, *"His Word shines brighter than the darkness of this age."*

The words seemed to fade into silence. Selman pounded his fist on the table. "Louder!"

Smiling, Ian read through the paragraph, his mouth moving, but Selman couldn't hear him.

"Don't play with me, boy!" Selman leaned forward and slapped his face to make the point. He felt his hand strike the boy's cheek, yet it made no sound, nor did it take away the smile. He backhanded him with enough force to send Ian reeling into the wall. Silence. In fact, he could hear nothing at all, not even his own breathing.

"What have you done to me?" he said, grasping his knife and

moving around the table, blocking Ian from a clear run out the door. At least he thought he said it, because he felt the sensation of speaking, but nothing reached his ears.

Ian backed toward the wall, shifting his gaze from the blade pointed his way, to the door.

"What kind of trick is this?" mouthed Selman, taking a step forward.

Ian faked left, drawing a lunge from Selman, then darted to the right around the table and fled the room, passing Zoe and Runt on the way in.

Selman brandished the knife as he backed around the table.

"Drop it!" Zoe shouted.

He couldn't hear her. His eyes flashed to Runt, who was moving sideways across the room.

"Drop the knife!" repeated Zoe.

Selman edged around the far side of the table, moving closer to Zoe, who was stepping sideways to put herself between him and Runt.

In a single motion, Runt grabbed the Common Faith flag, yanked the pole out of the base, and approached from around the other side of table. Selman grinned at the girl's pluck and determination. Sadly, she chose a useless weapon. Atop the pole in her hand rested the Common Faith's symbol. The Circle and Line was no sharper than her bare fingers. To his amazement, she broke the pole over her thigh, dropping the upper half with the symbol and flag to the floor. She aimed the splintered end of the lower portion at his chest.

Blocked by Zoe and caught between the table and the wall, Selman could do nothing but deflect Runt's improvised spear when she charged. He chopped at it with his free hand, diverting the shaft downward. The tip missed his torso but pierced his upper thigh. He dropped the knife to take hold of the pole. There they stood for three long seconds until Runt withdrew the point, releasing a gush of blood. He collapsed to the floor, both hands pressed over the gaping wound.

Zoe stood over Selman, who was trying to tell her something. She stooped closer but for some reason the words weren't audible. Seconds later his eyelids fluttered, and his body went slack.

Runt tossed the broken pole to the side. "Grab the book!" she said to Zoe.

The woman who had been the Common Faith's most effective compliance specialist stood in awe at the crude assembly that was Father Carroll's testament. It sat in the middle of the table, undisturbed by the action in the room, the cross on the cover gleaming bright. In the course of her career, she'd recovered dozens of Christian artifacts. All of them had been objects based on the past. This one, she believed, was one for the future.

"Come on, Philly Chick," Runt urged. "We have a bus to catch."

CHAPTER 36.

Per Bartok's plan, they drove east to the checkpoint. A trooper there climbed aboard the bus for a look at the two prisoners.

"What'd this one do?" he asked, pointing at Jagger's battered face.

"Resisted arrest," Crush answered.

The trooper poked Jagger's shoulder with his rifle barrel and said, "Learn your lesson or need some more persuasion?"

"All set," mumbled Jagger.

"Better be."

He walked all the way to the end of the vehicle, tilting his head for an angled view beneath the seats. "Hey there, driver, what's them wrapped parcels in the back?"

"Gutted pigs for roasting."

"Ain't nobody got beef anymore?"

"Not that I seen. Trouble with them miners is bad for every-thing," Boyle answered, scratching his newly shaved face.

"I heard that's over," the trooper said on his way forward. "Some dead coal diggers and a couple of Jesus freaks, too." He paused next to Zoe, who still showed dirt and filth from Selman's dungeon floor. "Should have hosed this one down before she got on."

"Ain't my job," Boyle remarked.

"Have a safe trip."

With that they were waved through.

Bartok, Whip, and Runt rolled up next. They got a flashlight poked in their faces, a few questions, and a look at Bartok's ID, the one he pilfered from a dead guy years ago.

"Where're you going?"

"Hazleton Hospital. Kid might have Red Death."

"Why didn't you say so right away?" the trooper barked, noticing dried blood on Runt's shirt. "Get the hell out of here!"

An hour later the seven of them wedged into Bartok's Chevy. They wound through the small towns along Route 209 to the Pennsylvania Turnpike which no longer charged tolls. Zoe wished she could have used the time to read Father Carroll's testament, but it was too dark.

They arrived in Philadelphia at one in the morning. After much discussion, they parted ways at the railyard near the Delaware River. The piles of export coal loomed like giant black pyramids near the docks where Chinese ships were loaded. Rows of shipping containers converted to bunkrooms bordered the fence.

"The Boxes, they're called," Zoe said, explaining that temporary workers rented them during the busiest times. They accepted only cash and required a week's deposit in advance. She'd busted Surviving Few members here in August.

Before he left, Bartok offered Jerry Boyle a partnership in the swamps of Florida with the idea that "Gator skins got to be worth something to the shoemakers."

"I think I'll use your money to buy a boat instead," Boyle said. "Hire these ladies to crew it and try my luck on the water."

Jagger liked the idea. "Told you we'd get to the beach," she said to Whip.

The last one to speak to Bartok was Zoe. She pressed him as to why he aided their escape.

"Hedging my bets," he explained. "Might be something in that book. And Jagger has an angel looking out for her sorry ass or she would have been dead a dozen times. Could say the same about you, or even myself. Either way, I figure I'm on the right side of things. For now."

They got the slow-season rate with a ten-dollar penalty for waking up the manager. He installed them in a pair of side-by-side boxes that each had two bedrooms, a bathroom, and small kitchen. The Mollies were most impressed by the hot running water.

Exhausted as she was, Zoe took a chair at the kitchen table to read Father Carroll's testament. After the snippets revealed by Runt, she was nervous about what was to come. She dared to page through, scanning the words, looking for something relevant, but her tired eyes struggled to focus.

Suddenly overcome by grief, she closed the book, folded her hands atop it, and bowed her head. Her mother was a prisoner. Her brother and Sara Darcy most likely dead. She was a wanted person, soon to be sought by skilled compliance specialists looking to notch their careers with her capture. She'd have to say goodbye to the Mollies tomorrow or risk putting them in danger. She would be alone in the search for the Surviving Few. How to convince them she was no longer their enemy? What if she didn't?

Runt padded out from the bedroom, took a seat on the other side of the table, and unwrapped a chocolate bar. She broke it in half, sliding a piece to Zoe, keeping the other for herself.

"Did your parents give you a name?" Zoe asked.

"Not that I remember, but Preacher John gave me one," Runt replied, "It's kind of strange, but I like it."

"Tell me."

"It's in there. Middle of page ten."

Zoe found the reference.

"Near the end of my time in the forest, I came upon the youngest of the group, who offered to bind these words in the nature of a book. Immediately, the Spirit transformed my vision to see her not as the fragile creature she was but as the indomitable leader she would become. Soon after, we met again. I baptized her by the stream, giving her the name given to me by the Spirit, the one all who read this after the Time of Gathering already know for heroic deeds assisting the Messenger and in the difficulties beyond."

Zoe looked up and said, *"Her name is Valerie Valda."*

EPILOGUE.

What does a system do when one of its own rebels? It drops the hammer. The hierarchy lives to feed itself and enforces conformity because dissent leads to self-destruction. There can be no questions asked, no doubts raised, no truths exposed, or else the lies believed in desperate times unravel. A compliant population then becomes restless as they realize how they've been misled in the name of the greater good, which, in fact and practice, is the much greater good for those few doing the misleading.

As foretold by Father Carroll, Zoe Whelan became the Messenger and thereby enemy number one of the Common Faith. Former colleagues led by Hester Thompson rallied to eradicate the Surviving Few along with anyone suspected of aiding Whelan. Martin Selman, hellbent on revenge and minus his right leg, joined the hunt by forming a cult of deadly adherents to his own brand of idolatry.

Unlike during the run-up to the Second Civil War, people paid attention to the warning signs, which was helpful and not. There was a generation looking to better their existence not just economically but spiritually. There were also plenty of tired souls who wanted to leave well enough alone. Between these two Zoe Whelan bounced, as both clashed with her and each other. It was a concentrated conflict, bloody only for those directly involved and with minimal collateral damage. Nonetheless, after the Time of Gathering, the resulting benefits accrued to everyone. Why and how is another story.

I'm grateful to have lived through the end of a dark age into a brighter one. Many were less fortunate. If there is one thing I can pass on from my experience, it is this: We are God's most exotic experiment. He gave us free will to explore our greatest potential. See it as an opportunity to create goodness. Keep a careful watch for those who don't see it that way. If not, the past will catch up and claim your present.

ACKNOWLEDGMENTS

I would like to thank Reverend Robert Kitchen,
Pastor John Hoff, Reverend Tony Villareal, Father Quinn,
Father Lawrence, and Randall Perry, all of whom
provided guidance and wisdom over the years.

Editors are instrumental in making
a story the best it can be, and
I am grateful for their insight.

As always, my wife, Heather,
remains a calming influence in my
tumultuous creative process.

ABOUT THE
AUTHOR

Daniel Putkowski, a graduate of New York University's
Tisch School of the Arts, resides in Chapel Hill, NC, with his
wife and two cats. *The Next Testament* is his sixth novel.

danielputkowski.com

www.ingramcontent.com/pod-product-compliance
Lightning Source LLC
Chambersburg PA
CBHW030549260626
47157CB00006B/2240